THE FAST LANE

BOOKS BY SHARON M. PETERSON

The Do-Over

The Fake Out

SHARON M. PETERSON

THE FAST LANE

bookouture

Published by Bookouture in 2024

An imprint of Storyfire Ltd.
Carmelite House
50 Victoria Embankment
London EC4Y 0DZ

www.bookouture.com

ISBN: 978-1-83525-014-3
eBook ISBN: 978-1-83525-013-6

To Daniel
It has been an honor
to watch you grow into
an amazing, funny, charming
young man who greets every
day, every person, every challenge
with a smile. I'm so blessed
to be your mom... even if you did
once tell me that I wasn't allowed to
die because then who would make
dinner?
Never change.
Love you,
Mom

ONE

Note to self:
When padlocking yourself to a tree, make sure you have the key.

Friday, three weeks, two days before the wedding

Two Harts, Texas

"I want her arrested." Peter Stone glowered down at me where I sat propped against the best tree in the entire world, a heavy silver chain wrapped around both of us several times. While this may have been a spur-of-the-moment decision, I liked to be prepared for any situation.

One should always have heavy chain laying around for such things. It also works well for chaining one's neighbor's lawnmower parts to various immovable objects after one has disassembled said lawnmower because the neighbor wouldn't stop using it at six in the morning when one's sick grandmother was trying to sleep.

Hypothetically speaking, of course.

I narrowed my eyes and jutted my chin in the air. My father

called me Ali the Mule when I wore this expression because it meant I planned to dig my feet in. He was not wrong.

Peter, the mayor of Two Harts, and all-around jackass, brought this side out in me and I'd made it my life's mission to annoy the crap out of him whenever the chance arose.

"I'd rather not arrest her," said the man next to Peter. Mario Alvarez was the county sheriff; he was also my dad's best friend and my brother's boss.

"I'm doing nothing wrong. It is my constitutional right to peacefully protest."

The chains rattled as I tucked a piece of flyaway hair behind my ear. I hadn't exactly had time to dress for the occasion. Whatever I was supposed to wear to a protest, it probably wasn't green basketball shorts I'd stolen from my brother Frankie a million years ago, hot-pink running shoes, and an oversized *Spock for President* t-shirt. My hair was still in the exact same state as when I lifted it off the pillow this morning. It was possible I'd slept in these clothes.

Peter yanked a hand through his floppy, dark-blond hair. "How did you know?"

"Know what?" I blinked at him in what I hoped signaled innocence.

I was totally not innocent. His assistant was Maria Connell, my cousin Patrick's ex-wife, and although she hated Patrick with the passion of a thousand fiery lakes, she still liked me. Probably because I made sure to keep her well-stocked with homemade baked goods. In return, she made sure to feed me bits of information now and then. Like Peter's 11 a.m. meeting with land developers to discuss selling this park to fund the stupid expensive high school stadium he was obsessed with.

With a growl, Peter glanced at his phone. His face turned a satisfying shade of greenish-white. "They'll be here in ten minutes. What the hell am I going to do?" He stabbed a finger in Mario's face. "Get her out of here now."

Mario hooked his thumbs into his belt loops and tracked Peter with narrowed eyes as he stomped toward the parking lot and disappeared. Then with a sigh that could be heard in the next county, he crouched beside me. "Alicia."

"Mario," I replied with all the sunshine and rainbows I could put into one word. Stay positive. Talk fast. Mostly tell the truth. Words to live by.

"You need to get out of here."

"Absolutely. There's just a tiny, itty-bitty little problem."

With a slow shake of his head, Mario's eyes slid shut. I knew that look, of course. This was not the first time Peter Stone had demanded Mario arrest me. Hell, it wasn't even the first time this month.

I spoke before he could. "Problem's not the right word. Just a little... issue."

"With what?"

"It seems the key may have not made it here with me." I could already picture it sitting on the kitchen counter where I set it while loading my backpack with three bottles of water, which I'd already chugged, and it wasn't even midday yet.

Note to self: Next time I chained myself to a tree in protest, consider how in the world I was gonna be able to pee.

Truly, I was usually more prepared than this, but Maria had texted me just before nine this morning with the details of the meeting, and I hadn't had time to plan properly. To be fair, it was also the first time I'd ever chained myself to a tree. A few hiccups were to be expected.

"Well, get yourself unchained. I do not want to call your mother," Mario said, a distinct note of pleading in his voice. "Please don't make me."

My mother, Stephanie Ramos, did not have a chill bone in her body. A true *smother* of the highest order. Nothing got her more worked up than when anyone messed with her sweet angel—her youngest and only daughter—me.

I really, really didn't want her help.

I use the word "help" loosely. Mom's special brand involved racing to my side, uncontrollable tears, strong words for whomever dared threaten her child, more tears, taking down badge numbers and making it clear she'd be calling to talk to someone's boss. That was all before she'd insist on taking me back to her house and suffocating me for the rest of the day.

Nope. Not calling Mom.

"No, no. Let's not do that. I'll find someone to quick bring me the key." I tapped a finger on my lips.

Ellie would be busy with the lunch rush. Frankie worked nights and was likely dead asleep. Not that he was a great option since he wouldn't be able to resist ratting me out; Mom would know eleven seconds after I hung up.

I peered at Mario, who peered back with a dark raised eyebrow. "Any time now, Alicia."

"Alright, alright," I grumbled, and hastily scrolled through the contacts on my phone. This is why I prepared for these things in advance.

Most of the time my best friend, Mae, was my backup plan and my backup plan's backup plan. But she was out of town visiting her fiancé's family; a big inconvenience for me. A year ago, I would have called Cal, my oldest brother, but he'd since taken a position in Portland. I liked to make him feel guilty about it often; it was how I showed love.

This was getting kind of pathetic. My list of emergency contacts (and by emergency, I meant rescuing me from sticky situations) had dwindled steadily over the last couple of years. I'd lost them to new love, engagements, career moves, life. Meanwhile, I was chained to a tree.

If that didn't say something about my life...

My eye snagged on a name and my heart thumped happily. But my heart had always been stupidly optimistic, a habit I'd vowed to break after my split with Alec the Awful.

I startled when Peter barked, "Why is she still here?"

"Shut up, Peter," Mario said, his eyes hidden behind mirrored sunglasses. But I knew he was staring at me just the same. "Alicia, get a move on."

I shot him a pleasant (and totally fake) smile. "I'm on it. I'll be out of your way before you know it."

Quickly, I composed a text message and hit send.

I pulled my sticky t-shirt from my body and stretched my legs. Shifting my weight, I shook out my arms. I didn't know which was worse—my urgent need to find a bathroom or the red tinge my skin was taking on by the second. At least I didn't have Peter scowling at me. He'd stomped off ten minutes ago after he made Mario promise he'd have me "taken care of" before he came back at one.

I patted the tree. "You're worth it."

This tree had been the center of our town since the two Hart brothers had settled here after the Civil War. It was right in front of this tree, maybe even where I was sitting, that the oldest brother married Emily. However, if the rumors were true, the large heart with the initials in the middle was made by the younger brother for the love of his life. Who also happened to be Emily.

Love was complicated, even back then. Love was also stupid, nonsensical, illogical, and downright exhausting. Which is why I was on a Love Sabbatical.

Alec had been clear our break-up was a Me Problem and not a Him Problem. At first, I'd been angry. Now I wondered if he was right. Maybe I was the problem. The unsolvable kind. All of it had felt like my heart had been run through a meat tenderizer. I was in no mood to relive that.

After adjusting my oversized sunglasses, I leaned my head against the trunk of the tree, ignoring how pieces of my light-brown hair snagged on the bark. My eyes drifted shut, the heat of the July sun making my limbs heavy and reminding me I hadn't slept well last night. Sleep was important; a lack of it was one of the few things I knew triggered my seizures. It had been eight months (or two years, depending on who you asked) since I'd had one and I'd like to keep it that way.

I must have dozed off because it was the grumbly voice of Mario saying, "Finally," that woke me. I cracked open one eye behind my glasses, then the other and watched Theo Goodnight head toward me, a ring of keys dangling from his fingers and a small, quiet smile hovering around his mouth.

I braced myself for the inevitable flutter of dragon wings—butterflies were much too small and delicate to create this sensation—in my stomach like they did each time I saw Theo. It was a sickness, and one I'd had since the age of fourteen, the summer I began to see Theo as something other than my brother's best friend.

A total cliché but I did everything in my power to get him to notice me back then, including: the two solid months I wore high heels every single day because I read men loved a woman in heels, the anonymous letters I slid into his locker and the final straw, tracking him down in his college dorm room and professing my undying love.

There was also the poetry. The kind of poetry you'd expect a lovesick teenage girl, whose working knowledge of poetry was limited to Dr. Seuss, might write.

The worst thing? A part of me would always have a crush on Theo.

Pausing at my feet, his smile grew as he took in the situation. "New hobby?"

I'd found that the easiest way to deal with Theo, to deal with anyone, was to pretend you were fine. Smile, joke around, make everyone comfortable, even if I wasn't, especially when I wasn't. It had become my superpower.

I shoved my sunglasses on top of my head. "Yep. City Hall's on the calendar for next week."

"Don't even think about it," Mario said from where he stood ten feet away, staring at his phone. "You get one free protest. After that, there will be consequences."

I rolled my eyes. "You're no fun."

"I saw that." Mario glared in my direction. "Get her out of here. I'm hungry and it's meatloaf day at the café."

"Yes, sir," Theo said. We both watched Mario head toward the parking lot, clearly finished with me. Theo's blue gaze slid sideways toward me, the corners of his eyes crinkling as they always did when he was amused.

I rattled the chains impatiently. "Hurry and get this off me. I have to, you know, go."

"Go where?"

"Go. You know, *go*."

The grin started as it always did with Theo—in his eyes first, his cheeks rising and causing his eyes to squint, and then moved to his mouth. I wouldn't call Theo shy, but he could be quiet, thoughtful. He ruminated before he acted. The man could take weeks to make a decision, but he always made the right one. It was his strength and his weakness.

"I have to go to the little girls' room. Please get these," I shook the chains, "off me."

Pressing his lips together, he ran a hand under his chin, which was covered in a light dusting of dark-blond hair—like a permanent five o'clock shadow. He'd started wearing it that way the last year or so. I liked it. A lot. "I don't know. I had to go out of my way to rescue you today."

I scoffed. "First, I'd like to point out you haven't done any rescuing yet. And second, you were at the high school, watching football practice and talking to the coach." Theo worked as a sports reporter for a big Houston newspaper. His job was to cover high school sports in the west side of the sprawling metro area. While it was technically summer, high school football camps were in full swing.

"True."

"The high school is a five-minute walk away from here." I flapped a hand in the general direction of the school. "And you drove."

He tapped a finger on his mouth right next to the tiny white scar that cut into his lip. He'd gotten it when he was twelve and he and my brothers decided to learn to juggle. With glass Coke bottles. "Also, true."

"Theodore Henry Goodnight, if you do not get me out of these chains, I will... I will... I'll think of something."

One dirty-blond brow arched. He tossed the keys in the air and caught them. "Threats? I don't know if that's the best strategy here."

"Please?"

He tsked. "Was that really sincere?"

"Yes. The lock. Now."

He took a couple of shuffling steps backwards. "I don't know."

"Theo."

"Let me know if you come up with something better." With that, he turned and began walking away.

"Get back here." My legs began to jiggle. Things were about to get real serious. I pulled out the big guns. "I have banana bread!"

He froze. "Chocolate chip banana bread?"

"Of course, with chocolate chips. I am not a monster. Next, you'll be asking me if it's gluten- and dairy-free."

He was unlocking me before I finished speaking. "You should have led with that. Let's go."

"Thank God some things never change." The chains loosened around me, and I wiggled free. Theo held his hand out and I took it, ignoring how solid and strong his grip was, how his fingers were a little rough on my skin. Or how the stupid dragon wings were trying to beat my ribs into dust.

I'd become very good at ignoring such things. Years of practice.

He squeezed my hand. "What's that mean?"

I shrugged. "You are easily swayed by baked goods."

"I am not." He dropped my hand and set his fist on his hip.

"Oh, yes sir, you are."

Two little ticks appeared between his eyebrows. "Only if chocolate is involved."

"Well, duh." I patted him on the cheek, the scruff there cool and surprisingly soft. "I know you like the back of my hand."

"I might have secrets."

I huffed a laugh and stepped away. "Sure."

Theo tilted his head, a fleeting sly glint in his eye. My stomach dipped, but by the time I blinked, the look had passed, replaced by thoughtful Theo. "You know, you might be surprised."

"You have a packet of gum in your left pocket."

He reached a hand into his left pocket and... pulled out a pack of gum. "How did you...?"

"Because you always have gum in your left pocket. Never your right. You had an orange for breakfast today and yesterday and the day before yesterday." I gave his chest a poke and caught a whiff of citrus that always followed him. "Because you have one for breakfast every morning."

"Fine. Yes." He frowned. "But I'm not that predictable."

I raised my eyebrows.

"I'm not."

"I've known you since I was six. You're basically my brother." I was pretty proud of myself for saying that with a straight face. Theo had never been and would never be "basically my brother." Or I was going to hell for my very un-sisterly thoughts about him.

He scowled, and I knew what he was going to say before he even said it. I knew it because I knew everything about Theo. I knew he was exactly five feet ten and a half inches tall. I knew when he let his hair grow out, it became unruly curls. I knew he loved being outdoors and he'd rather hike than spend time in a gym. I knew he favored faded t-shirts under long-sleeve plaid shirts with snap buttons that were never snapped. I knew he loved black licorice, hated olives, and could recite the lyrics to every Rush song ever produced. I knew he could be incredibly patient, he never forgot a birthday, and he could rattle off stats for hundreds of baseball players.

With a grin, I walked backwards. "I'm going to the bathroom. I'll meet you at your car."

"Fine." He waited until I'd flipped around and had my back to him before he said, "But, Alicia, I am—"

"Not your brother," I yelled. Without turning, I waved a hand in the air. "Knew you were gonna say that."

I knew because while a lot of things had been changing the last year, I could always count on Theo to be exactly who he was—a little predictable, comfortable—and I liked that about him.

Some people had comfort food; I had a comfort person. And I'd been two-thirds in love with him for half my life.

TWO

Note to self:
Online dating is a real MEAT market.
Think about becoming a vegetarian.

Monday, three weeks minus a day before the wedding

"Alright, spill." Ellie Sterns leaned on the counter, a bright-yellow apron with the words "Sit-n-Eat Café" embroidered across the front hanging from her neck. It was a little after one o'clock and the lunch rush had died down to a handful of regulars. "I heard you almost got arrested."

"My reputation precedes me, I see." I stuffed another bite of chili in my mouth. "This is amazing. I can't believe Ollie let you make something new."

The Sit-n-Eat Café was a Two Harts staple. The owner, Ollie Holder, a curmudgeon of a man somewhere between seventy-five and a hundred and seventy-five years old was very clear that the menu never, ever changed. Mondays were always fried chicken day, chicken-fried steak on Tuesdays, and so on.

The café was not open on weekends, and it only served lunch. There were no exceptions.

Once I asked if he had leftover tamales on a Friday. Not only did I not get an answer, but he also refused to talk to me for two weeks. Which was awkward because that was the summer I worked for him.

"I've been bugging him for months. I think he got tired of me asking." Ellie flipped her long braid over her shoulder and frowned. "Actually, I'm a little worried about him. He left early today because he wasn't feeling well."

"Ollie?" I said around a mouthful of cornbread. My table manners were on point. "I'm pretty sure he's indestructible. He's like Chuck Norris but shorter and with crazy eyebrows."

She huffed a laugh. "You're probably right. You've known him longer."

Ellie Sterns had landed in Two Harts a little over a year ago, her little boy Oliver in tow. Her brother, Chris, was Mae's fiancé and a defensive end for the Oklahoma Stars. He was kind of a football god, if I'm being honest, and I was a fan. But really, I loved him the most for loving Mae the way he did.

Ellie had come to Two Harts with the intention of meeting Mae and then heading to her parents' home in Oklahoma. But Two Harts can worm its way into a person's heart.

Ollie had had a permanent HELP WANTED sign in the café window until Ellie came along and became his newest employee. She'd found an apartment above the Spencers' garage to rent and settled into life at Two Harts like a champ. I liked Ellie. She was a little unpredictable, a little impulsive, a damn good cook, and a solid friend.

The bell on the door jangled announcing Mae's arrival. She slid onto the stool next to me.

"Sorry I'm late. Chris is headed back to Oklahoma for foot-ball camp, or whatever they call it. He came to say goodbye and

I got distracted with... stuff." Her red hair was half falling out of its ponytail, blue eyes sparkling, cheeks flushed, and—

"Maebell Sampson, is that a hickey on your neck?" I asked. Okay, maybe a little louder than I should since Mae slapped a hand over my mouth.

"It is not a hickey," she whispered. "I'm sure it's... it's..."

"Gross." Ellie screwed up her face in pretend disgust. "My brother gave you a hickey."

"A love bite," I said, or rather mumbled, behind Mae's hand.

Ellie grinned. "A sucker stamp."

I pulled Mae's hand away. "An affection affliction."

"Oooh. Nice one. How about"—Ellie placed the back of her hand on her forehead dramatically—"a passion patch."

Mae's face was about the same color as a beet. "Could you two stop, please?"

"Sure. Sure." I laughed so hard, I had to brace myself against the counter before I faceplanted in my chili. No need to waste good food. "I won't mention that lip legacy one more time."

"Me neither." Ellie held up her hand in the universal sign for "scout's honor." "Not one word about that sweetheart stain on your neck."

Mae covered her face with her hands as the two of us cackled. It was so fun to tease her these days. She'd spent a few years so stressed out and worried about everything and everyone, she'd had no time for fun. Chris gave her fun... and apparently hickeys.

"I'm going to kill him," Mae muttered. "There will be no wedding. Only a funeral and I will dance on his grave."

Murderous thoughts aside, they were so cute together. I was happy for her, truly, deeply, a hundred percent happy for her. Well, maybe ninety-seven percent happy and three percent jealous.

Still giggling, Ellie straightened. "Let me get you something to eat," she said to Mae, and then pointed at me. "And you have some explaining to do. I've only heard fifteen different versions from fifteen different people at this point."

Ellie disappeared behind the kitchen partition.

Mae arched an eyebrow in my direction. "I can't wait to hear what it was this time."

"First, you owe me an apology." I kept my voice light. "You're supposed to be around to rescue me."

"We've talked about this. I can't be here to rescue you all the time." She gave me a shoulder bump.

I sighed. "I know. I know."

Ellie reappeared and slid a bowl of chili in front of Mae. She rested her elbows on the counter in front of me. "Talk, lady."

"I will." I took a long sip of my sweet tea. "But first I want to hear how your date went on Saturday."

Ellie groaned. "It was bad. The sort of bad where I excused myself to the bathroom and never came back."

"Why?" Mae and I asked at the same time. Ellie's dates were legendary... for being awful.

She pulled out a dishtowel from her apron pocket and began scrubbing the already clean counter. "He was normal on the computer. His name was Ryan. Ryan is a perfectly normal name for a perfectly normal man, right?"

"Sure," I said.

"Wrong." She tossed the towel on her shoulder. "We met at a restaurant in Houston. It's this new place where the whole schtick is serving burgers made from exotic meat. So, we sit, we talk. He's nice. Like, really nice. Great smile. Dimples. Teaches high school history. That sort of thing. I say, 'Oh, they have ostrich burgers.'"

"Sounds gross," Mae murmured.

"Actually, I've heard ostrich meat is delicious," I said. "I read this article about—"

"Excuse me, focus." Ellie snapped her fingers. "I'm telling the story."

I grinned. "So sorry, go ahead."

"Then he says, 'Oh, ostrich is on my bucket list. It's a goal of mine to try as many different types of meat as I can before I die.' So, we order and we're chatting while we wait and then he says, 'Have you ever wondered what human meat tastes like?'"

"Shut up!" I said.

Ellie's braid whipped around as she shook her head. "I didn't say anything. I just stared at him. He looked at me like he wanted an answer, and he didn't blink. Not once. My creep-meter freaked out. 'No, I haven't ever wondered that,' I said. Then he shrugged and took a roll from the breadbasket, slapped some butter on it and all I could think was I might be the next thing he slapped butter on if I wasn't careful. So, I snuck out the first chance I got."

Mae and I gaped at her in stunned silence.

She shrugged, looking forlorn. "I'm beginning to think something is wrong with me. I attract deadbeats, losers, and now possible cannibals. My man picker is broken."

"Wow. I'm never dating again," I said. "Like, never."

Mae patted my arm. "Yes, you will. Not every guy wants to eat your face for dinner. Look at Chris."

"You sure about that?" I pointed to her neck; Mae did not look amused.

"Alright, I want to hear what happened on Friday," Ellie said as a customer arrived at the counter to pay. "Duty calls. Be right back."

My best friend turned a speculative eye in my direction. "You know, it has been a while since the break-up with Alec and—"

I hissed.

"Sorry. I forgot we're not supposed to say his name." She patted my arm.

"I gave you a list of acceptable things you could say instead."

"Yeah. Somehow Pea-Brained Coward doesn't roll off the tongue," Mae said in a dry voice.

"Alright, sorry to break up the moment," Ellie said, back in front of us. "But we close in twenty minutes, and I still don't know what you did."

With a wave of my hand, I straightened. "I chained myself to the Legacy Tree."

Ellie shook her head, baffled. "That's it? That doesn't seem your normal MO."

"It was spur-of-the-moment."

"Why?" Mae asked.

I pushed my empty bowl away. "It seems our illustrious mayor wants to sell Legacy Park."

"He wouldn't," Mae said.

"He wants that stupid football stadium and he's willing to do anything to get it. Including sell the park to some skeezy developers who'll tear down the tree and turn it into a strip mall. I really hate that guy."

"Same." Mae hated him even more than I did. That's what happens when your boss is also your ex-boyfriend. As the librarian, she'd had to fight him last year to keep her budget from being decimated.

"He can't do that, can he?" Ellie asked. "Doesn't he have to get it approved first?

"I'm sure it would have to go through the city council." Mae frowned. "But that council is full of people who would love to get more business in town. Even at the cost of our history."

"That tree has my parents' names carved on it. My dad proposed to my mom right in front of it." I propped my elbow on the counter and rested my chin in my palm, feeling more than a little disgruntled.

Mae patted me on the back. "We won't let it happen."

"So, who was your rescuer?" Ellie asked when I explained I'd forgotten the key to the padlock.

I squirmed in my seat, looking anywhere but at Mae. "Theo."

"Theo, of course." Mae smirked. "So nice of him."

"Who's Theo?" Ellie asked.

"He grew up with Ali and her brothers. Ali had the biggest crush on him when we were in high school. He lives in Houston now. Personally, I think Theo might ha—"

Cheeks heating, I cut her off. "Thank you for your thoughts, Mae."

"Have I seen him around? What's he look like?" Ellie asked, eyes bright with even the passing thought of something interesting to latch onto. She liked a little drama with her chili.

"Yes, Ali, do you happen to have any pictures to show us?" Mae arched an eyebrow because she knew I did.

I cleared my throat and stabbed around on my phone until I found a photo of him I especially enjoyed. It had been Cal's engagement party in my parents' backyard before he and Melanie moved cross country, a casual barbecue with some friends and family. He wore a regular old t-shirt and a regular old pair of shorts. I'd yelled at him to smile right before I snapped it and hadn't quite given him enough time, so his mouth was only tipped up one side, but his eyes were crinkled at the corners, and he was looking straight at me. Like he was seeing right into me and for some reason, what he saw made him... happy. I knew it was a question of timing and light, but I always wondered exactly what he was thinking at that moment.

"This is him." I handed the phone to Ellie.

After studying the photo, she let out a low cat whistle. "Oh, he's a cutie. He doesn't look like he's at the gym every spare minute or on some weird caveman diet."

I took the phone back and inspected the picture. Theo wasn't a gym rat like Frankie or extra lean like Cal who ran marathons for fun (I know, gross). He was somewhere in the middle. No six pack or bulging muscles. A normal guy. And so handsome.

"I see what you mean," Ellie said. "Her eyes are getting all dreamy and she's got a big, dopey smile."

Mae nodded. "Exactly. You should have seen her in high school when—"

"Nope," I cut in. "I'm way over all that."

I had to be. I was a realist when it came to Theo. The roles for he and me were cemented in years of friendship—minus that stupid little teenage crush—and that's exactly where it needed to stay.

Ellie and Mae didn't look convinced, both staring at me with dubious expressions.

"I am."

Mae arched an eyebrow. "No need to get defensive."

"I'm not defensive," I said very defensively.

"You know, Ellie hasn't been having much luck in the dating department." Mae tapped a finger on her chin. "We should fix her up with Theo. They'd get along great, don't you think?"

I narrowed my eyes. "No, I do not."

"Why? Something wrong with him?" Ellie asked.

"Yes, he... he smells."

Mae burst out laughing, and Ellie followed suit. "You are so full of it."

"It's alright." Ellie giggled. "You keep him all for yourself."

"You're both hilarious." I stood and slapped some money on the counter to cover my lunch. "I'm leaving now. Have your fun at my expense."

Before I left, I pulled my phone out and snapped a photo of Mae while she was still too overcome with laughter to stop me. With a wicked grin, I began to type a text message as I took slow steps toward the door.

"Did you take a picture of me?" Mae called out. "What are you doing?"

"Don't worry about it," I said over my shoulder, almost at the door. "I'm just letting Chris know how much you bragged about that little lip love note of yours."

"Ali! Do not encourage him!" She yelled right about the time I hit SEND.

THREE

Note to self:
If it looks like a jerk and acts like a jerk,
it's probably Peter Stone.

I took the long way home, which involved walking two extra blocks and cutting through the town square. Most people would have opted for driving given the heat of the day, but I didn't drive. I *could* drive but I hadn't been behind the wheel since I was sixteen. The handful of times I'd attempted to get over my crippling fear, I'd had panic attacks.

So, I walked. Everything I needed, I could walk to around here, and for the things I couldn't, I could usually con a friend or brother into taking me. Besides, walking meant I saw people, I chatted with them, I found out who was getting married or divorced, or having baby number three. I knew who was thinking about moving or whose business might be struggling.

Years ago, when the freeway was put in, all the traffic that used to come through town was diverted. Nowadays, our biggest rush of people came during our Founder's Day Festival. On the weekends, the city dwellers would stop by to pick through the antique stores. Mostly, Two Harts was a sleepy town, looking a little ragged around the edges and in need of a makeover. But it was my home and I loved it. Every worn brick and cracked sidewalk.

We had a small but busy public library with a kickass librarian to run it. (Spoiler: It's Mae, she's the librarian.) *Three* stoplights now. A few antique stores, a couple of restaurants *and* a taco truck. And we had the Legacy Tree. All located within a forty-minute drive to Houston.

Small-Town Heart; Big-City Neighbors. That was the winner of last year's slogan contest.

A dark-haired woman waved as she jogged past me pushing a double stroller—Deborah O'Brien, although I knew her as Debbie Cutter in high school. She was two years ahead of me back in school and now one marriage and two babies ahead of me in life.

Not that I was keeping track.

Don't get me wrong. I liked my life fine. But the break-up with Alec had forced me to take a long look at myself and while I wasn't a failure, I also wasn't content. The problem was that I wasn't sure what I was missing. Or maybe it's that I was missing out *on* something?

All Mae's talk at lunch of Theo hadn't helped. He was just a friend. Nothing more. And, if my heart had other feelings on the subject, it could get over it. Except I'd been trying to get over Theo Goodnight for years and doing a terrible job at it. I'd have to try harder, I suppose.

He's just a friend. He's just a friend.

Note to self: get that tattooed on your forehead. Maybe it will sink in then.

With a sigh, I turned the corner at Pappy's Market and came to an abrupt stop. Across the street sat a cheerful little yellow house with a white picket fence and a tidy yard.

The tiny, slightly stooped frame of Sarah Ellis, one of our

oldest Two Harts residents, was yanking on the arm of the wooden bench that had been in her front yard for as long as I could remember. The bench was not cooperating.

I jogged across the street and leaned against the fence. "Mrs. Ellis, do you need some help?"

She slapped her hand on her chest and wrapped her fingers around the ever-present pearl necklace she wore. Yes, ladies and gentlemen, she clutched her pearls. "Alicia, you scared me. I could use a bit of help, dear. If you don't mind."

"No problem." I let myself in the yard and hurried over to her. "Where are we moving this to? Other side of the yard?"

Mrs. Ellis looked harmless, like everyone's grandmother with her pale-blue polyester pants, matching floral shirt, and sensible white Velcro tennis shoes. (I bet they had great arch support.) But I'd once seen her smack Jackson Tillis, a grown man, over the head with her purse because he said something out of place. I'm not sure what she carried in that purse, but it was enough for him to wear a knot on his head for a week.

I had to give it to Mrs. Ellis; I liked her style.

"I got a notice I was breaking a city ordinance. I'm not allowed to have a bench in my front yard anymore." She pointed to the collection of garden gnomes piled together on the driveway. "My gnomes, too."

"No gnomes?"

"No gnomes."

"But..." Mrs. Ellis's garden gnomes were kind of a thing. Each holiday, she "dressed" them up for the season. Little Santa hats for Christmas, flags for the Fourth of July, peeking out of baskets for Easter. All the kids in town knew you had to walk by her house around any holiday to see what the gnomes were doing.

"I even special-ordered a whole set of reindeer gnomes for this Christmas." She shook her head.

"Did you say city ordinance?"

She pulled a folded yellow sheet of paper from her pocket. It was the back end of one of those triplicate forms and right across the top it read, CITY OF TWO HARTS ORDINANCE VIOLATION.

"Twenty-five dollars a day in fines for a bench and some garden gnomes," I read aloud. "But you've had this in your yard forever."

Mrs. Ellis stroked the top of the bench. "My husband, may God rest his soul, made that bench for me in nineteen sixty-seven. I sit in it every evening to enjoy the sunset and visit with the neighbors."

"This is ridiculous."

Mrs. Ellis lowered herself onto the bench. "I talked to Peter Stone. He said the ordinance has been on the books for years and the council decided it was time to start enforcing it. Between you and me, I think he's trying to make money for that football stadium, the rat bastard."

Pressing my lips together, I nodded. Peter freaking Stone, Mayor of Himself-ville, population one.

A couple of high school-aged boys walked by and I roped them into helping move the bench to Mrs. Ellis's backyard. After promising to come back soon to visit, I marched down the sidewalk. My walk took me past Two Harts High School. A large faded blue banner hung above the front entrance, which read:

Home of the Two Harts Blue Tarts: A-1 State Football Champions 1976.

Our high school was small, and it had been a long, long time since we'd made it past the playoffs in our division. Peter's obsession with a new high school football stadium was plain... stupid.

Two Harts didn't need a new stadium. We needed to put in a bit of hard work and grow some pride in our town. If we wanted to attract tourists, there were so many things we could do: a fireworks show on the Fourth of July, a Christmas parade, Easter egg hunts, movies in the park. Lean into the small-town quaintness of Two Harts. *That* would bring people here, not an overpriced football stadium.

I might not be able to fix an entire town, but Peter's obsession was a problem I *could* tackle right now. A little payback was in order. In the name of Mrs. Ellis's gnomes. A smile spread across my face as an idea began to form. I almost felt sorry for Peter.

I snorted. No, I didn't. Not even a little bit.

FOUR

Note to self:
Become a more adult-like adult ASAP.

Tuesday, two and a half weeks before the wedding

"Less than three weeks now. Are you ready for darkness to descend upon you?" I asked, grinning at my oldest brother on the phone screen. Since moving to Portland, the only time I got to "see" him were the couple of times a week we talked on the phone.

He snickered. "Don't talk about Mom like that."

"Be nice." Cal's fiancée, Melanie, leaned against him to fit into the frame. "You know she means well. Her methods are a little..." Her voice trailed off, unsure how to best complete that sentence.

Cal and I laughed. Melanie was sweet and kind and stupidly in love with my brother. I liked her a lot, even if she'd been the one to encourage my brother to apply for a job two thousand miles away.

"You two are impossible." Melanie rolled her eyes and then shoved Cal out of the frame. "I did want to ask you one more time..."

I sighed. "Melanie."

"I just want to make sure you're not going to be uncomfortable." She squeezed her hands together under her chin. "I want everyone happy that day and I don't want to have to worry about a screaming match between members of the wedding party."

"I have never had a screaming match in my life," I said, offended.

No need to waste that sort of energy when there are other ways to deal with someone.

"It's not you I'm worried about doing the yelling," Melanie muttered. "I know Alec—"

"I'll be fine, I promise."

Here's another thing about Melanie—she was Alec's older sister. Yes, that Alec. In fact, Alec and I had been the ones to introduce her to Cal. And look at us now. Cal and Melanie were about to get married, and I'd gladly spend a lot of money to never be in the same room with Alec again. But I've been determined to be the bigger person. I could get through a couple of days of being around him and not cause trouble.

Probably.

Melanie nibbled her bottom lip, concern flitting across her face. "Are you sure? We could figure something out."

"He's your brother. He has every right to be at your wedding. We're both adults."

Big words from me. Big, lying words. Sure, the fresh fish I hid in his car after the break-up wasn't exactly mature on my part. And giving every realtor in the Dallas/Fort Worth area his phone number and email address wasn't totally on the up and up.

But he started it. How he broke up with me. What he was doing forty-eight hours later. Yeah, he definitely started it.

"If you're sure?"

"Totally." I grinned so wide my cheeks hurt but I'm really trying to sell it. For Cal and Melanie, I would suck it up. It's not like I would have to talk to him except to be polite.

"Alright then." Melanie stared at me for a beat longer, maybe waiting for me to break into a blubbery mess of tears. Not happening. "Have you gotten your dress?"

"Yup. And I have to say I look pretty damn good in it." We'd had a choice of dress styles all in the same soft-pink color. I'd gone with an A-line dress that hit me just below the knee. It was tank-style with a deep V neckline and a belted waist.

"Always humble."

"Always," I repeated with a grin.

As a member of the Pear-Shaped Body Society, I had narrower shoulders, wide hips, and enough junk in the trunk to outfit an antique store. Because I didn't drive, I walked everywhere, ran a couple of times a week, and was always up for a friendly game of soccer. I liked to move my body when I could but I wasn't doing it so I could look better; I did it because it made me *feel* better.

However, it did not change the shape of my body, and that was cool. If not being a size 8 (or 10, or... okay, fine, I was a size 14) meant still getting to eat homemade lasagna and snickerdoodles, I was just fine. (Even if trying to find a pair of jeans that didn't gap at my waist was near impossible.)

"And the shoes?" she asked, her voice a touch sharp. "You returned the other ones and got the right ones."

"Um..."

"Ali," she snapped. "You need the right shoes, or you'll ruin the entire mood of the wedding party."

Melanie was an elementary art teacher and about the sweetest, gentlest person I knew. She caught spiders in the bathroom and escorted them outside after she'd given them names and backstories. Besides already being poor ('cause teacher), she often bought extras for the students she worried about—school supplies, shoes, coats. She was a bona fide saint.

But planning a wedding could bring out another side in a person. A scary, demanding, irrational side.

For the record, I had gotten the correct style of shoes but in pure white instead of cream. Clearly a mistake worthy of ruining everything. "I'm going later this week. I still have time, I swear."

Melanie stared at me for a long, uncomfortable moment and then suddenly smiled. "I can't wait to see you. I'm so excited. I'm giving you back to your brother. He's starting to pout. Talk to you soon."

Cal's face reappeared. "Hey, kid, I wanted to ask you something."

"Don't call me kid." I knew he wouldn't stop and I kind of liked it anyway. It was our thing.

Calvin Coolidge was the oldest of my brothers, seven years my senior. Our parents named each of the boys after presidents, the other two being Franklin Roosevelt and Abraham Lincoln. You can guess why they all preferred nicknames.

As for me, I was named for my two grandmothers: Alicia Grace. When I was about six or so, I asked why I hadn't been named after a president and Mom told me there hadn't been one to name me after. Family lore states I sighed deeply, and said very seriously, "Well, I guess I'll do it then."

As my oldest brother, Cal gave the best advice and if trouble was brewing, he'd step in in a heartbeat to take the heat. Now, I'm not saying I got in trouble a lot... let's say a moderate amount... but there's never been a bully or an injustice I could pass up without at least doing something about it. If I needed an alibi, Cal always provided it, no questions asked.

"I have a favor," he said, his voice pensive.

"I promised I wouldn't pull any pranks on the wedding day. Although, I think you should reconsider my idea of *The Muppets'* theme song for the recessional."

"No," Melanie yelled in the background. "Just no."

"I'll bring the sheet music. I can just slip it to the piano player. Sometimes it's better to ask for forgiveness than permission."

Melanie's face popped back onto the screen. "If I hear even a note of that song, I will tell your mother that living alone scares you."

I sucked in a breath. "You wouldn't."

"Try me, lady."

"Fine. Yes, I promise. Go yell at your florist or something. You're freaking me out."

"Alright, honey, she understands," Cal said, his voice gentle. He pried the phone away from his intended, who was still staring at me with freakishly violent eyes. Finally, she turned, and I watched her walk through the doorway to the kitchen behind Cal's head.

Cal shook his head. "I can't wait for this wedding to be over."

"I heard that," Melanie bellowed. "Don't think I can't hear you even if you're whispering."

He smacked a palm against his forehead, and I bit back a laugh.

"So, this favor..."

"It's a big one." He rubbed the back of his neck. "I asked Abe to come to the wedding."

"Really?"

"He hasn't said yes." A sadness seeped into his eyes. "I want this. I want to have everyone together. It's time, you know?"

"Yeah," I whispered.

Abe was the youngest of my brothers, four years—almost to

the day—older than me. And perhaps because he was the nearest in age to me, he'd been the one I was closest to growing up. Abe had a soft, mushy heart he'd hid under a surly, teenage boy attitude. He was great with his hands, an out-of-the-box kind of thinker, but he struggled in school, never making the grades our brothers did.

He and Dad fought constantly. Dad called him lazy and unambitious. When Abe graduated (still not quite sure how that happened) and decided to forego college for a job working at an auto shop in Houston, Dad was livid. The accident was the last straw. The fight between them that night was huge, the things they said to each other, things that couldn't be unsaid. Painful things. The next morning when I woke, Abe was gone.

One day, I had my brother, one of my best friends, and the next, he wasn't there. He never came back.

Oh, we talked on the phone. Sometimes I even got him to send a photo, or video-chat with me. In Colorado now, he was doing well for himself. He was part owner of a successful auto shop. He seemed happy, and I was happy for him.

But he hadn't spoken to our parents in eleven long years or been back to Two Harts. He'd missed birthdays and holidays and celebrations and hugs from our mom. He hadn't even come home when Grandma Grace died a year ago.

We talked about most things in our lives. I knew about the girlfriends he'd had; he knew about Alec. Movies, music, TV shows, pet peeves, almost anything, except for the accident. Neither of us ever brought that up. But the guilt was like a living thing inside me.

"I think if it came from you, he might seriously consider it."

My pulse thumped in my ears; sweat gathered at the back of my neck. "I'm not sure this is a good idea."

"He always had a hard time saying no to you." He paused, clearing his throat. My big brother, who'd always had my back since I was a scrawny tagalong kid sister, had to look away before I saw the tears welling up. “I miss him, Ali. He should be there.”

“I miss him, too.” So much.

But Cal didn’t know the whole story. No one did. Abe wasn’t the reason for that accident, as everyone thought; I was.

FIVE

Note to self:
Remember that your best friend can read you like a book, and as a librarian, she's really, really good at reading.

Wednesday, two and a half weeks before the wedding

Next morning, I knocked on the library door a half hour before it opened, clutching a bag from our local bakery and two iced white chocolate coffees with whole milk because this was not the time to worry about calories and too much caffeine consumption.

The best part about working as a virtual assistant was the hours. The worst part about working as a virtual assistant was also the hours. I tended to start a project at the worst time (oh, say two in the morning after the adrenaline from extracurricular activities kept me from falling asleep) and get so wrapped up, stopping was an impossibility. Flash forward four hours later and I wake up to my cheek resting on the keyboard and fifty-seven pages of the letter X on my Word document.

Which is why it looks like I rolled right out of bed this morning. Because I did.

So. Yes. I needed the caffeine.

"Oh, you brought me presents." Mae took the bag from me.

We made our way to her small office, which had recently been painted a sunny yellow. Her desk, like everything else about the library, was organized and neat. Several pictures were hanging on the corkboard above it. Mae with her mom and sister, Mae and Chris, Mae and me, all normal-sized photos. But crowding them were oversized photos, all featuring Chris—an action shot of him during a game, another of him posing shirtless while snuggling a puppy, another of him dressed in a suit that had clearly been tailored for him, and yet another of he and Mae kissing.

"When did you get a shrine to Chris?" I asked, pointing at the photos. "Not that I'm complaining."

Football god and actual Eagle Scout. I was not coveting; I was appreciating.

"That was all his handiwork." Mae slid into a chair at the small round table we often had meals at and peeked in the bag. "Uh-oh, chocolate croissants."

Having been my person since the fifth grade, Mae knew everything there was to know about me, including what happened on the day of that accident. She also knew chocolate croissants were harbingers of bad news.

"First, the croissants, and second, you've not made a single comment about this scarf." She set out a couple of napkins and placed a croissant on each before leaning back in her chair.

I hadn't even noticed the scarf—a gauzy blue number roped around her neck, which stood out even more with her snarky librarian t-shirt (this one read, *Don't Make Me Shush You*) and jeans.

I smirked. "Okay, Captain Obvious. You know, you can use

make-up to cover it. Or be loud and proud. Your hot football player fiancé likes you a lot. Besides, who's going to notice?"

"You think?" She pulled off the scarf and tossed it on the table.

Yikes. The hickey was even more pronounced today than it had been yesterday. I took an overlarge bite of my croissant and mumbled around it, "Yeah. You're good."

"Alright, enough about me. Tell me what's going on."

"So, the thing is..." But instead of talking, I fiddled with the hem of my t-shirt, then pulled my hair out of its ponytail and reworked it into a messy bun, and then took another huge bite of my croissant and chewed. Slowly.

Mae waited me out, eyeballing me over her iced coffee with concern.

Finally, I wiped my fingers off on my thighs. "Cal asked me to do something."

"Does it involve anything illegal?"

"No." Although I don't think Cal would be opposed to me drugging and kidnapping Abe. I took a deep breath and told her what Cal asked.

He wanted me to swing by Colorado, surprise my brother, hug it out, and convince/force him to come to the wedding. Oh, and keep it all a secret from our parents.

No. Big. Deal. What could possibly go wrong?

I stuffed the rest of my croissant in my mouth and waited for Mae to say something.

"That's... a lot." She frowned. "But how would that work? Aren't you riding out there with your parents?"

The transportation of the Ramos family to Oregon had become quite the ordeal. Mom had roughly seventy-three thousand "wedding things" to bring with her plus her father, my grandpa Mack, who refused to fly. Frankie could only take off a few days for the weekend, so he and his girlfriend, Ruth, were arriving on their own, and then there was me. I went wherever they told me. Which happened to be in the backseat of my parents' car.

Or that's what the plan had been.

I took a sip, the tang of the overly sweet coffee giving me a jolt. "Cal thought of that. Mom's been panicking about fitting all the wedding crap and me and Dad and Mack in the same car. Then she wanted to take two cars, but Dad put his foot down."

"How many centerpieces can one woman make?"

My mother had gone all out, put all her years of pent-up crafting to work after having given birth to a daughter who would rather eat live spiders than do things like needlepoint and quilling—whatever that is. Don't get me wrong, I was creative, but not in the arts and crafts way. My creativity tended toward more colorful pursuits.

But Mom had made candles and origami flowers, name cards for the rehearsal dinner and the reception. And there was the wedding arch, which disassembled for easy transport.

"A lot, apparently."

"Back to my original question, you're not going to be able to ride with them. How are you getting there?"

"Well," I cleared my throat, "Theo is driving out and, according to Cal, said I could go with him." I pushed the second croissant I'd dug out of the bag aside and laid my cheek on the table. It was cool on my skin. If there was one subject that made me flush, it was Theo.

"Oh, really?"

"Don't say it," I muttered, closing my eyes so I couldn't see her smirk.

"I bet he volunteered for that job. All those long, long hours in a car, only the two of you."

I groaned. "We won't even be alone for long. We're picking up Mack in Amarillo."

"What's the big deal? You like hanging out with him."

"Yes. It's just..."

How do I explain I tried so hard to limit my time around Theo because I didn't want to get too attached, too hopeful? He wasn't interested in me like that, no matter what Mae thought. He'd made that clear years ago and we'd managed to find a way to get over the awkwardness and keep our friendship. It had taken years to make everyone forget Theo-besotted teenage Ali and her earnestness. It had taken years to (mostly) forget how banged up my heart got, too.

"Is it because of Al—er, the Spawn of Satan?" she asked hesitantly. "Do you still miss him?"

"Ugh. No." I didn't miss him. I missed the idea of having a person. I missed cuddling and laughing and kissing. But I didn't miss Alec. He could go jump in a piranha-infested lake and die a slow, painful death.

It was going to be so great seeing him at the wedding, a real highlight of my summer. Obviously.

The honest truth was I was still hurt because of what Alec *said* when he broke up with me. How he labelled me as "emotionally unavailable" and "closed off" and said that I "deflected" when things got "real." He went on to say I was "too set in my ways" and "unwilling to bend." It was like he'd taken a crash course from Dr. Phil.

He wasn't wrong about some of it.

When we graduated, he moved to Dallas for a job he landed; I headed back to Two Harts. We decided to keep dating despite the five-hour drive between us and our relationship being so new. For the first year or so, it seemed to work. He came to see me; I'd bribe someone to drive me there. We did it; we were one of those couples that could survive long-distance dating.

I actually bragged about this.

Until it became clear Alec was starting to get frustrated. He began to occasionally bring up the idea of me moving to Dallas.

Wouldn't it be great if we lived in the same city, like before? We could see each other all the time. Or, what if I started driving again? That would make things easier. But I had never told Alec the reason behind my fear of driving.

At first, the comments were small and infrequent, easy for me to brush off, to pretend the idea of either of those things didn't make me nauseated. Then his questions got more direct and forceful. He wanted answers.

My dream had always been to live in Two Harts, raise a family here, give them the kind of idyllic, small-town childhood I'd had. I hated Dallas with its skyscrapers and traffic and fake country chic twist on everything. I tried to explain this to Alec, tried to make him understand. When the bitterness began to seep in, we ignored it. It was another two years of phone calls and text messages and trips to see each other, of sly comments and rolled eyes, of hurt feelings and misunderstandings. But I still stuck with it. At least I had a person, right?

Then one Saturday afternoon, he threw up all the feelings he'd been keeping inside. Looking back, Alec had done us a favor. I even respected him for it, for not trying to shield me from the truth like I was a delicate flower who couldn't handle it. Like the way my parents insisted on treating me.

What I didn't respect was how he'd broken up with me. Via text message.

He got to say all the things he wanted to say and then he blocked my number like the rotten coward he was. I hadn't told anyone, including Mae, that. I couldn't bear to say it out loud. Four years of my life and all I was worth to him was a long, ranty text message and the cost of postage to mail back the few things he had of mine.

"Maybe," Mae said, interrupting my thoughts, "this is a chance to see how you feel about Theo and how he feels about you."

"I don't think I'm relationship material." I picked at the

flaky bits on my croissant, not meeting her eyes. "Maybe I'm too selfish."

Mae's lips thinned. "That doesn't sound like the Ali I know. It sounds like something that gaslighting, insensitive, narcissistic jackass tried to make you believe." Mae had never been a big fan of Alec. She scooted her chair next to mine and put an arm around my shoulders. "I'm worried about you."

"I know," I whispered. "I'm kind of worried about me, too."

"It's like Alec broke up with you and he took all your sunshine with him." I put my head on her shoulder. "I hate him."

That's the kind of friendship we had; we showed our love with mutual hate. True loyalty.

My nose stung, but I sat up and flashed Mae a big smile. "Hey, I'm still a freaking ray of sunshine, what are you talking about?"

Mae's return smile was small. "Yes, you are."

"I like my life. It's a great life."

Arms crossed, she sat back in the chair. "Totally."

"I love living in Two Harts. Most of my family is here." I waved a hand in her direction. "You. Ellie. My life is full. So, I've been feeling a little... I don't know, lost? But that will go away with time."

Mae kept her silence, waiting me out.

"It feels like a lot of things are changing," I blurted out. "I don't know what that means for me exactly. Am I supposed to be making big life moves right now? Is it okay to live a quiet life in a quiet town?"

"There's not a thing wrong with that. As long as that's the life you want. I'm saying the Ali I've always known doesn't do anything quietly." Mae straightened, her expression thoughtful. "Maybe it's time for change."

"Like how?"

"That's up to you, I guess. What do you want your life to look like?"

"Geez. Being engaged makes you get all deep," I muttered.

I let her words sink in and quietly admitted to myself what I wanted my life to look like; one where fear didn't hold me back. I fiddled with my cup of iced coffee, swiping at the condensation.

The library door flew open.

"Mae," a man bellowed.

Mae's eyes narrowed. "Peter."

He barreled around the checkout counter and appeared in the doorway to Mae's office. His eyes landed on me instantly. "Alicia Ramos."

I turned extra slowly in my seat until I faced him, already knowing why he was looking for me. His face was flushed, and he was breathing hard, like he'd run all the way here. Beside me, Mae's back went rigid, her arms across her chest as though she was prepared for battle—the consummate Mama Bear.

"You." His fists curled at his sides like he wished there weren't witnesses.

Excellent. I smiled widely.

"Garden gnomes," Peter ground out. "Everywhere. All over."

"Do you think you could try to talk in complete sentences?" Mae asked. "You're not making any sense."

He stabbed a finger in my direction. "She knows exactly what I mean. They're all over my front lawn. And... and those gnomes are all placed in indecent positions. Indecent!"

"Indecent gnomes? I don't know a thing about that." I tapped my chin thoughtfully. "I did hear having benches and other lawn ornaments comes with a hefty fine from the city these days."

"I don't know how you did it," he leaned closer, "but I know it was you."

Blinking innocently, I pulled back to put more room in between us. I wasn't like Mae, who could cut a person down to size with one sharp-tongued insult; my preferred method of dealing with people was to put them in their place more... creatively. The man in front of me had been on the receiving end of many, many, many of my revenge pranks. It was not my fault; if he'd quit acting like a giant jackass, I could stop.

Peter's eyes seemed to bulge right out of his head, his face turning purple. He loomed over me, bracketing me in with his arms on the table. "You are the most annoying, childish, pathetic person I have ever met."

Mae stood, her voice sharp. "That's enough, Peter."

He adjusted the cuffs of his long-sleeved shirt. "I'm the mayor of this town. Remember that."

With that, he stormed off. I turned back around in my chair. "Did you get the feeling he was angry?"

"Indecent gnomes?"

"Sounds like whoever thought of that is a genius."

"*Someone* who needs to retire from her questionable activities." Mae plopped in her seat.

"Then who would keep Peter on his toes? He has to have someone challenge him or he'll claim he's king and we are all merely his peasants, here to do his bidding."

Mae's eyes narrowed. "He does need someone to challenge him."

"Yes, he does." I took a huge bite of my second croissant, suddenly feeling ten times better than five minutes before.

Mae's fingers began tapping on the counter. "You know what would be amazing? If someone finally ran against him in the mayoral race. The elections are this spring."

Peter has run unopposed for his last two (and only) races. Like his father who'd been mayor before him and his grandfather before that. They had a monopoly on the Two Harts political scene.

I laughed. "I'd support anyone who ran against him. It could be an inanimate object, maybe one of those gnomes, and I'd still vote for it."

Mae's blue eyes fixed on me with intensity.

"You're creeping me out."

"Just thinking that person would need spunk to run against him." She flicked a finger up. "Someone who loves this town." Another finger. "Someone who Peter can't intimidate." Yet another finger. "Someone who has a strong sense of justice." Suddenly, one long finger was pointed at me. "Someone like you."

My mouth dropped open. "Are you kidding?"

"Not even a little." She smirked. "Think how angry Peter would be."

"You cannot be serious."

Ignoring me, Mae pulled out a sheet of paper and a pen and began writing. "Oh, man. I would *pay* to see his face when he found out. I could be your campaign manager and we could make signs." She paused and tapped the pen on her mouth, staring off into the distance.

I snapped my fingers in her face. "Mae. I am not running for mayor. People would laugh their heads off."

She rolled her eyes. "No, they wouldn't. They would absolutely support you. The more I think about this, the more I know you'd be amazing."

"No."

"We were just talking about how it's time for a change."

"I was thinking more along the lines of changing out the curtains in my living room or getting a new phone, not running for public office." Agitated, I stood and dumped the other half of my croissant in the garbage can. "All I wanted to do was cry over chocolate croissants with my sensible, practical best friend. Instead, it appears she has lost her ever-lovin' mind."

Mae leaned back in her chair, unperturbed by my outburst.

"I am in total control of my faculties, thank you very much, and I'm serious."

"Whatever," I mumbled and marched out of the office, around the counter and was almost to the door when it opened and Mrs. Katz, my now-retired sixth-grade teacher and, because he was never far behind her, Horace Otismeyer, former train conductor, breezed in. Mrs. Katz had scared the crap out of me when I was a kid, and it wasn't much better now I was an adult. She had a brisk, no-nonsense way about her that tended to get under my skin. Probably because I prided myself on being as indirect as possible when it suited my needs.

I pasted on a smile and waved. "Hi, Mrs. Katz."

"Alicia," she said as she sailed past me, clearly on a mission.

I'd just pulled the door open when I heard her exclaim, "Maebell Sampson, is that a hickey on your neck?"

SIX

Note to self:
Rearrange all of Frankie's kitchen cabinets while he's at work.
And hide his hair gel.

Frankie was waiting by my front door when I arrived home, still in his uniform from working a ten-hour shift overnight. Like everything in his life, Frankie took his job seriously, right down to the creases in his uniform pants. He worked out every day, ate the recommended number of calories to maintain his physique, and made sure to get the right amount of sleep to keep him alert.

And although he'd never admit it, he spray-tanned on the regular. Ruth happened to work at a tanning salon. I couldn't confirm which came first—the spray tan or the girlfriend—but it all led down the same path. My meathead brother, with his obsession for rules, and slightly orange skin.

He was also my next-door neighbor. Mom loved this arrangement. She had a built-in snitch.

"Hello, brother, dear." I bounced up the steps to my front door and opened it.

Frankie pursed his lips. "You left it unlocked again."

"Oh, whoops." Of course, I left my apartment unlocked. This was Two Harts. I did lock it at night but otherwise, technically anyone could walk right in and make themselves at home when I was gone.

After slipping off my shoes, I wandered into the kitchen to fetch a bottle of water for Frankie and me and then wandered back into the living room and flopped on the recliner. I loved my little apartment with its big picture windows that allowed light to stream in in the mornings. The couch was an indiscriminate tan but covered in colorful throw pillows to distract from its boringness. Any space that could hold a picture frame, did. The walls were crammed with photographs of all the people I loved—my parents, my brothers, Mae, and, yes, Theo.

"You need to lock it, Ali." He followed me inside. "Things happen. Last night, we got called to the Sinclairs for a possible prowler."

The Sinclairs lived two streets over from me and a block away from a certain mayor. "Oh, a prowler? What happened?"

Frankie threw himself on my couch and caught the water bottle I tossed him. "Someone stole their garden gnomes."

"No way." I took a gulp of my water to hide my grin.

"Yep." He stretched out on the couch, the hand with the water bottle dangling over the side and his other arm over his eyes.

"That's crazy."

"Crazy is one way to describe it," he muttered. "The funny thing is that we got called to Peter Stone's house this morning and can you guess what we found?"

"A whiny man-child with strong narcissistic leanings?"

He lifted his arm and turned his head enough to glare at me. "We found the gnomes, doing very un-gnomelike things, by the way."

"Do we know what gnomes do in their private lives? Sounds pretty judgmental if you ask me."

He grunted. "We also found lots of other things that came from a lot of neighbors' yards. All over Peter's lawn."

I tsked. "Who would have thought the mayor was behind all this? I hope he was arrested. It's not safe for him to roam around. You know the saying: gnomes today, public statues tomorrow."

Ignoring me, he waved his water bottle in my direction. "I managed to divert their attention away from you, sis. You're welcome."

"Aw, shucks. You do love me."

"However, I could always tell Mom."

"You wouldn't." But it had been established long ago that he could.

"Unless you can make it worth it for me to keep my mouth closed."

"Does your boss the sheriff know about your proclivity to blackmail me?"

Frankie swung his feet to the floor and sat up. "Mario actively encourages it."

"Whatever."

He stood and waltzed to the door. "Two dozen chocolate chip cookies should do it."

"Fine." I sighed. "Hey, before you go, can I ask you a question?"

"Sure."

"Hypothetically, if Abe showed up to Cal's wedding, what do you think Dad would do?"

Frankie blinked, surprise written on his face. After a moment of thought, he shrugged. "Honestly, I don't know. I wish I could say I knew for sure he could forgive and move on, but Dad and Abe were always butting heads over every little thing. It sure would be nice to see him, though."

"Yeah, I know." I sat, staring at the door long after Frankie left, wondering if this might be my chance to finally correct the mistake I'd made eleven years ago. Or if it was a disaster waiting to happen.

SEVEN

Note to self:
Go over boundaries with Mom again.
And again.
And yet again, just to be sure.

Friday, nine days until the wedding

"Oh, wait a minute," my mom said after she recounted the boxes she'd made my father and Theo stack in the back of Theo's SUV. "I think I'm missing the two boxes of centerpiece candles."

My father gave a long-suffering sigh and ran a hand over his shiny bald head. "Stephy, how in the hell can you have this much stuff? It's one wedding."

"Excuse me, Eli. This is our baby boy getting married. It's only the most important day of our lives."

Mom's knack for hyperbole was renowned. In fact, if hyperbole was a person, my mother would win the Ms. Hyperbole USA Pageant hands down.

"Not even the birth of your children," I murmured. "Wow."

From his spot across from me, Theo lowered his head and adjusted his baseball cap. I didn't miss his smile.

"Well, of course, the birth of my children was important." Mom fussed with her short blonde hair, looking only slightly embarrassed. "I just meant this wedding is a very special occasion and I've spent months making these things because I want everything to be perfect."

Dad ground his teeth together. "Woman, this wedding can't come soon enough."

Mom put her hands on her hips. "What does that mean?"

With a sigh, I crossed my arms and rested a hip on the tailgate of Theo's SUV. I knew where this was headed. Theo's eyes found mine.

Here we go, he mouthed.

I rolled my eyes. *Of course.*

Dad arched one dark eyebrow. "You've lost your ever-lovin' mind is what it means. We haven't had a home-cooked meal in a month. You haven't been to bed before one in weeks and our house looks like a craft store and a wedding cake had a baby, a real ugly baby."

Theo shook his head, visibly biting back a laugh. *Uh-oh.*

"Well, excuse me, O Great and Mighty Man of the House. I'm so sorry I haven't been pampering you like a good little wife should."

I made a tick mark in the air. *Point goes to Mom.*

"Where's this damn box?" Dad roared.

"In the craft room," Mom yelled right back.

"Theo," Dad barked, glaring at my mother.

Theo snapped to attention. "Yes, sir."

"Come help me." Dad stomped off. Theo shot me an amused look before following my dad into the house.

My parents had been married for thirty-six years and for as long as I could remember, they drove each other crazy, but not in a way I ever thought they didn't love each other. They bickered in love. Once when I was eight and a boy in my class announced his parents fought all the time and so they were getting a divorce, I'd gone home in tears, certain my parents would be next.

Mom had explained all couples communicated differently, but that she loved my father very much. She and Daddy enjoyed sharing their feelings loudly. "Although, the best part is making up after. You should be thanking us. The reason all you kids exist is because of our yelling."

Eight-year-old me hadn't understood that. Thankfully.

While they did enjoy an argument, I'd also seen them weather tragedy and hardships and do it together. They were a good team when they had a common enemy.

Mom shook her head but stared at Dad the entire time he walked away, a hint of appreciation in her eyes. "That man does drive me crazy, but the backside on him is—"

"Gross, Mom."

"You should be grateful to have parents still married after all these years."

I shrugged. "I don't know. Divorced-parent guilt and step-parents would have meant more presents at Christmas."

"Alicia!"

With a grin, I slung an arm around her waist. "Love you."

After a moment, she unfolded her arms and hugged me back. "Did you pack your medication?"

"Yes." I sighed.

"And your rescue meds?"

"Yes."

"What about the first aid kit?" After I nodded, she continued, "I can print you out another page with all the important phone numbers on it if you need it."

"Mom." I dropped my arm and took a step back.

"I want you to be prepared. You never know when you'll have another seizure."

I slumped. That was the real crux of it.

Ever since that first seizure when I was sixteen, my mother had made it her mission to keep me safe. If she could get away with covering me in feathers and bubble wrap and writing "Fragile" on my forehead in permanent marker, she would. I understood her worry. Really, I did. I tried to be patient with her.

I'd had to deal with so many aspects of having epilepsy—the years of breakthrough seizures before finding the right combination of medications; the knowledge I'd probably take that medication my entire life; the fear that even after years of being seizure-free, they could return with no warning. But sometimes the hardest part was the guilt, the guilt that I caused so much worry in the people I loved.

"Mom," I said gently. "We've talked about this."

"I know. I know. I just worry." That was an understatement. My mother took worry to Olympic gold medal heights.

"And?"

"And I need to respect your boundaries and give you the space to be independent," she said, like a kid reciting the state capitals in class.

That was because it was, word for word, the "contract" I'd had her sign six months ago after a particularly alarming episode involving my mother bursting into my apartment after I hadn't answered my phone. I had been in the shower; Naked Ali had not been happy. We'd had a long talk after that and came up with a contract of sorts. It was still pretty touch-and-go.

You know those women who have a passel of boy children, get pregnant again and people ask them things like, "Trying for a girl, huh?" Most are quick to say, "Oh, no, I just want a healthy baby."

Not my mom though. I'd heard the tales of her proclaiming she would only be giving birth to a girl and that was that. God, perhaps not willing to deal with the amount of complaining that would come from my mother if she didn't get one, obliged. And thus, I liked to say she pretty much willed me into existence.

From as early as I could remember, I was wearing frilly pink dresses and giant hairbows. Gymnastics and dance classes started when I was four. We had girls' nights from the time I was ten. We'd curl up in bed and watch a movie together, paint our nails, and try out face masks. My mom and I were close. Did she make me want to pull my hair out sometimes? Sure. Was she a lot to handle? Also, yes. But my mom was the best even in those moments, too.

"So. The centerpieces." I pointed at the boxes and boxes of stuff in the back of Theo's SUV. It was a good thing it had third row seating. He'd already packed it with his camping gear. After the wedding, he'd be going on a month-long, solo camping trip, something he did every summer, and I'd drive back home with my parents.

"Yes, the candles." She clapped her hands with excitement. "They are darling. In fact, I've started selling them online and they've been a big hit."

"Oh, really?"

"I posted a video of my newest candle and people are ordering so fast I can't keep up. I had to start a waitlist." Mom whipped her phone out. "Let me see if I can find the pictures."

I tuned her out as she began describing with intricate detail the candles and centerpieces and I don't know what else.

Dad and Theo returned, shoving the two boxes in the car.

"There. Happy?" Dad raised a dark eyebrow.

"Thank you, honey." She pressed a kiss to his forehead, seeing as how she was a couple of inches taller than him. While she was tall, blonde and a card-carrying member of the Peach-shaped Body Society, Dad was stocky and his light-brown skin, which stayed permanently tan in the Texas sun, had been passed to him by his father. Grandpa Ramos's family had been of Mexican descent, although they'd been in Texas for generations. Grandpa had married a blonde woman with big blue eyes, too. So, while I was a Ramos, I was more white than Mexican, and my Spanish was only competent enough to order *arroz con pollo* at the Taco Truck.

In high school, I'd taken Japanese, since I was deep into my manga era then. Turns out there aren't many opportunities to use Japanese in small-town Texas.

Theo's arm brushed against my shoulder as he came to stand next to me. "You ready to go?"

I gave him a friendly punch to the shoulder. "You betcha."

Just normal old Ali who is in no way panicking at the thought of hours upon hours of alone time with him.

The corner of his mouth tipped in amusement. Sometimes I swore he could read my thoughts. Another reason to panic. 'Cause where Theo was concerned, my thoughts were... often, um, private.

"Do you have snacks?" Mom asked.

Theo nodded. "Yes."

"Jumper cables?" She turned to my dad without waiting for an answer. "Eli, do we have extra jumper cables for them?"

"I have jumper cables, a spare tire, my car insurance is up to date, I'm CPR-certified, all my seatbelts and airbags are in working condition and I made sure my zombie apocalypse kit is stocked for two."

"Alright." Mom held her arms out and gave Theo a hug.

To my mother, Theo was like a fourth son. He and his mom moved next door to us when I was six; Theo was nine. Becky and my mom became fast friends. My brothers—only three years separating the oldest from the youngest—found a kindred spirit in Theo, but it was Abe he was always the closest to, in both age and friendship.

Becky had been a single mom, Theo's father having left when he wasn't yet two and never heard from again. When she'd gotten a position as an overnight ICU nurse at a nearby hospital, she and my mom hatched a plan. In the evenings when she left for work, Theo came to our house. He ate dinner with us. He did his homework at the table with us. He listened to Mom read to us before bed. He slept on a trundle bed in the bedroom all three of my brothers shared.

He was just always there. Another brother. But not. Mom had been like a second mom to him. Now with Becky gone, Mom was even more determined that Theo always felt like he was part of our family.

"Well, you should probably be going then." She released Theo from the stranglehold of a hug. "Drive safe. You have precious cargo with you."

"I'm sure the centerpieces will be fine," I said.

"Very funny," she muttered as she wrapped me in her arms next.

"Stephy," Dad said when she was still hugging me a full thirty seconds later. "Let go of her."

Her grasp only grew tighter. "But she's leaving me."

"Mom." My voice muffled against her shoulder. "You're going to see us in a few days."

"Oh, fine." She let go. Finally.

Dad rolled his eyes but slung an arm around Mom's shoulders and pulled her close. "We'll see you in Portland."

I nudged Theo with my shoulder. "Quick, let's go, before she tries to handcuff us to the dining room table and load us up with so much meatloaf and apple pie, we won't be able to move."

Theo's head tilted in my direction. "Did you say apple pie, though? Isn't there always time for pie?"

Without a word, I linked my arm through his and dragged him to the car. My mother, Lord help us, stood in the driveway and waved until we were out of sight.

EIGHT

Note to self:
Do not get distracted by Theo's hands...
You know what? Don't look directly at Theo at all.

"Your mom doesn't do anything halfway, does she?" Theo asked as we pulled onto the freeway.

Grinning, I slid on my sunglasses. "You know her motto. Why keep it simple when we can make it as complicated as possible."

When she used her powers for good, the results were pretty damn amazing. I think my mom could solve the world food shortage, advise the president on any number of issues, and still have a full-course dinner on the table. However, when you were the object of her obsession, she was a downright menace. Her intentions were good though. I'd give her that.

"Is she still doing the needlepoint?" he asked, amusement laced in his voice.

Mom had discovered needlepoint a year ago and it had consumed her. She talked about needlepoint, watched needlepoint videos, joined online needlepoint groups, made her own needlepoint designs. Last year, all of us had received framed needlepoint pictures on our birthdays *and* Christmas. I hung one of mine, a scene of a dog dressed as a bumble bee with the words BEE HAPPY underneath it, in the bathroom.

But she hadn't stopped there. Convinced she could make a business out of it, she became a needlepoint machine, cranking out one after the other, and then peddling them at craft shows. While she'd often leave with several boxes of projects to sell, she'd return with even more things she'd purchased. Dad would huff and growl over the money she was spending. But it seemed to make Mom happy.

Like the sewing phase had. The interior design phase. The pottery phase. The pastry chef phase. The knitting. Oh, the knitting. So many hats and mittens and scarves, and we lived in Texas.

"She's moved on to candle making. The last one she showed me were candles in the shapes of hedgehogs and squirrels."

"Squirrels?"

"Yep, and chipmunks, bunnies, birds, trees. She's in her woodland creatures era." I leaned forward and fiddled with the radio.

"Nope." He swatted my hand away. "Driver picks the music."

"That's not fair. You know I don't drive. That's how you got into this mess."

"What mess?"

I snorted. "Me. I'm the mess. You have to cart me halfway across the country. I bet you were looking forward to a quiet, solo trip and you managed to get stuck with me."

"I don't mind. I don't get you all to myself that often," he said in a low, quiet voice.

Oh, that voice sent a shiver through me. He didn't mean anything by that, of course. Stare out the window like a good friend and ignore it, Ramos.

But I couldn't help myself. I snuck a peek at him and studied his profile. The scruffy jaw, the straight nose, the golden hue of his skin. His hat covered his eyes, which was a shame. But I could picture them anyway. He was better-than-model handsome. The sort of guy who grew more handsome every time he made me laugh or feel special without even realizing it.

Like saying stuff like that.

That was not good. Stay alert, Ramos.

But still I kept looking.

His left hand curled around the steering wheel, his right resting on his knee. The sun touched the silver ring he wore on his right ring finger—a gift from his mom years ago. I'm not sure he ever took it off.

One of my (numerous and detailed) Theo fantasies began to form before I could stop it. I'd slide my hand across the console between us and cover his hand. It would be warm from the sun, larger than mine, a little rougher too. I'd trace the veins I found there, reveling in the strength and solidness.

He'd shoot me one of his devastating half-smiles and my breath would catch. He'd turn his hand over and link our fingers, resting it on his thigh. We'd spend the next eight and a half hours like this, my hand nestled in his. In this fantasy, we'd never have to pee, nor did we run out of gas.

The dragon wings fluttered in my stomach, enjoying this fantasy very much. Then again, they'd been ever-present since he'd picked me up this morning because that meant I was within ten feet of him.

"What do you think?" he asked.

I blinked. "What?"

"About what I said."

Crap. What had he said? I'd been too busy obsessing over a hand-holding fantasy. Who even does that? A. Hand-holding. Fantasy. That was like a dog fantasizing about half a tennis ball, or a toddler getting excited over a baby doll without a head.

This is why I limited my Theo time. It had taken years, and I do mean years, to live down the "Stalker Ali" reputation I'd earned for my Theo-Induced Antics as a teenager. My brothers hadn't let me forget any of the embarrassing things I'd done to get his attention. I know it was all jokes and laughs for them. I played along even, but deep down, it hurt—my heart had been more bruised than I'd let on.

But it had also taken just as many years for me to set boundaries. I saw him regularly at family meals and holidays. We'd get together for game nights, a hike, to see a movie or catch a meal, but I always made sure someone else was joining us. These were the rules I'd made for myself. If he realized it, he never said a thing. It was easier since he'd moved to Houston a few years ago. Out of sight, out of mind, and all that.

Besides, I'd just been a kid when I'd been in my deepest Theo feels. We'd grown up, dated other people, shared laughs and tragedies, even a family vacation or two. As an adult, I proved I was able to handle a friendship without all these... invasive thoughts.

Theo was too important to me. If keeping him in my life meant only as a friend, then that's exactly where he would stay. In the friend zone.

If only he wasn't so adorable.

Also, I needed to up my fantasy game.

Theo shot me a confused look. "Did you say something about fantasies?"

My cheeks heated. Please tell me I didn't say that out loud. When I spoke, I sounded like a mouse after a shot of helium. "Nothing. I didn't say anything."

"Are you okay?" He shot a quick glance in my direction.

I cleared my throat and grinned. "I'm good."

His hand, *the* hand, rose and hovered in the air. Was he going to touch me?

He pointed at the radio. "So, you're okay with this?"

"Sure. Sounds good."

"Really?"

"Yeah, of course," I said with confidence although I had no idea what I was agreeing with. He could have asked if, at the next rest stop, we both stripped naked and ran around the parking lot.

Theo made a sound of disbelief. "I thought you'd put up more of a fight."

"Who, me? I'm like the queen of agreeability. Practically my middle name."

He scoffed, and with reason. "I wasn't aware of that, especially after our last road trip."

I grinned. The last time I'd been on a road trip with Theo was a few years ago when I'd hitched a ride to Dallas to see Alec. Theo'd "surprised" me by bringing along a date. Her name was Terra. It wasn't that I minded he brought her; it was that I would have liked to be prepared. See, the thing was, Theo had terrible taste in women. Or at least, I thought he did.

For example:

1. Angel Miller, his first real girlfriend, in high school. Although her given name was Angela, she insisted on answering only to Angel. With her bouncy hair, sultry smile, and love of being the center of attention, she'd naturally been a cheerleader. I hated her on principle. It made matters worse that I was deep into my Theo obsession, and she'd picked up on it. Oh, yes, she figured it out three minutes after meeting me and took the first chance she could to tell me to back off. Like I'd even been a threat. I often thought fondly of that one time when she received her new team cheerleading outfit only to find out her name had been misspelled. There'd been some mix-up, you see. Poor *Angle* had to wear

the thing for weeks before the mistake could be corrected.

2. Carly Whitman: Theo had met her in college, and they'd become an item almost immediately. They dated for three years and everyone, me included, was sure they'd eventually get married. Carly wasn't horrible at first. But her campaign to change pretty much everything about Theo started within a few months of their relationship—from his clothes, to his hair, to the personal trainer sessions she gave him for Christmas. When she insisted he change his college major to accounting so he could work for her father one day, Theo finally saw the light.
3. Most recently, Maddison with the Double Ds, and those Double Ds referred to more than the spelling of her name. Maddison of the hourglass figure and long legs, the pretty blue eyes, and the long blonde hair. Was I a little jealous? She was the exact opposite of me in almost every way and I guess that stung more than a little. Not that it mattered though. I was dating Alec anyway. Plus, I had zero say in who Theo spent his time with. Except she was so uninterested in doing all the things Theo liked to do—hiking or game night. But she did like to take selfies pretending to do those things. Thankfully, the relationship didn't last as long as the other two. As a dedicated friend, I was relieved when they broke up.

So that afternoon over two years ago, I hadn't been excited to see Terra in the car. "This is a surprise. Theo didn't tell me you were coming."

"Oh, it was last-minute," Terra had said, her dark eyes

watching me carefully. "I had to meet the woman Theo talks about all the time."

Sure, my heart beat a little faster hearing that. But just as quickly, I'd reminded myself that maybe he'd told her some of the stories about our growing up days. The five of us had gotten into some pretty epic adventures.

Theo, dumbly, gave me control of the music, probably as an apology for bringing Terra along. I made him pay for it, too. For the entire four-and-a-half-hour drive. Two boy bands' songs. On repeat.

I fidgeted in my seat. "I don't like surprises."

"You love surprises."

Which was true. "I—"

"You just didn't like Terra."

"There was nothing wrong with Terra," I said. Very maturely, I might add.

"You told me she pronounced her Ts too much."

"Nobody pronounces the T in exactly. That's weird." So much for mature. "As your friend, I need to have your back. Did you really want all those hard Ts in your life?"

He laughed. "Sure."

"Anyway." I patted my phone. "I have my boy band playlist all ready to go."

"No. Driver picks."

I groaned. "It's Rush, isn't it? It's always Rush."

"Hey, there's some Dream Theater and Porcupine Tree mixed in. For variety."

"Oh. Goody." I slumped in resignation. "Only two thousand long, long miles to go." He grinned. And dang it, I found I didn't care about the music as long as I got to see that see grin.

NINE

Note to self:
Change my phone number.
DO NOT TELL MOM THE NEW NUMBER.

Trying to doze off to drum solos—accompanied by Theo's rhythmic tapping on the steering wheel—was a challenge but nothing I couldn't handle. I was in the middle of a lovely dream where a man with smiling eyes and nice hands was about to confess his undying love for me when I jerked awake. My phone was ringing.

"Is it eleven forty-five?"

The ringing stopped and immediately started back up.

Theo chuckled. "How did you guess?"

With a sigh, I answered. "Hi, Mom."

The phone calls had started the day I moved out of my parents' house and into my duplex in town. My mother called me twice a day—11:45 a.m. and 8:00 p.m. sharp. It was in my best interest to answer, or she'd have every state trooper in Texas hunting us down.

"Your little phone picture thing seems to be moving very fast," she said in way of a greeting.

Frankie had been a hall monitor when he was in school, a job he'd taken very seriously. Furthermore, he'd always been the kid who ratted us out when we got in trouble. I mostly looked past his need to follow the rules. But he'd crossed a line a few months ago when he showed Mom how to stalk us by using the GPS on all our phones.

He was getting the best worst Christmas present ever this year.

"That's what happens when you're in a car. They go real fast."

She huffed in annoyance. "Don't get smart with me."

We passed a sign for a rest stop ahead. Theo flicked the blinker on, and we pulled off onto the exit ramp.

"We're pulling into a rest stop right now so you can relax."

"A rest stop? Oh, sweet Jesus. Be careful. People get murdered at rest stops."

"We are not going to get murdered."

Theo parked and waited, the car still running. I felt rather than saw his eyes on me. He was probably smiling that little crooked grin and I forced myself not to look.

"You could be kidnapped," Mom said, her voice jumping an octave.

"I am not going to get kidnapped."

Theo snickered. I raised an eyebrow in his direction.

"What if you're attacked by a wild animal? I hope you're wearing clean underwear because the last thing I need is for someone to discover your mangled body and find out you—"

"Yes, I'm wearing clean underwear." Theo choked on a laugh, and I sent him my meanest glare. "Do I need to talk to Dad about cutting you off from the true crime documentaries again?"

"Those shows are educational. I'm your mother. I am allowed to be worried."

"There's worried and then there's up-in-my-business-and-asking-weird-questions worried. Boundaries, remember?"

A dimple peeked out high on Theo's right cheek—the result of an injury when he and my brothers decided to teach themselves the art of stick fighting—and that only happened when he was highly amused.

I loved that stupid dimple.

Mom sniffled. When she spoke again, her voice was quieter. "Fine. Sorry. I'm overstepping."

"Thank you." Next to me, Theo's laughter bubbled over, and he pressed his forehead on the steering wheel. I smacked him on the shoulder but that only set him off more.

Another sniffle on the phone. "You are okay, though, right?"

"Yes, we're fine. Although Theo had a question for you." Theo's head came up, his mouth clamped tight, but those blue eyes were sparkling with humor. "About curtains. He was telling me how much he needed new ones."

"Tell him not to buy any." Mom's voice shifted out of the danger zone. "I'll make them for him."

"Oh, I'm sure he would love that. I think he mentioned something about fabric with dancing teddy bears?"

His eyes narrowed in response; I grinned widely. With lots of teeth.

"Dancing teddy bears. Hmm, I'm not sure I have any fabric like that. Oh, but I do have some leftover baseball fabric. It's darling. I used it to make a baby shower gi—"

"You know, he's right here, and we are just sitting at a rest stop. He'd love to tell you what he's thinking. Let me pass him the phone."

With a snicker, I held the phone out to Theo. He grabbed it, and my hand in the process. He mouthed, *I'll get you for this*.

I batted my lashes at him innocently. *Little old me?*

Yes, you. The glint in his eye was playful. But there was something else there, something I couldn't put a name to, nor could I look away from it. For a suspended moment, the two of us stared at each other. I'd never realized how little space there was between the front seats of a car.

If we both moved an inch or two, we'd be close. Very close. Maybe he'd lean forward and press his lips to mine, and I'd reach for him. I'd knock his hat off and run my fingers through his hair and then—

"Hello? Theo? Alicia?" Mom's voice called from the phone. "Is everything okay? Eli, I told you we should have put that tracking device on his car. He never would have known. What if they're being kidnapped this very minute and..."

I untangled my hand from his. "You better get that before she calls in the National Guard."

"Hi, Stephanie." He said into the phone, his voice respectful, but still holding my gaze with a look that was a little less respectful. It was only a second, that look, but that didn't stop my pulse from stampeding.

With a quick smile, I got myself out of that car as fast as possible.

TEN

Note to self:
A flirty Theo is a dangerous Theo.

"This place reminds me of the Sit-n-Eat." I glanced around Love Café—a greasy spoon just outside Fort Worth—it was small, about ten tables or so. The place looked like it had seen better days with its worn linoleum flooring, chipping paint, and wobbly tables, but it was clean and smelled heavenly.

"What do you think that's about?" I nodded my head at the photos of smiling couples wallpapering the back wall, most of them dressed in wedding garb.

Theo glanced at it and tapped his menu. "Says here the owner, Jolette Love, can look at a couple and tell them if they're meant to be together. Apparently, she has an accuracy rate of ninety-five percent."

"That's a weird superpower. I'd rather be invisible."

"I think mind reading would be the best." He took off his baseball hat, combed his hair back with his fingers and replaced the hat, this time backwards.

Because, you see, he was trying to kill me. Theo in a regular hat was handsome. Theo in a backwards hat was hot. Super-hot. I couldn't explain it. I didn't understand it. It just was. In fact, it was his actual superpower. That one move, and he went from Clark Kent to Superman, and woo boy, did I need rescuing in the worst way.

I must have some weird backwards-hat kink. That was the only explanation.

Our server, a dark-haired woman who looked about twenty-five months pregnant, stopped by our table for our orders. We handed her our menus, and she promised our food would be out quickly.

"Who gets orange juice with a burger?" I asked.

Theo smirked. "Who asks for olives on their burger?"

I flipped my hair over my shoulder. "Someone with a sophisticated palate."

"Sure," he said, drawing the word out. "Is this the same person who puts ranch dressing on their pizza?"

"Excuse me? That is the only way pizza can be properly enjoyed, Mr. I Don't Like My Food Touching on My Plate."

"That is not the burn you think it is. There is nothing wrong with being a fastidious eater."

"Fastidious." I put a hand to my chest in mock astonishment. "Such a big writer word."

"Very big. Huge. Lots more where that came from." He gave me an exaggerated eyebrow waggle.

This felt good and right and friendly. Silly, innocent ribbing. For maybe the first time that day, my shoulders relaxed.

I laughed. "What does that even mean?"

"Just wanted to make you laugh." He grinned, flashing straight white teeth—I remembered when he'd had the braces to make them that way. "I like when you laugh."

My heart flopped over. Sort of like a puppy begging for belly rubs. This was the second time today one of his comments had caught me off guard.

His phone vibrated on the table, and he glanced down to see who it was. His smile morphed into a small frown. The phone stopped and started right back up again a few seconds later. He flipped it over and tried to ignore it.

I glanced from him to the phone. "You can take that if you need to."

"You sure?"

"Go on."

"I'll be quick." He slid out of the booth and wandered toward the door, phone to his ear. I watched him through the window as he paced back and forth in front of the restaurant, the hitch in his step so slight most people wouldn't notice it.

That hitch was from the ankle-busting injury he sustained when he was hit by a car his senior year of high school. While it had ruined his chance at a baseball scholarship, that little rocking step of his had become his *thing*.

Ruth, Frankie's girlfriend, said his walk was sexy. But then Ruth called everything sexy. At our last family dinner, she called the Brussels sprouts sexy.

"Oh, he's a handsome one," a voice said behind me. A woman around my mother's age, her gray hair cut in a neat shoulder-length bob, smiled when I turned around. "I didn't mean to eavesdrop. Couldn't help myself."

"It's okay."

Her eyes lit up. "Are you here to see Jolette?"

"No, passing through on a road trip."

"You must see her. She's never wrong."

I squirmed in my seat. "We're not, um, together."

"She was right for me. Twice."

"Twice?"

"The first time she told me we weren't a good match, but I ignored her. We got divorced after three years. But the second time," she sighed dreamily, "she said we made a great couple and I listened. In fact, if you look on the wall, you'll find a photo from our wedding."

"So, she was right."

"Oh, yes. We were married twenty-seven years before he passed away." Her smile turned sad. "I miss him every day. Sometimes when I feel especially sad, I come have lunch here. It's a bit of a drive but it makes me feel like he's close. Silly, aren't I?"

"Not silly at all."

She peered out the window, a wistful smile on her face. "Thank you for listening to a sad, old woman ramble. I'll let you get back to your young man."

"He's not my—"

But she was already sliding out of her booth and walking away. Theo held the door for her with a smile, the phone still pressed to his ear, and wandered back to the table.

"August twentieth at ten," he said. "Yes, I have the address." Pause. "I look forward to meeting with you then. Thank you for the opportunity."

After sliding into his seat, he pressed end and tapped away on his phone like I wasn't sitting right in front of him.

"What's happening on August twentieth?"

"A thing I have to go to." He didn't look up.

"And this thing is...?"

He set his phone down and scratched the back of his neck. "It's for an article I'm working on."

"What's the article about?"

"Sports."

"What sport?"

His eyes crinkled in the corners in amusement. "All of them."

"A sports article about all the sports written by a sportswriter. Wow. You are the worst liar."

He smirked. "Am I, though?"

"Theo Goodnight, do you have a secret?"

"Maybe."

I leaned forward, propped up on my elbows. "Are you going to tell me what it is?"

"What if the secret is about you?"

Somehow despite an entire table between us, it felt like he was inches away. His eyes sparkled with sly humor. I couldn't honestly say I'd seen this side of Theo, at least not directed toward me. It was potent stuff, powerful, and kind of... sneaky.

I narrowed my eyes. "Are you flirting with me, so I'll stop asking about this article?"

He grinned and opened his mouth to speak, but our burgers arrived just then.

"Here you go." An older, round woman grinned at us; her hair was dyed an unnatural shade of red that matched her lipstick. Based on the height of her hair, she subscribed to the "bigger the hair, closer to God" theory. "Is there anything else I can get you?"

"I think we're good." I picked up a fry and stuffed it in my mouth.

"Thanks," Theo said.

The woman did not move. In fact, I'd say she took a step closer and waited. Every now and then she'd make a little humming noise in the back of her throat.

"Did you need something?" I asked.

"Oh, no." She pulled a chair over from a neighboring table and sat. "Y'all keep eating. I'm trying to get a read on you two."

"A read?" Theo asked, his burger halfway to his mouth.

She nodded, her hair moving as one helmet-like unit. "Of course. It's what I do. I'm Jolette."

"The lady with the superpower?" I asked.

She barked out a laugh. "I've never called it a superpower, but I do have a gift. I see you looking at me like I'm one donut short of a dozen but I'm not ever wrong."

Theo took a swig of his orange juice. "The menu said you had an accuracy rate of ninety-five percent."

"Pssht." She waved a hand, fingertips painted the same red as her hair. "I can't go claiming a hundred percent, my lawyer said. Might get me in trouble." She leaned in as though to tell us a secret. "My lawyer's my cousin, Big Mike. I pay him in pancakes. Works out real well for us."

"Nice to meet you," I said. Although I wasn't sure if that was exactly true. This woman was weird.

Jolette cracked her knuckles. "Now the two of you are awful cute together and I think—"

Choking on a bite of my hamburger, I held up my hand.

"I think she's trying to say we aren't a couple," Theo said, his voice dry.

"Is that so?" Jolette inspected us with shrewd brown eyes.

After chugging half my water, I waved a hand toward Theo. "What he said."

She didn't speak. I looked at Theo and shrugged. His eyes crinkled in the corners like he found this amusing. I raised my eyebrows; he winked. My mouth dropped open.

"Nope. You two are meant to be." She stood abruptly. The chair scraped the floor as she put it away. "Make sure you send me a photo when you get hitched."

Then she was gone.

"You winked," I accused. "You don't wink. You're the least winky person I know."

He frowned. "I wink."

"Winking is very flirty behavior." I stabbed a finger at him. "You are not flirty and yet, you've been flirty twice this meal alone. Do you have a brain tumor I don't know about?"

He was especially not flirty with me. He *couldn't* do things like that. It would go very badly for my heart.

His eyes widened before narrowing into some unreadable

expression. When he spoke, his voice was low. "Alicia, trust me. I know how to flirt."

I swallowed, my face growing warm. "But you don't flirt with me. That's not how our relationship works."

His expression shifted into a scowl. "Enlighten me. How does our relationship work?"

"Oh, don't act all offended. You know we're friends, not the flirty kind of friends"—I might not want it to be true but over the years, Theo had made it apparent that he felt it—"you're basically another one of my brothers."

His scowl turned into a fierce frown. Again, something he'd never leveled at me before. What was happening?

"I'm going to the bathroom." Theo tossed his napkin on the table and slid out of the bench. Instead of storming off, he turned away and hesitated. His shoulders rose and fell with a slow breath. When he turned around, he'd arranged his face into something more friendly.

Bracing a hand on the table, he leaned close. "I'm beginning to think you don't know me as well as you think you do."

My breath caught at the low, gravelly sound of his voice.

He shifted closer, his mouth stopping an inch from my ear. His warm breath on my skin sent a zing of awareness through me. "And I am definitely not your brother."

Then he walked away. I willed myself not to turn around and watch him. I fanned my face with my hand, wondering at this strange turn of events. Maybe the Theo I thought I knew was that teenage boy I made a fool of myself over.

But based on my racing heart, I think I might like this Theo even more.

Damn it.

ELEVEN

Note to self:
Sometimes ice cream is just ice cream.
Sometimes, it's not.

Back in the car, we were both quiet. Theo seemed lost in thought and I, desperate to distract myself, decided to check in with Cal.

Me: *What are your thoughts on singing telegrams?*

Cal: *Why?*

Me: *Hypothetically, it could be a nice gift to liven up the rehearsal dinner. Think about it.*

Cal: *Hilarious. How about a marching band and petting zoo while you're at it?*

Me: *I can't tell if you're joking so I'm going to err on the side of caution and say you're serious.*

The three telltale dots started and stopped at least three times. Then:

Cal: *THERE WILL BE NO SINGING TELEGRAMS AT THE REHEARSAL DINNER. YOU WILL COME, SIT IN YOUR ASSIGNED SEAT, AND SMILE FOR PICTURES. GOT IT?*

Me: *Hi Melanie*

Cal: *DO YOU PROMISE?*

Me: *No singing telegrams. Got it.*

Cal: *GOOD.*

Me: *Is my brother still alive, or have you offed him and stuffed his body in the freezer already?*

Cal: *First, I am not an amateur. A freezer is no place to hide a body. Second, he's right here. Third, I'm not kidding.* NO SINGING TELEGRAMS.

Me: *I hear you loud and clear.*

Cal: *Thank you.*

Me: *No problem. Gotta go. I'm going to go price out petting zoos. For no reason at all.*

Cal: *ALI!*

The trouble began twenty minutes later.

Our plan had been to make it to Mack's place in Amarillo, crash at his house, and leave the next morning to head to Colorado. We were traveling along a particularly desolate stretch of a state highway when it happened. It had been a while since we'd passed through a town, even a tiny one. In fact, the only other thing I'd seen was an exit or two, and sparsely treed roads, miles and miles of that.

Theo turned down the music. "Do you hear that?"

"The delightful, harmonic sounds of One Direction? No, you wouldn't let me pick the music, remember?"

"No, listen."

It didn't take long for a high-pitched whine to make its way to my ears. After Theo opened his window, it only got louder and more pronounced.

"Is that coming from the car?" But no sooner had I asked, when the temperature warning light flashed red on the SUV's dashboard.

"That's not good," Theo muttered.

"Is that smoke?" It was definitely smoke, billowing out from under the hood of the car.

Frantically, Theo pulled off onto the shoulder of the highway. He threw it into park, and we both scrambled out of the car. After backing away a good twenty feet, we watched as smoke poured like a chimney from the car.

"Well, that's going to be a problem," Theo said.

What else was there to say?

"I hate the heat." I swiped at the sweat dripping from my hairline into my eyes... again. "And sweat. I really hate sweat."

After we realized we had no cell service, our options were limited to lay down and die (not advisable) or start hoofing it to the resort I'd seen a sign for a couple of miles back. It wouldn't have been so bad except the sun was relentless and I was wearing flip-flops, and I hated the heat and sweating, and I was starting to feel very stabby.

"Tell us how you're really feeling," Theo said from his spot a few paces in front of me. He'd taken off his plaid button-down and it was dangling from his neck.

"This place is so desolate. Do you see those vultures?" Pausing, I pointed in front of us at what appeared to be a group circling high in the air over something, probably very dead.

"Yeah, I see them," Theo said, not stopping at all.

"Do you know how many bodies are probably buried out here?"

"We could make it one more," Theo said without turning around.

I planted my feet and stuck my fists on my hips. "Wow."

He took his baseball hat off, his curls shooting out in all directions, and used the sleeve of his plaid shirt to swipe at his forehead. His band t-shirt was a little tighter than what he normally wore, or maybe it was because he wasn't wearing the button-down, or maybe the sun had begun to fry what few brain cells I had left. Whatever the reason, it pulled across his chest with the movement and I didn't bother to not stare.

There was something overwhelmingly attractive about Theo, an understated coolness. He might not have the bulging muscles or a rebellious vibe, but I saw women glance his way. At the last convenience store, one woman chatted him up a good five minutes near the potato chip aisle. I'd wanted to toss a can of Pringles at her head.

"You coming?" Theo asked.

Get your head in the game, Ramos.

"I'm coming," I said with about as much enthusiasm as I could muster.

When I caught up to him, he shoulder-bumped me. "We have to be close to this place. Did you say it was a resort?"

"That's what the sign said. Resort and spa. Or something like that." At this point, I'd take a pay-by-the-hour motel with those vibrating beds, as long as there was air-conditioning.

"Bet they have a pool. That sounds nice, doesn't it?"

I sucked in a breath. "That sounds so nice."

"And ice water."

"And... and... ice cream?"

Theo slung an arm around my shoulders. "We'll find you ice cream."

"With whipped cream?"

"And a cherry."

"Yes." I groaned and slowed down, my eyes sliding shut as I imagined the taste of the cool sweetness on my tongue. "Rainbow, no, chocolate sprinkles. And cookie dough crumbles. Maybe some nuts."

I opened my eyes and was startled to discover we'd stopped moving. Theo's arm rested heavy on my shoulders, but his gaze felt heavier. His eyes drifted to my mouth. He frowned, two ticks appearing between his eyebrows. My feet rooted right there, fascinated by whatever was going on behind his eyes. I wanted to stand there and stare at him forever.

"In a cone or a cup?" His voice was low and gruff. My stomach swooped.

I licked my bottom lip, the one he was still staring at. "A cup."

He made a funny little half-groan and swayed closer, just a touch, but I noticed. "One scoop or two?"

"Three. Definitely three." Was that my voice? I sounded like I'd just run three miles. Uphill.

"Chocolate or caramel syrup?" His eyes moved to mine, bright and piercing.

"Oh, chocolate," I breathed. "Lots of chocolate syrup."

"I love chocolate." He inched closer. I didn't think my skin could get any hotter than it already was given the sun beating down on us, but I was wrong.

A vulture swooped and landed not ten feet from us, breaking whatever strange ice cream-flavored coma had settled over the two of us. Stupid bird.

Startled, I squawked. Theo dropped his arm. I clapped my hands at it; it didn't move. The dang thing stood there, drilling into us with beady dark eyes.

"It's huge." I shuffled away. "It's got to be at least two feet tall. Do something, Theo. I-I think it's trying to figure out what part of me to eat first."

"He's not going to eat you. You aren't dead."

I gulped. "Yet."

"Let's go get you that ice cream." With a soft laugh, Theo patted me on the back and started moving down the road, his limp far more pronounced than normal.

"Your ankle doing okay?" I called, still staring at the vulture that was staring at me.

"It's fine." He waved a hand of dismissal in the air.

"You're lying again."

"Hurry up. I want to find this place before we really are vulture food."

The bird took a small hop toward me. That was enough to get my feet unstuck fast.

TWELVE

Note to self:
Always carry a change of clothes.
And maybe a blindfold.

The large wooden sign to the Longhorn Natural Retreat and Spa finally came into view twenty long, hot, sweaty minutes later. Hands on my hips, I paused and read the sentence under the name: *Bare Yourself to Nature.*

Instead of finding a cheery group of cabins or a sprawling lodge, we found a stone fence at least ten feet tall with an equally tall iron gate. The gate stood open and revealed a long gravel driveway.

I groaned. "More walking?"

"Come on. It can't be that far."

"What are the chances we get the car fixed today?" I asked hopefully as we started down the winding road lined with oak trees. The cicadas provided an irritating and insistent playlist for the walk. The endless, endless walking.

"We'll figure it out. The worst thing that could happen is we're stuck here for a day or two."

"Oh, good. In the middle of nowhere." I pulled my phone to check again for a signal. "Nothing. Do you think my mom has filed a missing persons report yet?"

"Probably already contacted the local news."

"And organized a search party."

"Candlelight prayer vigil scheduled for tonight."

"I hope she uses that picture of me at Christmas last year when she's making the missing flyers," I said. "That was a good picture."

"In the red dress?"

I stumbled and caught myself before I faceplanted. "You remember that?"

He shrugged. "I pay attention. I remember things."

"No... it just seems like a weird detail for you to remember." But, boy, did I like the idea he did. I had looked smoking in that dress—a form-fitting knee-length skirt, off-the-shoulders cap sleeves that showed the perfect amount of cleavage, and both worked to make my waist tiny. I'd even worn heels and taken extra time with my make-up and hair. I might look like a mess nine days out of ten, but that tenth day, I liked to put in the effort.

"You were kind of hard to forget that night," he said so quietly, I almost asked him to repeat himself.

Stop it, Ramos, before you get actual heart eyes.

Before I could say something, Theo wrapped a hand around my forearm and pulled me to a stop. I jerked around to face him. With a finger, he tapped his mouth and pointed toward the trees behind where they'd thickened and formed a small cluster. He squinted, watchful. After a full minute of silence, he took a breath and released me.

"What was that about?" I asked.

"I thought I saw someone."

I peered into the trees. "It is on the resort property. Maybe it's a guest."

"Maybe. But... ah... you're gonna think I'm nuts."

"What?"

He put his hands on his hips. "I thought he was, well, naked."

I laughed. "Okay, the heat is starting to get to you. Let's go find this place."

The building appeared out of nowhere, a small wooden structure with a sign stuck in the front that read OFFICE/CHECK-IN. A crooked OPEN sign peeked out of a small window.

Theo opened the door and waved me through first. A blast of icy cold AC hit me, and I almost crumbled in joy. A dog of undeterminable pedigree raised a large brown head from his spot in the corner and stared at me with bored dark eyes.

"Howdy." The guy behind the counter looked to be about my dad's age with hair more gray than brown and dark-rimmed glasses perched on the end of his nose. His blue Hawaiian shirt hung loose on his frame, as not a single button was fastened. A thick pelt of graying hair covered his chest. There were crumbs caught in it. It was hot out, don't get me wrong, but this seemed a little on the unprofessional side.

"H-hi," I said, not knowing exactly where to plant my eyes.

Theo closed the door behind me and put his hand low on my back to gently push me forward. The dog emitted a soft growl before laying his head back down with a groan.

"Don't worry none about him," the man said, a friendly smile carved on his face. "He's grumpy 'cause he don't like the heat. Come on in. I'm Zip. What can I do for you?"

Theo and I stepped closer to the counter, his hand warm and solid on my back. Small bottles of sunscreen, bug spray, travel-sized tubes of itch cream, and bottles of pain reliever, all with outrageous price tags, cluttered the countertop.

"Our car broke down about a mile or so down the road and we don't have cell service," Theo explained.

"Oh, yeah, a total dead zone. You two walk here then?"

Theo nodded. "We were hoping we'd get some service near you."

My eyes drifted around the small office. A poster hung on the wall behind the counter of a man and woman's silhouette with the words *Free to Be Me!* Above them. On the opposite wall, handwritten announcements for board games in the community center on Wednesday nights covered a large bulletin board. Friday, there was a karaoke competition. A more professional flyer advertised a 5K next month called the Bun Run.

"We won't let them put a cell tower on the property," Zip said. "This place is supposed to be a sanctuary, a place to be free, if you know what I mean."

I shot Theo an uneasy look.

He shifted on his feet. "Would you have a phone we could use? And possibly the name of a mechanic close by?"

"Well, there's no mechanic round here exactly. You'd have to go into Amarillo." Zip scratched his chest, dislodging the crumbs. "But George, our maintenance guy, is pretty handy, so he might could have a look."

"That would be great."

"Let me go get him." Zip rounded the end of the counter to head toward the door, and that's when Theo and I discovered that aside from his Hawaiian shirt and a smile, Zip was very, *very* naked.

THIRTEEN

Note to self:
Eye contact is key to making new (naked) friends.

The second the door swung shut behind Zip, I turned to Theo and clutched his arm. "He was naked."

"I think that pretty much covers it."

"No, nothing was covered." I bit back the urge to laugh. "*His little zipper* wasn't covered at all."

"Ali," Theo said, his voice sounding choked like he too found this situation hilarious.

"Oh," I breathed. "Do you think this is some kind of weird cult? Did we stumble into a Netflix docuseries?"

The door opened as I asked that, and Zip chuckled. "No, ma'am. Just a resort for nudists. It's our busy season, being the summer, and we're packed full right now."

"With naked people?" I asked, my voice faint.

Keep your eyes above the waist, Ramos. Do. Not. Look. Down. Do not.

A small frown creased Zip's face. "Well, sure. We like to think we're born exactly the way we should live."

Theo cleared his throat and my eyes darted to his face. His cheeks were flushed pink, but his eyes danced with amusement. "We appreciate any help you can give us."

"Of course. Always best to help someone in need when you can." He opened the door and waved us outside. "Come out here and meet George."

George, as it had turned out, was a giant of a man who was wisely clothed seeing as how he worked with tools and whatnot. He offered to take us back to the car for a look. The three of us squeezed together in the front cab of George's truck and headed out.

While I'd packed my backpack with a change of clothes, toiletries, and my medication, George explained our water pump was shot. The good news? He could replace it. The bad news? He wouldn't be able to get the part from Amarillo until morning.

When it became clear we'd be stuck here for the night, Zip offered us an empty cabin.

"You're in luck," he said. "We're all booked, but this one was out of commission until the AC got fixed and that happened today. It's small but it will do, I think."

Zip wasn't kidding. The cabin was a tiny little one-room wooden structure, rough around the edges but charming. It had two twin-sized beds, a round table with two chairs, one dresser, a microwave, coffeemaker, and a TV we were warned got one channel "sometimes." But it was neat and clean, had AC, and a small shower so I wasn't complaining.

After Zip had gotten us settled in the cabin, he explained there was only one hot spot for the entire seventy-acre property. He lent us a golf cart, gave us directions to the community center a half a mile away, and the Wi-Fi password to use when we got there.

"Help yourself to whatever's in the kitchen," he said.

"Should be something to make sandwiches with. It's on the house."

"This place kind of reminds me of that summer camp we went to," Theo said, as we bounced along the faint dirt road in hopes of finding that great and hopeful sign of civilization, Wi-Fi. "Remember that one summer we all went?"

"Naked guy. Three o'clock," I whispered.

"Noted."

"I hated that camp." The next year, I'd flat-out refused to go, and no amount of cajoling or bribing had worked to change my mind.

"What? It was great. There was swimming and archery and campfires and all kinds of things to do."

"Yeah, that's because you were at the boys' camp." I swatted at a mosquito. "The girls had lots of arts and crafts. Lots."

"Naked couple on our left," Theo said.

"Not totally naked," I pointed out. "They're both wearing tennis shoes and socks. Very sensible."

He choked back a laugh and raised a hand when the couple called out a greeting in passing. "It wasn't all that bad."

"I mean, I would have gone with a sandal but to each their own."

He bumped me with his shoulder. "The camp, I mean."

"I was forced to make five thousand macaroni necklaces."

"I remember that. I still have the one you gave me." He turned left on the path. The motion caused me to lean into his side. I caught a whiff of soap on his skin; we'd showered after we'd gotten to the cabin.

"You do? That was a long time ago."

"I guess I'm good at holding onto things." He shot me a small smile.

I hummed, secretly pleased. Granted, I'd been nine at the time and had made said necklace under extreme duress and everyone I knew had gotten their very own handcrafted macaroni necklace, too. But I bet none of my brothers had kept theirs.

"You really didn't like camping?" Theo asked.

"I didn't like that summer camp. I loved camping. Remember that place we used to go to on the Frio River?"

For years, our parents would pack up all us kids, Theo included, and we'd head for a campground on the Frio. It was days of living in our swimsuits and playing in the water until our fingers pruned and our arms got tired. (Or I saw a water snake.) Then we'd beg my parents for a few dollars and race to the camp store to buy the cheap popsicles they sold. At night, we'd make s'mores on the campfire and lay out under the stars listening to Cal point out the constellations the rest of us could never see.

"It's been a while since we've all gone," Theo said.

The last camping trip we'd taken had been about four years ago. Alec had come with me; Theo had brought his girlfriend at the time whose name I couldn't even remember now. She'd been nice though. Frankie brought Ruth; Cal and Melanie were there too; in fact, that would have been when they met for the first time. It had been bittersweet. I remember sitting around the fire one night, longing for the day when it had just been my brothers and Theo and me, when Abe was with us, and we were kids.

Growing up really sucked sometimes.

"We should go again," Theo said, pulling me out of my memories. "It would be fun."

I smiled. "It would be. Maybe we can talk Abe into coming with us, too. It's not the same without him."

"That would be nice." He turned his head, a mixture of sadness and hope swimming in those blue, blue eyes. I felt that in my bones. This mission Cal had sent me on seemed important for so many reasons. It was more than just getting Abe to agree to come to the wedding. It felt bigger than that.

"Do you talk to him a lot?" I traced the edge of my shorts. "I mean, I know you talk. Abe's mentioned that to me. I know how close you two were. I never really thought about how hard it was for you when he left."

He paused, his knuckles turned white as he gripped the steering wheel. "We talk a lot. At least once a week."

"Good, I'm glad because—"

But Theo leaned down and whispered, "Naked guy on a bike coming right at us."

I turned my head away. "I don't want to look."

"Then don't."

"But I have to."

"You do not."

"I can't not look. It's like passing by an accident or coming across a pimple-popping video."

He huffed a laugh and then waved at the man as we passed.

I looked, hoping my red face would be taken for extreme sunburn and not a level of embarrassment I had yet to experience in my life. "Ouch. That looks so uncomfortable."

"Yes, it does," he said with feeling.

You know what's weird? Being unexpectedly stranded at a nudist resort. Even weirder? Being unexpectedly stranded at a nudist resort with your brother's best friend whom you've secretly been half in love with for half your life and there are naked people everywhere.

EVERYWHERE.

Shiny, happy, smiling naked people.

The community center was a long, one-story building, much bigger than I expected. We parked the golf cart and climbed the porch steps. The large set of doors, flanked by bulky wooden rocking chairs on each side, was unlocked. They opened to reveal a long, wide room that took up most of the building, sort of an all-purpose area to hold large gatherings.

A handful of people crowded around a table playing a

heated game of (naked) Monopoly. At the other end of the room, a (naked) group of people were seated on couches around a television in a sectioned-off area.

"Hello there," a voice called out. A woman easily in her seventies sat (nakedly) knitting. "You two lost?"

Theo and I looked at each other and grinned.

"Why would you think that?" Theo asked.

"Looking a little overdressed for this party." She winked and then directed us to the corner of the room for the strongest signal.

While Theo checked his messages, I called my mother. That phone conversation went about as well as I expected. She was beside herself. When she asked the name of the place where we were staying, I made up something generic but assured her we were safe.

"Do you get any strange feelings from the owner?" she asked.

"Why?"

"Does he seem like a man who is looking to make a dress from your skin?"

She had no idea why I laughed so hard, and I wasn't about to explain. "Please stop watching true crime documentaries. Please."

"Oh, honey," she said, after she was sufficiently convinced I wasn't going to be murdered in my sleep, "I sent you the link to my video online. It's getting so many views. Watch it and tell me what you think."

Next, I called Mack to let him know we'd see him in the morning and then listened to him tell me about the WWII documentary he'd watched earlier in the day. And while I wasn't at all interested in Operation Overlord, I'd sensed lately that Mack was lonely. It had been a year now since Grandma Grace died and the History Channel was not a substitute for human interaction.

Both of us were quieter on the trip back to the cabin.

"I've never stared at so many foreheads in my life," I said after a while.

"Or ears." Theo grinned. "This has been the weirdest day of my life."

I nodded. "We're never telling anyone about this."

"Not a soul."

FOURTEEN

Note to self:
Why does becoming a nudist sound easier than sharing my feelings?

"Did you know Texas ranks third in the states with the most practicing nudists?" I was stretched out on one of the two beds in our tiny little cabin. "Behind Florida and California."

"The mosquitoes must love that," Theo said, from behind his laptop, where he'd studiously been typing away for over an hour.

I chuckled and flipped over on my back, wondering how this day had started out so normal. Here I was, staying in a cabin at a nudist retreat with Theo Goodnight. A sentence I never even imagined existed, let alone one that would be true.

I'd spent the last hour lounging on a bed while Theo got some work done. Right next to the Gideon Bible in the nightstand, I'd found a welcome packet with all kinds of interesting info.

"It's bingo night tonight."

"I'll pass," he mumbled, not looking up.

"Yoga in the morning, too."

Now his head came up. "Naked yoga?"

"That's what it says." I waggled my eyebrows. "You interested?"

"No, thank you." He paused, the corner of his mouth curling ever so slightly. "Not in public, if you know what I mean."

I gasped and threw a pillow in his general direction. "There is it again. That was flirty."

His cheeks turned pink in the most adorable way as he went back to typing.

I stared at the wood plank ceiling. From what I'd seen so far, the Longhorn was a nice place, secluded and quiet. As the brochure explained, the entire property gave guests lots of room to roam... freely. There were cabins, yurts, RV sites, and even primitive tent camping.

While I had no desire to strip off my clothes and join them, I had begrudging respect for people who didn't have a lick of concern about their bodies and weren't afraid to let it all hang out. The people I'd seen hadn't had rock star bodies or movie star good looks; they were just normal. Like neighbors or the high school counselor or the guy who worked the deli counter at the grocery store.

I propped my head up and peeked at Theo. His mouth quirked to the side as he concentrated, and the dragon wings fluttered for no reason except Theo was Theo.

With a grunt, I buried my face in a pillow. What would happen if I stood up right now and confessed my feelings for Theo? The thought terrified me, opening myself up like that, knowing that the chances of him returning those feelings were zero. Or was this the fear talking again? Either way, I couldn't even handle revealing feelings I'd harbored for years. In fact, stripping naked sounded easier.

"I think I'm going to get ready for bed," I announced.

Tap. Tap. Pause. "It's only eight-thirty."

"Yeah, but it's been a long day. I'm beat. You can keep working. The light won't bother me." I dragged myself out of bed and over to my backpack next to the desk where Theo sat. I bent down to grab it and jumped at the sudden loud click of his laptop snapping shut. Frowning, I turned toward him.

"What are you doing?" he asked, his eyes darting between me and the laptop.

Slowly, I held up the backpack. "Getting ready for bed. I just told you that."

"Oh, right. I'll do that too." Abruptly he stood, but I didn't have a chance to take a step back to give him room. I stumbled. His hands wrapped around my shoulders to steady me, pulling me closer to him.

I had to tilt my head to see his face. Blue eyes peered at me cautiously; one of his curls was smack in the middle of his forehead and I itched to reach up and brush it aside.

"Bed sounds like a great idea," he said, his voice a little rough.

"Flirty," I whispered. "Definitely flirty."

His gaze moved between my eyes and dropped to my mouth. I swallowed, my breath becoming shallow. If he leaned down and I rose on my tippy-toes, we'd meet in the middle.

Stop it, Ramos. Love Sabbatical, remember.

With a shake of his head, he dropped his hands and stepped back. "You want the bathroom first?"

"You go ahead." Disappointment reared its head. I plopped in his seat.

He hesitated, then plunked the laptop off the table and stuffed it into his messenger bag.

"Oookay. That wasn't suspicious."

"What?"

"What kind of project are you working on?"

He licked his bottom lip and, not gonna lie, I watched. I was *impossible*. "Something for work."

"At the paper? Like the same sport article about all the sports you were talking about earlier?"

He shrugged, a definite non-answer if there ever was one.

"Can I read it?"

With a sigh, he set his hands on his hips. "What are the chances you'll forget about this project?"

I pretended to think about it for a millisecond. "Zero. The chances are zero."

"That's what I thought." He skirted around me and headed for the bathroom without another word.

"You still do that?" Theo asked from his bed where he'd been reading for the last fifteen minutes.

I held up my current journal. Leatherbound with scrollwork stamped into it, it had been a gift from Mom on my last birthday. Mom had given me my first journal on my eighth birthday and every birthday since.

"It's habit now." Every night before bed, I wrote something. Some days, there wasn't much to say. One entire entry last week read, "I'm here."

Today's entry was much, much longer.

He laid his book on his lap. "What do you write about?"

"Everything and nothing." I made an exaggerated period, closed the journal, and set it on the nightstand.

"I remember you doing it as a kid."

"Oh, yeah, do you also remember the time you boys found my journals and decided to read them?" I asked in a most salty voice and stretched out on the bed.

I'd been ten years old and mortified. Back then, my deepest, darkest thoughts ran more toward how much I hated them all because they were so mean. Except Theo. He wasn't mean to me.

He grinned sheepishly. "It was Abe's idea."

"Shocking."

"If it makes you feel any better, I thought you had really nice handwriting."

I threw a pillow at his head. "Go to sleep."

With a laugh, he snapped off the lamp. "I did like reading your list of the reasons boys are the worst. 'Boys are smelly. Boys think farts are funny. Boys think girls can't do the same things boys can do.'"

"I still stand by that." I turned over so I was facing him. The cabin was pitch-black, but I could barely make out the faint lines of his body under the covers. "I can't believe you remember that."

"It might have been the itching powder prank that came a few days later that has kept it fresh in my mind."

I burst into laughter, remembering how I'd carefully planned out how and when to douse their gym clothes. "That was a classic."

He groaned. "Imagine being in fifth period gym class playing basketball, and the itching starts."

"Good."

"Where is your sympathy, woman?"

"Buried deep in my cold, black heart, of course."

Our laughter trailed off and both of us grew quiet. Sleepiness washed over me and just as my eyes slid shut, I thought I heard Theo whisper, "I'm really glad you're here with me."

FIFTEEN

Note to self:
Might be time to see a counselor.
Or just ask Theo to move in with me.

The dream was always the same. I'm watching myself from above as I sleep. The bed I'm in is taller than any bed I've ever seen, at least six feet off the ground. On either side are equally tall wooden nightstands with razor-sharp edges. On one, a large lamp sits. On the other, a phone and a stack of books. It looks like my bedroom at home but taller, more imposing, dangerous.

I'm curled under the covers but I'm restless, tossing and turning. After several minutes, I fling the covers off. I toss once more but this time I don't stop, I keep rolling until I'm at the edge of the bed. There's a thud as my head connects with the corner of a nightstand on the way down. When I land, my body is motionless and there's so much blood.

With a gasp, I sat up. My heart knocked around in my chest and I pulled in breaths as fast as I could. It took me another few seconds to remember where I was. Naked people. The cabin. Theo.

I whipped my head to stare at his bed, praying he hadn't woken. After my eyes adjusted, I could tell he was out cold, the blankets half kicked off, his hair wild on his pillow.

After climbing out of bed, I tiptoed to the bathroom. I flipped on the light and blinked against the stinging, sudden brightness. I splashed my face with water and stared at myself in the mirror.

"You have got to get over this." It had been eight months now and I had this stupid dream at least twice a week. It didn't take a genius to guess why. Going back to sleep on the bed would be impossible now.

Quietly, I shuffled back into the main room and pulled the sheet, blanket and pillow off the bed, glancing occasionally at Theo. On the floor at the foot of the bed, I made a nest and curled up in it. I tried not to think about what things this floor had seen. Nope, not thinking about that.

Within minutes, I was sound asleep.

It could have been fifteen minutes or three hours later when the insistent tapping on my foot woke me. Pushing my hair from my eyes, I rolled over to find the shadowy figure of Theo staring at me.

"Why are you on the floor?" he asked. He'd switched on the light in the tiny bathroom and cracked the door. A soft glow haloed his head.

"That bed was way too soft." I sat up. "I like my bed like I like my men."

"Dirty and possibly contagious?" He crossed his arms and his t-shirt bunched up to reveal a strip of skin which I did not look at.

"No, dummy. Firm."

He crouched beside me, tucked a strand of hair behind my ear, and asked again. "Why are you on the floor?"

I picked at the blanket on my lap. If there was anyone on this earth who might understand, it would be Theo. My last seizure had not been two years ago, as everyone thought. It had been eight months ago.

Most people don't realize there are a lot of different kinds of seizures and reasons for having them. Focal seizures look as though the person is staring off in space, but they can't respond, or speak. Sometimes people go years without realizing they're having them. The ones I have are tonic-clonic seizures—the fall-on-the-floor, body-jarring convulsions. Frankie liked to joke I was "dramatic" even when I was having a seizure.

Like about fifty percent of people with epilepsy, I had no idea why my seizures started that day on the soccer field when I was sixteen. I only remember feeling the slightest bit nauseated and then—like someone hit a fast-forward button on my life—I was in an ambulance, and it was so hard to focus. My limbs had felt heavy, and I couldn't keep my eyes open.

See, I never remembered having a seizure. But according to those that have witnessed one, I fall or slump wherever I am, and my body goes stiff, then the convulsing starts. When that's over, my face turns bluish-gray, and I stop breathing for thirty seconds or so. The actual seizure lasts less than five minutes but recovering takes much longer.

That time is lost, a hole in my memory. Another little piece epilepsy has stolen from me. But it's a mercy, I think. If I remembered it, I think the fear would drag me down until I couldn't function, being trapped like that by my own body. The first fifteen minutes or so after a seizure, I'm unconscious. Dead weight, my dad called it. And then the vomiting comes. For hours after, I'm unsteady on my feet and so, so exhausted. I'll sleep for hours, and my brain feels slippery, like what I need to remember is right there but keeps slithering away.

That night eight months ago was different. I'd gone to bed around ten; I woke on the floor hours later. A wave of nausea greeted me. My head throbbed, and when I put my hand to the back of my head, it came away bloody.

The best I could guess, I'd had a seizure, fallen off the bed and my head hit the nightstand on the way down. After laying on the floor until I felt steady enough to attempt to move, I'd half stumbled, half crawled to the bathroom. Despite the fuzziness of my vision, I managed to make it just in time to puke.

It had been two in the morning, and I needed to go to the hospital to get checked out. I couldn't call my parents. My mother would lose her mind, and I'd finally gotten her used to me living on my own.

I didn't want to call Frankie who would turn around and call my parents. I could have called Mae, and she would have come to rescue me. But I was starting to get real tired of the imbalance in our friendship. If there was a giant scale with FRIENDS WHO GOT IN TROUBLE on one side and FRIENDS WHO RESCUED FRIENDS on the other, I knew what side I was on.

So, I called Theo. Even though we weren't nearly as close as we'd been as kids, given my whole Theo Thirst Era, the fallout from that, and my strict Friend Zone rule, I called and he came. Because he was Theo, he didn't ask questions; he just showed up, wearing gym shorts and an inside-out t-shirt, his hair protesting the early wake-up call by practically standing on end.

He'd taken one look at me, still not quite steady on my feet, a towel pressed to the cut on my head, and carefully, gently, like I was made of something fragile and precious—and at that moment, maybe I was—he'd wrapped his arms around me and held me. It had taken everything in me not to burst into tears. It soothed something in me, him being there, quietly comforting me.

After, he'd helped me to his car and taken me to the emergency room.

I'd ended up with a mild concussion that required I stay off screens for a couple of weeks, and a phone call to my neurologist who changed up my medication for the first time in over a year.

Theo had taken me home afterward and insisted on staying with me for the day. "To make sure you don't knock your head on anything else."

He hadn't hovered like my mom. He didn't make me feel guilty for needing someone, like Mae would without meaning to. He was just there, quietly checking on me while I slept off the aftereffects.

And he'd never breathed a word of it to anyone.

Although it had been eight months since, I still found myself spooked some nights. I'd never been one of those people who could predict when a seizure was coming. A few minutes before, a sense of foreboding might slither up my spine. But sometimes the seizure came, and sometimes Peter Stone appeared.

"I have this dream." My voice cracked slightly.

"About what?"

"Falling off a tall bed, hitting my head, and landing like a bleeding, crumpled piece of paper. Not very original, right? Whatever could it be about?" I tried to keep my voice light.

"So, you sleep on the floor."

"Not every night. Just the nights I dream. I get... tense." And terrified and unable to close my eyes if I'm lying in bed. The only way I'd been able to go back to sleep, I'd discovered, was moving to the floor. I'd never had to deal with nightmares before, even as a kid. I could watch the creepiest of horror movies (and I did because three older brothers) and they never affected me.

I guess that's the difference between a fake movie and a very real accident.

I yanked out the scrunchie holding my hair back and reworked it into a ponytail. "I'll be fine. Go back to sleep."

He gave me a long look. "Come on."

"Come where?"

"I'm not letting you sleep on the floor." He held his hand out and wiggled his fingers. "Come on."

I took his hand and disregarded the sleepy dragons, their wings fluttering ever so gently. "I really am fine."

Ignoring me, he led me to the small table. "Stay there."

Quickly, he swept up the pillows and blankets I'd made my nest out of and threw them on the foot of my bed. Then he shoved the bed against the wall, boxing it between two walls and a dresser now at the foot of the bed.

He clasped my hand and tugged me toward it. "Now you won't have to worry about rolling off."

Nibbling on my bottom lip. I hesitated. "What about the other side?"

"I have that covered, too. But first we need to get you in bed." Then without any warning, he turned, slid an arm under my knees and behind my shoulders and unceremoniously dumped me on the bed.

I squeaked out something unintelligible in surprise. Ignoring me, he covered me with the blanket and stuffed a pillow under my head. I laid there like a stunned fish, mouth opening and closing in disbelief.

"Give me a second." While I watched, he dragged away the nightstand from between the beds. Thirty seconds later, he'd pushed his twin bed against mine. He snapped off the bathroom light and crawled into his bed. "There. Now you can't roll off this way either. Better?"

"Yes?" It was better and worse at the same time. I mean, his solution was a good idea, but this also put us in the same bed practically.

"I can't let you sleep on the floor." He yawned. "We both need to sleep and now we both can."

He sounded so close, and the thing is, he *was*.

Stunned, I held myself perfectly still. The Theo-obsessed

fifteen-year-old inside me, that girl was about to incinerate with excitement. I'd had this dream many times. Theo, me, a bed... It was like one of those scenes from the cheesy romance novels Mae pretended not to read.

The part of me that was a grown-up was also equally excited. But smarter. Wiser. This was probably a terrible idea. But I didn't move.

"Thank you," I whispered.

Something warm brushed against my hand. My breath caught when Theo slid his fingers between mine, his hold strong and firm, reassuring.

"It must be scary to have that dream."

I made a small sound.

"Especially when you're alone," he said, his voice quiet and sure.

Out of nowhere, tears pricked the backs of my eyes and I blinked rapidly to get rid of them.

"But you're not alone right now, okay? I won't let you fall." He squeezed my hand. "Now, close your eyes and try to get some sleep."

So, I did. My last thought before I drifted off was that something monumental had shifted in the region of my heart in the last ten minutes. That once dormant crush on Theo I'd worked so hard to pretend didn't exist had woken with a vengeance.

Great. Just great.

SIXTEEN

Note to self:
Research how much text can go on a tombstone.

Saturday, eight days until the wedding

An hour or so outside Amarillo, Texas

A blinding ray of sunshine landed on my face, let in by a tiny crack where the curtains didn't quite meet. With a groan, I burrowed farther into the blankets to get away from it. My eyes drifted closed as I drew in a deep breath of oranges and sunshine and soap, a comforting smell. A familiar one. A Theo sort of scent.

I froze and took stock of where I was. I remembered falling asleep holding his hand on one side of the bed. But I was now pressed against him, my face buried in his side. One of my hands was resting on his chest, which was rising and falling steadily, and his fingers were tangled in my hair, and it was so comfortable and lovely and perfect and... oh, crap.

I'd had this dream too. Usually involving us trapped somewhere in the mountains during a blizzard. Alone. With one bed and...

Okay. Right. This was the opposite of Friend Zone and even if my feelings were starting to grow, it was all so confusing. Not just my own feelings but Theo, too. He'd been different since we'd left for this trip, and I had no idea what any of this meant.

Time for a plan. I'd extract myself quietly and calmly.

I raised my head slowly to find the easiest escape route. Then it all came back to me. Theo pushing the beds together and laying next to me for my safety.

Sweet, wonderful, thoughtful Theo who had taken care of me last night. The same Theo who currently had one hand in my hair and another on my back, the tips of his fingers grazing the strip of skin exposed from my tank top rising up during the night. The same Theo who I was now certainly seventy-five percent in love with.

Oh, this was not good.

Inching back slowly, I tried to free myself so as not to wake him. But his hand on my back pulled me closer as he shifted. We were now, somehow, by some weird Jenga bed magic, facing one another, one of his legs curled around mine. I sucked in a breath, afraid to move. But he seemed to sleep on.

I realized I'd been granted a rare moment to stare at him without it being weird. So, I gave in to the temptation. Like I was strong enough to turn down this opportunity. I studied the way the tips of his dark-blond eyelashes rested on his cheeks. How the right side of his mouth tipped up ever so slightly in a half-smile. I wondered if he was dreaming. And yes, I wondered if I was in those dreams.

Maybe I'd go back to sleep for a bit and when I woke up, I'd realize I'd been the one dreaming. I snuggled in, my eyelids growing heavy again. Sleep was a breath or two away when my nose started to itch. The sneeze was inevitable and loud enough to wake most of the county.

Theo startled. Reflexively, his arm squeezed me tighter and hauled me closer. I squawked at the bone-cracking embrace and held my breath as his sleepy blue eyes met mine. He blinked slowly. He seemed to take stock of his body. His leg slid from mine. Which was kind of sad. The hand on my back eased off.

I cleared my throat, my face hot. "Hi."

"Hi?" His hand in my hair began to move through my hair. And then again. And then again.

"Are you petting me?" I whispered.

The hand stopped. "I, um..."

I sat up quickly, taking the blanket with me, and stared at him. Which was a terrible idea. Awake and alert Theo I could handle (barely). Sleepy, rumpled Theo with his hair askew and his eyes lazy. Whoa, Mama. This was going to be how I died.

Please put the following on my tombstone:

Here Lies Alicia Ramos

Daughter, Sister, Friend

She died doing what she loved:

Staring at Theo Goodnight in wonder

Maybe I was *in* a dream?

I saw the second his brain clicked online. His eyes widened and a faint blush dusted his cheeks. He sat up slowly. Our eyes met for half a second before we both looked away. That's when I noticed we'd managed to squish ourselves on his bed, the one he pushed next to mine. At some point last night, I'd crossed the imaginary line to plaster myself to him. I could not be trusted. Seriously.

"I, ah... I wasn't... I mean, it must have..." He raked his fingers through his hair which only made it stand on end. "I don't know what I'm trying to say here."

"Hey, no biggie. It happens, right?" I shrugged.

He nodded. "Right. Yeah. It happens."

"Totally."

"Yup."

"All the time, I'm sure."

He frowned. "What are we talking about?"

I opened my mouth and closed it, then huffed a laugh. "I have no idea."

His mouth tipped in a crooked smile. Our gazes locked and held. I pressed a hand to my stomach where the dragons were engaged in some kind of aerial routine.

Somewhere outside a dog barked and broke the Theo-induced trance I was under. "I'll just get out of your way."

Blanket in a death grip, I scooted down the bed and slipped off the bottom, almost falling when I tripped on a flip-flop. I leaned an elbow on the dresser at the foot of the bed. "So, busy day ahead, and all."

I was proud of myself for how calm and cool I sounded. Since it was the exact opposite of what was going on inside. There, the dragons seemed to be growing in strength and number. I peeled a curtain back from the window above the dresser, anything to distract me from red-cheeked, messy-headed, totally adorable Theo, in time to see a man stroll by walking his dog. Naked, except for the sandals and a belt bag. With a shudder, I flipped back around.

Seconds turned to minutes filled with awkward silence. I played with the edge of my shirt, studied the wood plank floor, watched an ant make its way toward the dresser. My skin felt itchy. Suddenly, I couldn't stand there one more breath.

"I am going to the bathroom. To, um, get dressed and brush my teeth. Unless you want to go first," I said to the general area above Theo's head.

He cleared his throat. "Nope, you, ah, go first."

"Alright. Well, then..." I sidestepped toward my backpack. "I will go get ready. In the bathroom. Right now."

I skittered into the bathroom and hastily shut the door.

After dumping my backpack on the counter, I gazed at myself in the mirror.

"Okay, that was awkward."

Things were never awkward between us anymore because I made sure they weren't. I'd had years to get over this teenage infatuation with him. I mean, after that one time he made it very clear I needed to get over it.

And then Mom and Dad sat me down and told me I needed to get over it.

And Abe had sat me down and... well, you get the picture.

So, I'd hiked up my big girl soccer shorts and did it; I got over him. It was a mind over matter thing really. All about willpower and self-control. I hardly had a passing thought of Theo Goodnight and his crinkly, laughing eyes and his slow smiles and...

But just now, neither one of us could look the other in the eye and we had days, *days*, still stuck in a car together. I couldn't stand it if this awkwardness followed us for the whole trip. I needed to fix this.

Resolved, I ripped the bathroom door open and stomped back into the room. Theo was in the same place I left him, sitting up in bed, a curious expression in his blue eyes. It would help if he wasn't so dang handsome; it made my knees weak sometimes.

Then again, I feared Theo could one day decide to take up playing the recorder while wearing a foam cheese wedge hat every day of his life and I'd find it sexy. Not that there was anything wrong with occasionally admiring from afar. As long as I didn't start writing poetry again and naming our children.

"I want you to know I won't make things weird," I blurted out and kept going before I lost the nerve. "I mean, I'm not a teenage girl with a crush anymore."

Theo's eyes widened.

"This morning was weird, okay? We... you know." My eyes

landed on the bed with emphasis. "It looks like I invaded your personal space and—"

"Ali—"

I held my hand up. "No, let me talk. I know you don't think of me as anything besides a friend, a little sister, whatever, and that's okay. I'm over all that. I promise."

And the understatement of the year goes to Ali Ramos.

I forged on, determined to get this out even if I melted from pure embarrassment in the process. "I made things very uncomfortable for you back then. But I'm not a dumb kid anymore and I don't want what happened last time to happen again."

It had been awful. After my latest scheme to get Theo to notice me, which involved a series of increasingly obvious anonymous love letters I mailed to him at college, it had all come to a head when I'd shown up at his dorm room unannounced. I'd only had my license for a week, skipped school, wore what I'd deemed my most alluring outfit, drove to College Station and surprised him on a random Thursday morning with one last letter and a truly horrid poem I'd written.

Then, because I didn't do things by half, after professing my undying love, I'd gone for it. I'd tried to kiss him.

I still cringed just thinking about how gentle and kind and patient he'd been. How he'd sidestepped the kiss and carefully explained I was too young and didn't know what I was saying. How I'd put on a brave face and laughed it off as a huge prank.

"I really got you, didn't I?" I'd bragged, grinning so widely my face had hurt.

I was sure he'd seen right through me, but Theo being Theo, his kindness had won out and he'd gone with it. Then I'd punched him in the arm good-naturedly even though my heart had been shriveling up at that very moment. God, I'd been so young and clueless.

Despite all that, the next three years were strained and awkward between us. I made myself scarce when he was around. We didn't joke around anymore; I didn't clamor to sit next to him at every meal. I couldn't look him in the eye, and sometimes, I'd catch him staring at me across a room, confusion and hurt in his eyes. We barely spoke two words to each other, and when we did, they were painfully polite.

It had been too much, and I'd missed his friendship. So, I'd willed myself to get over it. By the time I got home from my first year at college, I'd made the decision we would be friends again. I willed that into existence too.

Things had been fine for years between us. Sure, sure, the feelings tended to rear their ugly head when I least expected them, but I pushed them down and went on. I dated, Theo dated, and we were okay. I'd rather have Theo as a friend. I chose that over some dumb crush.

Now, with Theo in front of me, watching me with serious blue eyes, I knew I'd made the right decision.

"I just want to say thanks for being my friend. It was sweet of you to help me last night. I want you to know there will be absolutely no weirdness from me. Nope. We can both agree we'll forget about all this and, you know, go back to being completely un-weird." Like a dork, I shot him with a finger-gun with the sound and everything. "So, we good?"

There. That felt better. But then the silence stretched from uncomfortable to very uncomfortable territory. And Theo wasn't saying anything; in fact, he looked partially stunned, partially something else and his eyes were so... intense.

Should I have said all that? No. Or yes? I don't know. I thought of Alec telling me I was emotionally unavailable. Which was basically a fancy way of saying I didn't share my feelings. This was why. When I did, it came out like this.

"I'm sorry," I whispered, inching back to the bathroom. "I made it weird trying to reassure you I wouldn't make it weird."

Quickly, I skittered inside the bathroom, closing the door and leaning against it. Huge gulps of air filled my lungs. I stood there waiting for the embarrassment to put me out of my misery by spontaneous combustion.

A quiet knock on the door startled me.

"Oh, hey," I said, scrambling to open my backpack and pull my clothes out. "I'll just be a few more minutes."

Theo's voice came through the door. "I promise it won't be weird, okay?"

Relief roared through me, relaxing body parts I hadn't realized I'd been clenching. "Okay."

"And Alicia?"

"Yeah?"

"Just so we're clear, you are not my sister."

My smile was small. "I knew you were going to say that."

SEVENTEEN

Note to self:
Everything is fine.
Probably.

True to his word, things went right back to normal between us. Kind of. If I ignored the slightly stilted conversation while we sat on opposite beds after we'd put the room to rights and ate granola bars for breakfast. Or when I'd brushed against him as we packed our stuff to leave, and he'd made a strange noise and practically leapt on top of the table to get away from me.

Message received.

Zip met us at the office at eight. He'd kindly put shorts on with his Hawaiian shirt, out of deference to us "textiles." That's what they call us clothing-dependent people: textiles.

George finished replacing the water pump by eleven and we were back on the road by eleven thirty, now one open invitation to "come on back to the Longhorn Resort and Spa anytime" richer.

Yeah, no. Although I briefly toyed with the idea of getting

Cal and Melanie a gift certificate as a wedding gift. Just for funsies.

As soon as we picked up a cell signal, my notifications went off in a series of frantic dings. Twenty-seven missed calls. Eight voicemails. And too many texts to count.

"Oh, thank God," Mom said when she answered. "I've been worried sick."

"You talked to me last night. We're fine. No one even tried to murder us."

"Yes, but then I worried you'd been abducted, and someone was making you say that so I wouldn't be suspicious."

Next to me, Theo snickered.

"Or what if you'd been attacked by a wild animal?"

"I think we're pretty safe from that."

"I watched a news report about a python that came up through someone's toilet. What if that had happened?"

"I don't even know how to reply to that."

She tsked. "You have to think about these things so you can be prepared."

"How do you prepare for a snake coming up through the toilet? Never mind. You're making my brain hurt."

"A headache?" I could *hear* her worried expression through the phone. "Did you get enough sleep last night?"

"I called to let you know we're back on the road. The car is fixed, and we'll be at Mack's in an hour."

She huffed. "How are you feeling? You know stress can trigger seizures."

"I'm fine."

"Are you sure?"

Okay, enough was enough. I pulled the phone a good foot away and half yelled. "Sorry, the service is getting spotty again. You're breaking up."

Her voice came through the phone, clearly yelling my name.

"I'm going to hang up now. I'll call back when I can. Bye. Love you." I groaned. "My mother is a menace."

"Like mother, like daughter," Theo murmured, his eyes on the road.

With a gasp, I slugged him in the arm. "Excuse me? I'm not like my mother. You take it back."

His mouth curled into a grin. "You have your own brand of menace."

"I do not," I said, purely on stubbornness.

He held up two fingers. "Two words: toothpaste Oreos."

I tried to hold back a laugh and failed. "You all asked for it. All I wanted was to hang out with you and the boys."

My brothers and Theo, all teenagers at that point, had been locked in the TV room watching some stupid horror movie. I didn't even want to watch it; I just wanted to be with them. They were older, cooler, and dead set against me joining them. Worse, my mother took their side.

After several failed attempts, I knew I wasn't going to win. Or at least, I wasn't getting into that room with them. It's possible I waited until Mom was in the shower, unscrewed and de-creamed about twenty Oreos and refilled them with white toothpaste.

Along with four glasses of milk, I arranged them on a tray and set it in front of the closed door to the TV room and knocked.

"Go away, Ali," several annoyed voices shouted.

"I wanted to say I'm sorry and I brought you some cookies and I'm going to bed." I'd scurried to the end of the hallway and peeked around the corner until someone opened the door and the tray disappeared. Then I scurried into bed. My eyes had just slid shut when I heard the shouts and feet racing down the hallway to the kitchen. I'd fallen asleep smiling that night.

Next to me in the car, Theo shuddered. "I haven't touched an Oreo in over fifteen years. I can't even look at them."

I laughed in an I-am-an-evil-scientist way.

"So yes, you were a menace." He tossed a pointed look in my direction. "You're still a menace."

"Whatever." He wasn't exactly wrong. "Your life would be boring without me."

His dimple appeared. "Very boring."

I scrolled through my messages, both voicemail and texts—did I even know this many people? Of course, there were messages from my mother to tell me she was worried, my father to tell me my mother was worried; Melanie texted to make sure we were safe, and Frankie texted to say Mom had asked him to contact the police department in Amarillo.

And then there were the others—my childhood pediatrician, Miss Mary, who'd been my Sunday school teacher a million years ago and now worked at the grocery store in town; the middle school counselor, and my mail carrier—who just wanted to make sure I was okay. I hated to cause all this worry but having that first seizure seemed to set in motion a kind of protectiveness from the entire town. There was always a possibility I could have another, and everyone felt it was their duty to worry over me. If they did forget, my mother was sure to remind them.

It was exhausting.

I loved Two Harts but every now and then I had a fantasy about moving away, changing my name, and keeping my medical history to myself.

I pulled up my group text with Mae and Ellie:

Me: *The car broke down yesterday.*

Mae: *I heard. I had to talk your mom out of calling up the Texas Rangers and that was after she added your missing status to the church prayer chain.*

Me: *We were not missing.*

Mae: *So, has Theo made his move?*

Me: *Stop it.*

Mae: *No then. Bummer. He likes to take his time, doesn't he? Really playing the long game.*

Ellie: *I'm trying to work here. What did I miss?*

Mae: *Nothing. Unfortunately.*

Ellie: *Damn. I was hoping for something juicy.*

Me: *I'm not talking to either of you ever again.*

Mae: *You love us.*

I glared at the phone like they could see me.

Mae: *Did you see the surprise I put in the front pocket of your backpack?*

Me: *Still not talking to you.*

Mae: *Text later?*

Me: *Fine.*

After rummaging through my backpack, I found the "surprise" Mae was talking about. I flattened out the folded piece of paper and frowned at it.

"What's that?"

"Nothing." I moved to stuff the paper in my backpack, but Theo gently tugged it out of my hand. "Hey, give that back. You're driving."

"Declaration of Candidate for Mayoral Election: Town of Two Harts, Texas," he managed to read.

When he didn't say anything, embarrassment rolled through me. I swallowed and picked at the raw edge of my denim cutoff shorts.

"It's a dumb joke. Mae put it in my backpack. She's not serious."

"I don't think it's dumb," he said quietly and handed me back the paper.

"Oh, sure. Could you see it? Alicia Ramos for Mayor."

"Huh." Nothing else. Just a little sound from the back of his throat.

I turned and pressed my forehead against the passenger side window and tried to sort through this knot of humiliation in my chest. Me as mayor *was* a dumb idea. I had zero experience. Zero political aspirations. Zero knowledge of how to be a mayor, let alone do it successfully.

Yet—and I was going to beat Mae with a wet noodle for this—a teeny, itty-bitty part of me was thinking about it. And everyone knew, when I got to thinking about something, things happened.

EIGHTEEN

Note to self:
Become a cat person.

Amarillo

The little yellow house on the corner of Oak and Delmont had always been my favorite place to visit when I was younger. It still looked exactly the same, too. Like time hadn't touched this magical place where homemade cookies were always available, and hugs were given out freely.

Theo and I climbed out of the car and were immediately serenaded with a rich, hearty baritone coming from the back corner of the yard where Grandma Grace's prized roses lived.

"Is he singing a Taylor Swift song?" Theo asked.

I paused at the gate to the front yard and listened. Mack seemed to hit his stride when he got to the chorus and started to really "shake it off." I couldn't help smiling.

Mack and Grandma Grace had been a case of opposites attracting. Michael "Mack" Sullivan was the life of the party, quick to make friends, and always willing to chat with a stranger. He could charm anyone he met within minutes. So, it wasn't a surprise he'd started as a salesman at a furniture store after he got out of the Navy and worked his way up to regional manager by the time he retired.

Grandma Grace was quiet and thoughtful, happy to be in the background, allowing Mack to have his fun, but always by his side. They went everywhere together. I'd never known a time when they were separated.

Grandma Grace had been my person. As the youngest of four, I always felt lost in the shuffle. The boys all had each other; they shared a room, friends, and a camaraderie between them I wouldn't ever understand. While I had lots of friends, it wasn't the same as a sister. Plus, no one ever listened to me.

When I was seven, I campaigned to get a little sister. That is until Mom sat me down and told me how babies were made. If her plan was to gross me out enough to never ask again, it worked.

But Grandma Grace *always* remembered me. I loved making the long drive to Amarillo because she'd be there waiting. Grandma Grace, with her faded blue eyes and soft gray hair, asked me questions about school, and what my favorite color was and my favorite food, and she listened to the answers. She'd been gone a little over a year now and I missed her. Mack missed her too, even if he pretended he was fine.

Mack was starting to fully commit to the song, belting it out without any care of pitch or correct lyrics. Theo and I caught sight of him repurposing a pair of garden shears as a microphone. His hips shimmied to the music.

He was in his "gardening" outfit which consisted of cargo shorts, socks and clogs, and... that was about it. His shirt was tossed on the grass and his shoulders and back had taken the brunt of the sun.

"He's got some moves, doesn't he?" Theo said.

I bumped his hip with mine. "Runs in the family."

Mack moved on from singing to chatting up the roses.

"Now, listen here," he said in a stern voice. "You'll do well to listen to the neighbor while I'm gone. Don't go getting any ideas about withering away."

He paused, his ear tilted toward the roses.

"Well, of course, I'll be back. I'm headed to Oregon to see my grandson get married. I have to go, there's no way around it."

Mack had always been a little eccentric. I'm not sure being alone helped any. There was no one around to rein him in like Grandma had done. Mom had brought up the topic of him selling the house and moving closer. But Mack was having none of it. This was the home he and Grandma had lived in for over fifty years, raised their kids there, made lots of happy memories. It was the last place Grandma Grace had been alive and I think a part of him worried leaving would mean letting go of her completely.

"Mack." I called from across the yard.

He turned and grinned. "Ali-Cat!"

I was three steps away from him when The Thing appeared. A tiny little hairy ball of... something scampered out from behind the rose bushes and launched itself in my path. It emitted a low growl that gave off, GET AWAY. I'M SUPER-SCARY. Which might have been true if it didn't look like it weighed more than five pounds and three of those were hair. The sandy-brown fur looked wiry and thick, and stuck out in all directions, like the thing had been electrocuted. It made the small, random patches of baldness even more noticeable. It could have been a large rat, a very small raccoon, a possible alien life-form, or a tiny dog with an attitude. It was hard to tell based on appearance alone.

Startled, I jumped back. Theo caught me and pulled me against him.

"What is that?" I straightened, but for some reason, Theo kept his hands on my hips.

"Karen, now, stop that," Mack scolded as he bent and picked it up. "That's my granddaughter. We like her." The Thing yipped and proceeded to lick every inch of Mack's face its tongue could reach.

"That cannot be a dog," I said.

Mack frowned. "Be nice. Karen is very sensitive."

"When did you get a dog?"

"Last month from the county shelter." He brushed the hair off her face and that did not make things any better. Karen's bottom teeth protruded from her mouth in an unfortunate underbite. It made her look wicked angry even without all the growling and barking.

"Does she have a lazy eye?" I asked.

"Yes. But she sees just fine, don't you, little one." He held her up, so they were face to face. Karen went to town, licking all the spots she hadn't been able to reach before.

"Mack," I said, "that is the ugliest dog I have ever seen."

"Don't listen to her, my sweet baby," Mack said to the dog. "She's just jealous of all your charm."

I snorted. "Yeah. That's not it."

Theo slowly approached, holding his hand out. Karen growled but leaned forward enough to sniff him out. He seemed to pass muster because she allowed him to pet her.

"She's not so bad," Theo said. "Come pet her."

So, I tried. I followed Theo's example and approached cautiously, holding my hand out. I got within a foot of her, and Karen's angry little face grew angrier. She escalated from a growl to full-on, there's-a-stranger-in-my-house level barking to snapping at my fingers, her whole body vibrating with rage.

"Wow. I don't think she likes you," Theo said.

"Oh, don't worry," Mack said, pulling Karen closer to him. "She'll have plenty of time to get used to you on this trip."

"Wait," I said. "She's going with us?"

"I can't leave her here with someone else. She has separation anxiety." He looked at the dog cradled in his arms with adoration. "Don't you, sweet girl?"

"There's not a neighbor that could keep her while you're gone?"

"I think she'll be fine. She is pretty sweet." Theo reached over and began scratching Karen under the chin. She let out a contented little sigh and went boneless in Mack's arms.

She did have that "so ugly, she's cute" thing going on for her. I lifted my hand to scratch her like Theo had. Before I even touched her, she cracked open one eye and growled.

I yanked my hand back. "A whole week in the car with her. That sounds like... fun." Right up there with root canals, letters from the IRS, and jogging on a street paved with Legos.

"My two girls can get to know each other." Mack rocked back on his heels. "Watch, you and Karen will be best friends by the end of this."

Somehow, I doubted that.

Mack's mischievous blue eyes darted between Theo and me and a wide grin spread across his face. "It's good to see you, Theodore. When are you going to put a ring on this one?"

I gasped. "Mack."

"I'm just saying I'd like to see it happen before I die."

"We are not dating. We're friends."

"Sure. Sure. Gracie and I were friends before we fell in love. I met her when I was seven, did you know that?"

Of course, I knew that. I'd heard the story many times.

Mack had been in his second-grade class when the door had opened and a new student arrived, a quiet girl with long blonde braided pigtails and enormous blue eyes.

"Love at first sight. Decided that day I was going to marry her." His eyes turned soft and dreamy. "'Course, she hated me at first, but I was persistent."

I smiled. "And it took fifteen years before she agreed to go out with you."

He paused and winked at Theo. "Married her three months later. Take it from an old man, Theodore, you find a good woman like our Ali, you get her hitched to you as fast as you can."

Theo smiled, his dimple peeking out. The look he shot my way could only be described as sly.

Mack threw his arm around my shoulder; Karen growled softly. "Alright. Alright. I'm an old man, what do I know? Now, let's go inside. You can relax while I get myself situated."

Shaking my head, I trailed behind Theo and Mack. That's when it hit me: Theo hadn't tried to correct Mack, not even once. What the heck did that mean?

NINETEEN

Note to self:
Mistakes, like bad seafood, have a way of coming up again.
Plan accordingly.

A gas station somewhere in Colorado

While Mack showered, Theo and I sat on opposite ends of the same brown couch that had been in my grandparents' living room since I was a kid. In fact, not much had changed at all. It still had the slightly dated, homey feeling of my childhood, and the smell of baby powder and vanilla was faint but still there.

Karen was nestled on Theo's lap, limp with joy as he stroked her. She was also watching me with unblinking dark eyes.

"She's staring at me," I whispered.

"She is not," Theo said, amusement in his voice.

"That dog is planning my murder right this instant." Karen's head cocked to the side. I think she was sizing me up to estimate the lethal amount of poison she'd need.

"Since when do you not like dogs?"

"I like dogs. Normal-sized dogs who like to play fetch and cuddle and don't want to bury my body in a shallow grave. That is not a dog."

Theo grinned and Karen continued to bask in his attention. I might have been a little jealous of her. I too would be limp with joy if Theo decided to stroke me... my hair... stroke my hair.

"Let's get this show on the road." Mack waltzed into the living room.

Mack had always been a jeans and t-shirt kind of guy at home, suits and ties for work. But this Mack was a different model: Mack 2.0. He wore loose-fitting tan pants that I thought were linen, a blue guayabera shirt with yellow embroidery, brown leather sandals, and a fedora at a jaunty angle. In all, he looked like he might be heading on vacation to a Mexican beach resort.

"Oh, wow. This is different," I said.

Mack glanced down at his clothes. "Thought I'd try out something new." He did a spin. "What do you think?"

"You look great."

"It was time for a change." He grabbed his suitcase and pulled open the front door. "After you, madam."

Mack insisted on sitting in the backseat and refused to change his mind no matter how much I protested. "Karen will do better back here and you two can keep each other company."

"I'd rather you sit in front. It will be easier for you."

"Stop playing so hard to get, Ali-Cat. Throw the man a bone." With a wink, Mack patted me on the cheek and climbed into the backseat as though he hadn't heard me.

"We are not dat—"

"Close the door for me," he said. "I plan to take a nap."

Fifteen minutes later, the sound of a small army of growling bears filled the car as Mack and Karen drifted off, his face pressed against the window and her face pressing into his lap.

I cringed. "I think Karen snores louder than he does."

"That's going to be fun to sleep in the same room with," Theo said.

It turned out Mack had the same size bladder as a goldfish.

Two hours later (and our second pit stop of the day), we ended up at a gas station just past Lamar, Colorado. While Theo got gas, I stretched my legs, bought a variety of snacks that would have made a nine-year-old with a credit card proud, and asked Gus, the grizzled, bearded guy behind the counter for the key to the bathroom. The key was tied to an actual bicycle wheel and unlocked a dingy white door to reveal an even dingier bathroom.

Unfortunately, by the time I returned, Mack, Karen cradled in his arms like a newborn, and Gus were chatting away like long-lost brothers. I heard mention of local historical landmarks, and I knew we were done for.

"Mack's gonna be a while." I pointed to a picnic table on the side of the store. "Might as well sit outside and enjoy the weather."

I climbed to sit atop the table and leaned back on my hands. The heat from the sun was soft and warm and a nice breeze rippled through my hair. The weather here was a dream, nothing like back home in Two Harts. It was beautiful, too, with sweeping views and mountains and fresh, clean air. The appeal was obvious. I could understand why Abe had settled in Colorado.

Theo sat on the bench, close enough that his shoulder brushed my knee. I rummaged through my bag of goodies and tossed a snack in his lap.

"Oreos?" With a grimace, he pinched the corner of the package and dangled it over my lap. "Not funny."

Giggling, I snatched the cookies back and searched through the bag again. "I think it's hilarious."

This time when I tossed something at Theo, he held it up and grinned. "Black licorice. Much better."

"Disgusting," I said, around the sour gummy worm I'd already stuffed in my mouth.

"The great people of the Netherlands eat more black licorice every year than any other country." He chewed thoughtfully. "Those are my people."

"How are we even friends?" I asked the sky.

He pressed his shoulder a bit more into my knee. It would have been so easy to reach down and run my fingers through all that unruly hair. I wondered if it was as soft as it looked.

Theo pulled out his phone to check his email. From my position, I could see the subject line of the message he opened and began to read.

SUBJECT: re: re: Current address and contact information.

And while I knew it wasn't my business, I still leaned in a little more, to see if I could make out any of the message itself when Theo seemed to remember I was there.

He stood abruptly and pressed his phone to his chest, tapping his fingertips on it. "I need to take care of something."

I nodded and watched him as he wandered off toward the car. Yet another thing to add to the increasing list of weirdness. In the span of a day, we'd already ended up at a nudist resort, I'd woken up in Theo's arms, and discovered Theo could flirt (and do it well).

Maybe that was the theme of this whole trip: Weird. Tomorrow, things were about to get even weirder. I rubbed my chest, trying to dislodge the uneasiness there.

By tomorrow morning, I would be looking my brother in the eye, and I had no idea the sort of reception I should expect. He could resent me. He should hate me. Although he'd never even once hinted at any such feelings over our phone calls and texts and emails, I had to believe my actions the day of that car accident replayed in his mind.

It had been a normal Tuesday, nothing out of the ordinary. I'd gone home with Mae on the bus, which sixteen-year-old Ali hated. But I'd had three seizures in the last four months. Legally, I wasn't allowed to drive until I'd been at least six months seizure-free. So I was again stuck riding the bus. I had a real concern that, once that six-month mark finally arrived, my parents wouldn't even allow me to drive. My overprotective mother had gone next-level after my epilepsy diagnosis, and I'd been forced to cut back on most of my activities.

No more soccer. No more driving. I wasn't allowed to be alone. Walks by myself? No. A run? I had to take a brother with me. Embarrassingly, Mom had set up a baby monitor in my room in case I had a seizure at night. I'm surprised I was still allowed to shower without a safety officer.

The resentment had built quickly—with my parents and my body. Through the last few months of testing, the EEG, the photosensitivity and sleep deprivation tests, the introduction of daily medications and their side effects (hello, grumpy, tired, hungry Ali), I'd tried to stay positive. Most people lived perfectly productive lives with epilepsy. My new pediatric neurologist even said I may grow out of them. But sometimes, the frustration with a body I could not control was so overwhelming.

To make matters worse, living in a small town meant everyone knew everything. I had teachers, friends' parents, the school janitor asking me if I felt okay, if I needed to sit down, if I needed water. I just wanted everything to go back to before the seizures started.

On the day of the accident, my parents had refused to let me sleep over at Mae's because they'd wanted to "keep an eye on me." By the time Abe had picked me up, all my teenage emotions, all the restrictions, all the lack of control had bubbled over.

"You okay?" he'd asked when I'd slid into the car. "You look like you want to punch someone."

I'd scowled. "Are you volunteering?"

Grinning, he'd leaned away from me. "Okay, then. Someone's not in a good mood today."

Back then, Abe had been quite the flirt. Girls had loved his dark, messy hair, big smile, easy laugh, and the ever-growing collection of tattoos. He and Theo had been quite a pair. Abe, all dark and flirty. Theo, with his blond hair and quiet, thoughtful way. Somehow the two of them had been the very best of friends.

"Whatever," I'd muttered.

"Ooo-kay." He'd pulled onto the quiet, country road Mae's family lived on. With my arms crossed, I'd leaned against the passenger window and sulked.

Five minutes of uncomfortable silence had been his limit. He'd pulled over next to the Richardsons' pasture. "Alright, start talking. We aren't moving until you do."

I'd turned to him and vomited every frustrated, angry, annoyed, angsty feeling I had in me. When I was done, I'd swiped at the tears on my cheeks. "I'm sixteen but I can't do anything. I can't spend the night at my best friend's house. I can't play soccer anymore. I can't even drive." I threw myself back against the seat in disgust. "I hate my life."

"It's just that everyone's w—"

"Worried about me. Yeah. Yeah. I just want a little freedom. I feel like I can't breathe some days."

"What can I do to make it better?"

I still don't know where the idea came from. There I was in Abe's car, and he'd asked me so earnestly and I'd blurted it out. "Can I drive the car? Just for a little while?"

Abe's hands had tightened on the steering wheel. "Is that such a great idea?"

"See? Even you!" I'd slumped in my seat.

"Okay. Yeah, okay. Sure. You can drive."

"Really?"

"Come on," he'd said with conviction.

Abe had never been good at saying no to me the way Frankie and Cal were. I'd eagerly slid behind the wheel of the car. Since it was November, the sun had long since set and minutes after I took over, rain began to pelt the car. I'd only had a few weeks of driving with my license before the first seizure. I was not, by any means, an experienced driver. Add in my mood, the chilly darkness of an early winter evening, the rain, the dark country road, the dangerous and intoxicating feeling of doing something I knew I shouldn't, all formed the perfect storm.

That's when I had the seizure.

The second before it started, I'd been hit with a wave of dizziness and then nothing. I'd woken to Abe yelling my name and shaking me so hard my teeth rattled.

My stomach had roiled, my vision was blurred and unfocused; I couldn't form words, let alone sentences. I hadn't been sure where I was, only that my head hurt, and I was going to puke any second.

Abe hadn't flinched when I'd done just that a second later, all over him. "Oh, hell, Ali. You're bleeding. Are you okay?"

I'd puked again and fallen back against the seat, the tinny, metallic taste of blood in my mouth. I'd bitten my tongue.

"You had a seizure." Abe's voice had sounded frantic. "We... uh, you ran into a tree."

Everything that happened next were snapshots I'd later have to piece together. Abe getting out of the car, pulling me out, and propping me against a nearby tree. EMS arriving, my parents right behind them. My father yelling at Abe in the background. A trip to the hospital in the ambulance. My mother's tearful face. Doctors. Blood draws and vital checks. The bone-deep exhaustion that lasted for hours after a seizure.

By the time I'd made it home in the wee hours of the morning, the house had been silent. Mom had helped to get me settled in bed. When I'd woken the next morning, Abe was gone. The note he'd slipped under the door said he'd miss me, and he'd written, "Don't worry about the accident. I told Dad I was driving."

I'd carried that secret with me for eleven long years, gotten so close to telling my parents the truth and then swallowing the words at the last minute. It wasn't just that I'd caused the accident, it was the reason for the accident, that I'd been driving when I knew I shouldn't be. It was that Mom would never let me out of her sight again if she knew. But mostly, it was because I was a coward.

Theo returned, pulling me from my memories. He stopped in front of me, his brow furrowed, and laid a hand on my knee. "Hey, you okay?"

"Do you think Abe will come to the wedding?" I worried my bottom lip.

"I know he misses you and your brothers and mom. Even your dad."

"He's told you that?"

He hesitated, as though he were debating what to say. "I've visited him a few times. Here, in Colorado. We've talked a lot about the whole situation."

"You've visited him?" I crossed my arms over my chest. A surprisingly sharp zing of pain sliced through my heart.

"In the summers. Sometimes I'll fly out for a long weekend."

"You've never said anything."

He gave me a weary look. "I didn't want to put myself between him and your parents. Abe's my best friend and your parents are like my family. I don't want them to think I've chosen sides or anything."

My chest tightened as I turned my face away. "You could have told me. You could have trusted me. I—"

"Ali." His fingers grazed my cheek, gently turning my head back. His eyes, those impossibly blue eyes, were tender as they gazed at me. I sucked in a breath. "It's what Abe wanted."

"It was?" I whispered and that hurt too, maybe worse. My own brother. Theo. I was so tired of everyone protecting me like I was fragile.

He pressed his lips together, his shoulders rising and falling with a sigh. "I know about the accident."

I jerked back. "He told you?"

"Hey, lovebirds," Mack yelled. "Let's get a move on it. We don't have all day."

I tried to hop off the picnic table, but Theo stopped me with a hand on my hip. A jolt of warmth radiated from the spot, and it made me even angrier. Because I was mad at him and I didn't get mad, and even though I was, he still had this stupid power over me, a power he didn't even realize he had.

"Are you okay?" he asked me; his eyes seemed to reach right inside my head.

I forced a stiff smile. "You know all my secrets and I'm beginning to think I don't know any of yours."

TWENTY

Note to self:
Fighting is dumb.
Making ~~out~~ up is better.

Theo beat his fingers on the steering wheel, playing some anonymous drum solo. The sound rode my nerves, but I tried to ignore it. Mack was no help in the distraction department. He'd slipped in some earbuds, pulled up a WWII movie on his phone, and proceeded to pretend we weren't even in the car.

Everything about the last two days was a jumbled mess in my head. I tried to parse it, pick out the important threads and throw the broken ones away but it was all a mess, impossible to untangle. Plus, I didn't like being angry with Theo but, dang, it stung. This was all so confusing.

I rubbed my forehead, feeling a headache coming on. That incessant finger tapping was not helping. "Okay, you have to stop. I can't take it."

He tightened both hands, the knuckles turning white. "Sorry."

"What's wrong?"

"Nothing."

"You've been tapping your fingers for almost forty-five minutes. You do that when you're anxious or nervous."

"I do not."

I rolled my eyes. "If you say so."

With a huff, he shifted in his seat. "I don't like that you're mad at me."

"I'm not mad at you," I lied. "I'm fine."

"That never means fine," he muttered.

"Excuse me?"

"Nothing," he said. "Abe thought it would be better if you weren't in the middle of him and your parents. He asked me not to tell you and..." His voice trailed off. "I trust you, Ali. More than almost any other person I know."

I barked a humorless laugh. "Really? Because it doesn't feel like it."

Theo opened his mouth and then closed it, pressing his lips together until they turned white at the corners. The silence between us was heavy and uncomfortable. We'd been on this trip for just over a day and it was becoming more and more apparent—shockingly so—that I didn't know Theo at all. We'd never had an argument. Oh, sure, good-natured ribbing, verbal sparring, but nothing like this. I'd happily strangle him right now, and I prided myself on never getting angry. Yet, here I was, angrier than Peter that one time someone placed an online ad selling ostrich eggs and told interested parties to text his number for information.

"I was serious. I trust you. You're one of the most important people in my life." His voice was all soft and thoughtful and it made my insides all gooey. Jerk. "I don't want to ever lose you. And, you know, our friendship."

That took most of the bluster out of me. Dang him. "I'm not going anywhere."

He nodded once. "Good."

"Great."

"Did we just have our first grown-up fight?" he asked.

"It didn't involve water balloons or shaving cream, so yeah, I guess so."

The corner of his mouth tipped in amusement. "Who won, do you think?"

"Obviously, me. That's how these things work."

"Because you're a woman?"

"Um, no, because I'm me."

With a snort, he settled back in his seat, shoulders relaxed. But before long, he was back to his drumbeats, then fiddling with the radio, and shooting several anxious glances in my direction. I pretended to ignore him. If he didn't want to share his secrets with me, fine. Whatever. It was—

"Can I talk to you about something?" he asked. Finally.

"Maybe."

"I haven't talked to anyone else about this."

I side-eyed him. "Really?"

"Yes."

"Is this bribery?"

"Kind of?" He sounded serious and a touch nervous. "Please."

"Sure. Go ahead."

"After Mom passed, I put all her stuff in storage." He stared intently at the road. "I wasn't in a good headspace to deal with it."

I murmured a soft encouragement for him to continue.

"So, I've been going through it lately. It's been a couple of years and... it was time." He swallowed. "I found information about my father."

"What kind of information?"

"Things I didn't know. His birthplace, his parents' names, his high school diploma. Hell, I didn't even know his birthday until I found all that stuff."

Theo hadn't talked much about his father growing up, mainly because he didn't know anything to talk about. The man had left his wife and son somewhere before Theo turned two. Becky had taken on the job of mother and father from then on. But she never talked about his father. Ever. He was a taboo subject in the Goodnight house. It never seemed to bother Theo, but there had to be a part of him that always wondered.

"That must have been weird."

"It was." He frowned. "It is. There was his last known address, too. I guess Mom had someone track him down for child support and stuff. So, I did some searching online and contacted a private investigator. I guess I'm curious about him, you know. He's lived around Las Vegas, for over twenty years."

"Oh."

"I'd always assumed he'd been a drifter or a junkie, or maybe got in trouble with the law and has been in prison this whole time. Or he was dead. Some reason he never came back." He took one white-knuckled hand from the steering wheel and shook it out. "I guess that was easier to believe than he didn't want us."

My heart cracked right down the middle for him. I didn't think, just took the hand he'd dropped to the console between us and cradled it between both of mine.

"It's his loss," I said fiercely.

"Yeah." His jaw ticked but he laced his fingers through mine and squeezed. A few dragons stretched their wings, and I ignored them. Now was not the time to fangirl over Theo. He needed a friend.

"Have you tried to contact him?"

"I don't know if I should. I've lived my whole life without him. Do I want to open myself up to that? I don't hate him, but I don't love him." He frowned. "I don't feel anything for him; he's a stranger."

I worried my bottom lip. "Do you want to know what I think?"

"Yeah. I do."

"I think you should see him."

He glanced at me curiously.

"It can't be too far out of our way. We could go to his house. Maybe you don't even get out of the car. We can set up surveillance and wear all black and eat bad convenience store hot dogs and spy on him."

He allowed a small smile. "That's a very specific plan."

I squeezed his hand this time. "You don't have to do it alone, you know. I'm right here."

"I thought you were mad at me."

"Please. I don't get mad," I lied. "I know we might not see each other all the time like we did as kids but I'd never, ever not be there for you. You have to know that. You're, you're..." Special. Wonderful. The man with whom I was pretty sure I was eighty percent in love. "You're Theo."

His thumb drew small circles on the back of my hand. "I don't believe you."

I stared down at our hands. "Anger and hurt look a lot alike sometimes."

"I don't want to hurt you, Ali. I've never wanted to do that," he said, his voice low.

A lump lodged in my throat. Swallowing hard, I pasted on a smile. "So, staking out your dad's house? What do you think?"

"Honestly, I don't know."

"It's a big decision, I get it. Think of me as your right-hand woman. I'm the Robin to your Batman, the chocolate to your peanut butter, the chicken to your waffle, the Bonnie to your Clyde, the cat to your empty box."

He laughed. "Okay. Okay. I get it. I promise I'll think about it."

"Good."

We didn't talk much after that. I found myself growing drowsy as I stared down at our hands still laced together. My last thought before I drifted to sleep was that I hoped he'd never let go.

TWENTY-ONE

Note to self:
If you can't beat 'em, join 'em.

"This is good stuff," Mack said, a spoonful of clam chowder halfway to his mouth.

Yes. Clam chowder. From an Elvis-themed café in a tiny, nameless town in Colorado where the closest ocean was a thousand miles away. Mack might be the bravest man I knew.

After a couple more hours of driving, we decided to stop for dinner and to find a hotel nearby. If those existed in this place. This day had seemed impossibly long, and Theo had been driving for hours without a real break.

I set my crossed arms on the table and tried to ignore how Theo's brushed up against mine. Mack had insisted we sit next to each other. I couldn't tell if he was a conniving, interfering old man, or legitimately confused about our relationship status.

Theo reached up to get his glass, his arm sliding against mine. Every time his arm gently bumped mine or the faint scent of citrus and soap assaulted me if I leaned even an inch closer, I got a little more antsy. I started to work up a fantasy where he turned and pulled me onto his lap and then right in the middle of this café and in front of my grandpa, he kissed me and...

I shook my head before I let my mind travel too far. He has to sit this close, Ramos. Stop making up stories.

"Glad I got to ride with you two." Mack smirked. "Even if you only have eyes for each other."

"Lay off, old man."

He ignored me. "I love Stephanie but, whoa boy, can she smother a person. Last time I saw her, we went out to dinner, and she tried to cut my steak for me. Into little, tiny pieces so I wouldn't choke. Can you imagine? I'm the one who taught *her* how to cut up a steak."

"She means well." Theo stole a tater tot from my plate.

Mack wagged his spoon at us, mindless of the tiny droplets of clam chowder that splattered on the table. "She does. But I'm nervous to tell her about my plan."

"Knock it off." I slapped Theo's hand as he tried to liberate another tot.

"They taste better when they're from your plate," he said.

"That is not true."

"It is."

"What's this plan?" I asked Mack, and in the split second my attention was diverted, Theo grabbed yet another tater tot.

I glared at him and moved my plate as far away as I could.

"I'm going to start dating." Mack shoved another spoonful in his mouth.

"Oh." I sat back, surprised. "I mean, I guess it's been a little over a year since... you know."

Mack pushed his bowl to the side. "Since Gracie died."

I flinched at his bluntness. "Yeah, since Grandma died."

"I loved your grandmother with my whole heart, I'll always love her, but," he put a hand on my arm, "I'm lonely. Real lonely. I talk to plants. I adopted possibly the ugliest dog in the world and sometimes I put clothes on her."

Karen's head popped up from where she was tucked in between Mack and the wall. It had been too hot to leave her in the car and Mack had wielded his charm enough that the restaurant staff looked the other way.

Mack patted her head. "You are the prettiest little puppy."

"You lie to your dog?" Theo asked.

"I told you, she's delicate."

Karen caught sight of me and bared her teeth.

"Yeah, delicate," I muttered. "How does this plan work exactly?"

"First, a makeover." He spread his arms out to showcase his outfit.

"That explains the hat."

He frowned. "The woman at JCPenney said it made me look dashing."

"Absolutely. I like it."

"Second, my counselor says I need to be open to new experiences."

"You're seeing a counselor?"

"Don't act so surprised. She's been helping me get all my feelings sorted. It's not so bad. You should try it," he said sagely.

"For what?"

"Think of it like taking your vitamins. You take your vitamins every day to keep your body healthy. You take your therapy to keep your mind healthy."

"I... wow."

"I've been reading a lot of self-help books." He nodded matter-of-factly. "And I enrolled in a Zumba class at the Y."

"Zumba?"

"Good exercise. Lots of women." He winked. "Joined some online dating websites, too."

My mouth dropped open. "You've refused to get an email address for years."

"Well, I have one now."

"Are you on a lot of these sites?"

"Keenage Dreams and Senior Friends with Benefits are my big ones."

Theo covered his mouth to muffle his laughter. I nudged him with my elbow.

"Senior Friends with Benefits?"

"I've met some very nice women. Younger women." He waggled his eyebrows.

"Younger?"

"Sure. One I'm talking to right now is only sixty-two." He pulled out his phone. "Let me show you a picture."

"That's okay," I said hastily.

"The point is that I'm ready to get out there. I'm tired of hiding away. I don't think Gracie would want that for me."

He was right. Grandma wouldn't want him to lock himself away. But still, I guess I couldn't keep the sad look from my eyes.

Mack squeezed my arm. "She is always in my heart. Always. I'm not replacing her."

I nodded. "I get it. I... this will be good for you. Mom will come around eventually." After she takes to her bed for three days and then figures out how to stalk Mack online.

"I knew you'd see it my way." Mack pushed his empty bowl to the side and picked up the check. "And to thank you, dinner is on me."

"I'll leave the tip." Theo pulled out his wallet. I reached over his shoulder and snagged a twenty-dollar bill.

"Hey, that's mine."

"I know, but it feels better to spend your money." With a wink, I folded the bill and tucked it in my bra.

Mack laughed. "When did you two say your wedding was?"

"No wedding. Not a couple," I said. Again.

Mack smiled widely. "Sure thing, Ali-Cat. Sure thing."

TWENTY-TWO

Note to self:
You can admire someone and
also want to cause them great bodily harm at the same time.

The only motel in town was called The Wagon Wheel, one of those theme places with a huge smiling cowboy on the sign and where the complimentary breakfast was served in "the chuck wagon" every morning. It looked like it had seen much better days. The VACANCY sign only read CAN, the cowboy was faded and tired and someone, probably some teenager on a dare, had given him a Hitler-style mustache and boobs so big, the guy had to have a backache.

While Theo helped Mack dig out Karen's food from the trunk, I went to the office to get us some rooms. A woman who looked to be in her mid-thirties with pink-streaked blonde hair leaned against the counter. Her badge announced her name was Tammy. Tammy was currently chatting it up with someone on the phone. She didn't acknowledge me.

"Pu-lease. I am so tired of the men in this town," she said. "I'd take about anybody at this point."

I stepped closer to the counter and tried to catch her eye. No luck.

"We need a girls' weekend in Denver." She giggled at whatever the reply was. "Oh, yeah. Definitely. I heard that place is a regular meat market."

I tapped my knuckles on the counter. "Hi. I was hoping to get a couple of rooms for tonight."

Tammy scowled. "Hold on. I'm obviously on the phone here."

I pressed my lips together and tried to tune out her conversation. But this was not a large room and the fake dark wood paneling and carpet of indeterminate color, circa 1975, made the office area seem even smaller and more cramped.

"I have next Friday and Saturday off. We should do it." Tammy twisted a piece of pink hair around her finger, her eyes growing unfocused. "I want to meet someone new and exciting."

With a sigh, I leaned an elbow on the counter, my foot tapping a frustrated beat. There was a service bell three inches away from me. My fingers crept closer and closer until the bell was snatched away. I jerked up to find Tammy doing her best to make my brain explode with only her eyes, bell in hand. Holding my gaze, she yanked open a drawer behind the counter and tossed it inside.

"Yeah, all night. You should come keep me company," she said into the phone sweetly, even though her face screwed up as though she'd bitten into a lemon.

The door opened.

Tammy's eyes drifted above my head and her expression went from annoyed to predatory with cougar-like speed. "Tiff, I have to go. Got a guest."

After tossing her phone to the side, she smiled widely, showing too many teeth.

"Everything okay?" Theo asked, coming to a stop right next to me.

Tammy licked her bottom lip. "I was helping your sister here get all checked in."

"She's not my sister." Theo wrapped an arm around my shoulders. For a microsecond, I held myself stiff as a board and then I melted into his side. My dragon wings fluttered about happily.

"Oh?" Tammy traced her bottom lip with a finger, determination in her eye. She gave her t-shirt hem a tug, so the V-neck dipped lower. Might as well have hung a sign that said OPEN FOR BUSINESS on them. "Cousin, then?"

"Not a cousin. We're actua—"

She squinted at me. "Now that I got a good look, she's older than I thought. Aunt?"

I narrowed my eyes. Okay, lady? His aunt?

Theo chuckled. "We aren't related. Did we get rooms yet?"

"Oh, honey," Tammy said, her voice breathy. She ran a finger along the edge of her shirt collar. Was I stuck in a B-rated teen movie? "I can help you with anything you need."

"Great." Theo shot me an uneasy look.

Tammy straightened and began tapping away at her computer. She pulled a piece of paper off the printer and slid it across the counter. With a finger and a sly smile, she beckoned Theo to come closer. Theo pulled me with him. "I'm gonna need your name and an ID and your phone number."

"Sure."

She slid the paper toward him, making sure to brush his hand with her fingers. "Could you fill this out for me?"

"Do I need to do that too? For the other room," I said, not keeping the annoyance out of my voice.

"Hmm. Separate rooms." With a wink in Theo's direction, she shoved a piece of paper and half a pencil at me. "Do it."

"Thanks," I muttered.

"So, where you from, handsome?" She twirled a piece of pink hair around her finger while somehow managing to simultaneously yank down her shirt AGAIN and squish her boobs together. If I didn't want to scratch her eyes out, I might have been impressed.

"Oh, um, Texas," Theo said, not lifting his head.

Tammy giggled. "I've never been but I heard everything is bigger in Texas. Is that true, cowboy?"

Gag me now. I slapped the pencil down and gave her a grimace barely disguised as a smile. "Done. What about you, Theo? Almost done?"

"No rush on my part." She skated her fingernails over the back of Theo's hand, her voice breathy. "I'll be here all night long."

Theo froze and turned his head, his look of alarm causing a surge of anger in me. I had the strongest urge to scream at her to keep her hands to herself, perhaps shave her head and make a necklace out of her hair. Okay, not that. That was weird.

But, yelling never solved anything; action did.

"All done." Theo slid his paperwork across the counter and tugged me under his arm again like I was a powerful amulet standing between him and pure evil. "If you can get us the keys, we'll get out of your way."

Two ticks in Tammy's forehead indicated her annoyance but I had to give her credit; she rallied. She hustled around the counter and in less than a millisecond, had managed to hook an arm around Theo's and tugged him toward the window. "Let me just point out where you'll be at."

Theo hauled me with him. My foot tapped a rapid staccato as she carefully, slowly pointed out the laundry room, the ice machines, the vending machines, and finally the stairs we would need to get to our rooms. The whole while, she leaned into Theo, brushing his arm with her chest in the most calculated move yet. It was impressive, to be honest.

The last straw was when she got on her tippy-toes and stage-whispered her own room number to him.

An idea formed, and before giving it too much thought, I smiled adoringly at Theo. "Honey, I'm going to go check on Mack and Karen. Meet you outside."

I rose on my tippy-toes. Just to press a kiss to Theo's cheek. An affectionate little peck to give Tammy the idea we were much more than cousins, siblings, or aunt/nephew. I must have startled Theo because at the same time I went for his cheek, he turned his head and somehow, improbably, my lips landed on his.

TWENTY-THREE

Note to self:
Accidental kisses don't count, right?

I was kissing Theo Goodnight.

I. Was. Kissing. Theo. Goodnight.

Then something more astounding happened; Theo kissed me back.

That was the last coherent thought I had because what had started as my stupid attempt to make Tammy take a hint turned into what would have been illegal in most states if we *were* related.

The second our lips touched, I gasped and tried to back away and just as quickly, Theo's hand slid into my hair, angling my head, and this time he kissed me, his lips soft but firm. The scruff on his face tickled slightly. My eyes slid shut and I let myself fall into it, this dream that was suddenly a reality.

He tasted like bubble gum and black licorice, which instantly became my new favorite flavor combination in the entire world. Every part of my body vibrated, wanting to be closer, wanting more, wanting it to never end.

Like he could read my thoughts, his other hand moved to my lower back and pulled me closer. A tremor raced down my spine. My arms found their way around his neck and somehow, I was practically floating, the tips of my flip-flops skimming the floor as he took all my weight.

Relief settled in my bones, like a strange sort of déjà vu, except instead of being sure I'd done this before, it was a certainty we were meant to do this all along. A satisfied little hum made its way from my throat and Theo redoubled his efforts when he heard it.

I was going to die from this kiss.

That tombstone would read:

Here Lies Alicia Ramos,

Daughter, Sister, Friend

Although she'll be missed,

She died happy from Theo's kiss.

(Again, everyone be glad I didn't decide to make a living as a poet.)

"Get a room, you two." The voice of my grandfather cut through whatever dreamland I'd landed in.

Theo pulled his head back, his eyes dark and burning. I shivered. Gently, he let me slide back down to my feet, his hands dropping to his sides. Neither of us could seem to look away.

I touched my swollen mouth as though I needed proof that had really happened.

Heat started in my chest and crept up my neck to my cheeks. I took a few shuffling steps back and bumped into a rack of souvenirs. A waterfall of postcards and brochures and keychains rained on me.

"Oh, crap," I muttered and dropped to my knees. Hastily, I scooped up everything—an armload of flyers about a local chokecherry festival and postcards with panoramic nature shots—and stood. My eyes darted from Mack (grinning) to Tammy (scowling) before landing on Theo (frowning). I dumped everything on the counter, ignored Tammy's grouse of annoyance, and rushed to the door. "I'll wait outside."

As the door was closing behind me, I heard Tammy say, "So I guess that means you aren't related then?"

TWENTY-FOUR

Note to self:
Get a better inner voice.

I'd been staring at the ceiling of my hotel room for what felt like hours, asking myself the burning life questions we all had. What was the point of popcorn ceilings? Who thought that'd be a good idea? Was it a decorating decision?

Maybe back in the seventies, which was when this motel's décor had clearly last been updated, an interior designer decided a popcorn ceiling went great with this wood paneling. Or maybe it went well with the burnt orange wallpaper covered in stagecoaches and cowboys and saloon girls on one of the walls. Then again, the saloon doors in place of a bathroom door were pretty classy.

I was contemplating popcorn ceilings with way too much seriousness. But I wasn't sure what else to do with myself.

When Theo got back to the car, he handed me my room key —an actual key with an oversized plastic keychain in the shape of a cowboy hat—and I scurried away with a mumbled thanks. I'd begged off dinner, raided the motel vending machine, and holed up with my laptop and the spotty Wi-Fi to check on a few clients, googled horror stories of accidentally kissing your brother's best friend (which existed in spades, thank you, Reddit), talked to my mom (soothed her worries), texted Mae and Ellie something generic, took my meds, tried to write in my journal but couldn't form a proper complete sentence, and climbed into bed.

It was only nine twenty-four. For the last forty-five minutes, I'd been lying here, desperately trying to think of anything but the feel of Theo's lips on mine, the way his fingers had tangled in my hair, how right it had all felt.

What if he thought I'd kissed him on purpose? It had been an accident. A terrible, awful, wonderful, amazing accident.

You could have stopped it, a voice in my head said.

I think we both got caught up in the moment.

Uh-huh.

It didn't mean anything.

Sure. It meant nothing.

Does everyone's inner voice sound like a sarcastic customer service rep? It was a mistake.

Liar.

Oh, shut up.

I rolled over on my stomach and buried my face in a pillow. Get it together, Ramos. You are not sixteen. You are a grown woman. A grown woman who can handle one little accidental kiss. I'm sure it happened all the time, right?

Someone knocked on my door.

I sat up and stared, holding my breath.

More knocking, a bit more insistent.

"I'm sleeping," I said.

"Nice try," Theo said back.

"Go away."

"No."

Okay, fine, I'd play it cool, pretend like nothing happened. I grabbed a grungy old University of Texas hoodie I'd stolen from one of my brothers, slipped it over my sleep tank, and marched to the door.

"Hi," Theo said when I opened it. He was still in his shorts and t-shirt, his hair messy as though he'd been running his fingers through it. A takeout bag dangled from his fingers. "I got you something, in case you got hungry."

"Oh, um, thanks, I'm fine." My stomach rumbled loudly and with feeling.

The corners of his eyes crinkled. "Are you sure?"

"Alright, yes, I'm hungry, thank you." I took the bag, careful not to touch his fingers, and hightailed it back to the bed. "I don't know what this is, but it smells like Heaven."

Theo entered the room and closed the door slowly. He made his way to the only place to sit in the room that wasn't the bed—a rickety wooden chair tucked under a built-in desk.

"General Tso's Chicken. My favorite."

"Yeah, I know. I can't promise how good it is. The place also had pizza, hamburgers, lamb, and all-day breakfast on the menu."

"I don't care," I said, taking a bite. The spicy goodness hit my tongue. With a moan of glee, I slid my eyes shut. "It's so good."

Theo cleared his throat. My eyes popped open. His blue gaze was watching me intensely. That kiss, the one I was trying desperately to forget, came rushing back. Don't look at his mouth, Ramos. Do not do it.

But I did anyway. Who would have thought his lips would be so soft, or how fast he'd taken control? Had he wondered, too, about what it would be like to kiss me?

After setting the takeout box on the nightstand, I rubbed my hands on my thighs. "Thanks for dinner."

"No problem."

The ensuing silence was painful. PAINFUL.

"I should get to bed," I said at the same time he said, "We should talk."

With a groan, I fell back on the bed. "I hate talking."

"Nice try. I seem to remember you once vowed to talk for twenty-four hours straight just to annoy us."

I laughed. "You all never could find that walkie-talkie."

The four of them were having yet another boys-only sleepover. Eleven-year-old me was not invited. So, I'd put a fresh set of batteries in my walkie-talkies, hid one carefully and out of sight in my brothers' bedroom where they were spending the evening, and waited. When midnight hit, I started talking. I recited the Pledge of Allegiance about twenty times, listed off every person in my fifth-grade class and everything I knew about them, and then began reading one of Mom's pilfered romance novels aloud.

"I wonder how long I talked for?"

"At least three hours. You fell asleep mid-sentence."

I grinned at the ceiling. "I was a brat, wasn't I?"

"But you were fun to have around."

"Oh, I'm sure."

The chair squeaked and a moment later, Theo's face appeared above me. "We do need to talk."

"That sounds so grown up."

The bed bounced as he plopped next to me, close enough that his thigh brushed mine. Ignore it, Ali. "It's a good thing we're adults then."

I flung an arm across my eyes, the better to hide myself. "Speak for yourself."

Fingers closed around my arm and lifted it from my face. Blinking, I turned my head and found him studying me with steady blue eyes. He said nothing, just watched me, his expression unreadable.

"I didn't mean for that to happen. I was trying to get that woman off your back. I only meant to kiss you on the cheek. Then you turned and..." As my voice trailed off, the heat climbed up my face. Even my ears felt hot.

"It was a mistake," Theo said, his voice low and oddly tense.

It hadn't *felt* like a mistake though.

"Right." My voice cracked. I cleared my throat and said it more forcefully. "Right. A mistake. Because we're not like that, you and me. We're friends."

Sixteen-year-old Ali would have gnawed off her right hand for the chance to kiss Theo. That was the same Ali who had practically thrown herself at him one embarrassing never-to-be-spoken-of day. The same Ali whose heart was shattered in a million tiny little shards by the end of that same day.

Yet, here was twenty-seven-year-old Ali, and I wasn't sure I'd learned my lesson. Why did my heart always go back to Theo?

This day had been so weird. Had it only been this morning we'd woken with a naked man walking his dog outside our cabin?

"We're friends," he said carefully.

"And I don't want to mess that up." I turned to him, a note of pleading in my voice, remembering the painful three years in which we barely said two words to each other. "Please, let's forget about it, pretend it didn't happen, so we can go on as before."

After a moment, he nodded. "It's been a long day."

"Impossibly long."

"And tomorrow will be longer."

Tomorrow, I would see Abe. "Extremely impossibly long."

"No room for complications."

I rose up on an elbow. "Am I a complication?"

A corner of his mouth curled. My eyes drifted to the tiny

white scar by his lip. My fingers itched to touch it. Or maybe kiss it.

No, no, no, Ramos.

With a shrug, he stretched out next to me. It took all my willpower not to curl into his side and smell the comforting mix of citrus and soap that always lingered on him.

"Kinda."

"Excuse me, I'll have you know I'm a simple girl with simple needs."

"You are the least simple girl I know." A smile tugged at his mouth. "Never change."

TWENTY-FIVE

Note to self:
Do not even think the words "Theo" and "shower" in the same sentence.

Sunday, seven days until the wedding

A small town in Colorado

Next morning, I woke up full of nervous energy. I was dressed, packed, and ready to go by seven. I watched an episode of *Forensic Files*, then called Mom before she called me. She and Dad had left early that morning and planned on making it mostly out of Texas that day. She drilled me on the usual—health check, med check, Mack check.

"Did you get a chance to watch the video I sent you?" she asked. "The one with my candles?"

I hadn't even opened it. "Oh, um..."

"You will not believe all the interest I'm getting. Dad says I'm internet-famous," she said with no small amount of pride in her voice.

"Internet-famous, that's what I told her," Dad yelled in the background. "I'm married to a celebrity."

I snorted. I loved them but, just last month, I'd had to show my dad how to download an app on his phone. Again. Internet-famous to them was probably one stranger commenting on something they posted.

"I promise I'll check it out," I said and pressed my lips together. I had this desperate need to tell her about seeing Abe. But I knew I couldn't. For a lot of reasons. If he refused to go, the disappointment would crush her.

When Abe left, Mom had been overcome with a kind of grief. Although she'd never said it out loud, it was evident her heart had broken a little the day he left. I'd find her hiding in the pantry, crying. Or begging off a family movie night to curl up in bed. If possible, her incessant worry over me got worse. I think part of her reasoned that she'd lost one child; she would not lose another.

"Hey, I love you," I said softly.

"I love you, too." Mom paused. "Are you alright? You sound anxious."

"I do?"

"Yes, I know that voice. Do you need something? Did you forget something at home? We could turn around and get it."

"We are not turning around," Dad growled. "We've been on the road for four hours."

"You wouldn't make that sacrifice if one of our children needed us?"

"No. Not even if God sent an angel down. Do you know how much gas costs?"

"Stop saying things like that. When God strikes you with lightning, I don't want to be anywhere near you."

"Take me home, Lord, I'm ready," Dad shouted, as he often did.

"Mom, I'm still here." I laughed.

"Oh, honey," Mom said. "I'm so sorry. Your father was being a smartass again."

Dad's voice was faint but clear. "Better than being a dumbass."

"Okay, okay, you two. You don't have to turn around. I'm fine."

"If you're sure?"

"I'm sure. Go drive Dad crazy. You know he secretly loves it."

Mom giggled. "I know. You tell Theo we said hi. He's such a nice boy, isn't he?"

"Sure."

"I was just telling your father he'll make someone a fine husband one day."

Frowning, I pulled the phone from my ear and stared at it. Where was all this coming from? "Okay."

"I know you've always had that little cru—"

"I'm way over that."

What a lying liar I was. After lightning struck Dad, it was coming for me next.

"Oh, of course, honey," Mom said quickly. "Now, you all be safe today."

After hanging up with her, I slipped on my backpack and went next door to Mack and Theo's room.

Mack opened the door, cradling a swaddled Karen, only her small, ugly face visible. She growled at me; I growled back.

"Don't you look bright as a daisy," he said. "Are you hungry? I was about to go get me some of that free breakfast. But your boyfriend there is taking his sweet time."

"He's not my boyfriend." I breezed through the door, dropping a kiss on Mack's cheek. Karen growled louder.

Mack grinned. "Right. Right."

Theo grunted from his spot at the desk. "I'll be another minute. You can go without me."

"Go say good morning to the man. Might put him in a better mood. I'll slip on over and get me some coffee." Mack patted my arm and waltzed through the open door. Before it closed all the way, he peeked back inside. "Now, you kids, don't do anything I wouldn't do."

"Go away, Mack."

His laughter could be heard even with the door closed.

"How was sleeping in the same room as Grandpa?" I asked, after flopping on one of the beds.

Theo glanced at me over the top of his laptop. "Loud. That guy does not know the meaning of an inside voice, does he? I also had to run to the store last night for distilled water for his sleep machine and he was up by five this morning. Singing in the bathroom."

I snickered. "Sounds like fun."

"A real joy," he muttered and went back to typing furiously.

"Kind of grumpy this morning, huh?"

"Yeah," he said, not looking up. "Didn't sleep well."

Me neither, not that I'd tell him that. Then he might think I'd been up half the night replaying that kiss, and the other half having dreams about what *could* have happened after it. I'll say this: my fantasies were getting better. Sigh.

I slipped off my backpack and made myself comfortable. Whatever Theo was working on, it had him completely immersed and it seemed like I'd be here a while. I wondered if it was the same "project" he had been working on yesterday morning.

Theo had always liked writing. Reading, too. When I was younger, he'd make up stories for me, fantastical tales with dragons and princesses who kicked ass and the princes she rescued. (Say what you will, but Theo knew his audience.)

He'd also loved baseball. His senior year, he'd had offers from more than one university. When he'd crushed his ankle in that car accident, his chances to play in college were crushed too. He'd pivoted though, settling on a journalism degree with a history minor. His job working as a sports writer for one of the big papers in Houston seemed to be the perfect fit for him.

I got up and began to pace the room, that anxious energy from earlier making a comeback. In a couple of hours, I would be talking to my brother face-to-face. I shook my arms out, the nervousness settling in my limbs.

I stopped in front of Theo, tapping my fingertips on the table. With a grin, he pressed two more keys with a flourish. He leaned back, looking pleased with himself. "Done."

"Great." I rolled my hand at him in the universal "get a move on it" motion. "I'm starving."

"Give me a second and then we can go eat." He stood and stretched, revealing a stripe of pale skin between his shorts and t-shirt. Which I tried so hard not to notice. There was zero, zilch, nada, nothing remotely provocative or alluring about the move. The man was stretching. It wasn't even an important inch of skin.

But this is what my life had come to—a glance at an innocent piece of skin and I was scandalized in all the right ways. And yet... had I not, mere hours before, agreed that we were friends in a friendship who were friendly to each other? Said friendship did not include ogling. Or kissing. Definitely no more kissing.

God, I wanted to kiss him again.

I schooled my face into a friendly, innocent smile but my voice was much too loud when I spoke. "You do that."

"You nervous about seeing Abe?"

I nodded, my hands fussing with the hem of my t-shirt.

Rounding the table, he put his hands on my shoulders and turned me to face him. "It's going to be okay."

"Yeah, it will be okay."

"It will be. Believe it." Then before I could blink, he pressed a soft kiss to my forehead. "Be right back."

"Okay," I sighed and tried not to melt into a puddle of gooey, heart-eye emotions, or worse, throw myself at him.

Back to pacing. I juggled my phone between my hands and debated texting Mae and Ellie and asking for advice. Something like, "How about that Astros' game? What stocks should I invest in? Also, Theo and I accidentally kissed and even though we both swore it didn't mean anything, I can't help thinking it meant something."

That needed more than a text to work through. At least a phone call. Perhaps a weekend retreat with professional help.

The phone tumbled from my hands and landed by Theo's chair.

"Crap." I bent to pick it up, my hip bumping the table. When I stood up, the laptop screen was right in front of me, and it was awake and staring at me. I shouldn't have done it. I should have gone back to the other side of the room and waited on Theo, but it was right there, whatever he'd been working on so intently a few minutes ago. Who among us wouldn't look? I'm not that strong.

With a glance toward the bathroom door, I hunched over the laptop and began reading.

...he unhooked the buttons of her dress slowly, one at a time like the best kind of torture. Her chest rose and fell faster, her breath unsteady...

My mouth dropped open. Theo had been writing this? Oh, my...

I kept reading.

"We shouldn't," she whispered. "I'll be ruined."

I gasped.

More reading.

He chuckled, low and deep. "Darling, I'm a pirate. Don't you know I live to plunder and ruin?"

Fanned my face.

"No way." With a shaky hand, I moved the cursor down and perched on the chair.

His big, powerful hand slid the dress from her shoulders, breath hot on her—

So engrossed was I in this... this... *this* that I was reading, I didn't hear the bathroom door open.

"What are you doing?"

With a shriek, I fell back against the chair and stared up at Theo, my face hot. All of me was hot, if I were being honest. "I didn't... it was an accident. I mean, I dropped my phone and then the laptop screen woke up and..." I waved a weak hand toward the screen.

Two giant steps later, Theo grabbed the laptop and clicked it shut. He pressed his lips together and glared at me. It wasn't a look I often saw from Theo, and rarely was it directed toward me.

I swallowed audibly. "I, ah, what, um..."

Sliding his eyes shut, his chest rose and fell with huge, deep breaths. Pink crept up from his neck to his cheeks.

"I'm sorry?"

With a grunt, he grabbed his messenger bag from the floor and stuffed his laptop inside it. I watched incredulously as he grabbed his wallet and room key and marched to the door. He held it open and waved a hand. "Let's go eat."

I leapt to my feet. "Theo Goodnight, I'm not going anywhere until you tell me what I just read."

His scowl could only be described as murderous. A beat passed, then another. Finally, he slammed the door and shoved his hands through his hair, yanking on the ends in anger.

"What was that?" I stared at the place on the desk where the laptop had been.

Theo stalked toward me, stopped a few inches from me. "You were not supposed to see that. No one was."

I blinked slowly. Angry Theo was super... hot. His chest

rose and fell with each furious breath, eyes practically glowing. That kiss I was not supposed to remember began to replay in my head in slow motion.

No, stop that.

"I'm listening."

His eyes slid shut and I swore I heard him count to ten under his breath. When he opened them, he seemed more resigned than angry. "I write books."

"Those kinds of books?"

"Yes." He scowled. "Those kinds of books."

"I have so many questions. When did you start writing?"

With a sigh, he turned and plopped on a bed. "College. It was an assignment for a creative writing class I was taking. We had to write out of our preferred genre, so I went for it. I wrote a short story, a romance. Didn't think it was any good, but the professor told me I had talent, and I should consider publishing it. I did it as a joke, I guess. To see if I could. And, well, people bought it and then a lot more people bought it, so I kept writing them. The money helps out and... and... I like writing them, okay? I like it."

"But romance?"

He crossed his arms. "*Historical* romance."

Who was this guy? "Right. Historical romance. My bad."

"With pirates," he said quickly.

I arched a brow, trying hard to rein in my smile. "Historical pirate romance? That's... specific."

"I have a good fan base." His cheeks were a charming shade of bright pink. "They like pirates."

I grinned. "So, do these pirates kidnap innocent young women?"

"Sometimes."

"Are these all set on the high seas?"

"Mostly."

"Are they all swashbuckling bad boys?"

He sighed and stood. "You aren't going to forget about this, are you?"

I ignored such an obviously dumb question. "Oooh. Does someone have to walk the plank?"

He shrugged. "It happens, although it's not historically accurate. But the readers..."

"The readers like what the readers like, right?" I snapped my fingers. "This explains your thing with oranges. Keeps away the scurvy." With that, I collapsed into the chair overcome with laughter. Because this was hilarious. Theo Goodnight, romance author? My quiet, thoughtful Theo? "Who are you?"

Theo rubbed the back of his neck. "Look, no one knows about it. No one. I want to keep it that way."

"Not even my brothers?" Oh, man, they'd have a field day with this info.

The look he gave me had a tinge of panic to it. "Please don't tell them."

"Huh." I moseyed over to him. "So, how do I find these books?"

"Why?"

"What do you mean, why? Do you think now I know this I can forget it exists?"

His head dropped back, and he stared at the ceiling. "They're online. Under a pen name."

"Well, what is it?" I asked, already pulling out my phone.

"I don't want to tell you," he muttered.

"Why?" I put my hands on my hips.

He refused to make eye contact. Oh, this was bad. Or really, really good. "Because—"

The door burst open, and Karen raced into the room, yapping like she'd seen a robbery at a dog bone factory. She made a beeline for me and my ankles.

"Stop it, you gremlin," I said, but Karen was not playing around. She got ahold of one of my shoelaces and began to shake her head back and forth violently while yanking on it, all the while growling at the offending piece of string. "Someone get it off me."

I tried gently, and then not-so-gently, to remove her by shaking my leg. Teetering on one foot, I put a hand on Theo's shoulder, but it was a losing battle. While Mack laughed like this was the funniest thing he'd seen in ages, Theo attempted to shoo her away, but Karen got the shoelace untied and scrambled between my legs. And that was that.

One minute, I was standing and the next I was falling... right on top of Theo. His hands caught me at the waist but not fast enough to prevent the inevitable. Theo fell on the bed, and I went with him. We both landed with an "Oophf," followed by stunned silence.

Or rather, Theo and I were silent. Karen was well on her way to a barking-induced brain aneurysm and Mack was laughing so hard, he was wheezing. Our eyes collided in shock. I dropped my forehead on his chest and we both began to laugh. His laughter traveled through my body, and I was certain I'd found a new perfect moment. This one right here with Theo.

You are in the danger zone, Ramos. Abort. Abort.

I scrambled to get off him but instead of helping me, Theo's hands tightened on my waist. My hand rested on his chest, and I could feel his heartbeat, strong and fast.

"I should get up," I whispered.

"Yes." One of his hands traveled up to gently tuck a piece of hair behind my ear. "You probably should."

"Absolutely." But instead of doing that like a sane person, I found myself moving closer. Theo's fingers slid into my hair and encouraged me and then there we were, our mouths a whisper apart. All one of us had to do was shift and our lips would touch and then...

"You two lovebirds need a little alone time?" Mack scooped up Karen and smirked at us.

"Oh, my gosh." I scrambled off Theo and the bed. My cheeks flamed hot as I grabbed my backpack from the floor and tugged it on, carefully avoiding Theo. Or Mack. And definitely that damn dog.

"I'm... just going to go..." I could barely hear my thoughts over the pounding of my heart. I froze mid-step. Crap. Where was I going? "Food. I'm going to go get breakfast."

"Good idea," Mack called to my back. "You're gonna miss out on the good oatmeal flavors."

"Right. Don't want to do that," I yelled back. But it wasn't the oatmeal I cared about missing; it was that kiss.

TWENTY-SIX

Note to self:
You can never have too many brothers.

The ride to Denver went much too quickly, each spin of the wheels ratcheting up my anxiety. Between Mack's excitement, Karen's growls, and my nerves, a strange tension filled the car. Even thoughts of Theo Goodnight, Romance Author, were pushed out of my brain. I couldn't stop conjuring up every bad outcome possible. What if Abe slammed the door in my face? My stomach roiled at the thought.

"About time this got taken care of," Mack said from the backseat. "That boy has always had a good heart. It's a shame he's been gone so long. Been over a year since I've seen him."

"Wait. You saw him?" I twisted in my seat to look back at Mack. Karen turned up her nose like she'd smelled something rotten. Then she hopped off Mack's lap and disappeared under the seat as though my very image was offensive.

"Sure, when Gracie passed, he came after everyone left. Didn't want to run into your parents."

"I... Wow." Why hadn't he told me?

This whole road trip was a series of revelations I didn't know what to do with. I pressed my forehead to the window, letting the coolness soothe me on the outside. The inside was an entirely different story, spliced wires wiggling around in chaos.

Theo glanced over at me from the driver's side. "Doing okay?"

"Yeah," I whispered, then cleared my throat. "Yeah."

Forty-five minutes later, we pulled up to a row of generic houses on a regular street in a suburban neighborhood on the outskirts of Denver. The lawns were carefully mowed. The trees and bushes were trimmed. Flowerbeds burst with zinnias and marigolds and asters. One yard had a kid's bike propped against a tree. Another had a small pool set up, waiting for the chill of the morning to burn off.

It looked so... normal.

"Not what I was expecting," I said.

"What were you expecting?" Theo asked.

"Not the suburbs."

Abe had always been the rebel. I expected a sweet apartment downtown, maybe over a bar or something. Not a cookie-cutter with an attached garage. But I'm not sure how well I knew Abe anymore. Even with our phone calls, it appeared there were a lot of things he hadn't told me.

A middle-aged woman in hot-pink leggings speedwalking her way down the sidewalk smiled as she passed us.

"Ready, kiddo?" Mack asked, slinging an arm around my shoulders.

I nodded, my tongue glued to the top of my mouth. I needed water. And a chocolate croissant. And about seventeen more months before I did this.

Mack led the way to the door of the unit right across from us, Karen basking in his arms like an Egyptian queen. The house was white with black trim and shutters, the yard simple but neat. An older model Land Cruiser was parked in the driveway. I smiled, thinking of how Abe had always wanted one.

I wiped my sweaty palms on my shirt and took the last two steps, Theo just behind me. I held up my fist to knock and hesitated.

Theo leaned closer and whispered, his breath warm and citrus-y from his morning orange. "A.N."

I turned my head. "What?"

"A.N." he said again just as quietly and while I was still confused, he knocked on the door. "The initials of my pen name."

"You're telling me that no—"

The click of a lock halted me mid-sentence. The door swung open, and my chest grew tight.

"Hi," a tiny little voice said.

I shifted my gaze down, down, down to the source of the tiny little voice. It belonged to a tiny little girl with huge brown eyes and light-brown hair currently tied up in what had to be the worst excuse for a ponytail I'd ever seen. I guessed she was about four or five, around the same age as Ellie's son, Oliver.

"Oh, um, hi?" I turned back to Theo. "Are you sure we have the right address?"

He peered through the door. "I'm pretty sure we do."

I crouched in front of the tiny human. She had a doll, with a hairstyle that remarkably resembled her own, clutched against her chest. Up close, I could see the faintest dusting of freckles across her nose and cheeks. A little cupid bow of a mouth, long, dark eyelashes, and ears that stuck out a bit.

"Hey, is your mom or dad here?" I asked.

"I'm not a'pposed to talk to strangers."

"That's a good rule. Are you supposed to answer the door?"

Her eyes widened with surprise and perhaps a touch of guilt. Before anyone could say another word, she slammed the door.

I rounded on Theo and propped a fist on my hip. "What the heck is going on?"

Theo adjusted his baseball cap. "No idea."

"Who is this kid?" I asked.

"I'm Hallie and I'm four years old," the little voice shouted at us from behind the door.

"Hallie, it's nice to meet you," I yelled back. "Is your daddy home?"

"He's in the shower but I'm a'pposed to sit on the couch and watch a cartoon and not answer the door ever but..." She mumbled something I couldn't quite make out.

"What's your daddy's name?" I asked.

"His name is Daddy," she said, and I did not miss the hint of *Duh, Lady* in her tone.

"Not helpful at all," I muttered.

"Here he comes," Hallie said and then in a slightly quieter voice, "Don't say I opened the door, 'kay? 'Cause then I won't get to have ice cream for breakfast."

"Hallie, what are you doing by the door? Is someone out there? You're supposed to be sitting on the couch." My stomach dipped. I recognized that voice.

The door pulled open again and this time, my brother Abe stood in front of me. He froze, his eyes darting from Theo to Mack and then to me. "Ali?"

I nodded, the lump lodged in my throat making words a challenge. "Hi."

"Ali," he said again, a touch of awe in his voice. He wrapped me in a bone-crushing hug, practically lifting me off the ground. "I can't believe it."

"Me neither," I mumbled against his chest.

After unfolding his arms, he took a step back and inspected me from toes to hair. "You're so grown up."

"It's been a few years." Sniffling, I smiled. "You're looking pretty grown up, too."

In the eleven years since I'd seen him in person, the handful of blurry selfies notwithstanding, he'd gotten a little taller, his shoulders had filled out, his jaw sharper, his eyes older. Still wet from his shower, his hair hung just past his shoulders, leaving damp spots on his t-shirt.

And then there were the tattoos. A lot of them. He'd gotten one the day he turned eighteen (which Dad hated). From what I could see of his arms and the one that peeked out from the collar of his t-shirt, he'd clearly gotten more. But there was also a silver hoop in one of his eyebrows and nickel-sized gauges in his ears.

If I talked him into coming to this wedding, I could already hear my father now.

Abe cupped my cheek. "I've missed you."

The tears I'd been trying desperately to restrain lost the battle. "I missed you, too. So much."

"Shhh." He crushed me to his chest again. "It's okay."

"Let me get in there." Mack wrapped his arms around both of us.

Hallie peeked around our tangle of people. "Is that a puppy, Daddy?"

That's when it clicked. This little girl was talking to my brother, calling him... "Daddy?"

Abe wrapped an arm around the little girl's shoulders and gave us all a small, nervous smile. "Meet my daughter, Hallie. Hallie, say hi to your Aunt Ali."

TWENTY-SEVEN

Note to self:
Get a life.

Me: *I'm an aunt.*

Mae: *I'm sorry?*

Me: *Abe has a kid. A fully formed four-year-old daughter.*

Mae: *Wait? What? Where did he get her?*

Me: *Left on his doorstep.*

Mae: *Like by a stork?*

Me: *Something like that. I'll tell you later. My parents are going to flip.*

Mae: *Yes, they are.*

Mae: *Has he agreed to go to the wedding?*

Me: *I haven't even talked to him yet. HE HAS A KID.*

Mae: *Maybe we should throw him a baby shower?*

Me: *Too soon. Way, way too soon.*

"So, she just left her on your doorstep," I asked. "Is that even legal?"

Abe huffed a laugh and glanced over at Hallie. After her breakfast ice cream, she'd pulled on a princess dress over her shorts and t-shirt and was currently holding court on the couch. Theo and Mack sat on either side of her while she regaled them with stories about the many princes she'd loved and lost.

"I didn't even know she existed until three weeks ago. Celia, her mother, dropped Hallie off at her mom's house a year ago and hasn't been back since. She's been finding herself, whatever that means, somewhere in Arizona. Her mom isn't in the best health, so she drove from California and... surprise." He shoved his fingers through his hair. "We're still trying to get to know each other. I have no idea what I'm doing. She's so... little and needy and never stops asking questions."

"How... do you know she's yours?" I grinned as Hallie set a sparkly pink crown on Theo's head; Theo winked at her. Every single biological urge to procreate in my body stood and volunteered as tribute.

"The timing works. Celia and I broke up five years ago. She was pregnant and didn't even know it. Plus," he turned again to stare at Hallie, "she looks just like you at this age. It's almost uncanny."

"Really?"

"Definitely. Has a mind of her own like you, too." He turned back to the table, shaking his head. "I haven't had a good night's sleep since she got here. She's ended up in bed with me every night. I think she's scared."

"I don't blame her," I murmured and watched as Hallie handed Mack what had to be the fourth book she'd pulled out and demanded he read. "Must be scary to go from what you've known your whole life and suddenly everything is different."

"Don't I know it," he said.

"Mom would freak if she knew."

"Yeah, she would."

"She misses you."

"I miss her, too." Abe crossed his arms and leaned back in his chair, and I was struck by how different he seemed, but familiar, too. A wave of sadness washed over me. I'd never gotten to see him make that transformation from dumb, gangly teenager to fully functioning adult. It had all happened over the last eleven years. In my mind, he'd been perpetually a teenage kid with a big smile. But he was a grown man now, part owner in a business, homeowner, father.

"I almost feel like I don't know you. You aren't very good with the phone calls." I took a sip of coffee.

"You aren't so good at telling me about stuff either."

"Touché." I tilted my head. "Although it seems like Theo keeps you pretty informed."

Abe gave me a long look. "He's pretty good at it."

"He comes to visit." I stared at a small water stain on the table. "I didn't know that. He... he said you told him about the accident."

Abe put a hand on my arm. "He's my best friend. I couldn't disappear and not tell him why."

"I get it. You went and visited Mack, too."

"After Grandma died, yeah." He bobbed his head around to catch my eye. "What's wrong?"

I pushed the coffee away. "A little part of me has always thought you were mad at me for what happened, and then I heard you'd seen Theo and Mack and I thought, maybe that's the truth. Maybe you are still angry with me, and I don't blame you. I really don't. I missed you, have missed you so much. I wanted to come see you so badly. I haven't driven since the, ah, accident. Every time I try, I start to panic."

He squeezed my arm gently. "Ali, look at me."

Hesitantly, I met his eyes.

"That day wasn't your fault. You weren't supposed to be driving. But I let you anyway. I was the adult; you were the kid. You didn't will yourself to have a seizure. And you didn't force me to take the blame. I did that all on my own. Sometimes I replay that night and think I was looking for an excuse to leave, you know?"

"But maybe you could have worked it out, if I'd told the truth when I was able."

His mouth tipped in a sad sort of smile. "Nah, I don't think so. I was angry about so many things. It was tough for a while after I left. Didn't know where I was going. Ended up in California for a while and then made it out here to Denver."

"It's beautiful here. I can see why you stayed."

"It's been good. I'm happy here."

I tilted my head and inspected him. "I believe you. You seem, I don't know, content. Calmer, too."

"I guess I grew up. I even took some business classes at the community college."

"Really? That's amazing."

"Hey, don't sound so surprised."

Abe had struggled in school as a kid, squeaking by with a lot of extra credit and teachers who couldn't flunk a kid who kept showing up even when it was clearly hard. The weird thing was that he liked learning. I remember he once took apart an old radio to figure out how it worked, for fun. He'd loved watching documentaries with Mack and could discuss everything he'd learned. But put a book in front of him and he couldn't focus.

"I went to this tutoring center to get help with my writing. My tutor there thought I might have dyslexia. Turns out I do." He frowned into his coffee mug. "That's why school was always so damn hard no matter how much I tried."

"Mom and Dad didn't know?"

"I didn't even know. I thought everyone saw the words the way I did but I was too dumb to make sense of them. I always felt like I was a disappointment to them."

"They love you, Abe," I said quickly. "I-I don't know everything that went on with Dad, but I know he loves you and Mom, she cries on your birthday every year. She tries to pretend she doesn't, but we all know."

He raised an eyebrow. "So, you want to tell me why you're here?"

I smiled weakly. "Would you believe we took a wrong turn?"

"No."

"Cal asked me to come."

"I figured." He grabbed both our coffee cups, stood, and took them to the sink. There, he rested his hands on the edge of the counter, his shoulders tense, and stared out the small window.

"Could you? Would you come?"

"I'm good here, happy," he said, his voice low. "I don't know if I want to stir everything up again."

I rose and moved to him. I wrapped an arm around his waist and leaned into him. "It's been eleven years. It's time, don't you think? I mean, the choice is yours. I'm not going to make you do anything you don't want to do but there's Hallie to think about now."

A long silence hung between us, and I resisted the urge to fill it. Ultimately, it was Abe's decision, and I wouldn't force it.

Abe's life was his and he could spend it as he pleased. Sometimes, I wish I had the guts to do the same for myself—live my life by my rules. Right now, I was in a weird limbo, always worried about making my parents worried. I made concessions for them, lived that quiet life because that made them less anxious.

"Hallie would have to come with us," Abe said, interrupting my thoughts. "I can't leave her here, even if I had someone I trusted to take care of her. I'm not sure she'd understand another person leaving her, even if it's only for a few days."

"I agree," I said quickly. "Bring her."

"It could go very badly."

"Or it could be the thing that brings us together."

He nodded. "I'll think about it. That's the best I can do."

"Good. Yes. Do that." I hugged him tight.

"No promises."

"Absolutely." I drew back and saluted him. A maybe was not a no. I could work with that. "No promises. Got it."

Sighing, he leaned back against the counter. "Can I ask you something?"

"Sure."

He nodded his head toward the living room, where Theo and Mack now sported matching sparkly jewelry with their tiaras. "Is something going on between you and Theo?"

"I'm sorry, what?"

"I don't know. You two seem pretty chummy."

"I mean, we're friends." Who kissed. And apparently flirted.

"Is that it?"

"I... I, ah, well..."

"Okay. Got it."

"What do you get?" I asked in confusion. "I don't even get it."

"You were kind of crazy about him in high school. Remember that Valentine's Day with the—"

I slapped a hand on his mouth. "We are never speaking of that again."

I'd been fifteen that year and worked up the courage to ask his mom what Theo's favorite dessert was. She'd given me a recipe for a chocolate cake with caramel syrup, whipped cream, and bits of a candy bar crumbled on top. Then I'd invited Theo over for dessert on Valentine's Day. I might have made it sound like it was a family thing. He definitely did not expect to show up and find a table for two complete with cloth tablecloth and candles. His face when he realized what was happening... I'll never forget it.

It only got worse when Frankie came home early from his date and discovered us. Never one to keep his mouth shut, he alerted the whole family. My brothers came to snicker. My father came out of concern. But it was my mother who sent me over the edge. She walked in, took one look at the cake, and exclaimed, "Oh, is this Becky's Better Than Sex Cake?"

My teenage soul couldn't take the embarrassment. So, while the family and Theo ate cake, I made up a lame excuse about homework I forgot about and hid in my room.

Abe's laughter was muffled. He removed my hand and tweaked my nose. "You had it bad."

I had been fifteen; I was twenty-seven now. And I still had it bad.

"And you all never let me forget."

Abe shoulder-bumped me. "Hey, you were a kid."

"Yeah. I remember. I also remember you sitting me down and telling me to get over it."

"Well, yeah. You were in high school, and we were three years older. That was a big age difference then." He smiled, his eyes curious. "Plus, you did make things weird."

Couldn't even deny that. I slumped against the counter. "I did make things weird."

"Like I said, you were a kid. First crush and all that." He tapped a finger on his chin. "You're both adults now, you know?"

"And?"

His gaze moved from me to Theo and back again. "It'd be kind of cool to have Theo as a brother."

"Are we done talking about this yet?"

With a grin that reminded me of teenage Abe, he leaned in and lowered his voice. "You know, he keeps looking over at you like he's checking to make sure you haven't disappeared."

The dragons perked up. It took every fiber of my self-control to not whip my head around and see if what Abe said was true. I waved a hand. "He doesn't think of me like that. I'm like his little sister."

Abe snorted and pushed off from the counter. He sauntered past me. "He sure isn't looking at you like you're a little sister. Not even a little bit."

TWENTY-EIGHT

Note to self:
Be braver.

That afternoon, Abe and Theo went out for "a drive." My brothers and Theo had gone on many, many drives as teenagers. Mostly cruising along backroads to waste time. Every now and then, they'd take pity on me and let me tag along.

Cal had been the first to get his license, and Cal being Cal, he'd saved up every dollar he'd been given or made mowing lawns since the age of twelve and bought his first car, an old four-door sedan, for a thousand dollars.

When Abe and Theo, whose birthdays were only a couple of months apart, became licensed drivers, they were gone more than they were home. Football games, dates, the movies, and anything else they could get into. Abe told me those drives were sometimes an excuse. He went on to explain, "Sometimes guys need to talk about stuff, but they can't do that unless they're pretending to do something else."

I hoped Theo would do a lot of the talking on this drive. Maybe he'd be able to sway Abe into coming. After a solid week of worry and doubt over seeing Abe, it now seemed imperative that he come to the wedding.

If he didn't say yes, I might have to do something dramatic. Like take him hostage.

After Mack complained of being tired and needing a nap—I think he was over playing princess—I spent the afternoon with Hallie, who spent her afternoon showing me every single toy, book, dress, and movie she owned. Which was a lot. I think Abe may be leaning into that whole "buy her whatever she wants to keep her happy" parenting style. Not that I could blame him. He'd been given a fully grown four-year-old less than a month ago; he was in survival mode.

After Theo and Abe returned, and we'd feasted on a dinner of pizza, followed by an evening showing of a princess movie with required viewing, we all settled in for the night. Mack took the spare bedroom and that left the living room for Theo and me.

After a fifteen-minute argument (that I won), Theo got the couch, and I got the air mattress, which turned out to be pretty comfortable as long as I didn't move a muscle. We'd shut the lights off ten minutes before and the room had gone silent, the only sound the occasional squeak of my air mattress or, farther off, a car driving by.

"Thanks for helping me today," I whispered. "I don't know if I could have shown up here without you."

"You would have been fine," Theo said. A slice of pale light shone in through a gap in the large front window curtains, dividing the room. I was on one side, he on the other.

"I don't know about that." I shifted to my side and could just make out his profile, his hands resting on his chest, the long line of his body tucked under a light blanket.

A fantasy took shape. I'd slip off the air mattress with an excuse to fix the curtain—that slice of light was annoying, after all. Then on my way back to bed, I'd get a little turned around in the dark and somehow manage to trip and fall on Theo. But do it gracefully like the well-bred woman I was. Think of a delicate leaf falling gently to the ground. In this scenario, I am the leaf, Theo is the ground. I end up smack on his chest and he starts laughing and I start laughing and then we both stop laughing because we're gazing into each other's eyes with such intensity an earthquake couldn't keep us apart, and he lifts a hand and cups my cheek and then—

"Is it weird? Seeing him?" Theo asked, interrupting me.

I pressed my hand to my forehead. Get yourself together, Ramos.

"What?" I asked, my voice about three octaves too high.

"You okay?"

I laughed (think hyena). "Totally fine."

"Okay." He waited a beat. "I asked if it was weird seeing Abe?"

"I mean, at first. He's my brother but I don't know this version of him like I knew the other one. Plus, he has a kid. It's wild."

"I think for him, too." His voice sounded sleepy. "Just so you know, I didn't know about her either. I wasn't keeping that from you."

"Thanks."

"You're welcome." He yawned. The room went quiet. But I knew he wasn't asleep, so I wasn't surprised when he spoke. "I've been thinking I should go to Las Vegas."

"To see your dad?"

"I don't know. Maybe not actually meet him. But I guess I want the opportunity to decide if I want to meet him. Does that make sense?"

"Yes," I said softly.

"I still don't know if this is a good idea."

"If this was your last chance to meet him and you missed it, how would you feel?"

"Not good."

"I think that's your answer. You should go."

"Is it stupid though? The guy never even tried to come back and see me."

"At least you can ask him why."

"It's terrifying." The uncertainty I heard in his voice made my heart hurt for him. Confronting the guy who'd abandoned him as a baby was opening himself up to rejection a second time. Showing up at his house made him vulnerable to being rejected again. This was a huge decision and I wondered what I would do in his shoes. Would I be so quick to jump at the opportunity?

"Fear's a real pain in the ass," I said.

The list of things fear kept me from doing was long: driving; having a real, honest relationship; sleeping in my bed; running for mayor. My heart thrummed against my ribs. Maybe Mae was right. I had let fear allow me to live a quiet life.

The last time I'd been really brave was that day in Theo's dorm room all those years ago. Sure, the result had been spectacularly awful, but I'd done it. I think I was even glad it had happened. It forced me to realize some things that sixteen-year-old me needed to learn.

"I'll have to tell Mack. Las Vegas will add extra time on the drive."

"Somehow, I doubt he'll mind," I said dryly.

He yawned. "I'll sleep on it."

"You do that. But give me plenty of warning. I'll have to get my official stakeout outfit ready."

"You have a— You know what? Never mind."

I was almost asleep when I remembered I had a couple of questions for Theo.

"Is it Amanda Nicholas?"

"Huh?"

"A.N. Amanda Nicholas. Am I right?"

His laugh was a low rumble. "Nope."

"What about Ava Nash?"

"Not even close."

"Angela Nelson? Abbie Norris? Agatha Nightcrawler?"

A throw pillow sailed across the room and landed on my stomach. "Give me some credit. Who would read a romance novel written by someone named Agatha Nightcrawler?"

"So, no?"

"Go to sleep."

"I'm going to figure it out, you know."

"I know. Trust me, I know."

My phone dinged with a message.

Mae: *Someone started a rumor you were running for mayor.*

Me: *Oh, yeah. Wonder who that was?*

Mae: *I wish you could have seen Peter's face. I did not know a human could turn that color.*

Ellie: *It really was an unhealthy shade of red.*

Me: *You know I'm not doing it.*

Mae: *I've gotten about fifteen people signed up to work the campaign. Mrs. Katz had flyers printed and she's been passing them out.*

Me: *Are you even listening?*

Ellie: *I made the cutest Vote for Ali buttons.*

Mae: *And we settled on a campaign slogan.*

***Ellie**: Let's Rally for Ali!!!!!!!!*

With a groan, I tossed the phone on the bed.

"Everything okay?" Theo asked.

I sat up. "It's this stupid idea about me running for mayor. Mae's getting people all excited about it."

After a long breath in which I considered the many ways I could make Mae's life miserable (nothing permanent, of course), I texted back.

***Me**: I AM NOT RUNNING FOR MAYOR.*

***Mae**: Your words say that, but your heart says something different.*

***Me**: Can we change the subject? Please.*

***Mae**: Okay. So, has Theo made his move yet?*

***Ellie**: Please say yes. Tell us EVERYTHING. I want deets.*

***Me**: I hate you both.*

***Mae**: Talk to you tomorrow.*

After throwing the phone on the floor, I laid back down, grumbling under my breath about interfering best friends.

But did I still lay there long after I heard the steady rhythm of Theo's breathing and wonder what it would be like to hold a position as mayor? Yes, I did. It sounded ridiculous when I said it out loud. But in my head, the idea was growing on me. So many things could be done to improve life in Two Harts and not one of them involved an expensive-as-hell football stadium or tearing down the tree our town was built on.

Plus, the idea of making Peter squirm because, for once, he would have an opponent. Oh, that might be the strongest pull of all. It would be the sweetest kind of justice, the perfect revenge.

As quietly as I could, I got up and took my backpack into the bathroom. I pulled out the application and a pen and, before I could overthink it, I filled it out. Then I stared at it for a long time. Was I brave enough to do it?

I put it back in my backpack, still not sure of the answer.

TWENTY-NINE

Note to self:
The road to Hipster-ville starts with one man bun.

I woke somewhere around two in the morning and stumbled into the kitchen for a glass of water. Since I was there, I rooted around in Abe's refrigerator for a middle-of-the-night snack and hit gold.

Well, ice cream, anyway. There were about five different gallons in the freezer, and I wondered if Abe had bought them all because he wasn't sure what Hallie liked. I settled on chocolate chip cookie dough. After finding a spoon, I dug in. Bowls were for wimps. Clutching the container to my chest, I wandered the quiet kitchen, lit by a soft light over the sink.

I smiled at a photo of Hallie and Abe hanging on the fridge, obviously taken in the last couple of weeks. Hallie was in his lap, curled against his chest, Abe's chin resting on her head. It was precious and I was struck by how natural and at ease they looked, like they hadn't just met less than a month ago. Maybe that's how it was with parents and kids; the love was there always, even when there was confusion and contention. It gave me hope Dad and Abe would be okay, somehow, someway.

A small scraping noise made me freeze. It sounded close by although muffled, and after investigating, I discovered Abe was sitting outside on the patio. I grabbed a second spoon and stepped through the back door quietly.

"Couldn't sleep?" I asked.

"I did for a while, but Hallie woke me and fell back to sleep in my bed." He looked at me over his shoulder. "Try sleeping with a foot in your... well, never mind. I needed a little alone time."

"Should I leave you to it?"

"Nah, come sit."

I took a seat and offered him a spoon. "Want some?" The cool night air sent a shiver through me. "Kinda cold out here, isn't it?"

"You're not in Texas anymore, Dorothy."

"Ha. Ha." I handed over the ice cream and side-eyed him.

"What?" he asked around a huge bite.

I shrugged. "I can't get over you being a grown-up and all. Or that man bun? Seriously?"

Abe pointed his spoon at me. "My man bun is awesome."

"Ooo-kay. If you say so. Are you wearing t-shirts with ironic statements these days? Have you recently had a strong urge to grow a beard, start a record collection, or learn to play the banjo?"

"Are you done?"

"Have you started wearing," I laced my voice with over-the-top horror, "skinny jeans?"

"Whatever."

I laughed hard enough to snort. After glaring at me, Abe's mouth turned up into a grin.

"You love me."

He gave my ponytail a tug. "I love you."

"'Cause I am adorable."

"Don't push it."

The quiet and chill of the night settled around us as we sat in companionable silence. Abe took a few more bites of the ice cream and set it aside.

"You okay?" I asked.

He rested his elbows on his knees and dangled his hands between his legs. "I'm thinking."

"Got it." I curled my feet under me and waited him out.

After what felt like ten solid minutes, he straightened. "Theo told me about his dad this afternoon."

"Oh, yeah?"

"I tried to imagine what that would be like, to not know your dad."

I pictured my father with his gruff exterior and squishy inside. "It's hard to even think about."

Staring into the dark backyard, he rubbed his neck. "I've been living like I don't have a father for years now."

My breath caught at the mix of sadness and regret in his voice. But I didn't know what to say to that. Because I knew it was true.

"I'm going to the wedding," he said quietly.

"Seriously?"

"Yeah." His shoulders drooped a little. "I have no idea how this will go. But it's impossible to say no to you and Theo and Cal when you gang up on me."

My excitement curbed. "Don't go because of us. Go because you want to."

"That's the thing. Between the three of you, it's all I've been thinking of. I'm nervous but I think it's the right thing. I-I want to see Mom and Frankie and—"

"Dad?" I reached out and clutched his arm.

"Even Dad." He turned to me, half of his face illuminated by the dim back porch light. "I need to do it for me and for Hallie."

"It's going to be okay." I was going with blind optimism here. "At least you'll get cake out of it."

He snorted. "At least I'll get cake."

THIRTY

Note to self:
Don't get jealous;
get even.

Monday, six days until the wedding

Denver

A finger poked my cheek, then my closed eye, and from there, my mouth. I held perfectly still, listening to the soft giggles.

"Auntie Ali," Hallie whispered in a voice that could probably be heard three counties over. "Are you awake? Daddy said you can get me ice cream for breakfast."

I cracked open an eye and stared up at Hallie, her hair wild around her face like she'd walked through a wind tunnel at some point last night. "Your daddy said you could have ice cream for breakfast?"

She nodded. "Uh-huh. Daddy said ice cream is made of milk and that's what we put on cereal. Plus, it had fuut in it and Daddy said fuut is good for you. What's your favorite fuut?"

I squinted. I should remind Abe that ice cream was not its own food group. "That was a lot of words all at once, missy."

"What's your favorite fuut?" she asked again.

"Fuut?"

She nodded her head, her big brown eyes watching me expectantly. "Your favorite fuut."

What in the world was this child saying? "I-I don't..."

"Her favorite fruit is watermelon," a gravelly, low voice said from the direction of the couch.

"Oh, fruit. Yes, what he said. Watermelon is my favorite." I smiled, pleased Theo knew my favorite fruit, which was a pretty weird thing to be pleased about.

"Auntie." Hallie tugged on my arm. "Is that boy your boyfwiend?"

"Theo? Nope, not my boyfriend."

"Could he be my boyfriend then?" she asked.

I sat up and Hallie climbed onto my lap. "What kinds of things would you do with a boyfriend?"

"He could take me to the park and make me cookies with the sprinkles on top and watch all the princess movies with me, and I could paint his nails all kinds of colors and then we could sing songs together and he would always give me all the red M&Ms 'cause they're the best M&Ms."

"I like your priorities," I said, trying and failing to hold in a smile. "I think Theo would love to do all those things."

"I'm taken," Theo said, his voice muffled, and I thought he might be laughing. "Aunt Ali is my girlfriend."

I threw a pillow at him.

His head shot up and he shoved his hair out of his face. It looked like it had grown three sizes overnight.

Save me, please, he mouthed.

I rolled my eyes.

With his hands pressed together, he shot me sad puppy dog

eyes that made all my inside parts squeal. Why was he so damn adorable? It wasn't fair.

"Fine. I guess he's my boyfriend." I can just imagine that conversation with Abe. *No, not a real girlfriend. It's pretend. We're fake-dating to trick a four-year-old. Very mature.* "But you know what? I'll let you share him with me."

"Sharing is what fwiends do." Hallie grinned. "Does that mean we're fwiends?"

"Well, of course, we are." I ruffled her hair. "How about we get some breakfast ice cream?"

More enthusiastic nodding. She held her hand out. It was sticky and a little sweaty but so tiny. I took it and let her lead me to the kitchen.

Over my shoulder, I called out to Theo, "You coming?"

"Is my girlfriend asking?"

Hallie and I grinned at each other and answered at the same time, "Yes."

"Can a person eat too many oranges, I wonder?" I asked.

"No. Oranges are perfect." Theo held one up reverently. "They're like edible sunshine."

I bit back a laugh. "I thought black licorice was perfect."

"Pay attention. Black licorice is the perfect *snack*." He dropped the orange in the plastic sack with the others and tied it off before setting it in the cart. "Oranges are the perfect fruit."

"Ah, of course. What an idiot I am."

He shoulder-bumped me. "Stick with me. I'll smarten you up."

While Abe was in a whirlwind of washing clothes and packing, Theo announced he needed to gas up the car and check the tire pressure. Abe had given him a list of stuff to pick up at the grocery store on the way and I'd been told by Mack to go "help the poor man." And even though I was more than confident Theo could handle it on his own, I jumped at the chance.

Because it was alone time with Theo and I was pathetically eighty-five percent in love with the guy.

Theo pulled to a stop in front of the applesauce. From his pocket, he took the list Abe had written out for us. "Applesauce pouches."

We stared at the rows in front of us. There were a shocking number of choices, a smorgasbord of flavors—carrot applesauce, cherry applesauce, carrot-cherry applesauce.

"Who knew applesauce wasn't just applesauce anymore?" I asked.

"Another reason oranges are superior. You won't find them mixed with carrots in a pouch."

"You are such a weirdo sometimes." I found the plain old boring applesauce and tossed it into the cart.

Theo stuffed the list back in his pocket but when he pulled his hand out, a small slip of paper fluttered to the ground. I picked it up and discovered it was a phone number with the name Tammy written in curlicue letters above it.

I gasped in outrage. "She gave you her number?"

"I meant to throw it away. She slipped it to me when I checked out yesterday." He attempted to take it from me, but I stuffed it in my pocket.

"I cannot believe she gave you her number. What a... a... Oh!" With a growl, I pushed the shopping cart faster. "She knows we're a couple. We practically made out right in front of her."

Theo trotted next to me. "I don't know that we technically made out."

Abruptly I stopped and glared at him. "Excuse me? We definitely made out. I was there. What a... a... shrew for slipping you her phone number anyway."

"Technically, we aren't dating either."

"She doesn't *know* that." I began pushing the cart again, although I had no idea where we were headed. Also, I was absolutely not thinking about why Theo having this phone number in his possession annoyed me so much.

We weren't a thing. Despite what Mae, Mack, Hallie, and a strange café owner in Texas said. Get a grip, Ramos.

"I'll rip it up right now," Theo said from behind me. "You just have to give it back."

Stopping yet again in the middle of what was now the cookie aisle, I pulled out the slip of paper. "This? You want this?"

"Yes. I'll throw it away." His eyes gleamed with humor. Which was also annoying.

"Nope." I stared at the number, smiling like an evil queen in a fairy tale. "I have plans for this number."

Theo dropped his head and shook it, but I still saw the smile he tried to hide. "Ali."

"Theo."

"Don't do anything crazy."

"Pffsht, whatever." I folded the slip of paper and stuffed it in my bra. "Now let's finish shopping."

Theo stepped closer and leaned in, so his mouth was an inch from my ear. His breath was warm against my skin when he spoke. "You aren't jealous, are you?"

Ignoring the zing racing down my spine, I smacked him on the shoulder. "You wish, Theodore. You wish."

THIRTY-ONE

Note to self:
Don't forget to text Tammy in a couple of days.

After three false starts—once because Hallie decided she could not leave her four Barbies alone for a week, we finally hit the road. When Theo informed him of our Vegas detour, Mack seemed more than happy with the change of plans if his exclamation of "Vegas, baby!" was anything to go by.

I'd been relegated to the third row, surrounded by several boxes of wedding décor, a bag of Hallie's stuffed animals, and Theo's tent so that Abe and Hallie could have the middle row. This suited me just fine because I had a little business to take care of. I settled in for a fun game I called TAMMY WILL REGRET THIS. Using a free internet phone number (it came in handy) and pretending to be a bot, I texted a certain motel employee:

> ***Unknown number***: *Hook, Line, and Sinker: Thank you for signing up for America's premium fishing tackle monthly subscription service. Reply Y to agree to the terms and receive*

automated marketing txts. Msg&DataRatesApply. STOP to stop.

I tapped my fingers on the seatback in front of me, waiting for a reply. Karen's head popped up from her spot between Hallie and Abe, two people she had decided were worthy of her affection. Me, though? Oh, no. She pierced me with dark, angry eyes and growled.

"Why do you hate me?" I whispered.

Karen's reply was to stick her nose in the air and disappear. My phone buzzed.

Tammy: *I never signed up for any service*

Unknown number: *Hook, Line, and Sinker: You are now subscribed. Congrats! Your first tackle box will ship out in 5–7 business days. Each box always includes premium live bait such as nightcrawlers, waxworms, or maggots, plus a surprise to make your fishing experience more enjoyable. All shipped directly to you. To upgrade your box or see photos, please see our website. Happy fishing. Reply STOP at any time to opt out. Reply HELP for help.*

Tammy: *omg stop*

Unknown number: *Hook, Line, and Sinker: You are now subscribed. Congrats! Your first tackle box will ship out in 5–7 business days. Each box always includes premium live bait such as nightcrawlers, waxworms, or maggots, plus a surprise to make your fishing experience more enjoyable. All shipped directly to you. To upgrade your box or see photos, please see our website. Happy fishing. Reply STOP at any time to opt out. Reply HELP for help.*

Tammy: *STOP STOP STOP*

I didn't reply. At least not yet. Now was the time to let her relax and think she'd won before crushing her spirit in a day or two. Grinning, I set my phone down and cracked my knuckles like any genius mastermind. I was good. I was really good.

Of course, I'd had a lot of years of practice.

It started in the second grade when, while at recess, I saw Josh Metcalf push Melody Sinclair off the swings. Josh had always been a bully and it had only gotten worse as he got older and bigger. He seemed to especially relish picking on Melody. I liked Melody. She was a little shy, but real smart.

I don't know if it was stupidity, pure anger, or growing up with three big brothers, but I marched right over, balled my fist, and socked Josh right in the eye.

He'd bawled like a baby, and I got suspended for two days. Mom had caused such a scene at the school, demanding to talk to the superintendent and all, that Dad had to leave work in the middle of the day to intervene. But I hadn't budged, even when the principal agreed to walk back the suspension if I showed some remorse.

I refused to apologize. It wasn't fair when people got away with doing the wrong thing.

That evening, Dad had sat me down and explained that hitting someone out of anger was never the way to solve a problem.

"But he pushed her first," I'd said.

"Things have a way of coming back around."

"What's that mean?"

"Just means that when someone does bad things, it might take some time, but it comes back to them. You have to be patient. They'll get what's coming to them."

Looking back, I get that he was talking about karma but

eight-year-old me understood it differently. I had to be patient and I had to be smarter about how I put a person in their place.

And thus, a legend was born.

I was always careful about who my intended victim was. A person had to earn a spot by doing something particularly egregious. Well, unless your name was Peter Stone, then you were permanently on my radar. While the pranks were fun, and trust me, they were, I had two big rules. One, I never did anything that couldn't be reversed or easily fixed, and two, I never told anyone outright what I did. I'd learned, long ago, the best course of action was to deny, deny, deny and give others the chance of plausible deniability.

Satisfied I'd used my powers for good this day, I slipped in my ear pods and turned on some music and tried to doze off.

Until the reality of traveling with a kid set in.

First, there were the numerous bathroom breaks. As the only woman, guess who got to spend a lot of time in a public restroom begging a four-year-old wearing a princess tiara and a velvet dress in August to, "Please, please, please just go to the bathroom?"

Spoiler: me.

Second, the persistent demand for snacks. Goldfish crackers. Applesauce pouches. Cheese sticks. Water. And more water. And more water. Which, in hindsight, was probably the reason for the bathroom breaks.

Third, the endless questions.

"Are we there yet?" No, we've only been driving for half an hour.

"Can I have a puppy?" Maybe.

"Are you still my boyfriend, Teo?" Sure.

"Are we there yet?" No, we've only been driving for forty-five minutes.

"Are you still Auntie Ali's boyfriend?" Yup.

"Will someone read me a story?" Mack took one for the team.

"I wish I lived in a castle. Do you want to live in a castle?" Put me in the dungeon, as long as it's soundproof.

"Are we there yet?" No, Hallie. Just no.

And lastly, sometime after crossing into Utah, "I don't feel so good."

Which wasn't exactly a question, but close enough. Like the dummies we all were, we didn't take her seriously until fifteen minutes later.

"Daddy," Hallie said in a tiny voice, "my stomach feels wobbly."

In the few seconds it took for any of us to register what she'd said, Hallie blew the motherload of puke. When it was all over, Hallie was crying, Abe was holding a handful of vomit, and I was yelling at Theo to pull over.

That's how we found ourselves on the roadside of a desolate patch of I-70 unpacking everything in the backseat to search for a change of clothes for Hallie, a shirt for Abe, and something to mop up the mess with. Our attempt to clean up Hallie involved nine fast-food restaurant napkins, three bottles of water, and two towels all while hovering around her to block her from possible passing cars.

The inside of the car was an even bigger challenge.

"Isn't it easier to burn the car down and get a new one?" I asked, staring at the carnage.

Theo grunted. "I'm considering it."

"I'm sorry, man." Even with the clean shirt, Abe looked like a soldier returning home from a war where he had *seen* some things. "I had no idea."

Mack moseyed over, Karen trailing at his feet. "Welcome to fatherhood."

"Thanks," Abe muttered. He marched forth to drag the car

seat to the side of the road. Using our limited supplies, we went to work on both the car and the seat.

An hour later, exhausted and damp, Abe, Hallie, and Mack climbed into the car while Theo and I quickly repacked the back of the SUV.

"How did all this fit in here?" I asked, shoving another of Mom's boxes in.

"I don't know." Theo took off his cap and swiped at his forehead. "But I know it does."

I crammed the last thing, a duffel bag, in, then spent the next five minutes pushing and shoving, grunting and cursing to get it situated. "There. All done."

Relieved, I took a step back and put my hands on my hips.

"Perfect," Theo said.

That was when the trunk spewed out the duffel bag and two of Mom's boxes at my feet.

I groaned. "Someone owes me something after this."

Theo grabbed the bag and I bent to pick up a box. The lid on the one with CANDLES written across the top had come open. I peered inside and gasped. Slowly, I picked up one of the candles and stared at it in a combination of wonder and horror.

"What is that?" Theo asked.

Startled, I jumped and dropped the candle. It lay in the grass on the side of the road. I couldn't stop staring at it. Theo moved beside me. He glanced down and then did a double take.

"It's the... the," I paused and swallowed back the laughter fighting its way to the surface, "the c-candles my mom made for the wedding. For the centerpieces."

He crouched and picked it up. Except there wasn't a good way for him to hold it. His hands on that candle looked downright indecent. "Are they supposed to look like this?"

"Mom says they're called r-rolling hills."

Wide-eyed, Theo tossed the candle into the box like it was on fire. At his horrified expression, I exploded in laughter, the kind that made it impossible to speak. Or possibly remain upright. Theo watched me, amusement dancing in his eyes before he too began to laugh.

My heart lurched at the sound and those squinty eyes and that dimple. Somehow my forehead landed on his chest and his arms came around me. For a moment, I allowed myself to enjoy it, being surrounded by him, the way his laughter rumbled in his chest, and how he smelled of citrus and laundry soap.

I tipped my head to study him, my breath catching. He had always been handsome, but like this, he took my breath away. His eyes found mine and held them. His laughter morphed into a slow, devastating smile. Carefully, he brushed a piece of my hair from my face, his fingers tickling my cheek and leaving tingles in their wake.

"You're flirting again," I whispered. "You should really stop doing that."

He leaned down enough to bring his mouth close to my ear. "Maybe I don't want to stop."

I sucked in a breath, my brain screeching to a halt. What did that mean?

"You two okay?" Abe called from inside the car.

With a gasp, I jumped back and turned away, my heart thudding like I'd just played the meanest, dirtiest, best game of soccer ever.

"Yep, we're done," Theo called out. He turned to me. "Go ahead. I'll finish this."

I watched him for a beat before climbing back into the car, confused, my skin tingling, and wishing we hadn't been interrupted.

THIRTY-TWO

Note to self:
Nothing good ever comes from
An UNKNOWN number.

Between our late start and the reality of traveling with a child, we ended up stopping somewhere in small-town Utah for the night. Mack and Theo shared a room again; Abe and Hallie were with me.

We ordered dinner but all of us were more tired than awake and decided we'd make it an early evening to get an early start. After Hallie got ready for bed, I read her a few books until her eyes started to droop. After that, it was lights out for the room and I crawled into bed for a little investigative research.

I scoured the internet for mentions of Mom and her candles, and boy, did I find them. Turns out, she and Dad were correct; Mom was internet-famous. Or her candles were. And not exactly for their intoxicating scent or long-lasting burn time. Oh, no. Mom and Dad might not see it, but the internet was all over it. Gifs and memes were aplenty, most of them featuring my mom gushing about the beautiful "shape" of the candles.

In each one, she seemed oblivious to what those candles really looked like. To make matters worse, Melanie's wedding colors were cream and pale pink; the centerpieces matched. Two rounded pale pink "hills" with white snowcaps, the wicks sticking straight out of the top like flags.

Or tassels.

I couldn't help laughing—partly from secondhand embarrassment and partly from the absurdity of the situation. Melanie's head was going to explode when she saw these. I was sure of it.

After setting my phone on the nightstand, I curled up in bed and allowed myself to replay the scene earlier today with Theo, the one where I was dangerously close to blurting out that I was at least eighty-seven percent in love with him at this point. But being wrapped in his arms, laughing about those stupid candles, had felt so... so good.

I flipped over on my back and hugged a pillow to my chest. Was he flirting because he wanted to? I wasn't sure I could trust myself to read the signs. After all, Teenage Ali had been sure Theo felt the same way she had. I'd read any article in any teen or woman magazine titled something like, "Ten Signs He's Into You." I could convince myself that Theo displayed every single one.

First love, puppy love, a crush—that's what everyone had called it. I wasn't really in love with him. "You're only fifteen," Mom had told me. "You don't even know what love is."

Looking back, she was right, I guess. Yet as hard as I tried to ignore the feelings, push them aside, hide them away, they were always there, brimming under the surface. They'd never gone away.

It was a terrifying, exhilarating, wholly disconcerting feeling and every day I was with Theo, it only grew stronger. If only I knew for certain how he was feeling.

Life would be a lot easier if we all wore signs that

announced how we were feeling. Sure clear up a whole lot of confusion.

My phone buzzed with a notification.

Unknown number: *Hey, Ali. It's me.*

Frowning, I wondered who "me" could be. Normally, I brushed off random messages from random numbers sent at random times of the night but this person knew my name.

Me: *Who is this?*

Unknown number: *It's Alec. I wanted to talk.*

I scowled at the phone in disbelief. It had been over a year since he'd contacted me. In fact, he'd blocked me after sending his break-up text rant.

Unfortunately for him, he hadn't given too much thought to his social media pages, so when he posted a picture two days after we split all cuddled up with a new woman, I'd seen it immediately.

It had taken a little time and patience, but I'd managed to get a ride to Dallas, and if a catfish was shoved under one of the seats in his car, it might have happened then. The only sad thing was that I had no way of knowing his reaction. I hoped it took him weeks to find it. I hoped his car still smelled like rotten fish carcass. I hoped the smell clung to his person enough to make women cringe.

Mostly, I hoped I could get through the next few days avoiding him as much as possible. I'd made a promise to myself and to Cal and Melanie that we could be adults. So, I would adult the hell out of this wedding. There would be so much adulting, other adults would come to me for adulting advice, and I'd give it because that was the kind of adult I was.

But first, I had to get through this text conversation.

Me: *Talk about what?*

Alec: *I guess I thought we could hang out, for old times' sake.*

Was he joking? He had to be. After all, he was the one who sent me text after text listing everything wrong with our relationship and with me. He broke up with me. My finger hovered over the phone. Be an adult, Ramos.

Me: *I'm good. I don't need to catch up. Let's just get through the wedding.*

Alec: *Come on, Ali. At least think about it.*

Me: *No.*

Alec: *I'll get you to change your mind. I always could.*

With a grunt of disgust, I tossed the phone next to me on the bed. He'd never made me change my mind; he wore me down until I got tired of hearing him. What had I ever seen in this man?

I closed my eyes and turned my mind to better things—like Theo when his eyes crinkle in the corners when he's smiling. And Theo with his arms around me. And Theo when he says something flirty and makes my heart turn over. And just all of Theo.

Pretty sure I fell asleep with a smile on my face.

THIRTY-THREE

Note to self:
Send Cal a fruit basket.
For reasons.

Tuesday, five days before the wedding

Las Vegas

After a mostly good night's sleep—Hallie woke at the ungodly hour of four thirty—we got on the road before eight and arrived in Vegas in the afternoon. We drove down the Strip where, even during the day, there were hordes of people, flashing lights and so much activity, it was hard to know where to look. Blinking, neon signs called out to "come on in" or advertised an "all-you-can-eat" buffet or announced they had the best quickie wedding packages.

Cal called to check in after we'd made it to our hotel, a chain motel with an outdoor pool off the Strip. Melanie's parents and grandparents were arriving the next day, which had her racing around to make sure everything was "perfect."

"So, I guess now's not the time to tell you about the centerpieces."

"What about the centerpieces?" a voice yelled from the other room. Cal winced.

"She heard that?" I asked.

"It's like her senses are heightened." Cal shook his head. "The other day, she smelled Mexican food on my breath from three rooms away."

"That's because Mexican food seeps into your pores and lingers. It's gross." Melanie's face appeared on the screen, her hair pulled into a messy bun and dark smudges under her eyes. "Tell me about the centerpieces."

Why did I suddenly feel like I'd just poked the bear?

"Um, yeah, the centerpieces. Well, one of Mom's boxes of wedding stuff accidentally fell and opened and..."

"And?" Melanie's eyes narrowed. "Did you break something?"

"No, not that. Have you seen the centerpiece candles?"

"Of course. Your mom and I have been talking and planning for months."

With an apologetic smile, I held one up.

Cal gawked. "Are those brea—"

Melanie whapped the back of his head. "Calvin Coolidge Ramos! They are hills. Very clearly hills."

"Are they?" I bit the inside of my cheek to keep from laughing.

Shooting his beloved a disbelieving glance, Cal rubbed the back of his head. "Mel, honey. Those are not hills."

"Yes, they are," she snapped. "Ali, you can see they're hills, right?"

Cal glanced at me helplessly. I swallowed. They looked as much like hills as I looked like a kangaroo. If I had to guess, I'd say they looked like C cups. Being diplomatic seemed the best course of action. "I guess some could describe them as hills, but—"

"Well, there you go," Melanie cut in, looking victorious. "They are hills."

"...others could see something else entirely."

"Those people are idiots." She gave her future husband a pointed look and stomped off-screen.

"Wow," I whispered.

"Yeah."

Laughter bubbled to the surface. "I mean, I was just going to say they looked like, you know, melons."

"Ali."

"Or coconuts? Is there a fruit theme I don't know about?" I collapsed on the bed in a fit of giggles.

"Really helpful, Alicia. Thank you."

"Oh, oh, I've got it. Cantaloupes." I'm not sure he could even understand me though. Because laughing.

"I'm going now." He sounded resigned to his fate. "I'll talk to you later."

I tried to pull myself together. Really, I did. "Ta-ta for now. Or rather, ta-tas."

That's when he hung up.

THIRTY-FOUR

Note to self:
Think about getting a tattoo.
Maybe a pirate?

After the phone call, I dug out my trusty two-piece bathing suit with the high-waisted bottoms and tank-style top and headed for the pool to hang out with Hallie and Abe, who had headed there about four seconds after we checked into the hotel. Mack was camped out in a corner, lounging on a chair with his shirt off and sunglasses hiding his eyes.

"There you are." Mack held up a drink with an umbrella in it. "Look, I made a friend."

The woman stretched out in the chair next to him looked about his age. She was short and round and wore a cheetah-print one-piece bathing suit along with a gauzy black cover-up that covered up nothing. Her toes were painted fire engine red, which matched her lipstick.

"Hi, honey. Mack here was just telling me about you." The smile she beamed at me hinted she could be sweet and a whole lot sassy. I liked her immediately. "I'm Mona, but most everyone calls me Mimi."

"It's nice to meet you." I plopped down in the chair next to Mack.

"I was just telling Mack here that I came all the way from Texas for a little me time and look at this, I meet a handsome man," she winked at Mack, "from Texas."

With a grin, Mack preened under her attention. "It was meant to be."

"I am tickled pinker than a redhead's skin after a day at the beach." She poked him coyly in the arm.

"Are you here with family?" Mack leaned a bit closer.

"Oh, no, honey. I don't travel with them. My daughter is a bit of a stick-in-the-mud. What she doesn't see, she doesn't need to know about." Mimi laughed, low and sultry, and took a sip of whatever fruity cocktail she had.

"Well, I for one am glad to meet you." He held up his drink. "Cheers to new friends."

Giggling, Mimi tapped her glass to his.

I watched, fascinated. This was like a masterclass on flirting. Leave it to Mack to take this whole change thing by the horns and go for it.

After adjusting my chair, I slapped on sunscreen, tied my hair on the top of my head, and got comfortable. The pool was more crowded than I expected, mostly kids and parents and some loners over in the hot tub.

I scanned the area for familiar faces. "Where's Abe?"

"He took the car to be detailed," Mack said. "I don't think we can handle that smell any longer."

"Wise." The smell of regurgitated Goldfish crackers had lingered. "Did he take Hallie?"

"Left her with Theo." He pointed to the far end of the pool where the shallow water was. "They're over there."

I saw Hallie first, her hair in crooked, wet pigtails. She wore a bright-green swimsuit and arm floaties. The man beside her hooked her under the arms, held her high, and released her in the water with a splash. Her head popped right back up in a swoosh, spluttering and giggling.

The man, though... I wasn't sure how I'd missed him the first time I'd looked. Or maybe I could see why. His hair was wet and dark, slicked back, and he was shirtless. Obviously. He was at a pool. His wide chest was tanned but not particularly muscle-y, with a light dusting of hair. But it was the huge, colorful shoulder tattoo that threw me off. Theo had a tattoo?

Alec had a few tattoos, one on his forearm, a tribal patterned armband, and another on his calf. I hadn't had strong feelings about them. But Theo's tattoo was doing all kinds of things to me. My fingers itched to trace it, discover all the little details. I wanted to ask him what it meant and when he'd gotten it.

Was I into tattoos and never realized it? Was this another kink? Like the backwards hat?

Just then, Hallie pointed over at Mack and me. She waved her arms in the air to catch our attention. Theo turned, the blue of his eyes reflecting off the water and looking twice as bright.

Nope. It wasn't the tattoos. I was really into Theo. I had a Theo Goodnight kink.

I waved back, unable to help both my smile and the roaring thump of my heartbeat in my ears.

"Oh, now, is that the great-granddaughter you were telling me about?" Mimi pointed at Hallie. "She's precious."

"That's her." Mack pushed up his sunglasses and glanced my way. "Go get in that water with those two."

He didn't have to say it twice. I stood and slipped out of my flip-flops.

"Ali-Cat," Mack said as I started to walk away, "you might

want to move up the wedding date based on the look on that man's face."

"Are you engaged?" Mimi hit Mack on the shoulder. "You rascal, you didn't say anything about that."

"No." I shook my head. "We aren't together. Just friends."

Laughing, he slid his glasses into place. "Don't listen to a word she says. I give 'em six months."

I put my hands on my hips in exasperation. "Mack."

He wiggled his fingers in goodbye. "Have fun."

The pool was bean-shaped, the shallow end farther away. I took the long route, surreptitiously sneaking glances at Theo. Except every time I glanced at him, his eyes were following me, that secret little smile hovering around his mouth. It was instinct to walk taller, push back my shoulders, and put a little extra swing in my hips. I couldn't say I'd ever felt as sexy or noticed as I did just then, at a swimming pool somewhere in Nevada, by a blue-eyed man who wasn't supposed to make me feel this way anymore.

"Aunt Ali," Hallie cried, kicking her feet as fast as she could to meet me at the stairs. She scampered up the steps and reached for my hand, pulling me in.

The water felt heavenly, in cool contrast to the sun beating down. "Hey, you. Are you having fun?"

She nodded. "Teo's throwing me in the water. Come on."

But when we reached the spot Hallie had last seen Theo, he was gone.

"Where'd he go?" Her little forehead creased.

"He'll show back up."

The words weren't even out of my mouth when someone wrapped a hand around my ankle and pulled. I screeched and clawed at the pool ledge, but that hand skimmed my leg and hooked my waist. I lost the battle and fell backward onto the warm, solid wall of Theo. Which, not gonna lie, was a pretty great place to be.

"Arrr, I've got you now," he said.

I burst out laughing. "That is the worst pirate accent I've ever heard."

"Teo." Hallie wagged her finger. "You let her go."

"I'll not. For I am the Dread Pirate Goodnight."

"You really do have a thing for pirates, don't you?" I twisted my head enough to see him. "Should I be concerned?"

"Oh, definitely." His eyes shone with mischief. "Do you think to rescue her, little girl?"

"Save me, Hallie. Save me." I reached a hand to her dramatically.

Thus began a rousing game of Catch the Pirate. Theo moved comically slow, so Hallie had a chance of catching him, his arm still wrapped around me. Finally, Hallie caught up with us and demanded my release.

"And if I don't release her, heh? What then?" Theo asked in his awful pirate voice.

Hallie narrowed her eyes, her mind working overtime. She smiled. "My daddy will get you and tickle you. He's good at that."

"Captain Ramos? My most feared enemy." Theo clutched his heart. "Fine. Fine. I'll release her... for a kiss."

I gasped. "There will be no kissing, you cad."

"Aye, I am a cad. You best not forget it either." He tapped a finger on his cheek. "Right here, ya pretty thing, and then I'll let you go."

"Do it, Aunt Ali. Do it." Hallie clapped her hands.

"Fine. It will be a great sacrifice but for my freedom, I shall kiss you."

He waggled his eyebrows and Hallie giggled. In a move that made my stomach dip, Theo flipped me around in his arms, both his hands spread across my back. I gasped but when he pulled me closer, I didn't stop him.

"You're being flirty again."

His grin was wolfish. "Oh, not me. The Dread Pirate Goodnight though? Total reprobate. Demanding kisses, kidnapping women, and kicking puppies when the need arises. Now, kiss me, you wench."

I rolled my eyes and pressed a kiss to his cheek, my thoughts racing back to the last time I'd tried to kiss his cheek and missed. And maybe he was thinking the same thing because when I pulled back, his eyes, full of heat, dropped to my mouth. I licked my bottom lip. His hands dug a little deeper into my back. The pool, Hallie's laughter, Mack in the corner probably watching this, the reasons I'd fought whatever was happening between us —it was gone. I couldn't remember any of it.

I wanted him to kiss me, really kiss me, like I wanted my next breath.

But we'd said we were only friends. We'd both agreed to keep things that way. Yet every second since, it felt like I was sticking to the rules and Theo wasn't. I didn't know what that meant.

"Hey, what's going on over here?" Abe hopped into the water.

I pushed against Theo's chest and turned, plastering a smile on my face. "Playing a little pirate game."

"You're free. You're free." Hallie clapped her hands. "You got away."

"Aye, she did." Theo crept closer to Hallie, wiggling his fingers at her. "It means I'll need to find another wench to kidnap."

Hallie screeched and tried to kick away, but alas, she was no match for the dreaded Pirate Goodnight.

The four of us played for over an hour before I called it quits to take a break. Theo joined me. At the chairs, Mack was deep in conversation with Mimi. I caught bits and pieces of a story she was telling about a birthday dinner and, bizarrely, Spanx ending up on the meatloaf.

Theo took the empty lounge chair next to me. After drying off, I slid on my oversized sunglasses and arranged myself to receive maximum sunlight. The nice thing about sunglasses is that no one can quite see what you're looking at. My eyes drifted to one of my favorite things in the world—Theo.

The tattoo I'd noticed was even more beautiful up close. A large white and pink lily sat on his shoulder, the leaves and stem leading over and down his back. Without overthinking, I trailed a finger over it, feather-light.

"It's beautiful. For your mom?"

She'd loved lilies. Every inch of free space in the Goodnight yard had bloomed with rain lilies in the spring and summer, fat white blossoms that faded into pale pink. Just like Theo's tattoo.

His smile was small and a little sad. "Yeah. I started it after she passed and add a little more every few months. It's close to being finished now."

"She would have loved it." I dropped my hand.

"She probably would have gotten a matching one."

"Nothing like mother and son matching tattoos to up your street cred."

He laughed softly but his eyes were sad. "I miss her."

"Yeah. She was pretty special."

Slowly, as though afraid he might startle me, he picked my hand up. Carefully, gently, he turned it over and uncurled my fingers. Head bent, he traced the lines there with a whisper-soft touch. My breath caught at the small gesture. It felt wildly intimate, and it was only my hand.

I had it bad. And it was getting worse by the second.

"This will sound weird." His eyes met mine. "I miss her hands."

Tears welled at the heartache in his voice. I couldn't

imagine losing my mother. And for Theo, she'd been his only family.

"Remember how she always talked with her hands? Or how she was constantly putting lotion on because her hands were dry from washing them so much at work? The thing I miss the most though is when she'd touch right under her eye."

"I remember that. What was that about?"

He chuckled, his fingers still tracing my palm. "When I hit middle school, I started to get embarrassed when she would do the whole 'I love you, my sweet baby angel' act when we were in public. She was kind of upset when I told her I wanted her to stop. She said she understood I was growing up but she still wanted to say she loved me anytime she wanted. So, she decided that whenever we wanted to say I love you in public, we would touch just under our eye."

"That's sweet."

"Sorry." He let go of my hand and stretched out on his chair. "I didn't mean to get weird there."

I stared at him an extra beat... or five, taking in the view, so to speak. Then, I followed his lead and laid back in my chair.

"Athena Norwood," I said after a full five minutes had passed.

"Hmm?"

"A.N. Athena Norwood."

He chuckled. "Not even close."

"Amy North."

"Nope."

I threw my hands in the air. "Can I at least get a clue?"

"Alright. Let me think." Which he did for what felt like hours. "One of the initials is the same as someone who has a special place in my heart. She's loyal and smart and clever. Plus, she smells good, and she always makes me smile."

I scowled. Who was this woman and how do I get rid of

her? He sounded much too attached. "Do I know this person? She sounds way too perfect."

He barked out a laugh. "Oh, you know her, and trust me, she is not perfect. Honestly, she can be slightly unhinged at times. It's part of her charm."

Crossing my arms, I settled back into my seat, mulling over his clues for this mysterious woman. Whoever she was, I hated her.

THIRTY-FIVE

Note to self:
Go shopping for a new stakeout outfit.

"Nervous?" I asked.

Theo's tapping fingers on the steering wheel paused. "Maybe a little."

After we'd finished at the pool and cleaned up, we ate dinner at a Chinese buffet and played a cutthroat game of Go Fish! until Hallie began rubbing her eyes. Abe kicked me out of our room while he got her to sleep. Theo and I had been presented with the perfect time to complete our mission. His mission. The mission. Whatever.

Twenty minutes later, we pulled into a fancy subdivision in a Vegas suburb called Henderson. It was the kind of "community" with its own pools, playgrounds, clubhouse, and gym. Judging by the size of the houses, meticulously manicured lawns, and expensive cars in the driveways, people paid through the nose to live here.

Theo found the house quickly. We'd now driven past it four times, and each time he drove a little slower.

"We probably should at least park." I pointed at the sign we'd also passed four times. "Neighborhood watch patrol signs. We don't look suspicious at all."

He grunted, but pulled up to the curb across the street the next time we reached the house. It was a sprawling stucco ranch style with red accents that matched the tile roof. Instead of grass, the front lawn was made of rocks with two tall palm trees guarding the driveway.

"This is a nice neighborhood," I said.

"Yeah, it is." Theo's hands tightened on the steering wheel until his knuckles turned white.

"You want to sit here and see if anyone comes out?"

He gave a curt nod. Both of us stared at the dark-red door. Tension radiated off him in waves, evident in the lines of his face, the set of his shoulders.

I reached into my backpack and pulled out a bag of candy. "Licorice?"

"When did you get that?" He grabbed the bag and ripped it open.

"I have a stockpile."

"You're good to have around," he said around a mouthful of licorice bits.

"Yes, I am," I said primly.

We lapsed into a silence punctuated with the crinkling of the candy bag and the occasional barking dog. It was after seven and the sun was setting, leaving behind a sherbet sky of pinks and oranges.

I smoothed my shirt, the nicest one I'd packed, a wrap-style silk tank top with a tie at the waist. I'd paired it with my favorite jeans, the ones that molded to my curves and made me feel extra cute. Honestly, I'd spent way too much time pondering what one wore to meet the deadbeat father of the man you're mostly in love with.

"So."

"So." Theo stared intensely at the house.

"What's our plan?"

"I don't know. I guess..." His voice trailed off as the front door opened. A tall woman with dark hair stepped out and slid into the BMW in the driveway. Theo tugged his baseball cap lower and slumped in his seat. The car pulled out and went in the opposite direction.

"Who was that?"

Theo shrugged. "His new wife? Or maybe he doesn't live here. Maybe he rents it out. Maybe we're sitting here staring at a house like creeps for no reason."

"There's only one way to find out."

He nodded stiffly and opened his door. I waited, not presuming anything. He climbed out of the car and frowned at me. "Aren't you coming?"

"I'll understand if you'd rather be alone."

He braced himself on the hood and leaned in, his eyes dark and serious. "Please come with me. I don't think I can do it without you."

Nodding, I unbuckled my seatbelt and tried to ignore the warmth blooming in my chest. It was nice to be needed. Really nice. It felt like I was always the person who needed someone. I hadn't realized how powerful those words could be, especially coming from Theo.

At the door, Theo rubbed his hands on his shorts and frowned.

"Do you want me to knock?" I asked.

"No, I'll do it." After a long moment, he rapped on the door. Without missing a beat, his hand found its way to mine, linking our fingers. I squeezed back some encouragement.

Finally, the door whipped open. "Did you forget someth—?"

Standing in front of us was a young man, probably still in high school. Taller than Theo by an inch or two with tousled blond hair a shade or two lighter than Theo's. And with a square jaw like Theo's. And a straight nose, just like Theo's. But it was the eyes that gave him away; they were the exact same shade of blue as Theo's.

"Who are you?" the kid asked.

But if I were a betting woman, and hey, we *were* in Vegas, I would bet it all that this kid was Theo's brother.

THIRTY-SIX

Note to self:
Sometimes closure is just the beginning.

"Um, do you want something to drink? Or pizza? There's leftover pizza from dinner." The kid, whose name was Travis, swallowed and cranked his head to the side like he was cracking it, his nervousness practically another person in the room.

The resemblance between them was so strong, it was impossible to ignore. But neither of them said a word about it. Instead, after getting over the initial shock, Travis invited us inside.

We sat in a tastefully decorated formal living room with strong southwestern vibes. A trio of cowboy hats were arranged on the wall as "art." A collection of belt buckles filled a small curio cabinet. There was not one but two Longhorn skulls. It was all very southwest-décor-magazine perfect.

Theo and I sat on a leather couch. His grip on my hand was one second away from bone-crushing but I didn't let on.

The kid, Travis, stood awkwardly on the other side of the coffee table, fidgeting with the string to his hoodie, which read

Rawlings HS Swim Team across it. His eyes—I couldn't get over how they matched Theo's—wandered the room, avoiding the giant elephant, er, brother, he didn't know he had in the room.

"I think we're fine," I said.

"Oh. Okay. Good." He perched on the edge of a chair, looking as though he planned to make a run for it any minute. "So."

Theo frowned. "You probably shouldn't invite strangers into your house, kid."

"Something tells me you aren't really a stranger," Travis said.

Somewhere in the house a clock was tick-tick-ticking. Travis stuffed his hands in his hoodie pocket; Theo set our joined hands on his thigh.

"Is your father here?" Theo finally asked.

The kid opened his mouth, then closed it. "No. He's not home from work yet."

I saw Theo's shoulders go rigid. With my thumb, I began to make small circles on his hand as he'd done for me.

Theo and Travis stared at each other. Not in anger, more in curiosity.

"How old are you?" Travis blurted out.

"Thirty. How old are you?"

"Seventeen."

"In high school, huh?"

Travis nodded. "My senior year."

"Swim team?"

"Yeah. And baseball."

Theo perked up. "I played baseball."

"Oh, yeah, what position?"

"Second base."

Travis's eyes widened. "Me too." He pointed between Theo and me. "Are you two together?"

I opened my mouth to correct him, but Theo nodded. "Yeah, we are."

"We are?" I whispered.

With another squeeze of his hand, Theo turned his head just enough that I could see something like panic in his eyes.

"You know, I'll take that water," I said.

"Oh, yeah, sure." Travis left for the kitchen in a hurry like he'd been desperate for any excuse. I didn't blame him. This was all so... unexpected.

"Are you okay?" I asked, keeping an eye on the doorway Travis had gone through.

Theo stood abruptly. He pulled his hat off and ran his hand through his hair. "I don't know."

"He seems like a nice kid."

"Yeah." Theo wandered over to a row of photos sitting on a sofa table.

He picked one up and scrutinized it for so long, I got up to see what he was looking at. The photo showed Travis around age ten or eleven, a wide, toothy grin. The woman next to him was tall and dark-haired, an arm wrapped around him, showcasing the same grin. The man had his arm around the woman. With his blond curly hair, wide shoulders, and bluer than blue eyes, his resemblance to Theo was almost spooky.

Theo set the photo down and shoved his hands in his pockets without saying a word.

"We can leave any time you want, you know. Whatever you want to do."

He opened his mouth to say something but was interrupted by Travis. He handed us both a glass of ice water and we wandered back to the couches. Theo sat even closer this time, his thigh brushing mine.

"Do you know how much longer your dad will be?" Theo asked.

Travis twisted his hands. "I, ah, called him and told him about... that you were, you know, here. He said he was on his way. It's about a thirty-minute drive. My mom had a book club thing tonight. She won't be back until later."

In a move that would have made a synchronized swim team jealous, we all picked up our glasses and took a drink at the same time.

Abruptly, Theo stood. "I guess we'll be going."

But at that same moment, Travis blurted out, "Do you think... are we brothers?"

Theo sank back to the couch. He rested his elbows on his knees, his hands dangling between his legs. "Yeah, I think so."

"I didn't know you existed," Travis whispered, his face pale.

"That's funny. I didn't know you existed either."

The two stared at each other, this time, with open curiosity.

"When was the last time you saw him?"

"He left before I was two. I don't have any memories of him." After a moment, Theo straightened. "Is he a good dad?"

Travis nodded. "He's the best."

I bit my tongue. Sure, people can change but how do you forget an entire child? How?

"That's good." Theo rubbed his palms on his thighs. "I think I'm going to leave."

"A-are you sure? He said he was leaving as soon as he got off the phone with me."

"Yeah, I think I am sure. For now. I'm glad you get to have a dad, Travis. He's not really my father. He's just a guy I'm related to."

After a moment, Travis nodded. He seemed a little disappointed, like he wanted to say something else. "Yeah, okay."

He walked us out to the porch, his hands shoved in that hoodie pocket again. We said our goodbyes and had taken maybe three steps before Travis's voice stopped us.

"Do you think you and me, could we stay in touch? Maybe email or something."

Theo turned back. "Are you sure about that?"

Travis shrugged. "I've always wanted a brother."

"You don't know anything about me," Theo pointed out.

"Then I guess you should give me the chance to."

THIRTY-SEVEN

Note to self:
Never forget the healing power of pie...
and the blabbering power of pie-themed cocktails.

Theo hardly spoke on the drive back to the motel. It was a thoughtful silence, and I guessed after you met the brother you didn't know existed for the first time, you'd need time to process. But enough was enough.

"We need pie," I announced. "There's a place called Pie in the Sky a block from the hotel. Open twenty-four hours."

"Pie?"

I nodded firmly. "Yes. Pie. You're thinking too hard right now."

"I am not."

"Yes, you are. You're going to hurt yourself. To pie, my good man."

We decided to park at the motel and walk. Pie in the Sky was as if a hipster bar and a fifties diner had a baby. The décor was all shiny chrome and red faux leather with black and white squared flooring. There were matching red and chrome booths. But instead of a lunch counter, there was a tall, wooden bar and instead of milkshakes, they served pie-inspired cocktails like apple pie on the rocks or a key lime pie martini.

There was also actual pie. Several tall, spinning, glass display cases with oversize pieces full of crusty, sugary goodness.

"This place is Heaven." I eyed a slice of lemon meringue pie like it was the new love of my life. "It has to be."

"Clearly." Theo placed his hand low on my back and directed me to an open booth in the corner. "I'm going to run to the bathroom."

"Sure, sure," I mumbled, head already buried in the menu. The options were endless. I could splurge a little and have a drink or two. I was a lightweight because my anti-seizure meds interacted with alcohol in funny ways, one of them being it metabolized quickly and hit me hard.

A server arrived within seconds, dressed in a modern twist on fifties style with a flirty above-the-knee poodle skirt and a black shirt with off-the-shoulder sleeves. "Hiya, what can I get you?"

"All of it." I grinned. "But maybe just water until my friend comes back."

"No problem."

For a pie-themed bar (or maybe because of) it was a busy place. Most people seemed to land in the thirty to forty age range with some outliers, just for fun. The bar was packed and the two bartenders, dressed as modern-day soda jerks with red suspenders, matching bowtie and no shirts, were likely pulling in some very nice tips.

At the end of the bar sat a guy with dark hair, glasses, a sweater vest and a nice smile, radiating hot professor energy. He made eye contact with me, his smile widened, and he lifted his drink in my direction. I gave him a little nod in what I hoped was polite disinterest and swung my gaze back to our table and the menu.

Yes, the guy was hot, but he had nothing on Theo. I'd take dreamy blue eyes and small, secret smiles all day long.

Several minutes later, a glass slid onto the table.

"A Boston crème pie martini for you."

I looked at the drink and then the server. "I didn't order this."

"Sure didn't." She grinned and pointed with the tray in her hand right to Sexy Prof. "He did."

"Oh, um." My face heated. "I'm flattered."

Theo slid across from me into the booth. "Did you order something already?"

"Not exactly."

The server smirked. "The lady has an admirer. Maybe he didn't see your boyfriend when you came in."

"Okay. Wait." I pointed at Theo. "He's not..."

Theo crossed his arms and leaned back in the seat.

"I mean, we're not..."

Smirking, he arched an eyebrow.

"I can't accept this," I blurted, pushing the drink toward the server. "Could you tell him thanks but no, thanks."

"No problem." She winked at us and whisked the drink away. "I'll be back to get your orders in a few."

Face burning, I couldn't stop myself from mouthing *I'm sorry* to the guy at the bar.

Theo frowned. "You know, if you're interested, you could go over there. Us, just being friends and all." He glanced over at his shoulder. "I mean, he seems like the kind of guy you'd be into."

"What does that mean?"

"Reminds me of Alec."

"He does not."

But my eyes swung back to the Sexy Prof who was now

chatting it up with a tall blonde. He did have that slicked-back, put-together, finance bro feel. Less professor if I thought about it, more money talk. Which described Alec a lot. Not when we first started dating, but the longer he'd worked at that job in Dallas, the more he became the suit-and-tie, cocktail-party-attender schmoozer he was today.

Don't get me wrong. I love a man in a suit. I was looking forward to seeing Theo in his groomsman get-up at the wedding. I liked dressing up for a cocktail party every now and then, not that Two Harts gave many opportunities for that. But all the time? It just wasn't how I wanted to spend every Friday night.

"Fine." I sighed. "Maybe he does."

The server returned. I ordered an apple pie sangria and Theo went with a chocolate cream pie made with vodka, Rum Chata, chocolate liquor, and chocolate syrup. After some deliberation, we decided to split a piece of key lime pie.

"Can I ask you something?" Theo asked after the server left.

"Sure."

He tilted his head, his eyes fixed on my face. "What did you see in Alec? I never got it, the two of you."

"Oh." I swallowed. It was on the tip of my tongue to give a flippant answer about how handsome he was, or how he treated me well, or any number of things. I could admit, at least to myself, that Alec hadn't been all bad. Sure, he'd broken up with me in an epic asshat move but we'd had good times too.

But I went with the truth instead. "He was safe."

Theo stayed quiet, waiting me out. Damn him.

"There wasn't any real chance of us working out. I think some part of me knew that. His life is in Dallas, mine is in Two Harts. Neither one of us wanted to compromise on that. But it was easy too. We liked each other as people. We got along. Relationships have been built on less, you know." I traced the edge of the table with my thumbnail. "But I guess the real reason he was safe is because I wasn't ever in any danger of falling in love with him. Not the way a person should love their partner."

"Why?" Theo's voice was low, deep, and it rumbled across my skin.

"Mainly because my heart wasn't mine to begin with." I raised my head and looked him in the eye. "It's always belonged to someone else, I guess."

"Who?" he asked, his eyes soft.

You, dummy. You.

The server arrived with our drinks and the biggest, thickest wedge of pie I'd ever seen. A piece of pie I would be forever grateful for since it saved me from saying something stupid. I'd already made a fool of myself a long time ago over Theo; I wasn't about to do it again.

Thank God for pie. I should put that on my tombstone, too.

After consuming drink number two—a frozen French silk pie cocktail—and announcing I loved it so much, I wanted to marry it, Theo wisely paid our tab, and we headed back to the hotel. We'd spent two hours not talking about a single serious thing including: 1) my confession about Alec; 2) Theo's newfound family; or 3) the weird tension between us that had been growing steadily.

Sure, I tried to bring up the scene today at his father's house, but he wasn't interested in talking about it. I hoped he opened up about it later. But Theo was also a thinker. Never knew exactly what was going on in his head. Unless you were sixteen, showed up at his dorm room on a random Thursday morning, confessed your undying love, and tried to kiss him.

Then he told you exactly what he thought.

I giggled. I'd put him in an awful predicament, and he'd been kind about it, sweet even. Not that I recognized that at the time. I was a kid; he was in college. I was stalker-level intense about my feelings; he was sensible.

"Maybe this is the alcohol talking," I announced halfway back to our hotel. "But remember that time I came to your dorm room and told you I was in love with you?"

"I remember, trust me." His eyes crinkled in the corners.

"I'm sorry I did that. It was a dumb idea."

"It was definitely memorable."

"And embarrassing."

He shrugged, a corner of his mouth inching up. "I don't know. It was kind of sweet."

"Sweet?"

"Well, sure. And brave."

I wrinkled my nose. "I used to be brave."

"Telling someone you're in love with them and you're not sure how they feel takes a lot of guts." He stepped a tiny bit closer. A streetlight hit his eyes just right, making them look dark and liquid. "I'm not brave enough to do it now."

Carefully—I didn't want to poke him in the eyeball in my current state—I traced the lines at the corners of his eyes with my fingers. "I love these. They give you away sometimes."

Theo held himself very, very still. "What do they give away?"

"That you're thinking very hard. Or you have something important to say. Or you're amused. 'Cause I amuse you." Grinning, I threw my arms out, and spun in a circle. My stomach didn't like that. Also, I was pretty sure I'd stopped and yet the ground was still moving. Was it getting closer? Was I—

"Whoa, there," Theo said, his voice close to my ear. He'd hooked an arm around my waist and pulled me against his chest.

"I don't think I should have had that second drink, Theodore."

He snorted and turned me gently. "Think you might be right about that."

I blinked at him. "You look like an angel."

"That's the streetlight."

I shook my head and patted his chest where his heart was. Or should be, I thought. Not a doctor. "Nope. You're my angel. I'm sure of it."

His eyes did the crinkle thing again and then dropped to my mouth. My breath caught, my stomach clenched in anticipation and then... he slowly let go, his hands hovering around my shoulders just in case I tried to tip over.

I frowned. "I thought you were going to kiss me."

"Do you want me to?"

"So much, Theo. I want you to, so much. I have dreams about it," I whispered. "Do you want to kiss me?"

The moment stretched before he gave me a small, crooked smile. "What I want is to get you back to the hotel, safe and sound."

My whole body drooped in disappointment. "So, no?"

"I didn't say that, did I?" He took my hand and tugged so I'd start walking again.

"So, you do?"

With a long-suffering sigh I'd heard my father use with my mother on many, many occasions, he shook his head. "I think I am losing my mind."

"Don't do that. I like your mind." There were other things I liked about Theo. I should tell him. "And your hair. I want to run my fingers through it so badly. You have that one piece that falls in your eyes, and I have to sit on my hands sometimes, so I don't reach over and fix it. So, it's probably best you wear your baseball cap around me unless you'd like to be mauled one day. Oh, except don't wear it backwards, okay?"

Theo shot me a bewildered look. "Why?"

"I love it when you wear your hat backwards. It's hot. You're hot enough without trying to tempt me. It's not fair."

He made a funny, strangled sound. "Got it. No backwards hat."

"Well, not unless you want me to do something about it." I hip-bumped him. "If you know what I mean."

Theo huffed a laugh.

"I like your hands, too. How they're big and gentle, and I love when you make that little circle with your thumb when you hold my hand. I dream about that sometimes, too." I slapped a hand on my mouth and mumbled out, "I shouldn't tell you that, huh?"

"Please go on. I'm enjoying this."

I pulled my hand down. "Alright. I like that your tummy's a little soft because it makes for such great cuddling. I mean, I imagine it does. We've never cuddled. At least on purpose, I guess. But I want you to know I am available to give it a try." I grinned proudly like I'd just volunteered to serve my country.

"That's good to know."

"Ellie says you don't look like you eat caveman food or dead-lift cars and that's a good thing because it means you'd rather spend time with people and that's hot." I paused for a breath. "'Cause you're hot."

"You mentioned that."

"It bears repeating." I stopped and frowned, sure I'd seen that same garbage can in front of that same store front already. "Are we lost?"

"No, we've walked around the block about three times now. You seemed like you wanted to talk."

"Oh. Good." We started walking again, his hand still wrapped around mine. "I like how you're always kind and... and whenever I need you, you come. You don't ask questions. You don't make me feel like I'm broken. Mom, Dad, everyone, even the boys sometimes, always seem like they're waiting for me to have a breakdown. I mean, sure, I have epilepsy. Guess what? It's not a death sentence. Lots of people live with epilepsy and have active, normal lives. I know they care but it's suffocating sometimes. I hate that I make them worry."

"It's hard to see someone you love go through hard things," Theo said quietly. "We want to protect them, keep them safe."

"Yeah, I guess." I sighed and then tried to hide a yawn.

"You tired?"

I leaned my head against his arm as we walked, loving the feel of his skin on my cheek. "I guess so."

We were back at the motel in two minutes. Theo held my hand all the way to our neighboring rooms.

I turned to him. "Mostly, I think something inside me recognizes something inside you, and when I'm with you, there's excitement, sure, but there's this feeling of..." I shook my head, frowning. "I don't know, home? Like you're home, a safe place to land. You're my comfort person."

Those blue eyes stared at me so intensely, it felt like a caress. He cupped my cheeks and tilted my head. My heart dipped to my toes.

"Are you going to kiss me now?" I asked.

"No."

"I would really like you to."

"I really want to."

And my heart climbed back up... to my throat. "Okay."

"But not now. You're a little drunk and I don't want to take advantage."

"Oh my gosh, Theo, stop being such a good guy. Please take advantage of me."

He touched his lips to my forehead in the sweetest, gentlest gesture. Now my heart was in a puddle. "Go to bed, Alicia."

"Fine." I tried to get the key card in the slot at least three times before Theo took it from me and did it himself. Then something in my less than sober brain clicked, and I gasped. "Alicia. A.N. Is the A for Alicia?"

Theo winked. "I'll see you in the morning. Get some sleep."

THIRTY-EIGHT

Note to self:
Send a fan letter to my new favorite author.

Sleep, it turned out, was the furthest thing from my mind. After quietly changing, I climbed into bed and went to work searching for authors named Alicia who wrote pirate books.

It was no accident he'd chosen my name. It couldn't be. I thought back to the clue he'd given me at the pool. A warmth started in my stomach and moved through my body. I was the person he thought so highly of. Me.

What did it mean?

It didn't take long to find the name: Alicia Night, whose website proclaimed she wrote "Love Stories Set on the High Seas." She had quite an online following: reader art, reviews, devoted fans, and constant speculation about her identity.

I immediately downloaded every book to my reading app. Each cover featured scantily clad men and women. On pirate ships. In torrid embraces. With lustful eyes. Written by Theo. Mild-mannered Theo. *My Theo.*

My brain could not connect my quiet, thoughtful Theo with these stories. This must be like what happens when someone finds out there's a serial killer in the family and they say things like, "I can't believe it. He was such a nice guy."

Except no murder, of course.

It was after one in the morning, but that didn't stop me from opening one of the books and reading the first two chapters before I was interrupted by a soft knock on the door.

I scrambled to the window and peeked through the curtains. It was Theo.

Quietly as possible, I opened the door. "Is everything okay?"

He shook his head. "It's Mack."

Despite calling forty-three times and sending just as many text messages, Mack didn't respond to any of them.

"Straight to voicemail again." I rubbed grit from my eyes since it was now after two in the morning. Any pie cocktail buzz I'd had disappeared the second I realized we had a problem.

When Theo had returned to the room, he'd found a note from Mack saying he and Mimi were going out on the town. I gently woke Abe, who said he'd seen Mack before he went to bed around ten, which meant he'd left sometime between ten and one in the morning. Nothing good ever happened then.

I paced the length of Mack and Theo's room. "What do I do?"

Definitely not calling my mother, that was for sure. Why couldn't he answer his phone and let me know he was okay?

"He is a grown man," Theo said but when he got a look at my face, his voice trailed off.

"It's two o'clock in the morning."

"I know."

"In a city he doesn't know."

"Yes."

"With a strange woman he doesn't know."

He shrugged. "She seemed pretty nice."

"Theo!"

"Right."

"Mimi might not even be her real name. She could be planning to harvest his organs." I stopped in front of Theo and grabbed his shirt with two fists. "We have to find him."

He covered my hands. "Ali. I'm not going to say a word about how you sound like your mother right now."

"That's what you got out of all this?"

"We'll find him." He gently pried my hands from his shirt.

"How?" I threw myself on the nearest bed. "He could be anywhere."

My phone pinged. It was a text from Mack. I gasped, my jaw going slack.

"What?"

I handed Theo the phone to show him the photo my grandfather had sent. It was of Mimi and him, both wearing huge smiles. Mack had on a t-shirt that said, "What Happens in Vegas is Awesome", and Mimi had a "Vegas, Baby!" hat on. But that wasn't the part that made me gasp. Oh, no. It was that they were standing in front of a sign which read 24-HOUR WEDDING CHAPEL.

"He wouldn't, would he?" I asked for probably the fiftieth time as we left what might have been the fiftieth twenty-four-hour wedding chapel in this city. Turned out that twenty-four-hour sign was not unique. They were everywhere. Like the Vegas version of lawn flamingos.

"I'm sure it was a joke."

"I'm not laughing."

Theo threw an arm around my shoulders as we walked down the block. "You'll laugh about this later."

"No, I don't think I will."

The next chapel boasted that a couple could be married by Elvis, Britney Spears, or Michael Jackson. The lobby was clean and white with a long counter. Behind it, a large sign hung on the wall, which outlined their wedding packages starting at the "Sign and Go" for a mere seventy bucks, and going up to $2,300 for the "Grand Ultimate" package, which included all the bells and whistles, a hotel room, and a borrowed wedding dress. But wait, you could make your own package, too—à la carte style. It was like a fast-food menu but for matrimony.

"This is... classy."

A middle-aged woman in a pale-pink dress stabbed out a cigarette and shot us a practiced smile. "Hello, lovelies. Can I help you with anything?" She pulled a thick binder from under the counter. "You can flip through this to see our selection of flowers, wedding dresses and tuxes."

"We're not here to get married." With a yawn, I held out my phone with the photo of Mack and Mimi. "Have you seen these two tonight?"

She grinned. "Oh, yeah. They were the cutest. Sometimes you get some real idiots up here but these two were sweet."

My heart seemed to freeze mid-beat. "They were here."

Theo put his hands on my shoulders. "Do you have any idea where they went?"

"I think they said they were going to Casa Nostra, that Italian restaurant down the block, to celebrate."

"To celebrate," I repeated. Mack had done it. He'd gotten married to a woman he'd met all of eight hours ago.

"Thank you," Theo said after getting directions to the restaurant. He turned me and gently frog-marched me out of the chapel.

Somehow, we made it Casa Nostra without me realizing we'd even been walking. The restaurant was busy despite it being closer to four in the morning. We scoured the entire restaurant and when we found nothing, I pulled a chair out from the nearest table and sat.

The couple sitting at the table looked at me curiously. The woman held up a basket. "Breadstick?"

"Thanks." I pulled one out and took a bite. "Sorry for intruding."

She shrugged. "Eat up, honey. You look like you could use the carbs."

"You have no idea." I waved the breadstick at her. "This city is nuts."

Theo passed the table, then stopped and turned around, walking back. "No luck."

"Nope."

The woman offered Theo a breadstick too. "Who ya looking for?"

I showed her the photo and she smiled. "Oh, yay. I've seen them. They were sitting over there." She pointed at a table nearby, now occupied by a trio of women. "Not sure where they—"

That's when I heard it. Somewhere a man was belting out Taylor Swift at the top of his lungs. I grabbed Theo's hand. "Do you hear that?"

The restaurant bar boasted twenty-four-hour karaoke and while the place wasn't empty, it was a fairly small crowd of the very drunk, which included Mack and Mimi.

Mack was on the stage. Every lyric sort of tumbled out of his mouth in sloppy, drunken happiness. Despite that, he got an occasional catcall and random applause. Standing by the stage and swaying to Mack's caterwauling was Mimi, wearing bright-pink hot pants, four-inch heels, and a shirt that showed a whole lot of the girls she was currently shaking.

"What is happening?" I whispered.

"I would say Mack is having a really good time."

I plopped down at the bar, eyes on the stage. After Mack ended his song, Mimi joined him for a truly horrible rendition of "Islands in the Stream."

"A really, really good time," Theo said as we watched Mimi plant a kiss on Mack's cheek.

"Can I get you something?" the bartender asked.

"I'm with the band." I yawned. The adrenaline was fading fast, replaced by exhaustion.

Theo sat next to me, his baseball cap pulled low. I gazed longingly at his shoulder, wondering if he'd be okay with me putting my head on it. Or if he'd possibly let me curl up in his lap.

Theo turned to me and frowned. He brushed a piece of hair from my cheek and read my mind again. "You look tired."

"So do you." And I'd already noticed his limp was becoming more pronounced with each step. "And your ankle is hurting, isn't it?"

He gave me a weary smile. "And we still have a marriage to break up."

I groaned. "Do you think they have quickie divorces in Vegas?"

Mack and Mimi finished their song, and with linked hands, practically skipped off the stage.

We tracked the two back to a table full of people who looked to mostly be in their sixties and seventies. What had they done? Crashed a senior living group, got married, got drunk, and then decided to continue the celebration with karaoke, and not necessarily in that order.

"Mack," I said, much too loudly. Everyone at the table jerked their heads in my direction.

"Ali-Cat!" Mack stood and held his arms open. "I didn't know you were coming."

I blinked. "We've spent the last two hours searching for you. Your phone goes straight to voicemail. I've been worried sick."

"I didn't mean to worry you. I left a note. I sent you that text too, but then my phone died. Did you get it?" With a grin, he waved his hand around the table. "Mimi, look who came to visit."

"It's four o'clock in the morning. This isn't a visit."

Mack continued jovially like he hadn't heard a word I was saying. "Friends, this is my granddaughter, Ali, and her fiancé, Theo."

"He's not my..." A rowdy round of congratulations made it impossible for me to be heard. "Whatever."

After everyone settled down, Mimi pointed to the one unoccupied chair. "Well, you two, pull up a seat. We're celebratin'."

"Did you two get married?" I blurted out.

Mack's eyes widened and he plopped back down into his chair. "Now, Ali..."

"The picture you sent... it was in front of a wedding chapel, and I know you're a grown adult. Of course, you are, and I love you, and I know you have this plan and you're looking for a change, but meeting a woman and marrying her eight hours later is insanity. She could be a serial killer or a mouth breather or... I don't know." I paused and looked over at Mimi. "No offense, Mimi. You seem very nice."

"Oh, no offense taken." Her mouth twisted into an amused smirk. "But, sugar, I'll ease your mind right now. I got seconds on the day God handed out common sense. There's no way I'd let a man I just met put a ring on it. That would be nuttier than a squirrel turd."

A wave of relief coursed through me. "Thank God."

Mimi pointed to a man in a dress shirt and tie and a woman in a lavender dress who were sitting almost on top of each other, each wearing matching expressions of bliss. "Those two got hitched."

The couple waved and the woman held up her left hand and pointed to the wedding ring there.

"Congrats," I said weakly.

"They're friends from Texas. That's why I'm here," Mimi continued. "This was all planned, but then I met Mr. Charming here," she leaned over and gave Mack a kiss on the cheek, "and thought he looked like a man who liked to have fun. So, I invited him as my plus one. I didn't realize this would cause so much concern."

"Oh." That's all I could say. My face felt hot with embarrassment like I'd received a dressing-down from the principal (which had happened once... or twice... or, well, you get it).

Mimi's eyes danced from me to the man standing behind me. "You're here now. Why don't you have a seat and stay awhile."

"We should take Mack and get going," I protested. "We have a lot of driving ahead of us tomorrow."

Mimi raised a dark eyebrow and spoke in a firm voice. "Sit."

"Got it."

The table only had one empty seat and with Theo's ankle, I offered it up to him. "You take the chair. I'll find another one."

Theo frowned. "No, you sit. You're exhausted."

"And your ankle hurts."

"I'm fine."

I crossed my arms. "So am I."

"This is stupid," Theo muttered. He sat in the chair. Then, before I could blink, he grabbed my waist and pulled me onto his lap. "There. That's better."

"I'm not too heavy?"

"Don't even." He adjusted his arms around me, one hand going to my hip.

But I wasn't planning on arguing. I put my head on his shoulder, breathed in all the Theo sort of smells—soap and citrus and comfort. My eyelids began to droop, the world growing blurry and muddled. His hand, warm and gentle, slid under the hoodie and sleep tank I had on. It found a patch of skin on my lower back and his thumb began to make small, soothing circles. It was the last thing I remember before falling asleep.

THIRTY-NINE

Note to self:
Nieces and tickles make life more fun.

Wednesday, four days before the wedding

A tiny monster flung herself across my stomach. "Wake up. Wake up."

"Oophf." I groaned and pulled a pillow over my face.

"Auntie Ali," Hallie said in a sing-songy voice. "Time for wake up."

"Hallie-girl, what time is it?"

She rolled off me. "Daddy, what time is it?"

"Nine in the morning," Abe said.

I groaned louder. "I don't want to get up."

Abe tugged on one of my feet. "That's what you get for staying out until six in the morning."

Ripping the pillow from my head, I glared at my brother. "I was out all night looking for your grandfather."

"He's your grandfather, too."

"Nope. I have officially disowned him. You boys can have him. Good luck." I sat up and rubbed my eyes.

"I told Theo I'd drive today. You two can sleep in the car."

"That's so nice of you."

He smirked. "I know. That's the kind of guy I am."

Hallie tugged on my shirt. "Are you getting up now?"

"Yes, yes. I'm getting up." I yawned and stretched my arms high. "But first, I think it's time for tickle fingers."

Hallie screeched and tumbled onto the far side of the bed. "No, no tickles."

Or I think that's what she said. She was giggling pretty hard. I crawled toward her, my hands held like claws.

"Daddy, save me," she said through her laughter.

"You are on your own there." With a grin, he stretched out on the other bed and watched until Hallie was limp with laughter.

I leaned down and whispered in her ear; she nodded her head so hard, her crooked ponytail bounced around. Her eyes drifted to Abe, a hand clasped on her mouth to hide her excitement.

"Ready?" I held up three fingers and counted silently. On one, we leapt off the bed and attacked.

Abe yelled and tried to scramble away but he was no match for two very motivated tickle monsters. In no time, we had him begging for us to stop in between laughs.

I flopped on the bed next to Abe, Hallie wedging her way between us. Her little hand found its way into mine. "I like having an aunt."

"I like having a niece."

She patted Abe's arm. "I like having a daddy."

Abe melted. Right there, in front of me. He turned his face away for a moment, but I saw the tears shining in his eyes. He kissed her forehead. "I like having a daughter."

Hallie patted him on his cheek and then slid from between us. "I gotta go potty."

"Close the door," Abe said.

Smiling, I stared at him.

"What?"

"You're a dad. It's so weird to see. You're good at it."

Abe blew out a breath. "I don't feel like it."

"Then you're faking it pretty good. The way you caught her puke in your hands the other day? That was a top-tier parent move. Impressive."

Abe winced. "Let's never mention it again."

"It's going in my Christmas letter." I mimed writing with a pen in the air. "Saw Abe after eleven years. Surprise! He has a daughter, and he can catch vomit in his hands. He's still single, ladies. Get on this."

"Very funny."

Smiling, I studied his profile, and a wave of emotions overwhelmed me. I fought back the strange urge to cry.

"Stop staring at me. It's weird."

"I'm really, really glad you're here."

He turned his head. "I'm really glad I'm here too."

"Daddy," Hallie yelled from the bathroom. "Daaaaad-ddddyyyy."

Abe took a deep breath. "What's wrong?"

"I pooped. Can you come help me wipe?"

I was still laughing when he opened the door and disappeared inside.

FORTY

Note to self:
Always lock the bathroom door.
(*Or not.*)

After Hallie and Abe left to find breakfast, I grabbed my change of clothes, shower bag, and headed for the bathroom. A shower would wake me up and I needed to wash off the lingering smell of 4 a.m. karaoke and pie.

I pulled up a playlist on my phone and cranked the volume. As I was about to turn on the water, I was sure I'd heard something in the bedroom. I paused the music to listen, but nothing seemed out of the ordinary. Maybe Abe had forgotten something.

It was when I was in the middle of belting a song out while using the conditioner as a microphone when the bottle slipped and landed with a loud, ringing thump in the bathtub. I bent to pick it up just as the door to the bathroom flew open with so much force, it bounced against the wall. I screamed and dropped the bottle again.

"Alicia?"

Shoving wet hair from my face, I poked my head out from behind the shower curtain. "Theo?"

His whole body sagged. "Alicia. You scared me."

"I scared *you*." The nerve. I straightened, hearing my voice rise with each word. "You burst in on me while I was taking a shower. Why are you even in my room?"

Theo spun around to face the door. "Careful. The curtain's slipping."

I yanked it up. "Why are you in here?"

"Abe let me in. I know you didn't get a lot of sleep, so I thought I'd bring you coffee and I heard a crash and thought you'd..." His voice trailed off.

"Had a seizure?" I wanted to scream. "Get out of here. Now."

I finished the shower quickly and angrily. Yes, it turns out you can shower angrily. My loofah will never be the same and you know what else? I loved that loofah, and it was ruined now. Whose fault is that? I also applied body lotion angrily (good skin care should never be skipped, after all). I brushed my teeth angrily. I got dressed angrily. You get the picture. I. Was. Angry.

I whipped the door open to confront Theo. He was sitting on the bed with his elbows resting on his knees and his head hanging, a little like a man defeated.

"Seriously?" I marched up to him ready for a confrontation, my wet hair dripping everywhere.

Confront someone? This was not my MO. This was Mae's MO. But the anger vibrating through me needed a release.

"I'm sorry." Theo lifted his head, his skin pale. "You didn't get a lot of sleep and I know it can be a trigger for you. When I heard that crash, I thought something had happened and you'd fallen. Maybe you were hurt and... and it scared me."

"Did I not tell you last night you were the one person who didn't treat me like I was going to break any second?"

"Yes."

My hands curled into fists. "You can't be like them, Theo. I cannot handle one more person who treats me like that. Do you know what that feels like? To be the person everyone is always, always worried about?"

"No, I—"

I paced the area in front of the two beds, stepping over a pile of dolls Hallie had been playing with earlier. "Let me tell you. It's the worst. It's awful to know I keep my mom up at night with worry. It doesn't seem to matter I am a fully capable adult. All my family ever seems to see is a teenage girl who could blow any minute." I paused and pressed a hand to my chest. "You are different. Or you're supposed to be."

"Alicia..."

"No, don't you Alicia me and try to get on my good side."

"I'm not trying to get on your good side." He stood. "I'm trying to say I'm sorry."

"Fine. Whatever. I accept your stupid apology."

"Yeah, it sounds like it. I am sorry for bursting in on you. But I'm not sorry for being worried."

"Then I don't accept your stupid apology."

Throwing up his hands, he growled, "I don't want to see you get hurt. What is wrong with that?"

"Why would you even care?" I blurted out.

"Really?" he said with no small amount of amazement.

"Yes, really." I poked him in the chest. How had he gotten so close to me? "I could kick myself for saying all those things last night."

His eyes fixed on me with that laser-like intensity. "You remember what you said last night."

"You are missing the point here." I stuck my fists on my hips. "You could have knocked on the door at least."

"I did. You must have not heard me over the music. I want to go back to the thing about you remembering our conversation. Do you? Remember it?"

"I'm not sure." I bit my bottom lip.

"You're lying."

"How do you know that?"

"Because I know all about you, too, Ali. I know when you're sad or happy or about to bring down the patriarchy with one well-placed banana."

I took a tiny step back and crossed my arms. "I'm way past bananas at this point."

"Ali." He said my name, not in anger or exasperation, but I couldn't quite place the tone; it did strange things to my pulse.

I closed my eyes. "Yes, okay. I remember everything."

The air in the room changed, became almost electric.

"Open your eyes," he said quietly. He'd moved closer, close enough that I could feel his words on my skin, and I shuddered.

Swallowing the lump of pure, unadulterated fear in my stomach, I did as he asked. His hands hovering over my shoulders like he wanted to touch me but wasn't sure he should.

"I said some embarrassing things last night. And while I remember every single word, I was a little tipsy, so it wasn't like I was serious."

A corner of his mouth hitched. He could see right through me. "Have you been drinking this morning?"

"No."

"So, say it again."

"Say what?"

"Say you want me to kiss you again."

I sucked in a breath. "Why?"

His hands curled around my shoulders. Goosebumps exploded over my skin as they traveled from there slowly up my neck. "Because I want to kiss you. But I won't if you don't want me to."

One of his thumbs traced the line of my jaw and it was getting hard to think. I should ask questions. Like, what does it mean if we kiss? That was a pretty big question that needed a pretty big answer but as I stared up into those blue, blue eyes, nothing mattered. I'd worry about the consequences later.

"I really want you to kiss me," I whispered.

FORTY-ONE

Note to self:
Pretending like everything is fine is my fatal flaw.

That first kiss was tender, a million feelings packed into one little chaste brush of our lips. He placed that first one right on the center of my mouth. Then on each corner. The tip of my nose. My eyelids, and that tickled a little and made me smile. But every kiss felt reverent, like he had been given a gift and he was going to unwrap it slowly and savor it.

Tentatively, I rested my hands on his chest where his heart thumped as rapidly as mine. He was solid and warm through his t-shirt, and I wanted to sink into it. I ran a hand up to his head and into his hair. The curls were softer than I expected, and I made a little sound of approval.

He grew bolder. A nibble on my bottom lip made me gasp and he deepened the kiss. His hand, low on my back, pulled me closer until there was only room left to do much more than breathe and I was only doing that sparingly.

You know when you're a kid and you wanted something so badly, you begged, pleaded, dreamed, wished, and hoped for it?

But when you finally got it, you'd built it up so much in your mind, that the reality of it wasn't nearly as good as what was in your head.

This was not that.

This, I couldn't have dreamed up because nothing had ever felt so right, like coming home. With a groan, Theo pulled away and rested his forehead on mine, his breaths coming fast and erratic.

"Can we do that again?" I asked.

He laughed and cupped my face. This kiss started languid and slow and made all my insides pool at my feet. But not for long. He shuffled forward until I was forced to inch back or fall. My back hit the wall. One of his hands slid down to my hip, finding the strip of skin between my shorts and t-shirt and stroking. My whole body went hot and cold and then hot again.

Theo pulled away and rested his forehead on the wall by my head. Most of his body pinned me to the wall and I slumped there, too weak-kneed and in such a Theo-induced coma to even think about moving.

I did try to talk. Sort of. "I, you, we..."

His shoulders shook.

"You are not laughing right now."

He turned his head, smiling broadly. "That was one way to make you forget you were mad at me. I'll remember that."

I slugged him in the arm, pushed off the wall, and wandered across the room. I wished I could laugh, but instead of savoring the best kiss of my life, an unease settled in my chest. It must have been written on my face because when I turned around, Theo frowned and moved toward me.

"What's wrong?"

I swallowed and put some distance between us. "What did that mean? That kiss?"

"What do you mean?" Those two little tick marks between his eyebrows appeared, and his body tensed.

"I can't play pretend or... or just have fun. Not with you. If that didn't mean something to you, then I want to know now."

His shoulders relaxed. "Ali."

"Yeah."

"I thought I made that clear."

"No, no, you did not. You've been confusing me for the last five days." I began to pace. "You've been flirty and touchy-feely and, I don't know, all intense stares, and I have no idea what it means."

"It means..."

I held up my hand. "Let me finish." My stomach dipped. I didn't want to say any of this. Fight through it, Ramos. Be brave. "We both know I had a thing... no, I'm being brave, I *have* a thing for you. I-I really, really like you. It took a long time to get over it when I was a kid. You don't know how much you broke my heart. I know, I was sixteen and dumb, and you did the right thing, I'm not blaming you. But it still hurt. A lot. I've had to work hard to be okay with us being friends. Really hard."

Theo sat on the edge of the bed, his eyes following me as I walked back and forth.

"I don't know if I can handle getting over you again. I'm supposed to be on a Love Sabbatical. I'm taking a break from all this love crap but here I am, trapped with the guy I've been half in love with for half my life and he's been clear we're only friends and now he's kissing me. What am I supposed to do with that?"

My breath was coming quickly, and I wondered if I was having a panic attack. Wouldn't that be something?

Doctor: What triggers your panic attacks?

Me: Driving. Oh, and sharing my deeply held feelings with a man I am ninety-five percent in love with. Now, how about some Xanax?

"You done?" Theo asked quietly.

I steeled myself and nodded.

He waited until I walked by him again and snagged my hand to pull me closer until I stood between his legs. I stared at my bare feet. "I really, really like you, too, Ali. I haven't been trying to give you mixed signals. I've been trying to figure out how to tell you that."

I braved a glance at his face. Pink stained his cheeks, and I thought maybe he was having trouble getting this out too.

"I'm not sure I'm good relationship material." The words tumbled out of my mouth. "Maybe I'm too selfish or... or too emotionally distant... or just a little too damaged."

"Ali, you are not damaged."

A humorless laugh tumbled from my mouth. "I am, at least a little." I tapped a finger to my head. "Weirdly wired brain. I could short-circuit at any second and have a seizure. There's no guarantee that one won't happen fifteen minutes from now. I might never be able to drive and... and what if one day, I become someone's mom. It will always be in the back of my mind. I could have a seizure while I'm alone with my kid. And..."

He picked up both my hands and laced our fingers together. "I've never heard you talk like this. Where is this coming from?"

I shrugged. "Alec said some things when we broke up about how I was 'emotionally unavailable' and 'closed off.'"

Theo's eyes grew wide and then narrowed. "What an ass."

"He broke up with me through a text and blocked my number so I couldn't reply. Started dating two days after we broke up."

"I amend my previous statement," he said, his voice grim. "This is an ass and a tool."

I couldn't help but smile at how outraged he sounded on my behalf. "I've never told anyone that. Don't be too mad at him. I think he's right about some of those things. I don't share my feelings, my real feelings. I hide a lot. I'm in plain sight, but I'm hiding. Smiling and going with the flow. And no one seems to question it, you know?"

He tugged until I sat on one of his legs. One of his hands cupped my cheek. "I see you."

The thing was that I believed him. He did see me. Maybe he always had.

"Hey, no crying." He caught the tears with his thumbs.

I sniffled. "Sorry. I think this entire road trip has flipped me upside down."

"That's not a bad thing. Sometimes when we get flipped upside down, we start to see things for how they really are." He pressed his forehead to mine.

"Like you? Not that I didn't know you. I don't know all of you."

He kissed the tip of my nose. "I don't want to screw this up."

"What does that mean?"

His gaze turned thoughtful. "Maybe we take our time. I'm not going anywhere and you're not going anywhere."

"You promise?" My voice cracked. "Are you sure you want to see where this might go?"

"I know where I want it to go." His eyes locked on mine and my heart flipped right there in my chest. And something else happened at that moment.

I fell all the way, one hundred percent in love with Theo Goodnight.

FORTY-TWO

Note to self:
Make reading a daily habit.

Mae: *Question.*

Me: *Yes.*

Mae: *Would you rather have a fundraiser in September or October?*

Me: *For what?*

Mae: *Campaign funds. You'll need a little money for expenses. We're thinking of a nice luncheon. We'll charge per head.*

Ellie: *I'll do all the cooking. I was thinking chicken-fried steak with a side of mashed potatoes, sweet peas.*

Ellie: *I'll make my rolls. You know how good my rolls are.*

***Ellie**: They bring all the boys to the yard.*

***Me**: I am not running for mayor.*

***Ellie**: And pie. Lots of pie. So much pie.*

***Me**: Stop talking about food. I'm hungry now.*

***Mae**: I think we have Peter in a real panic. Someone leaked his plan for Legacy Park and the good people of Two Harts are not happy about it.*

***Me**: Really?*

***Mae**: Yup. You're going to kick his ass based on that alone.*

***Ellie**: You totally are. Everyone's wearing the t-shirts we made, too. I'm wearing mine right now. Look, here's a picture.*

A selfie of Ellie popped up, half her face cut off to showcase the shirt she was wearing.

***Me**: Is that my face on that shirt?!*

***Ellie**: You like it?*

***Me**: Can we please change the subject since I AM NOT RUNNING FOR MAYOR?*

***Mae**: Fine. Has Theo made his move yet?*

***Me**: MAYBE?*

***Ellie**: Wait? What?*

Mae: *What does that mean?*

Mae: *Alicia Grace Ramos! What? Does? That? Mean?*

Ellie: *Did something happen?*

Mae: *Ali!!!!!!*

Once we got on the road, my plan was to make up for the sleep I'd lost last night. And although my body was exhausted, my mind would not stop. It kept looping back around to this morning and those kisses and what it all meant.

It was smart for us to keep this all under wraps for now, of course it was. I would have to fight my natural urge to scream this news from the rooftops, then send out a group text, and start looking at wedding announcements. My journal entry tonight was going to be epic.

But taking it slow was good. If this didn't work out, I didn't want it to be ugly. My family was also Theo's family in all the ways that matter. I never wanted to put him in a place where he was alone in this world. But seeing him at family functions and dinners and going back to pretending we were just friends might break me. There were consequences to us being an us. We needed to think through those.

Then, with the wedding in a few days, I didn't want to overshadow Cal and Melanie's wedding or Abe's homecoming. There'd be time for us to figure everything out. Like Theo said, neither of us was going anywhere.

While that all sounded very mature and adult of me, sixteen-year-old me was losing her mind right now. Sixteen-year-old me was kicking her feet in the air and deciding when we'd have our first child. A giddy laugh bubbled up. I tried to swallow it, but Theo turned and raised an eyebrow.

I shook my head, grinning so widely my mouth hurt.

His return smile was small but no less potent. Because that smile was for me and me only. Giddy delight blossomed in my chest. I yawned and started shifting around to find a good position to sleep in.

"I'm going to take a nap," I said.

Then, because I could, I leaned forward and ran my fingertips over the back of Theo's neck. This time, he was the one who shivered.

After three blissful hours, I woke feeling oddly refreshed for a woman who had a crick in her neck from sleeping at a weird angle and drool all over her pillow. At some point, Theo and Abe changed seats and Theo was driving again. Hallie was out cold, her head dangling by the strap on her car seat. Next to her, Abe wore headphones, but the tinny sound of music was still audible. He'd always loved his music loud. Got in trouble all the time when we were growing up for it.

Since I was awake, I pulled out the Alicia Night book, *The Pirate's Booty*, the one I'd started last night before the hunt for Mack. It took no time for me to get hooked into the story: There's a young woman desperately trying to get away from her father who was forcing her to marry an old, lecherous, but very rich, lord. She hears of a pirate who has been known to help a damsel in distress... for a price. After a faked kidnapping, our lady finds herself on a pirate ship headed for the Americas. Trapped with a handsome, dashing pirate and so much extra time on her hands? Whatever could possibly happen?

A lot, it turns out.

"On the plank?" I gasped. "Is that even physically possible?"

"What's that?" Mack asked from the front seat.

Oh, no. I'd said that out loud.

Even though he'd gotten as little sleep as I did, Mack had been upbeat, happy, and smiling since the moment I saw him this morning. It could have been that goodbye kiss Mimi gave him right before we left though. Karen's head peeked around his arm and growled when she heard my voice.

"Oh, shut up, Karen," I muttered.

"Don't talk to her that way." Mack cradled the mutt in his arms. "She's sensitive."

"Yeah, yeah. She looks real fragile."

"Now what's this about a plank?"

"How about lunch?" Theo asked, his eyes making the briefest of contact with mine in the rearview mirror. "We should be hitting a bigger town in the next hour."

"Sure. Sure," Mack said, but then like an old man with a history obsession, he asked again. "What's this about a plank?"

"I'm reading a book."

"About pirates?"

"Yeah. About pirates on the high seas and all that."

"Sounds interesting. What's it called?"

"It's called... um..." I couldn't say the real title, of course. Too many questions from Mack and too much teasing from Abe when he discovered it was a romance novel. I scrambled to make something up. "Um, *Swashbucklers: The Historical Significance of Pirates From 1775 to 1850*. It's, ah, riveting."

"That does sound good."

"Theo recommended it," I blurted out. "He knows all about pirates. Practically a pirate expert."

Even from the back in the cheap seats, I saw Theo's ear grow red.

"Is that so?" Mack asked.

Theo cleared his throat. "Thanks for sharing that with everyone, Ali."

"You're welcome."

While Theo answered the bazillion questions Mack sent his way, I drew my phone back out and soon lost myself in the story again. We'd just pulled into the parking lot of a burger joint when I hit chapter fourteen.

My jaw dropped. "No. In the crow's nest?"

Theo began to cough.

"I got to read this book," Mack said. "I hope my library has a copy of it."

But I'll admit it, I wasn't listening; I was reading that scene again. For historical research purposes, of course.

FORTY-THREE

Note to self:
Put a tracking device on Mack.

Reno

The sun was setting, and the temperature was dropping with it when we checked into a hotel in Reno. We ate at a small diner, all crowded around a corner booth. At dinner, I made Mack swear he wouldn't meet some crazy woman and follow her all over the city.

"Mimi wasn't crazy." He held up his phone. "She gave me her number."

"Way to go, Gramps." Abe held up his fist and Mack bumped it with his. "I liked her."

"I liked her, too." I pointed with my fork. "What I didn't like was spending the wee hours of the morning traipsing around Vegas looking for you."

"And trying to wrangle both of you was not fun," Theo said. "That woman was very handsy."

"I know," Mack said like it was his favorite thing about her.

"Mack. Promise."

"Alright. I promise. I'll be a good boy tonight." He chuckled. "Have to say, I haven't felt that young in a long time. It felt good to get out and do something different. But all that dancing got to my knees."

"And I'm sure all that alcohol got to your liver."

"Daddy, what does handsy mean?" Hallie looked up from the coloring sheet the server had given her.

"Ah, it means," he shot me a bewildered look, "someone has nice hands."

"Oh." Hallie held her hands out. "Am I handsy?"

"Sure."

Hallie nodded and went back to coloring.

"So, tomorrow, we'll make it to Portland?" Abe stared into his empty soda glass.

"Yep. Should get there in early evening." Theo reached for the salt and pepper, leaning into me more than he needed to.

And that's also when he put his hand on my knee.

I'd somehow managed to sit between him and Abe, which didn't seem like a bad thing until Theo started to inch closer and closer. I wasn't even sure he was moving until his thigh pressed against my thigh and his foot captured my foot under the table.

But never once did his facial expression give anything away. Never once did he falter in conversation. I, on the other hand, not so much.

"You okay over there, Ali-Cat?" Mack asked. "You looked flushed. Are you getting sick?"

"No." I winced as my voice squeaked. "I'm totally fine. Just tired, I guess."

I shot Theo a pointed look, which he ignored. But his mouth curved into one of those secret smiles and his hand moved a tiny bit higher on my leg, fingertips brushing the edge of my shorts.

"How do you think it will go tomorrow?" Abe ran the back of his hand over his mouth.

"Nervous?" I asked.

"I guess. I don't know what to expect, you know? They really have no idea I'm coming."

"Cal wanted to keep it a surprise. He didn't even tell Frankie because Frankie..."

"...would tell Mom." Abe grinned. "At least some things never change. He used to be such a tattletale when we were kids. You remember?"

I snorted. "He still is. He is on my 'need-to-know' list and there are a lot of things he doesn't need to know."

"I love that guy," Abe said.

I wrinkled my nose. "He's alright."

Under the table, Theo's thumb began to make those little soft circles. I sucked in an audible breath. I knew I'd told him too much during that confession. Damn him.

"Are you sure you aren't getting sick?" Mack asked.

"I'm fine. I am not getting sick. Actually, I need to go to the restroom." I shoved at Theo's arm, urging him to stand.

When he finally took the hint, I scrambled out and hoofed it down the back hallway. Once I got a look at myself in the bathroom mirror, I understood why Mack was concerned. Two bright-red spots had taken over my cheeks. How could one man do this to me with a few small touches? And more importantly, would he do it again? Please.

With a giggle, I pulled open the door and stepped out, right into someone.

"Oh, I'm sorr—" I glanced up and smiled. "Are you stalking me?"

"Maybe." Theo grabbed my hand and pulled me deeper into the hallway. "I just wanted to do this."

I thought he might kiss me, which I was more than happy to go along with. Instead, his arms wrapped around me, and he pulled me close, burying his face in that sensitive spot where my neck meets my shoulder.

"Are you sniffing me?" I asked.

He nodded, still not moving.

"Are you okay?" But then I gasped when I felt the gentle scrape of teeth on my neck and goosebumps exploded on my skin. "Did you just bite me?"

He nodded again.

"Did you not get enough to eat at dinner?"

With a low laugh, he lifted his head. "I wanted to hug you, okay? Nothing wrong with that."

I bit my bottom lip. "Just... hug?"

His smile was slow. "What else did you have in mind?"

I grabbed a handful of his t-shirt and pulled him down just enough to give him a peck on his mouth. "Something like that."

"I don't know. That wasn't very exciting."

"No?" I tapped my lip with a finger. "What would make it more exciting, you think?"

"Maybe this?" His fingers slid into my hair. He leaned down and stopped a heartbeat from my mouth. "Hey, Ali?"

"Yeah?"

"I really, really like you." He whispered the words against my lips, his eyes watching me intently.

My stomach whooshed in the best way. "I really, really like you, too."

Then neither of us said another word seeing as how our mouths were otherwise occupied.

When we got back to the table, Abe took one look at me and raised a very suspicious eyebrow. Nervously, I ran my fingers through my hair but there was nothing I could do about the goofy, blissed-out expression on my face. I'd gone back into the bathroom; I'd tried to get myself together. This was the best I could do.

Thankfully, Mack was in the middle of lecturing him about seeing our parents tomorrow, so he didn't have time to comment. No, I bet he'd save that for tonight in our hotel room.

"You and your father have never been able to see eye to eye," Mack said. "Both of you, stubborn as rocks. I know he's made mistakes. And I know you've made mistakes. But it's time to fix it, get over it, do what needs to be done. You've wasted eleven years of your life. Don't waste one more."

Abe shifted in his seat. "It's not that easy, Mack. There's a lot of history there and—"

Max slammed his glass down and all of us at the table, even Hallie, jumped. "Damn it all. When Gracie died, I wasn't sure life would go on for me. She was my best friend. We were married for fifty-seven years. She was my other half, my better half. I miss her every day." His eyes grew unfocused and misty.

I laid a hand on his arm. "We all miss her, Mack."

That snapped him out of his memories. He stabbed a finger on the table. "What I mean to say is this: you don't know how long you have with a person. It could be fifty-seven years, or it could be five months. What would happen if something happened to your father, and you never got the chance to make things right? Any time you have with someone you love is worth it. Don't waste it being angry."

"Daddy," Hallie whispered, her eyes concerned. "Is Mack okay?"

Mack stood and pulled his wallet from his back pocket. He dropped a few bills on the table and then held his hand out to Hallie. "Come on, darling, let's go see what trouble we can get into."

Hallie frowned. "I'm not a'pposed to get in trouble though."

"It's alright. Stick with me. I've been getting into trouble my whole life and look how old I am."

"I'm four but I'll be five on my next birthday soon. How old are you?"

"Why don't you guess?"

Hallie's face scrunched in concentration. "Twenty-seven?"

Mack grinned. "You got it. Twenty-seven years young. That's me." While Hallie climbed out of her chair, he gave Abe a hard look. "All I'm saying is sometimes you have to be the bigger person. Life is already too damn hard; don't make it harder on yourself if you can help it."

"Mack, if you can say damn, can I say damn?" Hallie asked as they walked away from the table leaving the rest of us in a stunned silence.

"I've never seen him that upset," I said.

"Yeah, I guess I said the wrong thing." He huffed a laugh and moved to the other side of the table now that we had more room.

"I think we're all a little nervous about how this will turn out. You aren't alone, though. Remember that."

He gave me a long, unwavering look. "I'll remember."

The server came by and refilled all our drinks.

"Speaking of how things turn out..." Crossing his arms, Abe sat back and gave Theo and me a speculative look. "So... you two are a thing now, huh?"

I almost spit out my water. "What?"

At the same time, Theo said, "Yes."

"Wait, what?" I glared at Theo. "I thought we agreed not to tell anyone until after the wedding and we figured out what this," I waved a hand between us, "is exactly."

Theo smirked. "Oh, right. I forgot."

I smacked him on the arm. "You forgot nothing."

"It's Abe. He's not going to tell anyone."

With a harrumph, I crossed my arms and scooted over to put a little space between us.

"I have eyeballs. There's no way you would have been able

to keep it a secret." With a grin, he pointed at Theo. "He can't stop staring at you like you hung the moon and," now he pointed at me, "you look like you're floating."

I ducked my head, my cheeks heating. "Are we that obvious?"

Abe rolled his eyes. "Yes."

"Whoops," Theo said. "That's too bad." He slid over, put an arm around my shoulders, and tucked me into his side. "I guess we're caught."

"It hasn't even been twenty-four hours." I frowned at Theo. "You're bad at this."

He leaned in, and right there in front of my brother, whispered, "That's not what you said a few minutes ago."

"Okay, well, that wasn't as quiet as you think it was, and gross, bro, that's my sister." Abe leaned forward, his expression serious. "You're two of my favorite people in this entire world. Don't screw this up, okay?"

Message received.

FORTY-FOUR

Note to self:
A good friend will tell you when you're wrong.
A best friend will bet on it.

"So, it finally happened. Yes!" Mae grinned at me from my phone screen. She had the phone propped up and was folding laundry. Which was a very Mae thing to do. Two birds, one stone, and all that. The woman did not know the meaning of taking it easy. "I knew it. This was my day. This was my day."

I narrowed my eyes. "Your day for what?"

She pressed her lips together, looking guilty. "We might have had a pool going on about you and Theo."

"What? Who?" I asked in outrage. "Who are these people?"

"I don't want to tell you now. I feel like there might be payback for this."

"Yeah, good feeling. I'll come for you first if you don't start sharing."

"We have a group text—"

"You have got to be kidding me."

"We're usually only active after the two of you have been seen together. But this whole trip has had us working overtime."

"What is the pool for?" I asked slowly.

She crushed a shirt to her chest. "Wellllll... It's a pool to see who can guess what day you two will finally figure it out. This was my day." She danced a little jig. "I won."

"You bet on my love life?"

"Just for the last couple of years."

"I was still dating Alec a couple of years ago," I said, not sure I should be outraged or amused.

"Pffsht. That thing with Alec was never gonna work out."

"You didn't know that."

"Yes, I did. I am your best friend. He was all wrong for you. It got even worse the longer you dated. In the beginning, he wasn't so bad, but there at the end, he was the worst. I wanted to punch him the last time he was in town and started talking about your clothes."

"I mean, I was wearing sweatpants on a date night."

"So? We were having a movie night. In your apartment. Wear a tutu and cowboy boots. How does that give him the right to get mad at you? Yeah, I should have punched him." She shook her head in disgust. "Theo cares about you, not what you wear or how messy your hair is or if you're too tired to go to a stupid cocktail party or that driving gives you panic attacks. Theo cares about *you*."

"Thanks," I said softly.

"Don't thank me for telling you the truth. Geez. Alec is a total juice canoe." She picked up a pair of socks and folded one into the other. "So, you get your man. Finally. I'm going to go collect my spoils."

"You never did tell me who else is in this pool."

"I'm not going to either. What happens in the group text, stays in the group text."

Smiling, I shook my head. "Mae."

"Yeah."
"I'm glad you're my friend."
"Same, Ali. Same."

Theo: *Are you awake?*

Theo: *Ali?*

Theo: *Alright then, just wanted to tell you goodnight.*

Theo: *And sweet dreams.*

Theo: *And that I really, really like you.*

FORTY-FIVE

Note to self:
The apple doesn't fall far from the tree.
Remember my family can be just as sneaky as me.

Thursday, three days before the wedding

Reno to Portland

A weird mix of nervousness and excitement filled the car when we left the next morning. Abe had gone silent and pensive, likely thinking about seeing our parents again. I was nervous, too. I didn't know how this would go and I worried it might all blow up in our faces.

But the other reason was that I knew I would have to confess my part in that accident. If it would help reunite my brother and parents, then it would be worth it. It was the right thing to do. I wanted to do it. Still, it felt huge and impossible, like scraping off a layer of skin so deep, the white meat was exposed.

Hallie must have sensed the mood because she happily put

on her headphones and settled in for a princess movie marathon. Even Mack was quieter than usual. Karen, on the other hand, had been restless. Instead of staying on Mack's lap, she'd crawled under our seats and was hiding somewhere. Probably planning my "accidental" death.

And Theo, too, had been off since earlier this morning when he'd gotten a phone call while we were eating breakfast. When he'd come back to the table, he'd seemed distracted.

"Everything okay?" I'd asked.

"Oh, yeah. Had a change in plans for that, uh, meeting. I'm going to have to take off after the wedding quicker than I thought. Especially since I need to get Abe home."

"Where is this meeting?"

"Chicago." His eyes widened ever so slightly as though he hadn't meant to say that out loud. "It's a work thing."

I stared at him an extra beat but let it drop. If I've learned anything over the last few days, there was a lot I didn't know about Theo. I wondered where he got his ideas for his books. And if he owned a pirate outfit. If I should invest in a wench costume. Was there cosplay involved? Yep, there were a lot of questions I had for Theo. I wanted the chance to ask them all, too.

He was familiar to me, and also not. My comfort person 2.0.

One more mystery would be fun to solve.

Famous last words, and all that.

Alec: *I hear you all are getting into Oregon today.*

I rolled my eyes and ignored the message.

Alec: *It would be nice to sit down before the wedding.*

Alec: *Dinner tonight?*

Alec: *Or we could go for drinks tonight.*

Me: *No, thank you.*

Alec: *Come on, Ali. Be an adult.*

With a growl, I tossed my phone down and glared out the window at the landscape of heavily treed mountains and rolling green hills.

Abe turned toward me. "You okay?"

"I..." I almost played it off as not a big deal. But for some reason, I didn't want to do that anymore. "Alec's been texting me. He wants to get together and talk."

Abe sneered. "That guy's an ass."

"You've never even met him," I pointed out.

"Don't need to. I've already heard enough about him."

"From who?"

"Take your pick. Theo. Mack. Cal. Even Frankie wasn't a fan."

"You didn't like him at all?" I raised my voice so the whole car could hear me.

"Who?" Mack asked.

"Alec. You didn't like him?"

"No," Mack and Theo said at the same time.

"Totally wrong for you," Mack said. "He seems like a fine enough man but I'm awfully glad he's gone."

"Why didn't anyone say something to me?" I demanded. "You could have saved me years of figuring that out on my own."

"Ali-Cat." Mack turned in his seat. "Sometimes you gotta let people come to things on their own. You are one of those people."

"I am?"

"Sure. You've never been one to let other people tell you

what to do. At least when it comes to the big things. We knew you'd figure that out. You have a good head on your shoulders. You get that from me."

"He wore way too much hair product," Theo muttered.

"That's for sure," Mack said.

"Hair product?" I repeated faintly, still not quite sure how to deal with these new revelations. But funnily enough, it wasn't anger I felt. Warmth tugged at my heart. It was nice to have so many people who were on your side.

"We're officially in Oregon," Mack said.

We all cheered, but not too much. Portland was still at least five hours away and the consensus was that that felt impossibly far.

Thirty-five minutes later, we pulled into the pizza place in Klamath Falls. After stocking up on snacks for the rest of the drive, we piled back into the car. I chatted with Mom for a little. They'd pushed themselves and had managed to make it to Oregon already. She gushed about how good Cal and Melanie looked and the precise placement of the tables at the reception and that she'd finally seen the Pacific Ocean.

"It was beautiful. And, oh, goodness, the Columbia Gorge, that's where the venue is, a little place called River Valley. It's not too far from Multnomah Falls. Wait until you see it."

"I can't wait," I said.

"So, you'll be here tonight?"

"About five hours."

She squealed. "Can't wait to see you. You've been feeling okay, right."

"Mom."

"Yes, yes. Chill out, Mom," she said with a little laugh. "By the way, I do have a bone to pick with you. I had my money on the day of the wedding. You know, Sunday, start of the new week, and I was sure that would be your moment."

"What are you talking about?"

"You and Theo, of course."

I gasped. "My own mother is part of that pool? I cannot believe it."

"Your father doubled down on Christmas last year. I don't know how many times he moved that mistletoe."

A funny little squeak comes from my throat. "Are you kidding? Is that how he fell off the ladder and sprained his ankle? Moving mistletoe because he was betting on my love life?"

Abe turned around, a question in his eyes. I shook my head.

"You know how competitive he is, honey," Mom said.

I dropped my forehead forward until my head hit the seat in front of me. "I cannot believe you people."

FORTY-SIX

Note to self:
~~*Kissing*~~ *Walking is a good form of exercise.*

Portland, Oregon

Cal and Melanie's apartment was located in northwest Portland, a fancy condo in an upscale neighborhood for "young professionals." We pulled up in front of it and I texted Cal to let him know we'd made it.

We all piled out onto the sidewalk, stretching legs and shaking arms to wake them up from the long drive. Mack clipped Karen to a leash, and she tiptoed in a circle, sniffing everything. Until she got to my feet. She growled, backed up, and barked.

"Shut up, Karen." I bent over and glared at her. "Why do you hate me?"

Being a dog, she couldn't answer back. Although she did bare her teeth.

"I am officially a cat person." I straightened.

Theo smiled. "And I was planning on getting you a dog for your birthday."

"Please don't."

He put his arm around my shoulders and pressed a kiss to my cheek. My eyes darted to Mack who smiled in an "I told you so" sort of way.

"Where are we, Daddy?" Hallie had her doll in a death grip against her chest. Her dark hair was mussed from traveling and she looked more than a little tired.

"We're here to see your Uncle Cal."

"I have an uncle?"

"You have two," his eyes dart to Theo, "no, make that three, uncles."

"And an aunt. And a grandma and grandpa." She shook her head like she couldn't quite believe it. "That's a lot of birthdays to 'member."

"Ali," a voice yelled from halfway down the block. The short, slender frame of my almost sister-in-law came barreling toward me. She didn't stop until her arms wrapped around me in a breath-stealing hug. "I can't believe you're here. Although, I am a little miffed. I lost a hundred bucks to Mae."

I detangled myself from her arms. "Is everyone in on this thing?"

"I lost two hundred. A fact Mae hasn't let me forget," Mack said. "Bit of a bragger, that one."

"Alright, that's enough. No more betting on Theo and me." I held my hand up to stop the chorus of protests. "Nope. No more. And someone owes us a cut of this."

"Aw, come on," Cal said, my own flesh-and-blood brother. "I just chose my days for the proposal."

"What?"

Cal grinned and hugged me. "You know I love you."

Abe cleared his throat. Hands tucked in his pockets, the vulnerability in his eyes made my heart squeeze.

Cal stepped toward him, inspecting him closely, his smile growing wider. "Brother."

"Brother." Abe nodded, his shoulders relaxing in relief.

And then they hugged; I wasn't the only one crying when they did.

* * *

"These are the seating arrangements." Melanie tapped yet another tab on the tablet resting on her lap, yet another category in her highly treasured digital Wedding Planner. Pages upon pages, crammed with décor ideas, venue choices, menu options, cake topper ideas, and anything else a person could possibly need for a wedding. Just looking at it overwhelmed me.

"This is what the boutonnieres look like. Aren't they beautiful? They go so well with the bouquets. I got a great deal on the flowers. And... Ali, are you listening?"

"Sort of."

With a sigh, Melanie put the tablet to sleep and held it against her chest like it was a precious thing. "I didn't mean to bore you."

"You aren't." It wasn't her fault Theo was fifteen feet away, in a little group with Abe and Cal. Every now and then, the three let out a roar of laughter that made me smile. It felt like when we were younger, before Abe left, before we all grew up and scattered.

It also wasn't her fault he'd turned his hat backwards and every time I stole a glance at him, his eyes were on me and they were smiling, and I wanted to forget about everything else and get him alone.

"Oh, my gosh. You have the cutest dreamy smile on your face right now. Whoever could you be thinking about?" Melanie's peal of laughter rang like a bell, her dark eyes twinkling. "You've got it bad."

"I do not." I totally did.

"You never looked at Alec that way." Her tone was matter-of-fact.

I jerked my eyes to her, the happy feeling draining from me. This was awkward. "I didn't... I don't..."

She smiled. "It's okay. I don't remember Alec looking at you the way Theo does either."

"Still, he's your brother and I don't want to make anything weird this weekend. I promise I won't. No weirdness."

"No weirdness. Got it." Melanie patted me on the leg. "Maybe the whole reason you and Alec met was to set Cal and me up."

"Four years of my life seems like a long game just to set someone up."

With a shrug, Melanie stood. "I guess I believe people come into your life for a reason, even if they don't stick around. Alec wasn't all bad, right?" She gave my ponytail a tug. "I'm going to put you out of your misery now. Besides, someone's coming your way."

"Wanna go for walk?" Theo held out a hand.

I took it with a smile. Before leaving, Cal promised to let me know when my parents planned to show up. Having arrived before noon, they'd decided to do some sightseeing.

Theo and I didn't speak as we made our way out onto the sidewalk and when we did, he kept his hand linked with mine. Trees canopied the hilly streets as we set out without a destination in mind.

A park boasting a walking trail appeared, and we found ourselves wandering a dirt trail, shaded by enormous pine trees, sprawling maples, and oak trees with great, thick trunks. A breeze rustled the leaves and cooled the air. All of it was so different from the endless plains of Texas, so flat you could watch the path of the sun until it sank below the horizon.

We stepped into a small clearing, most of the sunshine

blotted out by the trees. The birds chirped happily, and a few fat bees hovered over a grouping of bull thistle. I dropped Theo's hand and spun in a circle. "It's breathtaking."

"Yeah, it is." But when I looked back at him, he wasn't looking at the trees or a squirrel checking us out from behind a bush or the moss climbing a fallen limb. No, his eyes were on me. The dragon wings fluttered.

I blushed, unexpectedly shy. Suddenly, I wished I'd put a bit more effort into my outfit this morning, but cutoff shorts and an ancient Buc-ee's t-shirt would have to do.

Somehow both of us moved until we met in the middle of the clearing, only a few inches apart. A light breeze blew a piece of my hair across my face and Theo gently tucked it behind my ear.

He smiled, the corners of his eyes crinkling. "Hi."

My face grew warmer. "Hi."

"We made it."

"We did. It's been the longest six days of my life. Thanks for driving me. I know—"

But I never got to finish the sentence because he kissed me, slow and sweet, only our lips touching, and somehow that seemed the perfect thing in this perfect little hidden spot in the forest.

When he pulled back, my eyes drifted open. "That was nice."

"Ali." He took a huge breath, and something like apprehension slid into his eyes. "I really, really, really like you."

"That's a lot of reallys."

"All true." He brushed my cheek with his hand. "I need to talk to you about something and—"

My phone rang; I winced. "Sorry. I better get that."

Cal didn't even let me get a greeting out. "Hey, Mom and Dad are back."

FORTY-SEVEN

Note to self:
Kids are the perfect icebreaker.
Maybe ask to borrow Hallie.

By the time we made it back to the apartment, my parents were standing in the middle of a very silent living room. Mom's face was pale, her gaze darting between the son she hadn't seen in eleven years and the granddaughter she hadn't known existed. But it was Dad, his eyes shining with unshed tears, that we all watched. And we waited. To see how he would react, what he'd say.

If this meeting would go very, very badly.

It was Hallie who made the first move. Still clutching that baby doll with the wild hair, she marched up to Dad, tilted her head back, and pursed her lips. "You look like my daddy."

Dad's eye widened. "Hi."

"'Cept Daddy has hair on his head, and he has pictures all over him and he smiles all the time. You aren't smiling. Why?"

"Uh, well." He dropped to a knee. "I guess because I'm surprised."

"Oh," Hallie breathed. "I love 'sprises." Her brow wrinkled as she glanced around the room. "What's the 'sprise?"

Dad cleared his throat. "You are."

"You're funny." Hallie giggled. She held her hands out in front of her, fingers spread wide. "I got a 'sprise. I'm handsy."

"You are?" Dad shot a confused glance toward us.

"Uh-huh. It means I have nice hands. Are you handsy?"

"I've never thought about it." A smile spread across his face. "I'm your grandpa."

"Ooooh," she breathed. "I've never had a grandpa afore. Can I hug you?"

Dad sat on the floor and cleared his throat again. I will swear forever that my loud, disgruntled father, who laughed at the sad parts of movies, including the scene when Bambi's mother dies, had tears in his eyes. Real, actual tears. He held his arms open. "I'd like that a lot."

"Good idea getting a kid," I said quietly, sitting on the arm of the couch next to my brother. On his other side was our mother, who had been beside herself. She'd hugged Abe so long, even I got uncomfortable. We'd had to gently pry her arms from him, although she'd refused to completely let go of him and was even at this moment clinging to his arm.

Abe snorted. "Yes. It was my plan all along. Father a child I didn't know about and use her to unite our family."

"She is pretty awesome."

"Agreed."

Both of us looked over at Dad, who'd already been conned into wearing a princess tiara and reading books with Hallie curled up in his lap. They'd been cuddled up like that for over an hour and while it was hard not to smile when I looked at them together, it was clear Dad planned to avoid the elephant in the room as long as possible. The one with all the tattoos and piercings.

"Has he said anything to you?" I asked.

Abe's shoulders slumped. "No. He nodded his head in my general direction but otherwise, nothing."

"Don't get discouraged," I hurried to say. "Give him a little time. We sprung this on him."

"I hope you're right." But he didn't sound optimistic.

Frankie and Ruth joined us a little later. Abe teased Frankie for still being the shortest of the brothers.

"Hey, I have the biggest guns though," he said, and proceeded to take us all to the "gun show" by flexing his arms.

"You're such a meathead," I said.

"He's sexy," Ruth said, gazing at Frankie with hearts in her eyes. You know what they say about a lid for every pot. That pot and lid had definitely found each other.

Melanie burst into the middle of our group, her eyes wild, and waved her phone around. "No. No. No."

"Honey, what's wrong?" Cal put an arm around her shoulders.

"The weather forecast. It's just been updated and... and..." She shoved the phone in his face, her eyes filling with tears. "Rain. So much rain. It's supposed to start tomorrow and go for the next five days."

"We planned for this. Remember? We have that tent on backup."

"But... but it won't be the same. Everything is falling apart." Melanie threw her arms around Cal.

Mack stepped forward, cradling Karen in his arms. "I'm sure it will be okay."

Melanie straightened, sniffling. "Nothing is going to be okay. The personalized labels for the water bottles aren't going to make it. The deluxe nut mix I ordered in bulk is mostly peanuts. My mother hates Portland, and one of the bridesmaids and one of the groomsmen are probably going to get in a fist fight during the ceremony. And... and... the napkins are white instead of cream. It's all going to be a disaster."

Abruptly, Mom stood, a smile plastered on her face. "You know what we need."

We all swung our heads in her direction.

"We need pictures. We need pictures *now*."

So, we spent forty-five minutes getting more pictures than any one person needed. Theo offered to take them for us so the "whole family" could be in them, and the idea of that made me sad. Theo should be in these photos, too.

"What are you doing?" I said. "Set a timer and get in here with us. You're part of this family."

Theo hesitated.

"Of course, Theo." Mom waved him over. "You've always been part of our family."

Even through all of that, Dad was careful to stay on the opposite side of the room, never getting close enough to Abe to require words be spoken between the two of them. After we finished and someone ordered us pizza, I watched Dad duck out on the patio. I followed and found him sitting at a little wrought-iron table that had a citronella candle working overtime to keep the mosquitoes away.

"Can I join you?" I asked.

"Of course."

I sat next to him, but we didn't speak. At least not for a while. Dad and I were like that. We were okay with silence. Which was the exact opposite of Mom, who couldn't stop talking.

"Wish I had a cigarette."

"You don't smoke."

"Oh, I used to. When I met your mother in college, I

smoked all the time. Then she nagged and nagged until I stopped." He stretched his legs out and crossed them at the ankles. "I don't wish for one often, but tonight, a smoke sounds real nice."

"Sorry I can't help you there."

"Eh. It's not good for me, anyway." He rolled his eyes. "And God forbid I did, and your mother smelled it on me. I'd never hear the end of it."

"You and Mom are so weird."

His smile was small but sincere. "I love your mother. No other woman out there for me."

"Even if she drives you crazy sometimes."

"Especially when she drives me crazy."

I laughed softly. "Are you okay? I know we kind of sprung all this on you."

"Yes and no." I could tell he wanted to say more so I waited. "Yes, because I've missed him. Your mother, you kids, we've all missed him. He never should have been gone this long. And now there's a grandbaby. It's a lot to wrap my head around."

"She's pretty cute though."

He chuckled. "She looks just like you when you were little."

"Like I said, she's pretty cute."

"Yeah, yeah." He flicked the tip of my nose, like he's done since I was a kid.

"So, what's the part about you not being okay?"

A long breath escapes him. "Sometimes a person does things they regret. It's hard to face those things. Especially when that thing is the son you drove out of your house. He's so damn different from me, from your brothers. Look at all those tattoos, and what the hell is wrong with his ears? Are those holes on purpose?"

"They're called gauges and... you know, never mind. I'll explain later. You finish."

"I never knew how to talk to him. Still don't."

"Is that why you're avoiding him?"

"You noticed, huh?" His shoulders deflated. "I don't know how to mend it, how to make this better, and I regret all those years we missed out on having Abe in our lives because I was too stubborn to get over myself."

I swallowed a lump of my own regret. Dad and I, we had a lot in common when it came to this subject. Ironically, my regret was tied to his regret.

"I gotta figure out what to say to him." He frowned. "I don't want to screw it up again."

I put a hand on his arm. "Maybe the first step is telling *him* all this."

"Huh. Maybe so."

We settled back into silence, although it felt less comfortable now, more contemplative. It was funny how we forget our parents are people, too. My father was as human and riddled with as many fears and regrets as the next person. He also happened to be my dad. He wasn't the infallible superhero I was sure he was when I grew up.

From inside, I could hear Mom asking Hallie all sorts of questions about her favorite color to her favorite food. Like Grandma Grace used to ask me. Hallie giggled at something Mom said and I couldn't help smiling at the sound.

Any doubt I had about this surprise reunion disappeared. I had a feeling it wasn't going to be all sunshine and rainbows. Maybe this was the calm before the storm. But for now, bringing Abe here gave us all a chance to start to fix what was broken.

Eventually, Dad broke the silence.

"So, tell me about these holes in his ears. What did you call them again? Gadgets?"

FORTY-EIGHT

Note to self:
Make sure the next hotel I stay at is "pest" free.

"Oh, Karen, you didn't." But I was staring at the evidence. She totally did.

The open shoebox held one and a half perfectly intact cream-colored wedge sandals. And also, one half of a chewed up cream-colored wedge sandal.

"I found the box sort of wedged under the backseat. I don't know how she did it." Theo sounded almost impressed.

"Hate. She was fueled by pure hate for me." I held up the mangled shoe. It was still soggy. Gross. "Why does she hate me?"

"She doesn't hate you." He rubbed my back.

"Right." I dangled the poor damaged shoe by a finger. "Melanie is going to lose her mind."

"Over a shoe?"

I laughed a little too loud. "Did you not hear her earlier? She's been planning this wedding for a year. She has a vision. Any time something doesn't match up to the vision, it's a nightmare. Did you know she had a dream about her wedding colors?"

He shook his head.

"Oh, yeah. One morning, a couple of weeks after they got engaged, she sent a group text to all of us in which she described the color pink she saw in her dream as 'pink but not too pink with a bit of orange but not too much orange and a hint of purple.' That color does not exist."

"It is her wedding," Theo said.

"I swear if I ever get married, I want something simple. Like in the summer, maybe June before it gets too hot, in front of the Legacy Tree on a random Thursday afternoon with just family and a few friends." I began to picture this scene in my head. It would be small and romantic and perfect. "I don't even think I want a traditional wedding dress. Something white but simple, knee-length, and a few flowers in my hair. Afterward, we'll go to the Sit-n-Eat and have a big celebration."

"If you get married?"

"Someone has to ask me first." I patted him on the chest.

Theo peered at me, one of those small, secret smiles curving his mouth. For a moment, I got lost in his eyes and reached for him. Until I almost clocked him with the shoe in my hand.

"I'm going to have to see if I can track down another pair in my size." I stuffed the shoe back inside and put the lid on. "We aren't going to tell Melanie about this. It will only upset her."

Theo took the box and wedged it under the backseat. "What shoes? I don't know about any shoes."

"I knew I liked you." I shifted a little closer and walked two of my fingers up his chest.

"Really, really, really liked me?"

"I'd even go so far as to say really, really, really, *really*."

A hand landed on my hip and encouraged me to come closer. "I feel like I have to prove I'm worth that extra *really*."

My hands slid around his neck. "I think it's only fair."

And Theo, who never let me down, went ahead and did that.

Melanie, super-organized wedding diva, blocked two entire floors at a hotel close by for out-of-town wedding guests. In my room, I found a gift basket with water bottles, chocolate, microwave popcorn, hand sanitizer, maps to restaurants close by, local sightseeing opportunities, important phone numbers, and an itinerary of events over the next few days.

I flipped through the schedule, wincing at how every minute seemed to have something planned. Melanie had kindly highlighted the events I was required to attend in yellow, events that she highly suggested I attend in blue, and events I didn't need to worry about in pink.

Three pages of yellow. It was gonna be a long, long weekend.

With a groan, I stretched out on the bed without changing. I hadn't been this tired in a long, long time. I'd just lay here a minute and then finish unpacking and change for bed. Yeah, that's what I would do.

My limbs grew heavy, and my eyelids slid shut and before I realized it, I was asleep.

Until the alarm woke me.

At first, I didn't realize what it was, that loud, incessant ringing. A red light blinked at me from the ceiling. Someone knocked on my door. I stumbled to answer it.

"Ma'am," a man said, yelling over the alarm. He had on a vest and nametag that identified him as a hotel employee. "We need to evacuate the building. That's the fire alarm."

I blinked, my brain slowly catching up. "Fire alarm?"

"The emergency exit is that way." He pointed to the left and was gone before I could say another word.

Thankfully, I was still dressed. I yanked on my tennis shoes and had the foresight to grab my backpack. By the time I checked to make sure Mack, Abe, and Hallie (who all had rooms on my floor) didn't need help and made it down the eight flights of stairs, a large group of guests were huddled together in a far corner of the parking lot. No one knew what had happened but seeing as how it was three in the morning, no one was real happy about it. No signs of smoke billowed in the sky, although there were two fire trucks, an ambulance, and several police cars in the parking lot.

A chill ran through me in the cool night air. Above, the moon played peek-a-boo with the thick gray clouds. I sat on a nearby curb right by a streetlight, put my backpack in my lap, and curled my body around it until I found a comfortable position.

"Is Aunt Ali okay?" Hallie asked.

"Yeah, honey. She's just tired, I bet."

I groaned but didn't lift my head. Not even when someone sat on the other side of me and put an arm around me. Theo rubbed his hand up and down my arm. "You're freezing."

"Yes. Cold. Tired."

Theo chuckled. "Here, sit up."

I obeyed, my eyes barely open.

"Arms up." He pulled a sweatshirt over me. The arms were too long, but it was still warm from being on him and it smelled like him. I buried my nose in the collar.

"Hmm. Good." I slumped into him, doing an accurate impression of a cooked noodle.

"Ali?"

Frowning, I looked toward the voice. "Alec?"

"Yeah, it's me." His smile seemed forced as his eyes darted between the two of us. "Theo."

"Alec."

At least we all knew each other's names. I blew out a breath and waited to see who would speak first. This was so much more awkward than I expected.

Alec turned his body slightly, so he was facing me. "I hope we can have a chance to talk before the wedding. To catch up."

Theo's arm on my shoulders tightened and he hauled me closer. I put my hand on his knee.

"I don't have anything I need to say," I said. "So, I'm good."

He leaned closer. "I think I made a mistake. I thought," he smiled a little uncertainly, his eyes darting to Theo and then back to me, "you could go to the wedding with me. As my date. We could reconnect."

I was almost impressed he'd asked. He had bigger *cojones* than I had given him credit for. "No. We're not going anywhere together. You made that clear over a year ago. Like I said. I'm good."

"Oh, come on, Ali. We always have fun together and," again his gaze tripped to Theo and back to me, "I miss you."

My back went rigid. "Where is this coming from? You haven't spoken to me in months. You blocked my phone number. You were dating two days after you broke up with me."

"But—"

"She said no," Theo said, his voice hard.

Alec's eyes swung to Theo, giving him a quick assessment. He'd never said outright that he hadn't liked Theo when we dated but it had been obvious. Mae was right. Alec had changed when he got that job in Dallas. The more his boss praised him, the more time he spent with his work bros, the fancier his suits got, the more his arrogance grew.

I'd put the blame of our relationship's demise on me. It was my stubbornness, my selfishness, my inability to share my feelings that had caused all our problems. But that wasn't true. Alec had been just as complicit. He'd just never taken any responsibility for it.

Alec rocked back on his feet. "If you change your mind, let me know."

"I'm not going to," I said but he'd already walked away.

It took another twenty minutes before we discovered a guest had been smoking in his room and set off the fire alarms, and we were finally let back inside. Everyone rushed to the elevators, so Theo suggested we take the stairs. That sounded impossible but if it put me closer to being in bed, I was all for it.

Around the fourth flight of stairs, I gasped. "I forgot my room key."

I'd have to go all the way to the lobby and beg for another. I stopped and turned, ready to trudge back the way I'd come.

Theo laid a hand on my arm. "Do you have everything you need in your backpack?"

"Yes."

"You can stay in my room."

"Bed. Sleep." I nodded.

We started back up the stairs. "I might like this version of you. These one-word answers are nice."

"Jerk."

He laughed. "I deserved that."

When we reached his floor, the elevators were letting off a group of people. We waited for them to pass. Theo reached out and took one of my hands. I smiled sleepily and rested my head on his shoulder.

The last person exited the elevator and froze when he saw us. Of course, it was Alec.

He smirked and waved us to go first. Thus began the most awkward thirty seconds of my life. Alec followed us down one hallway and again when we turned left. Theo pulled me to a stop in front of his room. Alec stopped, too. At the room right next to Theo's.

Alec cleared his throat. "Like I said, think about it."

My jaw dropped but, as was Alec's way, he said what he

wanted to say and disappeared into his room before I could reply.

"Ignore him," Theo whispered. "He's not worth the effort."

Theo's room, like mine, only had one bed. I crawled in and curled on my side.

"Make yourself at home." Theo pulled my tennis shoes from my feet and tucked the covers around me. He snapped off the lights and climbed in next to me. I was mostly asleep when he rolled on his side behind me and wrapped an arm around me.

"Nice," I whispered.

The rain started a few hours later.

FORTY-NINE

Note to self:
Elope.

Friday, two days before the wedding

Rain in Texas was quick and dirty. A storm blows in fast, brings thunder and lightning, thirty minutes of heavy rain, and then it's done.

But we weren't in Texas; we were in Portland where rain worked differently. It started early Friday morning, an endless light drizzle. A few moments of more intense rain and then back to endless light rain. It didn't stop. Just continued for hours and hours, making everything damp and gray.

"So much rain." Melanie stared morosely out the window while a nail technician worked on her French manicure. She'd been on the verge of tears since yesterday.

"This is why I wanted you to have the wedding back home in Texas. We could have used the church and wouldn't have had to worry about the weather. But what do I know? I'm just your mother." Melanie's mother, Sonya, was an aggressively polite woman but always standoffish when Alec brought me around. All day, her snide comments had done nothing but drag the mood down.

I'd never liked that woman. There. I said it.

"Hallie," I said, in hopes of changing topics, and quickly, "how you doing?"

She smiled at me from the miniature pedicure chair next to me where she was getting a lovely pearl pink applied to her toes. "I feel like a princess."

My mom didn't take the hint. "A wedding in Texas would have been so nice."

"Mom." I turned my head and gave her a pointed look. "No, just no."

"That's what I told them. I said it would be so much more convenient." Sonya sighed. "But no, they insisted on having it here in Oregon."

Melanie drew in a slow breath, her cheeks flagged with red. Sonya was the biggest reason Melanie hadn't wanted the wedding in Texas. She would have taken over everything and done it "the right way." It was also the reason she and Cal had insisted on paying for the wedding themselves.

"It's so... soggy here, isn't it?" Sonya's mouth firmed in distaste.

"I think it's beautiful," I said lightly. "Mel, you said you got a tent as a backup, right?"

"Yes, from the chair rental company." Melanie gave me a grateful smile.

"There you go. Problem solved. It's going to be beautiful. I'll help however I can," I said.

I meant it too. I didn't like how stressed-out and exhausted Melanie was. That's not how a woman about to marry the love of her life should look. Time to do something about that.

"In fact, why don't you let me call the rental place and double-check everything. I can make all your last-minute calls, if you want. I bet I can con Theo into picking up anything that you need, too. I'd like to help."

"You'd do that?" Melanie beamed. "That would be great. It's been a lot, trying to plan a wedding in a place I just moved to."

"I did tell you to hire a wedding organizer," Sonya said.

I really didn't like that woman.

It turned out the rain was only the first problem.

Back at the hotel, Melanie and Cal had plans to take out both sets of parents for lunch. After some hemming and hawing, and eliciting many promises from me, Melanie trusted me with the Wedding Planner and left me with instructions to call a list of vendors to triple-check everything was in place for Sunday.

I found out quickly, things were not in place.

"But I have a signed contract right here," I said for the fifth time. "They reserved a tent in case there was rain. And guess what? It's raining."

"There was a little snafu." Ted, the nice, if somewhat disorganized, employee at the rental company, explained.

I'd learned he had a wife, two daughters, and a dog named Benji in our ten-minute phone call. I had, unfortunately, also learned that sometimes rental companies double-booked their equipment by mistake. Things like tents.

"I understand but I'm in a bind now. I need a tent for Sunday, and you all promised my soon to be sister-in-law. I need to tell you that right now, I am the calmer person to deal with, but I can always put the bride on the phone. I'm sure you know how sensible and understanding a bride can be two days before their wedding day."

"No, no," Ted said, a bit of panic in his voice. "I have a tent."

"Excellent." I grinned. "It's all set for delivery Sunday morning, correct?"

"Yes, but as I said, we're low on tents and while I do have one in the correct size, this might not be exactly what you were thinking."

"It's a big white tent. What's so hard about that?"

"If you'll notice, the contract doesn't specify color of tent."

"What does that mean?"

He promised to text me a photo and hung up quickly. Hmm. That didn't sound promising.

Next, I moved on to the photographer, who was nearly impossible to get ahold of. But after several phone calls, someone finally picked up.

"Did you say you were Luke's assistant?" I asked.

"No. I'm his son. He's not here."

The voice sounded young, like a prepubescent middle-school boy.

"How old are you?"

"Eleven."

Great. "Why can't I speak to your dad?"

I could practically hear this kid's shrug over the phone. "He's in Montana this weekend."

"But he'll be back for the wedding on Sunday, right?"

"I think he's not coming back until Wednesday."

I pulled up the PHOTOGRAPHER folder in the Wedding Planner. "I have receipts. He received all the payments. What am I supposed to do?"

"Um, I have a cousin who likes photography. He helps Dad sometimes."

I perked up. "Oh, really?"

"I can ask him. Sometimes his mom works on the weekends and then he won't have a ride."

"Wait. How old is he?"

"Fifteen."

I pulled the phone from my ear and stared at it. Was I getting punked?

It only got worse.

The caterers confirmed for Sunday but swore their receipts stated one hundred and fifty guests when it was supposed to be two hundred and fifty. The venue lost the reservation for the honeymoon suite and there was some convention in town starting on Sunday. Getting a new room was going to be a challenge.

The limousine company verified they'd be sending over a replacement since the white stretch limo had been in a car accident two days before.

The officiant had the flu, but he was pretty sure he'd be okay by Sunday. Then he proceeded to cough so hard and so long, I almost called 9-1-1 for him.

That was about the time the text came in from Ted. Oh, he had a tent for us. One with yellow and red stripes that said, WELCOME TO THE BIG TOP, in bold, bright letters above an oversized entrance. A literal circus tent.

"What am I supposed to do with this mess?" I asked my empty hotel room. I couldn't tell Melanie all this. She would curl in the fetal position and never speak again. Literally. I was not exaggerating. The rainy forecast almost killed her.

I'd have to fix it. I wasn't sure how, but it was going to happen.

I just needed a plan.

I called a meeting of the wedding party, minus parents and the bride and groom. By the time everyone arrived, I'd managed to talk the hotel into letting me borrow a small whiteboard from one of their conference rooms. My hotel room had become the Situation Room.

An hour before the rehearsal was to start, Mack, Karen in

tow, my brothers and Theo, plus Melanie's bridesmaids: her twin cousins, Lydia and Laura, Ruth, Frankie's girlfriend, and Melanie's best friend since college, Penny, were all crammed into my hotel room.

And Alec. Yeah, him, too.

"We have a problem." By the time I finished explaining the many, many things that were about to explode, no one was smiling. In fact, the room had grown eerily quiet. Except for Karen who began to growl when I accidentally made eye contact with her.

"I have a plan," I continued. "First, we don't tell anyone else about this. Second, we—"

"Not tell them?" Alec cut in from his spot leaning against the closet door, where he'd stared at his phone the entire time I'd talked. "Cal and Melanie need to know about this as soon as possible."

A chorus of "no ways" and "no's" rang out.

Penny shook her head. "Melanie is hanging on by a thread as it is."

"And Aunt Sonya would spend the rest of her life reminding Melanie about how the wedding should have been in Texas," Laura said. "She's kind of a Karen."

"She didn't mean that, sweetling." Mack rubbed the dog's tummy. "Could we please refrain from making Karen jokes? She's a very sensitive puppy."

"Our mom tends to be a little... highly strung," I said. "We're on our own here."

"Fine, we won't tell them." Alec pushed off the wall and walked to stand next to me. "Here's what I think we should do—"

"Sit down." Theo stood. "Ali's got it under control."

Alec smirked. "Is that so?"

Theo stepped closer and the two of them glared at each other. If it was Regency England, Alec would have slapped

Theo across the face with a glove and challenged him to a duel. Theo would be the dashing pirate in disguise who beat the bad guy and got the girl.

I tucked that little fantasy away to think about later.

Seeing the two side by side, the differences between them were stark. Alec with his dark hair slicked back and shrewd dark eyes versus Theo's blond curls and thoughtful blue eyes. Alec was a bit shorter, leaner, clean-shaven and dressed in designer jeans and a black t-shirt that probably cost three hundred dollars. On the other hand, Theo was taller with wider shoulders, and a permanent scruff. His shorts and t-shirt were probably ten years old.

Alec would be the kind of dad who left early every day to work out and stayed late at the office every night. The weekends would be for schmoozing on the golf course. His kids would never see him. Theo would hurry home after work. He'd take the kids swimming and on walks and to the playground. Surely, he'd invent twelve different pirate games to play with them.

I really had chosen Alec because he was so different from the man I wanted. He had been a safe choice. What an idiot I was. I almost felt bad for wasting Alec's time. Almost.

"Yeah, that is so. Ali's got it covered. She's smart and clever and thinks outside the box and she'll get the job done, no matter what. In fact, she makes a damn good leader." Theo gazed at me, his eyes steady and true. "I'd follow her anywhere."

"Thank you," I whispered, but inside the dragons were in a frenzy of swoops in pure adoration.

"No problem." Theo took a step toward Alec. "What she's not is a finance bro with more money than sense."

"Whatever. I think I know Ali pretty well and I can—"

Theo cut in. "I know you're the idiot who broke up with her on a text message and then blocked her number like a coward."

"That's how he broke it off with you?" Frankie inspected Alec from head to toe like he was a bug about to be squashed under his foot. He sneered. "We're going to talk about this later."

That wiped the smarmy, smirky expression off Alec's face.

"What can we do to help?" Lydia asked.

Everyone's eyes were on me (minus Alec, who had found something very interesting on the carpet), expectant, trusting, and a moment of real panic wedged its way into my chest. It must have shone on my face because Theo slid his hand into mine.

"You got this," he murmured.

He was right; I did have this. I straightened my shoulders and started talking.

FIFTY

Note to self:
Don't let Melanie plan my bachelorette party.

"Isn't this fun?" Melanie said as she carefully painted a bumble bee on a ceramic cup.

"Super-fun." Lydia haphazardly added black dots to the dalmatian she'd created on her teacup. Or maybe it was a spotted skunk?

Ruth held up her bowl. "Sexy, right?"

"Totally." I glared at the vase I'd attempted to paint stripes on, but it looked like the work of a four-year-old with a short attention span.

A few months ago, us bridesmaids had asked Melanie what she'd liked to do for her bachelorette party. We had expected the usual—wear a bride-to-be sash, drink too much, end up at a show à la the *Thunder from Down Under*, and come back to the hotel a giggling mess. But no, Melanie had replied she wanted to do something "fun and creative."

That's how we ended up at one of these paint-it-yourself places.

Not surprisingly, the elementary art teacher in Melanie was in Heaven. The rest of us, not so much. Although it was loads more fun than the rehearsal and dinner we'd had before this, and that was saying something.

"Hey, Ali," Lydia said, still placing black dots on her teacup. "Your mom looks so familiar. I've been trying to figure out where I know her from."

Laura nodded. "I noticed that yesterday, and it's been bugging me."

I shrugged. "No idea."

Lydia folded her arms across her chest. "It'll come to me."

"What are we doing after this?" Penny asked, her expression full of hope.

Melanie glanced around the table, her brow furrowed. "After this? Go back to the hotel and get some sleep. I'm exhausted."

"Mel," I said, "we could hit a bar, get a drink, live it up a little. You're going to be a married woman in less than forty-eight hours."

Melanie pointed her paintbrush at us. "Why aren't you all painting?"

"Because, like, I'm done." Ruth held up a bright-pink bowl with stenciled red hearts around it. "I wonder what the boys are doing?"

"Oh, let's find out." Laura brushed her long blonde hair behind her shoulder and set aside the tile she'd been painting a misshapen cat on.

I pulled out my phone and shot a text off.

Me: *How's it going?*

Theo: *Pretty good. Cal's having fun.*

Me: *Where are you?*

Lydia nudged me with her shoulder, a hopeful gleam in her eye. "So, um, are any of your brothers available?"

Abe was. Sort of. "Only one but his hands are pretty full right now. Single dad and all."

"Bummer." She set aside her teacup.

Theo: *A sports bar not too far from the hotel. Where are you?*

Me: *Strip club.*

Theo: *Liar.*

Me: *I brought all these dollar bills for nothing.*

Me: *We're painting teacups. Very respectable.*

Me: *And boring.*

"Now we just need to take these up so they can be fired in the kiln. I can get them after the honeymoon, and I'll mail them all to you." Melanie placed each painted piece on a tray. "How does that sound?"

A spattering of unenthusiastic agreements followed.

Penny groaned after Melanie left to drop off the ceramics. "I think we need an intervention. I love her but she needs to unwind. She's strung so tight; I expect her to snap any minute."

Theo: *Come join us.*

Me: *I don't want to crash the bachelor party.*

Theo: *Everyone said to come.*

I grinned at the group. "I know where we can take her."

FIFTY-ONE

Note to self:
Weaponizing cheesecake may be one of my greatest ideas yet.

Saturday, one day before the wedding

"Everything hurts." Melanie pulled down her sunglasses a tiny bit. "I feel like roadkill that was resuscitated and then run over again for fun."

I felt a twinge of guilt. Had I kept refilling Melanie's glass of beer every time she got up to play darts or pool? Yes, yes, I had. But if there had ever been a bride-to-be in history who needed to relax, it was her. My plan worked. Maybe a little too well. I had no idea Drunk Melanie knew all the words to "Pour Some Sugar on Me."

And she liked singing it while dancing on tables.

Let's just say some of us weren't allowed back at that sports bar.

"Melanie, take those sunglasses off. You're inside." Sonya glared down the table at her daughter. They'd not been happy to hear of our escapades last night.

As if they knew the half of it. I hadn't had anything to drink so when the police were almost called after Cal, Frankie, and Abe tried to play blind darts and narrowly missed nailing a guy in the head thereby resulting in a pissed-off guy who wanted to throw more than darts back at them (all of which my brothers found hilarious), it was me who got them *out* of trouble.

Yeah, we probably shouldn't even walk by that bar ever again.

But as it was the day after, the consequences for all that fun were front and center. Melanie was not the only one wearing sunglasses inside.

Melanie's father stood and tapped on a glass to get everyone's attention. "My wife and I invited you all to this brunch to thank you for your friendship, for traveling many miles to come to the wedding, and for your love and support for Melanie and Calvin."

Melanie pushed around the scrambled eggs on her plate. "I can't eat this. My stomach feels like a washing machine stuck on the spin cycle."

I patted her shoulder. She winced and pulled away.

"The tattoo?"

She shushed me. "Not too loud. I don't want my mom to know." She leaned closer. "Why did you let me get a tattoo?"

I smirked. "Because it took me almost an hour to talk you out of the eyebrow piercing."

She rubbed her forehead. "Oh, good grief."

"You were pretty set on it. Something about how eyebrow piercings were exotic."

She'd argued for that piercing with the same passion most people reserved for politics, religion and pizza toppings. When trying to rationalize with her hadn't worked, I'd finally resorted to showing her photos of what happened if that piercing were to get infected. She'd only let her disappointment get her down for about fourteen seconds before she'd moved on to her new passion: a tattoo.

Melanie groaned. "I'm never drinking again."

"You never were good at holding your liquor," Alec said from across the table.

Unfortunately, there was assigned seating at this gig. Theo and I were seated at different tables, while Alec and I were not. I was determined to not let him get under my skin, especially after yesterday. Strangely, I didn't feel angry when I thought of him now. Just pity and sadness we'd wasted so much time on a relationship that wasn't meant to be.

"Shut up, Alec," Melanie muttered. "I don't want a lecture right now."

"I wasn't going to lecture you. I was going to say I hoped you learned your lesson."

"My head hurts too much to deal with you right now." Melanie stood, grabbed her glass of water, and wandered over to Cal's table. My brother's smile when she came close was bright enough to light a stadium. He pulled her onto his lap, and she rested her head on his shoulder.

Maybe Melanie was right, and they were the whole reason Alec and I had ever dated, so Cal and Melanie could find each other.

"They're a good couple, aren't they?" Alec said.

He'd moved to the seat Melanie had vacated. Be an adult, Ramos.

"They are."

He peered at me over the glass of the Bloody Mary he was nursing. "So, you and Theo?"

"Yup. Me and Theo." My eyes found the man in question. Like he somehow knew, he turned his head and locked eyes with me, his slow smile warming me.

"I always figured he had feelings for you." He snorted. "I know you had feelings for him."

I turned to face him. "Excuse me?"

"It was always 'Theo this' and 'Theo that.' The guy could do no wrong." His words slurred, and I wondered how many Bloody Marys he'd had.

"I was never unfaithful to you, if that's what you're getting at."

He tossed back half his drink. "Don't matter now anyway, does it?"

"Actually, I do think it matters. I am not that kind of person, and I don't like you insinuating I am."

He shrugged. "I guess I am."

I froze. "Excuse me?"

"You wouldn't move to Dallas." He shrugged. "I was lonely."

"You were lonely?"

"Yeah. So, I saw other women."

"You saw other women?"

"Are you going to repeat everything I say?" He ran his fingers through his hair, his voice agitated.

"When you broke up with me, you said it was all my fault. That I—I wasn't emotionally mature enough for you." Tears welled up and I blinked to hold them back. He was not getting the pleasure of making me cry.

For a split second, guilt slid across his face and disappeared just as quickly.

"I've spent over a year picking myself apart, wondering how I could be a better person because of the things you said. Worried I was too selfish for someone to love me, and all this time, it was you spouting stuff, so you didn't have to feel bad." I slammed my hand down on the table hard enough to make the silverware rattle. "You ass."

Half the room's occupants were now looking at us with interest. I'd promised not to cause any problems. I really, really, really wanted to keep that promise. Keep it together, Ramos.

"Quiet down," Alec said.

I leaned in and stage-whispered, "You are an ass. Better?"

"Is everything okay?" Theo rested a hand on my shoulder.

"Theo, my man, how's it going?" Alec lifted his glass in an insincere toast.

"Ali, you okay?" he asked, ignoring Alec.

"I think I might need to leave early." I glared at Alec. "For reasons."

The smirkiest of smirks slid onto Alec's face. "Speaking of leaving, when's the big move?"

I blinked at the sudden change in topic. "Move? Who's moving?"

"Talk to your man here." Alec gestured toward Theo.

Theo's jaw ticked. "He doesn't know what he's talking about."

"Oh, did I hear wrong? I thought you were telling Cal and Abe about a job you're interviewing for in Chicago." He took a swig of his drink only to find it was empty.

"What job? Chicago?" I asked, my voice rising with each word.

"Chicago is pretty far away from Two Harts," Alec pointed out. "You couldn't even bring yourself to move five hours away."

"Do you have a job interview in Chicago?" I asked Theo.

Theo's eyes slid shut. He took a deep breath and opened them. "Yes."

"In Chicago. But... you said... and we're..." I growled in frustration. Why couldn't I get a coherent sentence out? And why did it feel like my chest was squeezing the breath out of my body?

"I need you to hear me out before you jump to the wrong conclusion. Please?"

I stood so quickly, my chair almost tipped. How had it gotten so hot in here? I needed air. And space. I needed to process all this.

"Oh, whoops." Alec's smirk morphed into a vicious grin. "Was I not supposed to tell anyone?"

"Shut up," Theo ground out. "Ali, listen to me. It's not what you think."

"Everything okay?" Cal appeared at my side. "You have an audience."

"This is so sad, really." Alec stretched out his legs. The Alec I knew was much too concerned with appearances to let himself drink so much in public. A part of me knew he'd regret this. "But gotta tell you, she's not worth all this drama."

"Okay, now," Cal said at the same time Theo turned toward Alec, his hands curling into fists.

"No! There's not going to be any fighting."

That would have been it. I would have picked up my sunglasses and purse and gone to my room right that second, but I made the mistake of giving Alec one final look. That smirk was back, and I wanted so badly to make it disappear. To make him disappear. To make all this stop.

"Melanie," I called out.

"Yes?"

"I'm sorry. I tried so hard to be an adult." I snatched a plate with a piece of cheesecake covered in strawberry preserves and a drizzle of chocolate syrup. I'd been looking forward to eating it.

Sigh.

"In my defense, he started it. But I am going to finish it." In the next blink, I leaned forward and smashed the dessert on the top of his head. The gratification of watching him fling his arms out as the syrupy trails of strawberry and graham cracker crust slid down his face more than made up for not getting to eat it.

I grabbed my sunglasses and purse. "I'm leaving. And no one is following me." I looked right at Theo. "No one."

. . .

I took the elevator up to my room, changed my clothes, turned my phone off, and crawled into bed.

The scene replayed in my head. Not the part about Alec. What he had said mattered little. I didn't even hate him; instead, the best I could feel was apathetic toward him. I'd had my say, and spending any more time dissecting his words wasn't worth it.

But the parts with Theo? Oh, that, I couldn't forget. I don't know what hurt worse. That he was considering a job so far away or that he hadn't told me about it. Maybe he wasn't so serious about this thing between us. What if I were the only one who felt that way? I couldn't watch him walk away and I couldn't see myself moving.

I thought of the almost panicked look in his eyes when he asked me not to jump to the wrong conclusion and drew in a long breath. I trusted Theo and that meant I had to trust what he said. He asked me to listen to him, and I hadn't.

Hugging a pillow to my chest, I curled on my side. That's what I would do. I would listen to him.

I must have dozed off because I was jerked awake by heavy pounding on my door.

"Go away."

"Ali-Cat, we need you," Mack said and the urgency in his voice was the only reason I forced myself out of bed.

"What's wrong?" I asked after I'd opened the door.

Karen growled at me from her place at Mack's feet. But I ignored her because the expression on Mack's face made the little hairs on the back of my neck prickle.

"I tried to call you. You need to come. It's Abe and your father."

FIFTY-TWO

Note to self:
First, the truth.
Then, the pie.

I could hear the yelling before we'd even reached the room. Dad and Abe, both of their voices raised in anger. I was immediately transported back to when I was a teenager, and they'd go at it constantly.

"What happened?"

Mack shook his head. "Your dad got upset because Abe had too much to drink last night. He started laying into him about how his choices affect Hallie now. One thing led to another. Same argument, different day."

As a kid, I would have never waded into the middle of one of their arguments. But now? Now I would not lose my brother again. Even when that meant telling the truth about everything. Even if that meant my parents' anger. Or worse, their disappointment.

"Where's Hallie?"

"With Frankie and Ruth."

"Okay." I knocked. Then I knocked louder. I wished Theo were here with me; that strong, quiet way of his always made me feel better. But Theo might be moving to Chicago, and I probably shouldn't depend on his presence. My chest squeezed painfully.

One thing at a time, Ramos.

Dad ripped the door open.

"What?" But when he saw it was me, he smiled although it didn't hide the anger in his eyes. "What do you need, honey?"

"Everything okay in there?" I leaned to the side to see who was in the room.

"Your mother and I are talking to your brother."

Mom didn't seem to be doing any of the talking, but whatever. "I want to come in."

"It's not a good time," he said, a mulish expression on his face.

But two could play that game. I crossed my arms and shot back the same stubborn look. "That's too bad. I want to be here."

He glared at me for a long beat and must have seen I was serious. "Fine."

Mack touched my shoulder. "You okay?"

I nodded, hoping I looked more confident than I felt. "Yeah, I'm going to be okay."

"Of course you will." Mack pressed a kiss to my cheek before turning around and heading back down the hallway, Karen trotting at his heels.

I breezed past Dad. Mom was perched on the bed, hands twisting in her lap. Tears stained her cheeks, but she gave me a trembling smile. I sat next to her and wrapped an arm around her shoulders.

Abe stood by the window, shoulders slumped, staring off into the distance. Probably wishing he were back in Denver about now.

"Happy now? You got your sister involved in this," Dad said, his tone harsh.

"Dad." Abe sounded defeated.

"Don't 'dad' me. You're a father now. You don't get to go out and get drunk and forget your kid."

"I didn't forget her. I already told you that. She was with Mack all night." Abe turned around to face Dad. "Why can't we ever just talk to each other? Why does it always end up with someone yelling? I can't do this anymore. I'm not a child; I'm an adult. I have a business, a house, a kid. Maybe you and me, we're not meant to have a relationship."

Mom gasped and clutched my hand.

Dad slumped. "I didn't mean—"

"We can say we tried, and it didn't work out. I'd like to stay for the wedding, and then you don't ever have to see me again." Abe stalked toward the door. I stood, trying to get my mouth to open to tell him to stop, but I couldn't seem to make my throat work.

"Run away again," Dad bit out. "That solved nothing eleven years ago, and it won't solve anything now."

"Dammit, Dad." Abe whipped around. "What do you want me to do? If I stay, you're upset. If I leave, you're upset. There's no good choice for me." He pointed to the bed. "Mom is crying. I don't want to make Mom cry, I don't want to run away. Last time, I left because it was the only thing I could do."

The two of them stared each other down, a strange mix of yearning and anger rolling off them in waves. Mack was right, they were too much alike. Abe was a younger version of Dad. I hoped for, no, I needed these two to find common ground. I wanted Abe back in our lives, but they couldn't keep circling each other like wounded animals, lashing out to hide their soft underbellies.

I licked my very dry lips. While that accident didn't start all this, it had played a part in widening this rift between them. I had to do this. I said a prayer and then I spoke.

"It's not Abe's fault."

Abe scowled. "Ali, stay out of thi—"

"No." I slashed a hand through the air in frustration. "No. I'm not going to anymore. Cal wanted so badly for Abe to be here, for our family to be together, and you are both so stubborn that you can't figure out how to admit when you're wrong."

"Alicia, honey," Mom said. "You know getting upset can trigger..."

"... a seizure? Yeah, yeah, I know. Oh, God, do I know it. You never let me forget. I've lived with epilepsy for over a decade and guess what, I'm doing just fine. I'm trying so hard to live my life but..." I forced myself to take a calming breath. "You'd think the hardest part of dealing with it is that I never know when I'll have another one. But that's not it. You know what keeps me awake at night? Feeling guilty because I have so many people worried about me."

I swiped at my cheeks, annoyed I'd started crying without realizing it.

"I want to live my life. I can't keep hiding out in my apartment or answering your calls twice a day. I can't keep worrying that you're worrying." I straightened. "I am not broken."

Mom's head jerked in surprise. "Of course you aren't broken."

"Then stop treating me like I am." Before she could answer, and since I was on a roll, I turned on my heels and faced my father. "Did you know Abe has dyslexia?"

Abe grunted. "Ali."

"Shut it. Stop trying to be an enigma and talk to your parents."

"Is that true?" Mom asked.

He nodded once. "I found out when I took some business classes in community college."

"That's why school was so hard for him," I said. "That's why he struggled. It wasn't because he was lazy or not trying hard enough."

Dad flinched at that. Good. Maybe something would get into that head of his. But I wasn't done yet.

"And the car accident?" Say it, Ramos. You can do this. "It wasn't Abe's fault."

"Yes, it was." Abe's eyes drilled into my head; I ignored him.

"No, it wasn't. I was driving the car. I knew I wasn't supposed to, but I begged him to let me."

A wave of exhaustion hit me, and it had nothing to do with lack of sleep. It was as though my body had been using so much energy holding this in for years and had finally found relief. "I was so angry at everything. The seizures, giving up almost all my independence, you and Dad with all the rules."

"The rules were to keep you safe."

"I couldn't drive or spend the night at friends' houses or go swimming without it being a big ordeal. I had to have someone come with me when I checked the mail at the end of the driveway."

Mom winced. "We didn't know when you'd have another one."

"I understand. As an adult, I get it. But I hated it. All the decisions were out of my hands. It made me so angry. So, yeah, I begged Abe to let me drive the car and he did."

"What happened?" Dad asked.

Keep going, Ramos. "I had a seizure while I was driving."

Mom gasped. "You could have died. What were you thinking?"

"I already told you what I was thinking. I was a dumb, angry kid who'd lost all her independence and I needed to feel a little bit of freedom."

"I never should have let her talk me into it. I thought a short drive wouldn't be a big deal," Abe said, his voice low. "I've never been so scared in my life."

I pressed my hands to my too-hot cheeks and found them wet. Damn tears. "And then this idiot took all the blame for it. By the time I figured out what he'd done, I couldn't bring myself to tell you. I was scared I'd disappoint you or you'd be so upset, you'd take away more from me. I've been scared since that accident. Scared to drive, scared to upset you and Dad, scared to do a lot of the things I want to do because I don't want to worry anyone. But being scared, it's holding me back from doing a lot of things."

"Oh, honey." Mom wrapped me in a smothering hug. "I don't know whether to be angry or relieved right now."

"Be both. I can handle it."

Mom stepped back and wiped my cheeks, her smile small but comforting. "We need pie."

"Yes, pie would be wonderful."

She took my hand. "Let's go find some and we'll talk."

"I'd like that."

I followed behind her but when Dad and Abe made to follow, too, I stopped and turned, glaring at them both. "You two do not deserve pie. The both of you need to sit down and figure out how to talk to each other. Talk, not yell, not ignore each other. Talk. What time is it, Mom?"

"A quarter after eight."

I poked them both in the chest with my finger. "You have two hours. Together in this room. No leaving and no yelling. Quit being so damn stubborn and figure it out."

Mom nodded. "What she said."

With a smile, I took Mom's hand. "Now, let's go find some pie."

FIFTY-THREE

Note to self:
Buy a second copy of How to Pirate Like a Professional *to keep in the car.*

Mom and I had a long talk at a little café we found a few blocks from the hotel. She cried; I cried. All the things I'd kept in came bursting out. I even told her about the seizure eight months ago. To her credit, she held it together.

"I can't just turn off my worrying, honey," she said.

"I need you to rein it in some."

Somehow, I knew we'd have this conversation again and I was okay with it. I was lucky to have people who loved me enough to worry about me. The alternative was pretty damn depressing.

Back at the hotel, Mom hugged me long and hard before heading back to her room to see the state Dad and Abe were in. It was when I was strolling by the lounge I saw him, a handsome man with curly blond hair, nursing a drink and staring at a game on the television.

Like the creeper I was, and had always been where Theo

was concerned, I watched him for a while. With his hunched shoulders and pensive, forlorn expression, he reminded me of a lost little boy. My heart squeezed.

I strolled in and slid onto the stool next to him. "Hi."

He turned. A tiny smile tugged at the corner of his mouth. "Hi."

"So, how's your grog?"

One dark-blond eyebrow lifted. "Pretty good."

The bartender moseyed down to us and asked if I wanted anything. "Can you make a Wrecked Pirate?"

Theo chuckled. "A Wrecked Pirate?"

"I've been doing my research."

Theo laughed softly, the sound sliding through me. "You have a thing for pirates?"

I turned my body and propped an elbow on the bar. "I might. You know any?"

The corners of his eyes crinkled. "Maybe."

My drink appeared, and I took a sip, pleasantly surprised at the taste. "Shiver me timbers, as the sea dogs would say."

He laughed. "Did you memorize a pirate dictionary?"

"Oh, no. I've been reading these pirate romances. So good." I leaned in closer and lowered my voice. "Very educational."

"You'll have to tell me more about these books," he said solemnly, although his eyes sparkled.

"I see that in our future. Although I should warn you, the author has a very active imagination." I slid closer.

Mouth stretched in a wicked little smile, he placed a hand on my knee. The skin there thrummed warm at his touch. "Are you flirting with me now?"

"Aye. How am I doing, matey?"

We stared into each other's eyes wearing matching dopey, smitten smiles like dopey, smitten lovebirds for far too long before Theo leaned forward to press a kiss to the tip of my nose.

Both of us straightened. I took a healthy sip of my drink to fortify myself.

"I'm sorry," we both blurted at the same time.

"I tried to call you a few times," he said. "Knocked on your room door, too."

"I turned off my phone then I fell asleep. Mack woke me because Dad and Abe got into it, and then I went for pie with my mom." I bit my lower lip. "I wasn't ignoring you, I promise."

"What kind of pie?"

I smirked. "That's your question."

He grinned. "I tried to tell you about the interview earlier, but we got distracted."

"So, there's really a job in Chicago you're considering?"

"I am." He shook his head. "I was."

I sat back, putting distance between us, and pretending my heart wasn't starting to ache. "Chicago is a long way away."

"After my mom died, I felt sort of alone, restless even. Like I should be doing something. And things were... hard. There was this woman I couldn't stop thinking about, but she was in a relationship. I thought I was in love with her, but I wasn't sure how she felt about me. So, I thought a change of scenery might be a good idea."

"Who's this woman?" I asked, sounding like the jealous girlfriend I totally was.

He gazed at me intensely. "You don't get it, do you?"

"Get what?"

"A few months before my mom died, we were at a family dinner at your parents' house. It was before Cal left and you and Alec were still together. You were sitting next to me, and you were teasing Frankie about his workout clothes."

Strangely, I remembered the family dinner he was talking about. Frankie had been deep in his wrestling onesie phase. Someone had to call him out.

"You turned to me and smiled and asked me to pass the salt and pepper. That's when it hit me."

"What hit you?"

He picked up my hand and began making those slow, small circles with his thumb, warming me from the inside out. "That I wanted to sit next to you all the time. That I liked hearing your laugh and seeing your smile and watching your eyes light up and listening to whatever you had to say. That I wanted you to ask me to pass the salt and pepper every day for the rest of my life."

"Oh," I breathed.

He huffed a laugh. "But you had a boyfriend. Then you didn't have a boyfriend, but I wasn't sure how you felt about me. I was scared to tell you how I felt." His gaze dropped to our hands, but he couldn't hide the pink blooming from his neck to his cheeks. He was nervous. Somehow, that made me want to throw myself in his arms even more.

"A friend from college works at a sports magazine based in Chicago. He got me an interview. It's right after the wedding."

I leaned down to try and catch his eye. "That's what the phone calls were about."

"Yeah. But a couple of weeks ago, Cal asked me if I'd be willing to go to Colorado and talk Abe into coming to the wedding. I got this idea that maybe if, well, if I could spend time with you, I could figure us," his gaze met mine, "out before I made any big decisions. So, I told Cal you should come with me for purely selfish reasons. I wanted to spend time with you."

"What did you figure out?" I held my breath; this seemed like the most important answer.

"I don't want to go to Chicago, Ali." Those blue eyes locked onto mine, full of so much emotion, my heart ached. "I'll cancel that interview in a heartbeat if you want me to, but you have to tell me."

I hesitated. Why wasn't I shouting my answer? Yes, cancel

the interview, marry me, let's have babies, and make everyone sick over our all-encompassing love. But I didn't say any of that. Why?

"You're scared." He cupped my cheek. "I know. This is terrifying."

I let out a wet laugh. "Yeah, it is. I don't want to screw it up."

He pressed his forehead to mine. "You won't. You can't. I'm already yours."

FIFTY-FOUR

Note to self:
I deserve someone who loves me.

Sunday, Wedding Day

"This is beautiful," Melanie breathed, walking slowly around the new location for the ceremony.

It had taken all I had to secure this room for Melanie. But it was gorgeous, all soft creamy walls and wainscoting, high cathedral ceilings with gold accents. But the best part was that wall of windows overlooking the Columbia River and providing impossibly gorgeous views.

It was about five thousand times better than a soggy circus tent pitched in the backyard. Sure, it had taken all my bargaining skills to get them to let us use it. We'd had to give up a few things and they'd required us to use their catering services. I might have promised them my firstborn.

Melanie hadn't been told any of this, and I planned to keep it that way. Maybe on their fiftieth anniversary if she hadn't figured it out by then.

The same room would also be used for the reception. It would require guests picking up their chairs and moving them, but they'd all survive, the poor dears. As for the décor, I'd put Penny and the twins on it, and they'd come through spectacularly. The room was beautiful, swathed in pale pink and cream with hints of gold. Classy and sweet, just like Melanie.

Well, almost.

"It's not quite finished. Mom still needs to get the centerpieces on the tables. That is if you still want to use those candles?"

"The ones your mom made?" She held her folded hands under her chin, giddy as a little kid at recess. "They'll be perfect."

They'll be... something.

"Oh, I love it." Melanie threw her arms around me. "How did you do all this?"

"No big deal at all. I had a lot of help." That was the truth. I'd made a list and delegated chores, right down to someone picking up the officiant at his house and tracking down a new photographer in twenty-four hours' time. This day would be perfect, damn it. "If I haven't said it, I'm glad you're about to become my sister."

"You're the best." Sniffling, she clung to me like a baby sloth. "It's all been so much, and I can't believe it's here and... and..." The sobs got to her.

"Hey. Whatever happens today, remember, at the end of it, you'll be married. That's the prize." I pulled her away gently so I could look at her. "But today is going to be great, fantastic, a day to remember for years to come." Melanie swiped at her cheeks, her face splotchy and red. "Now, let's get you upstairs. We have a wedding to get ready for."

. . .

I was in a bathrobe and fuzzy bunny slippers when I knocked on the room where the men were getting ready. But Melanie had insisted Cal get this gift right this instant. And I was here to do her bidding.

Abe answered, already dressed in his tux except for the jacket. "This is a good look for you. Bathrobe princess."

I scowled, but carefully as I was in full wedding make-up and hair. "I've been sent on an important mission." I beckoned him to come forward. "Now, come here, your bowtie is all crooked. Let me fix it."

Abe shuffled forward. A roar of laughter burst from the room behind him. "Hurry. I'm missing the good stuff."

"And what is this good stuff exactly?"

He grinned. "Mack is telling Cal what to expect on his wedding night."

I laughed. "No, he's not."

"He is."

"All finished." I patted his shoulders and took a step back. "I'd say you look handsome but you're my brother so that's gross."

"Compliment accepted." He leaned against the doorframe. "Hey, um, thanks for last night."

"How did it go after we left?"

"We talked for about twenty minutes. No one yelled or tried to storm out. It was awkward as hell. Then we watched *Terminator*."

"That sounds like some good father–son time. Think you'll do it again?" I asked hopefully.

"I'd like to. We have, like, five more *Terminator* movies to get through." His eyes are soft. "Thank you, Ali."

"No problem." If it means I get my brother back, I'd do just about anything.

"One question. What's going on with you and Theo? He's been all moody and pensive."

"He has?"

"Thinking way too much. I haven't gotten him to say two words all morning; it's going to make his speech at the reception kind of hard."

I bit the inside of my cheek. "I'll talk to him, I swear."

"I can get him right now."

I waved at my bathrobe. "We don't have time. I'm not even dressed yet, but I do need to see Cal. Please?"

"Promise me you'll fix Theo?'

"Promise."

When Cal came to the door, I couldn't help but grin at him. "You clean up pretty nice."

He fiddled with his tux jacket. "I'm so nervous."

"Why? Think she's going to wise up and make a run for it?"

"Nah. Worried about saying the vows in front of all those people."

"You have it memorized, right?"

He nodded. "I don't want to screw them up. They're kind of important."

"I think as long as you tell her exactly how you feel, you won't screw anything up. Melanie loves you, you big lug." I pulled the small package from the bathrobe pocket. "Speaking of your bride, I was sent to give you this."

"Thanks." He palmed the box. "You and Theo ar—"

"I promise I'll talk to him."

"Good." He hesitated. "You deserve to be with someone who loves you, too, you know."

My breath caught. "That obvious?"

Cal's head tilted to the side. "Has there ever been a time when you didn't love him?"

I opened my mouth, but nothing would come out. Because Cal was right. I'd always loved Theo. Always. Maybe not the way I felt now, but a part of me had always been drawn to him.

Nothing had changed. I was older, probably wiser, and just maybe crazy enough to take a chance on us.

I stood on my tippy-toes and pressed a kiss to Cal's cheek. "I guess we'll see what happens."

But I already knew, and I couldn't wait.

FIFTY-FIVE

Note to self:
If home is where your heart is,
I know exactly where to find mine.

The ceremony was beautiful.

The décor, the flowers, the wedding party, all of them gorgeous. But in the end, it was Melanie and Cal who took everyone's breath away.

Cal had been right to be nervous about forgetting his vows. When it was his turn to speak, he froze. His wild eyes found mine. I patted my chest and mouthed, *from your heart.* He blinked and something settled in him. I watched it happen. He went from terrified to self-assured in just a few seconds.

"I can't remember a word of the vows I wrote."

The guests tittered.

Cal cleared his throat. "But someone told me to speak from my heart, so I'll do that instead. Melanie, every day I am thankful for you, for your patience and kindness, for your love. For being my person, the one I want to see first thing in the morning and before I close my eyes at night."

I sniffled and tried to keep my eyes on the bride and groom. But my gaze wandered to Theo, so handsome, it made my heart ache. What would I do if he moved to Chicago? It felt like we'd just found each other and now I might have to let him go. That wasn't fair. Would I consider moving to Chicago? If he asked me?

When Alec wanted me to move to Dallas, my answer had been easy and fast. But Theo wasn't Alec. Theo was my heart.

"I doubt I'm worth all that," Cal continued, "but I'll spend every day working to be worthy. I love you, Melanie Harrison. I look forward to spending the rest of my life making sure you always know that."

Fifteen minutes later, Cal had a wife. Melanie had a husband.

* * *

"Excuse me," Mom said, a death grip on the microphone someone had given her. Smiling, she waited for the wedding guests seated for dinner to quieten down.

After the ceremony, it had been a whirlwind of guests moving their chairs, wedding party photos, introductions, and I'd only just made it to my seat at an extra-long table stretched across the front of the room. I was seated in the middle of the bridesmaids, exhausted, happy, and so hungry, I was beginning to wonder if the flowers in the bouquet I carried might be edible.

Melanie couldn't keep the smile off her face, nor was she paying attention to much of anything except Cal. I knew that to be true when she hadn't even noticed I'd forgotten to take care of one little wedding-related detail: replacing the shoes Karen had mauled. In my defense, I did remember about thirty minutes before the ceremony and with very little time or options, I wore my flip-flops down the aisle. I figured by the time Melanie got the photos back, I'd be safely back in Texas.

When the murmur of the guests quieted, Mom continued. "I wanted to extend to you our family's deepest gratitude for joining us today for Calvin and Melanie's wedding." She placed a hand on Cal's shoulder. "I'm so proud of the man you've become, and you've chosen a wonderful woman as your bride." She paused, sniffling. "You've made your own family. Of course, I'll be tickled when you decide to add to that family. Maybe by then, you'll move back to Texas, so I'll be able to see my grandbabies."

Several guests laughed.

"Mom," Cal groaned. "Please."

My mother managed to look contrite. "I'm sorry. I went off on a tangent. Anyway, I wanted to let you all know: to thank you, the centerpieces are yours to take home. They were made with love for you all to enjoy. And if you like the candles, you can find my shop online. Just search for *Candles by Stephanie*."

Mom managed to produce a candle like a magician and held it up, the twin peaks and their wicks standing tall and proud.

From my vantage point, I saw several guests press their lips together, holding in laughter. Some stared at their plates of chicken or steak. But no one, *no one* made a sound.

Cal rubbed his forehead, looking torn between laughter and tears. Same, bro.

Lydia turned to me, her eyes huge. "Your mom is the candle lady."

Laura choked on a roll. "Holy crap. She is."

"Who's the candle lady?" Penny asked.

"The candle lady." Lydia slapped her sister on the back as she coughed. "She's the one who makes the candles that look like boo—"

I stood and smiled brightly. "Thanks, Mom, for all your hard work."

I rushed over and took the microphone away from her. Still clutching her candle to her chest (oh, the irony), I walked her to her seat next to my father and the same table as Melanie's parents where Aggressively Polite Sonya looked apoplectic.

As I was walking back to my seat, I heard Dad say, "Did you know Stephanie is internet-famous?"

As the best man, Frankie gave the first speech at the reception after everyone was served. The maid of honor, Penny, followed. Then it was basically open mic night. Anyone who wanted to say something, could. And boy, did they.

One after another: cousins, parents, work friends, old friends, new friends, Mom for a second time, and then Theo.

"If you don't know me, I'm Theo Goodnight, and I've known Cal and his family since I was nine. We've been through a lot together and I have the battle wounds to prove it." He pointed to his chin and told the story of how he'd gotten it after my brothers dared him to jump off the roof onto our trampoline.

"We've shared a lot of memories—good ones, bad ones, a few illegal ones, that one time in... Well, I'm not supposed to talk about that." He paused for the laughter to subside. "But this last week might have been the most epic, most important week we've ever undertaken." His eyes found mine again. For a suspended second, it felt like we were the only two people in the room. At least, until he looked away.

"Cal is the first of us to get married so I'm not sure I can give you any solid marriage advice. But I've had this in my wallet for a long time. Someone very special gave it to me. And I thought I'd share it with you." From his pocket he produced a piece of paper. It looked brittle, the folds fragile, like something he'd pulled out often. "I've always thought if you find someone who makes you feel this way, do everything you can to hold onto them. It's called 'Home:'"

"A home is more than four walls and a roof.

"A home is protection from storms and rain."

My breath caught. I flashed back to sixteen-year-old me slaving over yet another poem dedicated to Theo, the same poem I had earnestly and foolishly used to profess my undying love to him there in his dorm room. That terrible, awful poem, the same one Theo was reading right now. It was one I'd given him all those years ago.

And he's kept it tucked away in his wallet. Tears gathered behind my eyes.

Theo continued:

"A home is strong and sturdy and faithful.

"A home is a place to rest your head at night.

"A home is where all your precious things live.

"But to me,

"A home is a person, a soft place to land.

"A home is the person who protects your heart.

"A home is the person who loves you on your worst days.

"A home is the person you can't imagine living without

"A home, my home, is you."

Carefully, Theo folded the piece of paper back up and tucked it back in his pocket. "Cal and Melanie, I think you've found your home."

He looked over at me just once after he sat, his eyes warm and full of love. The dragons and their wings were performing a Cirque du Soleil act in my stomach.

The dancing started soon after. Like we'd planned it, we found each other and met on the edge of the dance floor. Standing close, but not too close.

"That poem was terrible." I clasped my hands in front of me even though I wanted to touch him.

Smiling, he shook his head. "It's my favorite poem. I have it memorized."

"Have you really kept it in your wallet all these years?"

"Also, true."

"It's like I don't know you."

He took a step closer. "You know me. You know all the important things."

"I want to find out all the other things, too." I bit my lip. "But I'm scared this won't work out somehow. Or I'll screw it up. Or you'll realize I'm not worth the trouble."

"You don't think I'm not scared?" He slid a hand down my arm and threaded his fingers with mine. "I'm scared of all those things too. But you know what's bigger than the fear?"

I shook my head.

He brought our joined hands to rest on his chest, above his heart. "It's how I feel about you."

"Oh," I breathed.

"You're stuck with me. I'm not going anywhere," he said, his voice firm. "If I need to spend the next month, year, decade proving that to you, I will. I'll write you poems and bake you your favorite cake and scare off any man who starts looking a little too friendly and remind you every single minute that I love you."

"You will?"

"I will. Like I said, when you find the person who makes you feel like you're home, you do everything you can to hold onto them."

My mouth lifted slowly in a trembling smile. "I might drive you crazy sometimes."

"Go for it. Do your worst."

"I can be a menace."

He shrugged, not looking the least bit concerned. "Don't forget slightly unhinged."

"That, too."

"But you're also sweet and kind and funny and up for any challenge and loyal and fierce, and when you smile at me, I feel like I could do anything."

I stared up into his eyes, those blue, blue eyes shining back at me with such love. "I love you." A laugh escaped me. "I really, really love you."

One minute, he was smiling at me, the next I was wrapped in his arms, and he was kissing me, a slow, lingering kiss, a promise. When we broke apart, he rested his forehead on mine.

"I do have to tell you something," he said. "I'm moving."

I frowned and tried to pull away. His arms tightened around me. "What? You can't just say all that and then tell me you're moving to Chicag—"

He put a finger on my mouth. "To Two Harts. I'm moving to Two Harts. I want to make sure I'm able to vote in the next election. Someone I know is running for mayor. And she's smart and hardworking and loves that town. She's going to do amazing things."

My eyes narrowed. "I haven't even told you I planned to run."

He held his palm out. "Don't get mad."

"About what?"

"I snuck into your backpack to find that application form. I wanted to see what it all entailed and if I could convince you to send it in, but you'd filled it all out already."

I crossed my arms.

"And I sent it in for you. You'll be on the ballot this spring."

"What? I wasn't sure I was going to do it," I said in outrage.

He smirked. "Yes, you were."

"You didn't know that."

"Yes, I did."

"We're going to have a talk about this later."

"I understand." He tried, and failed, to look properly apologetic.

"I'm serious. That is the first rule of our relationship. We don't enter each other into mayoral races without expressed written consent."

"Deal."

"And no Rush during long car trips."

"Now, wait. I am not agreeing to that."

"We'll see." I raised on my tiptoes and whispered in his ear, "Kiss me, Goodnight."

So, he did. A toe-curling, breath-stealing, name-forgetting kind of kiss.

I think I heard a few catcalls. Someone announced that the limo for the bride and groom had arrived and that it was hot pink with the words PARTY TIME in huge letters and a stripper pole inside. And I'm pretty sure Mack walked by and asked if there was a pool for wedding dates yet.

But whatever.

Theo Goodnight loved me.

I think I won.

EPILOGUE

THEO

Note to self:
Like Mack said, time to put a ring on it.

A random Thursday in June, ten months after the wedding

Two Harts

"Are you sure about this?" Abe asked, checking himself out in the small, warped mirror.

The biggest drawback of holding a wedding at a county park was dealing with the restroom situation. There was nothing romantic about metal toilets, cement floors, no hand soap, and a scratched, dirty mirror that looked as though it had been purchased from a funhouse.

But bathrooms aside, today was exactly how Ali had described her perfect wedding to me all those months ago. Kind of funny to think it had been less than a year ago when I'd unchained her from the tree we were about to get married in front of.

Or hopefully married in front of. This was a surprise.

Everyone was in on the surprise but Ali. She could say no but, and I'm not being cocky here, she wouldn't.

I finished buttoning the sleeves on my dress shirt. It was chambray blue because Ali said it almost matched my eyes. "Very."

Abe raked his fingers through his long dark hair and winked at his reflection, clearly pleased. "Have you thought this through? You'll have to stay on your toes."

A huff of laughter escaped me. "You do remember I know who I'm dealing with, right? I can handle her."

Abe's face swung toward me, incredulous. "You're hilarious. Not a chance."

"Not a chance about what?" Cal asked as he strolled into the bathroom, also dressed in the simple white dress shirt and tie Abe sported. Behind him, the lanky form of Travis followed, also in the same outfit.

My brother—still so strange to think I had one—and I had stayed in contact, emailing, then texting and calling. In early January, he'd come for a visit, and we'd taken him to check out the University of Texas at Austin who'd been recruiting him for their swim team.

Scott—I couldn't call him my father—and I had communicated but only through email. And although I wasn't sure that would be a relationship I ever wholeheartedly pursued, it had given me closure I hadn't realized I needed.

And a brother.

"He says he can handle Ali." Abe shoved a thumb in my direction.

Cal patted my back. "Good luck with that."

With a slow smile, I nudged Abe away from the mirror and took his place. "I have my ways."

"Dude," Abe said, sounding disgusted. "That's my sister."

I laughed. "Get your mind out of the gutter."

Ten months of dating Alicia Ramos had taught me a few

things. Like her intense hate of towels not folded properly or how much she secretly loved Hallmark movies. Or that she had a spot right below her right ear that always made her giggle. Or how she'd cried for hours after she'd won the election.

It would take me a lifetime to learn all the little things about her.

Which was exactly what I intended.

"Do I look okay?" I asked.

Abe took his time inspecting me before nodding. "You look good. Calm, even. Why do I feel like I'm more nervous than you right now?"

I shrugged. "You've always been highly strung."

"Hilarious." He slapped my back. "Seriously, why?"

"Because I get to marry Ali today." Thinking of that sent a wave of peace through me, a rightness.

Abe threw his arms around me and pulled me into a fierce hug. "I'm glad. I'm really glad."

Frankie pushed through the bathroom door, crowding an already crowded room. "Break it up, you two. Mom says she wants everyone out and ready."

Abe released me. "We're coming."

Frankie held his hand out. "Welcome to the family."

With a grin, I shook it.

"He's always been a part of our family." Cal slung an arm around my shoulders.

"Well, now it's official," Frankie said. "And since you'll be married and all, any incidents involving gnomes in inappropriate positions fall on your shoulders."

"Should I ask?"

One of Frankie's eyebrows arched. "Do you really want to know?"

Ali's brothers looked at me and then we all said at once, "Plausible deniability."

We were still laughing when my phone dinged with a text.

Mae: *We're finally on our way. She stops to talk to everyone though so who knows when we'll get there.*

Me: *We're ready.*

"She's on her way." Excitement pulsed through me. "We should get out there."

Together, we filed out and walked down the dirt path to the clearing in front of the tree where several neat rows of rental chairs had been set up. Forty exactly—family and a few friends. Afterward, we'd go over to the Sit-n-Eat for a cookout the whole town was invited to.

"Oh, don't you look handsome." Stephanie paused in adjusting the bows at the ends of each row of chairs for the fortieth time.

"Thanks." Abe turned slowly. "I think I make this shirt look pretty good."

"Abraham." Stephanie waved a hand at him, grinning despite herself. "I meant Theo. But you look very handsome too."

Abe dropped a kiss on her cheek and stage-whispered, "I'm your favorite, aren't I?"

"You're too ugly to be her favorite." Frankie shoved him as he walked past. Abe shoved him back.

"Boys, it's your sister's wedding," Stephanie said, although her eyes gleamed with delight.

In the months since Abe had come back into our lives, the change had been remarkable. Eli and Abe were slowly building the kind of relationship they'd never had before. Oh, they still butt heads and sometimes refused to talk to each other for days, but they got over it, figured out how to move past it.

Abe brought Hallie to visit every other month or so. They'd come for Christmas this past year for a couple of weeks. Stephanie had been beside herself with happiness. Slowly, the family was reshaping itself to include this new version of Abe, an older one, a little more serious than he used to be as a teenager. But his smiles were still there, the ribbing between brothers, the easy comradery.

"He started it," Frankie muttered.

"And I'll finish it." Abe wrapped an arm around Frankie's neck and hovered a hand over Frankie's head. "I'd mess up your hair but then I'd be covered in hair gel."

"Eli," Stephanie called.

"Boys, listen to your mother," Eli yelled.

"Yes, Dad," they both grumbled. Abe released Frankie, who glared as he adjusted his shirt.

"Daddy," Hallie called from her place at the back, a basket clutched in her hands. She was decked out in a pink cupcake of a dress with two lopsided ponytails and shiny white shoes. "I'm ready to be a flower girl."

Another message came through.

Mae: *Mrs. Linton stopped her to discuss the Fourth of July parade.*

I smiled. The town's Fourth of July celebration was Ali's first big push to help bring business to Two Harts and she was intent on making it a success. Winning the election had been the first hurdle, but she had to prove herself now. My girl was determined and focused. That celebration didn't have a chance of failing.

Mae: *I'm about to put a paper bag over her head so we can get there before the next century.*

Mae: *Finally. We're moving again.*

Mae: *By the high school now.*

"They've made it to the high school," I announced.

Melanie, who'd taken over as coordinator the second she and Cal arrived two days ago, clapped her hands. "Places, people. Everyone in their seats. Eli and Stephanie, come back here with Hallie. Cal, Frankie, Abe, up to the front. Ellie, you too. Mack, where's Mack?"

"Ready to go." Mack stood in front of the tree, cradling Karen in his arms.

Melanie marched up to him. "We talked about this. You cannot officiate the wedding and hold Karen at the same time."

Mack frowned; Karen licked his cheek. "I don't see why not."

Melanie snapped her fingers. "Give me the dog."

"Fine."

Melanie tucked the dog under her arm and raced back over to the arch we'd set up where the dirt path opened into the clearing. She kissed my cheek. "You got this, Theo."

I smiled gratefully. "Thanks for all your help."

"Are you kidding? It's way more fun to plan someone else's wedding." With a sly smile, she lowered her voice. "Plus, guess who picked today in the wedding pool?"

She scurried down the aisle to stand next to Ellie, dumping the dog off on the lap belonging to Chris, Mae's husband, along the way.

Mae: *We have made it to the parking lot. T-minus thirty seconds.*

Mae: *I lied. She's inspecting the park sign now. Wants to update it.*

Me: *We're ready to go.*

Mae: *Good.*

***Mae**: Hey, Theo?*

***Me**: Yeah?*

***Mae**: I'm glad it's you Ali is marrying.*

A warmth spread through me. Mae's acceptance meant a lot, maybe more than the Ramos family's. Ali's family loved me, but Mae had always been a little harder to read, a little tougher to crack, and fiercely protective of those she loved.

***Me**: Thanks.*

I heard a murmur of voices and could just make out Ali's. The nerves I'd held at bay suddenly showed up and I ran my hands along my pants and took a few steps forward, wanting to meet her before she saw what lay ahead.

She was laughing when she appeared and, like it usually did, my heart flipped over at the sight of her. At the silky wave of her brown hair, the big dark eyes with the permanent glint of mischief, the freckles that dusted her cheeks, the sassy swing of her hips, how her head tilted ever so slightly, asking a question without words, when she saw me.

"What are you doing here?" Ali asked, her steps slowing. "You said you had a big meeting this afternoon in Houston."

I shrugged. "I lied."

She crossed her arms. "And you're all dressed up."

"So are you," I pointed out. Mae had concocted a fake photo shoot for a fake magazine article to get Ali in a white dress that cinched in at her waist and flared out to just below her knees. The top was held up by dainty straps and a scooped neckline that made my heart race for other reasons.

Mae clapped her hands. "My job here is done."

She turned to Ali and hugged her, whispering something

into her ear I couldn't hear. Whatever it was, Ali sucked in an audible breath and stared at Mae as she scooted down the path, stopping to give me a kiss on the cheek. "Go get her, tiger. Or should I say, that booty's all yours, Dread Pirate Goodnight?"

My cheeks flamed. "She told you?"

Smiling, Mae patted my back. "Your secret is safe with me."

With that she was gone, leaving Ali and me alone. We drifted together, pulled by the invisible string that seemed to link the two of us.

"You told her?"

"Just that you had a thing for pirates." With a shrug, she bit her lip. "I like your thing for pirates."

"Oh?"

Her cheeks flushed an adorable pink as she wrapped her arms around my neck. "I sure do."

I pulled her close and buried my nose in the spot where her shoulder met her neck, breathing in the familiar spice that clung to her skin.

"Not that I'm not enjoying this but," she pulled back a little to look up at me, "why are you here?"

"I have a surprise." I skated my hands down her arms and grasped her hands.

"I love surprises."

I took a deep breath and blurted it out. "I want to get married."

Ali froze, her eyes latched onto my face. "I-is that a proposal?"

Pulling her along, I took a few shuffles toward the clearing but not close enough for her to see anything. Yet.

"Because if that was a proposal, the answer is yes. I mean, I don't want to seem too easy but... well, when it comes to you, I'm easy."

Someone behind me laughed softly.

I pretended to frown. "You should make me work for it."

She shook her head. "No, really. I'm good. Let's get married. Could we go to Vegas? Knock it out in a weekend?" Her teeth latched onto her lower lip, her eyes staring somewhere into the middle distance. "Although Mom and Dad would be upset about that. And I would want Cal and Melanie there. And Abe and Hallie. Plus, Mae and Chris. Oh, and Ellie. That might be hard for her to get away to Vegas with work and all. And maybe Travis would want to come?"

"Ali..."

"No, no. I can figure this out." Her nose scrunched in concentration. I leaned forward and kissed it. She kept right on talking. "We could wait until school's out. Probably after the Fourth of July. That's going to take up a lot of my time. And then maybe..."

I tugged her around the bend until we were standing under the wooden arch. "Ali."

She blinked, glancing around her. Her gaze came back to mine, wide and shiny, like she was on the verge of tears. "W-what is all this?"

"Auntie Ali, you're getting married, and I get to be the flower girl." Hallie threw a handful of petals in the air with enthusiasm. Stephanie leaned down and shushed her.

"I'm getting married?" Ali breathed. "In front of the Legacy Tree?"

"On a random Thursday afternoon in June. With family and a few friends." I picked up her hand and placed it over my racing heart. "Just like you said."

"I said that?"

"About ten months ago. It took forever for June to get here." I pressed my forehead to hers. "What do you think? Want to get married?"

A tear slid down her cheek, but her smile was brighter than the sun. "Yes, please."

A LETTER FROM SHARON

Dearest Reader,

I cannot say thank you enough for choosing to read *The Fast Lane*. If you'd like to keep up to date with all my book news, just sign up at the following link. Never fear, your email address will never be shared, and you can unsubscribe at any time.

www.bookouture.com/sharon-m-peterson

Even though this is my third novel, I'm still wrapping my head around the idea that you—yes, you, dear reader—chose my book out of so many other choices. I know time is precious; thank you for using it to get to know Ali and Theo and the rest of the gang.

I'd love to hear what you think. Reviews are a great way to share that, and they make such a difference helping new readers to discover one of my books for the first time. If you ever have questions, want to chat, or need a random picture of a baby animal to brighten your day, please feel free to find me online.

You can find me on my Facebook page, oversharing on Instagram, tweeting nonsense on X/Twitter, adding too many books to my TBR list on Goodreads, making awkward videos on TikTok, or my website.

Happy reading,

Sharon

sharonmpeterson.com
goodreads.com/user/show/68003715-sharon-m-peterson

facebook.com/SharonMPetersonAuthor
x.com/stone4031
instagram.com/stone4031
tiktok.com/@stone4031

ACKNOWLEDGMENTS

On a mild January evening a few years ago, I was beginning the (thankless) job of making dinner for four children, chatting with my oldest son who, at the time, was fourteen. It was when I turned my back on him to open the refrigerator that I heard the crash. I whipped around to find him on the ground, his body stiff and unyielding, eyes rolled back in his head, unresponsive to his name. The convulsions came, then his face turned blue. That's not a figure of speech: it was blue. Terrified, I yelled for my husband and called 9-1-1.

That was his first seizure.

Over the next two years, he would be diagnosed with epilepsy, and it would take just as long to find anti-seizure medications that worked to keep them under control.

Like Ali's mother in *The Fast Lane*, I found myself panicking at the slightest noise, making sure he wasn't left on his own, rethinking how we kept doing things like swimming or bike riding and still keep him safe.

When I was writing my second book, *The Fake Out*, where we meet Ali for the first time, we were in the middle of those two years of questions and worry and trauma. Seeing a loved one have a seizure is just that—traumatic. I loved Ali from the beginning and right away, she told me she had seizures too. (Yes, the characters talk to me.) Maybe it was a way for me to deal with what we were going through at home.

When I knew that Ali's book was next, I knew I needed to do my research. And so, with the help of an online epilepsy support group, I found two lovely women about the same age and with a similar diagnosis as Ali who were willing to share their experiences. I could not have written this book without their help. Thank you, Ashley Nguyen and Victoria Carpenter. Thank you, thank you for your willingness to open up to a stranger on the internet. Your experiences helped me to shape Ali and how her epilepsy affects her life. I hope I've done Ali's story, and in many ways, your stories, justice.

Many, many thanks to my agent, Nalini Akolekar, who has been a constant support and who works tirelessly to get my books into the world. I'm forever grateful that you believed in me, sometimes when I did not believe in myself. Thanks also to the rest of the gang at Spencerhill Associates.

To my editor, Billi-Dee Jones, thank you for seeing something in my stories that touched you. My little book baby has grown fat and happy under your care. To the whole team at Bookouture, you've created such an amazing environment for authors to bloom in. Thank you for all you do.

To Christie, for telling everyone you know about your friend who writes books and for being a friend who has always been like family. To Noydena and Mat, for always being willing to answer my weird, random tech questions. To the rest of the gang—Andrea, Stephanie, and Shawn—thank you for letting me vent (a lot), for your encouragement, and for funny memes just when I need them. And Brian, FDR once again. You're welcome.

To Google, for always knowing the answer to the most random questions I ask. You truly make my job easier. I mean, just the searches for nudist resorts alone saved me a lot of real-life research and for that, I am eternally grateful. Plus, I'm sure I'm on a government watchlist somewhere because of you.

To Melissa Weisner. Thank you for being a listening ear and for answering countless questions. And for letting me vent. And for encouraging me. I'm really glad you're my friend.

To the ladies at the Eleventh Chapter. I'm so grateful to be part of a group of women writers who support each other in so many ways. You all rock!

To Courtney Lott, who has been cheering me on since the very first word of my first book, read countless drafts, and is the queen of encouragement. I could never, ever have finished writing my very first chapter without you.

To Maria Gonzalez-Gorosito, who, along with a group of moms who barely knew me, surprised me with a new laptop when mine broke. It remains one of the most remarkable gifts I've ever been given. It wasn't just a laptop you gave me; you gave me the courage to write. You're going to be thanked in every book, so just get used to it.

To the ladies of the Ink Tank. Your constant support and the safe place you've provided for me to vent/scream/cry/lament/laugh/celebrate is such an important part of my writing life. You are all amazing.

To Tracey Christensen. Thank you for always telling me the truth even when I might not want to hear it. Your wisdom and friendship have truly been a gift from God. I'm so very glad I know you, my friend. HONEYMOON BABY, forever!

Thank you to the members of the Women's Fiction Writers Association and the League of Romance Writers, for giving writers support and opportunities to grow.

To my mom and Aunt CC, thank you for being my cheerleaders and believing that I could make a dream like this a reality. Love you bunches.

To my sister Gabbie, who will never get to hold one of my books in her hands. I miss you always; love you forever. And I fully expect you to sell a copy of this book to every single angel in Heaven.

To Daniel, Benjamin, Gideon, and Katherine. I am incredibly blessed to be your mother. Thank you for putting up with a mom who makes you repeat everything you say at least twice because my mind was somewhere else the first time you said it. You are in my heart always.

To Carl. You've put up with my exhaustion, my tears, my anger, my disappointment, my excitement, my crazy ideas, my ramblings about made-up people in made-up worlds, and way too many pizza dinners. You've never wavered in your support of me. Ever. I love you.

To the many, many others I can't even begin to list here, but you know who you are. Your endless support, encouragement, and prayers have kept and continue to keep me going daily. Thank you for always believing in me.

Lastly, thank you to the readers. Aside from having really good reading taste, you all have been incredibly welcoming and kind to me over these two years. I'm humbled each time someone reaches out to me, writes a review, or spends time reading one of my books.

If you'd like to know more about epilepsy, please visit the Epilepsy Foundation at: https://www.epilepsy.com

P.S.: Any geographic inaccuracies are my fault. Forgive me.

P.P.S.: No nudist resorts were visited in the making of this book.

PUBLISHING TEAM

Turning a manuscript into a book requires the efforts of many people. The publishing team at Bookouture would like to acknowledge everyone who contributed to this publication.

Commercial
Lauren Morrissette
Hannah Richmond
Imogen Allport

Cover design
Head Design Ltd

Data and analysis
Mark Alder
Mohamed Bussuri

Editorial
Billi-Dee Jones
Charlotte Hegley

Copyeditor
Donna Hillyer

Proofreader
Jenny Page

Marketing
Alex Crow
Melanie Price
Occy Carr
Cíara Rosney
Martyna Młynarska

Operations and distribution
Marina Valles
Stephanie Straub

Production
Hannah Snetsinger
Mandy Kullar
Jen Shannon
Ria Clare

Publicity
Kim Nash
Noelle Holten
Jess Readett
Sarah Hardy

Rights and contracts
Peta Nightingale
Richard King
Saidah Graham

Printed in Great Britain
by Amazon